ACCLAIM F

NOW AND THEN AND ALWAYS

"Powerful. I've always loved Melissa Tagg's stories, but this one is something special. Lyrical, yes. Enchanting, of course. But her story about a broken man meeting an equally broken woman and their journey to healing touched unexpected places in my heart. An absolutely beautiful, compelling read."

-**Susan May Warren**, *USA Today* bestselling, RITA Award-winning author of the Montana Marshalls series

"Charming! Set in an old bed and breakfast in need of love, *Now and Then and Always* delights the reader with mystery and romance. Tagg continues to set herself apart as a classic romance storyteller."

-**Rachel Hauck**, *New York Times* bestselling author

"Melissa Tagg is the kind of writer who makes me fall in love with story every single time I read one of her novels. In *Now and Then and Always* she does it again. Tagg's writing draws you into the pages—into the Storyworld she creates in such a powerful way, threaded through with humor, romance and, yes, mystery. I closed the book happy and satisfied—except that I wished the story hadn't ended."

-**Beth K. Vogt**, Christy Award-winning author

"With her trademark wit and stunning word pictures, Melissa Tagg has penned a romance that drew me in from the very first sentence. *Now and Then and Always* is a heart-breakingly beautiful romance sprinkled with characters who felt more like friends. Truly, a story that will capture your heart."

-**Courtney Walsh**, *New York Times* and *USA Today* bestselling author

"*Now and Then and Always* is a beautiful story of an old house that brings people together to find healing and wholeness in their brokenness and the family they never expected. Tagg's well-written novel is the perfect blend of smiles, tears, and happily-ever-after with a touch of intrigue. The characters linger long after the pages have been turned and The Everwood makes me wish it was real so I could have my own life-changing experience."

-**Lisa Jordan**, Carol Award-winning author for Love Inspired

WALKER FAMILY SERIES

"Tagg crafts a beautiful romance filled with humor, mystery, and heartfelt emotion . . . Tagg's moving story beautifully explores themes of redemption and the nature of home."

-**Publisher's Weekly**, for *All This Time*

"Bear and Raegan are endearing and intriguing characters, and readers can't help but fall in love with them. Tagg excels at fleshing out the hints we've been given throughout the series and developing them into layered, authentic backstories...A doozy of a first kiss is completely worth the wait, and even a little suspense is skillfully worked into the plot—in case pulses weren't already racing. (They were.)"

-**RT Book Reviews**, 4½ Stars TOP PICK! for *All This Time*

"With her inimitable style, Melissa Tagg has penned a gem of a story, one that will delight longtime fans and entrance new ones. Replete with swoon-worthy moments, unwrapping Bear's complicated history and discovering Raegan's hidden struggles make this a love story that resonates on a deeper level."

-**RelzReviewz.com**, for *From the Start*

"With profound truths on one page and laugh-out-loud hilarity on the next, *Like Never Before* quickly becomes one of those novels I didn't want to end. Melissa Tagg has penned a delightful story that took hold of my heart and didn't let go. Superbly well done!"

-**Katie Ganshert**, bestselling, award-winning author

"In *Like Never Before,* readers are invited to revisit the much-loved Walker clan that delivers on the promise that even if lost once, love can be found again. In true Melissa Tagg style, the dialogue is smart and the romance is real and raw in all the right places. This series is witty story-telling at its best."

-**Kristy Cambron**, bestselling, award-winning author

"Tagg (*Made To Last; Here To Stay*) writes heartfelt and humorous gentle romances with a wisp of faith woven throughout. Fans of her previous two books will want this one. And devotees of Rachel Hauck and Robin Lee Hatcher will embrace a promising new author."

-**Library Journal**, for *From the Start*

"Tagg excels at creating wholesome romances featuring strong young career women, gentle humor, and an unobtrusive but heartfelt infusion of faith."

-**Booklist**, for *From the Start*

BOOKS BY MELISSA TAGG

MAPLE VALLEY SERIES
Now and Then and Always

WALKER FAMILY SERIES
Three Little Words (prequel e-novella)
From the Start
Like Never Before
Keep Holding On
All This Time

ENCHANTED CHRISTMAS COLLECTION
One Enchanted Christmas
One Enchanted Eve
One Enchanted Noël

WHERE LOVE BEGINS SERIES
Made to Last
Here to Stay

A Place to Belong (e-novella)

NOW
and
THEN
and
ALWAYS

MELISSA TAGG

To the readers who keep returning to Maple Valley with me. Ten stories in, I still ♡ this town.

But I ♡ you even more.

PROLOGUE

*I*t was just a house. Just a weathered old house in a hidden grove, shuttered and still under the shadowed reach of pale moonlight through listless clouds. It shouldn't beckon him so, prying him from the truck and that wrinkled magazine page from his pocket. The one with the white creases from his folding and unfolding and folding and . . .

Marshall Hawkins took a frayed breath, inhaling the musty scent of damp soil, exhaling memories that never quite dissolved, and, fingers numb, unfolded the paper. Not that he had to look to know what he'd see. Two stories, gaping windows, gleaming siding, and a towering elm tree out front. All under splashy letters advertising some construction company. He slid his thumb over the Victorian's deep-blue door at the center of the faded ad.

Just a house.

Except the image on the gloss-print now stared at him in real life too. An aged version, to be sure, with peeling wood and a sagging porch, naked, gnarled vines climbing one side. And this front door was brown. Still. It was

1

uncanny. Like looking at a decades-old photograph of a woman in her youth and then lifting your gaze to see the grandmother she'd become. It could almost be the same house.

And he could almost hear Laney's voice.

"It's perfect, Dad. It just needs a swing."

A sharp wind snagged the page and his grip tightened. A raindrop, or maybe a lone tear, landed on the paper. And the thudding in his head—the reason he'd pulled off the highway in the first place, followed a winding rural road until he came upon this copse and the house it secreted—turned to thunder.

This wasn't like the other headaches. And even if it were, he'd surrendered every last prescription bottle to his sister this morning. He'd swallowed a few measly aspirin earlier, probably right around the time he'd crossed the border into Iowa. But the throbbing had only worsened.

The pain squeezed until Marshall's knees landed in soggy grass and his vision fogged, Laney's house blurring in front of him.

But it's not. It's not Laney's house. Because Laney's not . . .

The page between his loosening fingers whipped in the wind as the house faded from view. The last thing he saw before he gave in to the darkness was a metal sign staked to the ground underneath a bowing tree, letters stenciled—The Everwood.

ONE DAY EARLIER

*T*he knock came midmorning—bellowing through the first floor of the Everwood Bed & Breakfast, rattling the rickety bones of the sluggish house and jarring Mara from sleep.

In her cocoon of throw pillows and a tangled herringbone blanket, in this cozy den where not so long ago she'd learned to live again, Mara blinked against a slant of sunlight from the picture window.

Was Lenora finally back? Or perhaps it was a guest.

Please, anyone but Garrett Lyman.

Another knock echoed. Or maybe that was just her heart, pulsing back and forth between hope and fear.

But no, no reason for fear. It *couldn't* be Garrett. It'd been ten months. Surely he'd stopped looking by now.

She made herself breathe and stretched her neck, gaze lifting to the water spots dappling the cedar planks of the den's pitched ceiling then down to the frayed oval rug that covered a hundred nicks and grooves in the hardwood floor.

As for the hope of Lenora—also a no-go. Lenora

wouldn't knock. As the owner of the Everwood, though absent these last five weeks, she'd have her own keys.

A guest then. *A real, live, paying guest.* The first one this month. So maybe there was reason to hope after all.

That is, if Mara could pull off her role. Step into Lenora's shoes and play the welcoming hostess. Pillows toppled to the floor as she lurched to her feet, the last, lingering fog of her momentary alarm lifting to make room for a nervous laugh. How many knocks had she just dawdled through?

She had to stop spending whole nights curled on the couch, waking up with cramped muscles that made her feel far older than thirty. And though she'd fallen asleep still wearing a presentable wraparound sweater, her snowflake-print leggings didn't exactly say professional innkeeper.

No time to worry about that now. She scrambled from the room. Aged floorboards creaked as she hurried through the sprawling dining room, its tarnished chandelier wobbling overhead, and the formal sitting room, long and spacious. Its antique furniture might be worn, but every piece was dusted and polished—from the twin trestle tables and lamps with rose glass shades to the wooden legs of the tufted green chaise lounge.

One thing about the Everwood—there was always another room to tidy, another tasseled rug to straighten, another mirror to Windex. How had Lenora ever thought to run this place on her own?

Mara passed between the mahogany pillars that led into the lobby as another knock echoed in the quiet.

She stopped, catching her breath and summoning her composure. She could do this. Smile like Lenora would and give a bright, "Welcome to the Everwood." Rattle off nightly rates and breakfast hours . . . keep her promise.

"I think you may love this raggedy old B&B even more than I do, dear Mara. Take care of it for me, won't you?"

With a nod of resolve, she twisted the front door's lock. *For Lenora.* "Welcome to the—"

"Took you long enough, young lady." A tall woman with silver hair piled high, suitcase in one hand and cane in the other, blustered in. "Please tell me this is not your usual modus operandi. Leaving old women out on porches on damp March mornings. Step aside, girl, step aside."

Mara backed up, bumping into the check-in desk. "I'm so sorry. I was at the other end of the house and . . ." She pasted on a stretchy grin and tried again. "Welcome to the Everwood."

Horn-rimmed glasses slid down the woman's narrow nose until she nudged them back up with her cane. "What kind of bed and breakfast keeps its front door locked?"

The kind that too often went whole weeks without guests. Whose owner had left on a trip more than a month ago and still hadn't returned.

And whose longtime boarder turned temporary caretaker had grown a little too jumpy in her extended isolation. Funny how loud and dramatic the nighttime sounds of a ramshackle house seemed when no one else was around to hear them—wind in the chimney, leaves scuttling over the porch, the way that ancient elm tree out front moaned on gusty days.

It was why Mara had taken to spending her evenings cozied up in the den at the back of the place—the part of the house meant to be the owner's private living quarters. The den felt homey, made her think of peaceful nights in front of the fire with Lenora, cups of tea, and the gradual unveiling of a whole new life.

No more nannying. No more existing on the periphery of others' families. No more wishing she had someplace to go on holidays or wondering what it'd be like to settle somewhere for more than a few years at a time.

No more Garrett Lyman.

She hadn't meant to stay long at the Everwood when she'd first arrived late last summer. Had only known of its existence thanks to a brochure in a rest stop along I-80. But in Lenora she'd found a friend and in the Everwood a safe harbor. And as each week drifted into the next, she'd felt it more and more—she belonged here.

"We don't get many visitors this time of year," Mara finally answered the woman. Not that she had been here at this time last year to know for sure.

No, last spring she'd been back in Illinois, still naively believing a little suburb south of Chicago was far enough away from Garrett for peace of mind.

She shoved the thought aside and skirted around the check-in desk. Paisley wallpaper made the space feel cloistered. Tall windows helped with that on sunny days, but today the sky was all rolling shadows. "My name is Mara, by the way. Can I get you checked in, Ms.—"

"*Mrs.* S.B. Jenkins." Her suitcase thumped onto the floor. "You seem quite young."

"Uh . . . thank you?"

Mrs. S.B. Jenkins sniffed. "I mean, too young to run a reputable bed and breakfast. If you make me check in by signing my name using my finger on one of those fancy touchscreen things . . ."

Was that an actual shudder? Mara clamped down on a laugh. "No worries, Mrs. Jenkins. We're quite traditional around here." *Old-school* was the term she'd used when joking with Lenora, who shared this woman's apparent aversion to technology. The computer at the check-in desk, the software they used to track reservations—both outdated. The Wi-Fi barely functioned. Lenora didn't even own a cell phone.

If she did, Mara could've tracked her down by now and

asked her when she was coming back and what to do about the stack of bills piling up in that basket on the corner of the desk.

She could've quelled her growing fear that maybe Lenora wasn't coming back at all. That she'd been abandoned all over again.

No. Not Lenora. Mara pressed the computer's power button. "Now, how long are you planning to stay?"

"Oh no you don't. I'm not committing to anything without a tour first. I have a book to finish writing, you see, and I need to make sure this is the adequate atmosphere."

"All right. I'd be happy to show you around."

With any luck, she'd have Mrs. Jenkins settled in a guestroom within an hour. Then Mara could scrounge through the pantry, make sure she had enough staples on hand to provide tomorrow's breakfast. At some point she'd probably have to venture into Maple Valley for groceries. She'd done that twice already during Lenora's absence, and both times she'd managed to avoid conversation with any locals.

"We'll start downstairs. The Everwood is full of personality, as you'll see. The owner is actually an award-winning travel photographer. Some of her original works are hanging in the hallway upstairs."

"So you aren't the owner." Mrs. Jenkins arched one gray eyebrow. "I'd like to meet this award-winning photographer. Where is she?"

Oh, what Mara wouldn't give to know.

"We missed a room."

At Mrs. Jenkins's rasped words, Mara paused in the

second floor hallway, hand on the decorative banister cap at the top of the open staircase.

It hadn't taken more than twenty minutes to lead Mrs. Jenkins through the house. First they'd strolled through the entire ground floor, including the only updated room in the whole house—the kitchen with slate gray appliances, bright white cupboards, and a modern subway tile backsplash. Mrs. Jenkins had clucked in approval.

Upstairs they'd peeked inside nearly every room that lined the narrow corridor. All but one—the first door at the top of the staircase.

Which she'd really hoped Mrs. Jenkins wouldn't notice.

No such luck. "Oh, that room's nothing special, Mrs. Jenkins."

The woman walloped her cane against the wall beside the cracked-open door. "Are you hiding something in there?"

"Of course not. I just—"

"It's not an outrageous thought. Perhaps you have a child, and as I told you I'm looking for quiet and solitude, you thought it best to hide him away."

"I don't have a child."

"Maybe a lover."

Mara tried to squelch a laugh. Failed. It came out a snort. "Uh, no lover."

"A dead body then."

She didn't even try this time. Her laughter echoed down the hallway. "What kind of writer did you say you are, Mrs. Jenkins? Suspense novels, perhaps? I promise, there aren't any dead bodies behind that door."

"Stranger things have happened, young lady. And you can't deny the smell of mystery hangs in the air of this decrepit old house."

Actually, that was probably just the lemony scent of the

homemade polish Mara had used on the woodwork yesterday. And "decrepit" was a little strong, wasn't it? Sure, all
five bathrooms—one downstairs, four up—needed a
complete gut job. The furnace rattled and old windows did
little to deny wintry drafts.

But couldn't Mrs. Jenkins see the charm underneath it
all? Hadn't she noticed the stained-glass window behind the
registration desk downstairs? Or the ornate woodwork of
the staircase banister? The tray ceilings and crown
molding?

Mrs. Jenkins thumped the wall again. "Shall we?"

Mara swallowed her sigh and skirted around the
woman. She nudged the door the rest of the way open,
stepped inside, and waited as her potential boarder shuffled
in behind her. And then, just like Mara had known she
would, Mrs. S.B. Jenkins gasped.

"I know. They're a bit much." Porcelain dolls—dozens of
them, with painted bow lips and beady glass eyes—peered
from ghostly white faces all around the room. They were
crowded onto every surface—the mahogany dresser, wall
shelves, even the window seat with its faded mustard
yellow cushion that matched the poster bed's lacy canopy.

The other guestrooms had their quirks, but this one was
just plain creepy, right down to the antique clock ticking
loudly in the corner.

"It's . . . it's . . ." Mrs. Jenkins stuttered.

A nightmare.

"Beautiful."

Mara nearly choked. "Wait. What?"

"Heaven only knows why you didn't show me this room
first. It's positively delightful." She straightened a doll's
dress. Opened a dresser drawer. Pushed aside a curtain,
letting in what little muted light the overcast day had to
offer, and wandered to the open closet.

"In that case, if you're thinking of staying, we have nightly and weekly rates. Breakfast is included, of course, and—"

Mara was cut off by a screech. Mrs. Jenkins jumped and backed up, bumping into the bed, glasses sliding down her nose.

A telltale meow drifted from the closet, and a second later a tawny feline sauntered to Mara's feet and batted at the hem of her sweater. So this is where the annoying furball had been hiding since last night.

Wrinkles folded into each other on Mrs. Jenkins's forehead. "You have a cat." Her voice was flat.

"*I* don't have a cat. He doesn't really belong to anybody." According to Lenora, the cat came with the place when she'd purchased the property last year. But as long as Mara had been here, he'd come and gone at will, sometimes disappearing for days at a time.

Mrs. Jenkins took off her glasses and stuffed them into her purse as if she'd seen enough—or too much, perhaps. "I don't do cats." She pulled a tissue from her purse, punctuating her irritation with a sneeze. "I'm dreadfully allergic."

She whisked from the room and Mara spun to follow, nearly tripping over the cat. "You just *had* to show up now, didn't you?" She hissed the words over her shoulder before hurrying after Mrs. Jenkins.

"I can keep away the cat. He won't come near you. Honestly, I don't like him all that much either."

Mrs. Jenkins's cane bopped against each step as she moved down the staircase. "Thank you, but no. The house is completely unsuitable."

"B-but the dolls. You liked the dolls."

In the lobby Mrs. Jenkins reached for her suitcase. "I was temporarily distracted from the rest of it. The atmosphere is most assuredly *not* adequate."

Mara followed her to the porch. "Mrs. Jenkins, please, I—"

But it was too late. The woman had made her decision and there was nothing to do but watch her march down the porch steps and across the lawn. Within minutes her Lincoln disappeared down the lane, its rumbling engine joined by the groaning of the stooping elm tree.

The wind carried off Mara's sigh and lifted her already unruly hair, reddish strands fluttering over her eyes. *I tried, Lenora. I really did.*

But apparently she didn't possess the same inviting warmth and knack for welcoming guests as the Everwood's owner. She never had been any good at impressing folks. But she'd thought the house's charm might make up for the lack of her own.

She cinched her sweater's belt. On a different day, she might make herself feel better with a stroll over the patchy lawn. She might pass under the arbor at the side of the house, imagining spring and flowers and rolling green reaching into the trees, while her heart tested out the word that never seemed to fit anywhere else—*home.*

But it was too cold for that on this March day and those bundled clouds overhead, too gray.

So she went only as far as the mailbox. She plucked a lone letter from the box and turned back toward the house.

And then froze halfway across the lawn, two boldfaced words on the outside of the envelope marching into focus —*Foreclosure Notice.*

The leaning elm whimpered again. So much for home.

Pounding his fist on his captain's desk was going too far.

Marshall knew it when a framed photo of the man's wife tipped. Knew it when stale coffee sloshed over the edge of a forgotten mug, slicking down to stain letterhead bearing the precinct's emblem.

But when Captain Wagner's granite gaze seized his . . . that's when he felt it, the sickening thud in his stomach an echo of his mistake. Only the latest in a reckless series.

It should've been enough to still his tongue.

But no. "You can't release him. I still have two hours."

"And what exactly are you going to accomplish in those two hours that you haven't been able to in the past forty-six?" Movements methodic, Captain Wagner angled in his chair, pulled a wad of tissues from the Kleenex box on the windowsill behind him, and wiped up the coffee. "I hope you realize how much restraint it's taking me right now not to make some snide comment about the irony of cleaning up your mess."

Any other time, a rumble of laughter might lighten his commanding officer's tone, even during a scolding. Not this time.

Too far.

Rain drizzled down the window in rivulets, the Milwaukee evening sky outside as gray as these unadorned office walls. He rubbed sweaty palms over his tan pants. Had he been wearing these since Saturday? "Captain—"

"Save it." With a final swipe, Captain Wagner shoved aside the wet mess and fastened his dark eyes on Marshall's once more. "You should never have brought him in. I know it. You know it. Every cop out there who's spent all weekend trying to dig up evidence just to make *your* arrest stick knows it."

Marshall couldn't make himself turn to glance where the captain pointed, to the glass overlooking the pod of desks that made up the detectives' bullpen. Didn't have to.

He'd already seen the circles under Tracy's eyes earlier this morning, after a night spent wading through street camera footage. He'd spotted Larry napping in the precinct lounge a couple hours ago. Must not have gone home last night either. Bailey and Lewis had been pulled off a case to help out too.

And Alex. His focused efforts over the past two days had nearly outrivaled Marshall's, so much so that his wife had taken to texting Marshall, asking if she was ever going to see her husband again.

A chore sometimes, having a sister married to his closest friend on the force.

A friend he'd let down. Just like he'd let down Captain Wagner and all the rest of them. He'd known on Saturday night when he brought in his suspect, Liam Price, that there wasn't enough evidence to charge him for the string of Westown burglaries. The chances of obtaining said evidence in the time they were allowed to hold the man before recommending charges? Slim to none.

The thing was . . . he hadn't cared.

And Captain Wagner knew it.

"I could lecture you, Hawkins. I could tell you how stupid it was, hauling in that kid. The son of a council member? Really?" Captain Wagner stood, not a single crinkle in his starched navy blue suit nor any hint of the exhaustion he must be feeling. He'd spent the bulk of his past two days here too, working just as doggedly as everyone else to fix Marshall's error.

Error? More like outright failure.

"I could go on and on about how the last thing we need right now is a PR scuffle." The captain rounded his desk, the steps of his polished shoes clacking. "I could waste time I don't have yelling 'til I'm blue in the face."

Marshall's gaze traced the groove in the floor, trekked

the diagonal line until it crossed with another and then trailed that one. A habit he'd picked up in the hospital, following lines or tracing patterns wherever they appeared —floors, ceilings, walls.

In the quilt over Laney's hospital bed. He'd memorized its every patch.

A too-familiar buzz lurked near the back of his brain. It would turn into an all-out pummeling if he didn't get out of this office soon, rummage through his locker until he found the spare pill bottle he hoped to high heaven was there. He hadn't allowed himself so much as Tylenol in the past two days, needing full alertness for the impossible task in front of him.

Lot of good that'd done.

"Marshall."

He forced his attention to the captain, the stern but kind man who'd mentored Marshall since his earliest days with the precinct. Alex might be his closest friend on the force, but there were times when Elias Wagner bordered on father figure.

"I could lecture you," he said again, lifting one hand as if to comb his fingers through nonexistent hair. His palm stayed there, resting on the back of his bald head until he let out a sigh. "But I don't think you'd even hear me."

Marshall shifted in his chair at the sudden softening in the captain's voice. *No*. No, not this. He knew what was coming and this was worse. "Cap—"

"Alex reminded me of the date. I'm sorry I didn't realize it on my own."

"Please. Don't." He spoke through gritted teeth.

"I won't try to imagine what you must be feeling, Marsh—"

"I said *don't*." He pitched from his chair so quickly that it swiveled behind him, knocking into the closed office door and rattling its glass pane. *Too far.* "I'd rather have your lecture."

He spun, facing away from Captain Wagner, accidentally catching Tracy's eye as she watched from her desk in the bullpen. There was pity there. He yanked his gaze away only to see Alex leading Liam Price down the hall, on his way to freedom. Liam *would* pick that moment to look up, glance Marshall's way, flash a smug grin.

"Fine then. Three months."

At the captain's voice, he whirled. "What?"

His boss had moved behind his desk, sitting once more. He held up the letterhead, a lingering drip of coffee dangling at the corner. "Administrative leave. You say one word in argument or hit my desk again, I'll retype this myself and replace 'leave' with 'suspension.'"

"I—" He clamped his lips at the tick in Captain Wagner's jaw. But no, he couldn't just stand here, defenseless. *Three* months' leave? He'd go crazy.

Or worse. With that much empty time, the quiet, the despair . . . he'd be helpless against it. And he'd rather feel a frigid nothing than feel helpless.

"Please, Captain." He didn't so much sit as wilt, limbs heavy and head cloudy.

"I wish you would've taken some extended time off two years ago. Right after . . ." The captain shook his head. "Perhaps I should've forced it on you then."

"You don't understand—"

"What I understand is you're not capable of doing your job right now, son. You haven't been for some time." He steepled his fingers atop his desk. "And I won't have the rest of the team paying for your stubbornness."

"My *stubbornness?*"

"Figured if I said pain or grief or depression, you'd jump out of your chair again."

"I'm not depressed." Mumbled words. Dishonest ones.

"I don't think you know what you are. But you *are* on leave. Starting now. Clean out your locker. Turn in your badge and firearm on the way out."

"Captain—"

"I meant what I said about changing this to a suspension."

Did it really matter, though? Call it administrative leave, call it a suspension, the end result was the same. Humiliation and far too many hollow days.

But the flint in Captain Wagner's expression, even rimmed as it was with compassion, warned him into silence. What more was there to say, anyway?

He rose, wordless, and moved in a bleary-eyed trance. Out of the office, past the bullpen, down a hallway to the lineup of officer lockers. Wouldn't take more than five minutes to empty his own, nothing more than bare essentials inside. No school pictures or crayon drawings anymore.

"Marsh?"

Alex had finished the paperwork for Liam's release already?

Marshall kept his back turned on his brother-in-law, yanking his duffel bag from the locker and stuffing in a pair of spare shoes. "Go home, Alex. Beth keeps texting."

"Keeps texting me too. I've been trying to convince myself it's because she loves and misses me, not just that she wants a hand with the twins."

Marshall hadn't seen his niece and nephew in weeks. Sometimes he wondered if Beth and Alex thought it was better that way. Better they not see the man he'd become. He stared at the small, square mirror on his locker door. Bloodshot eyes. Stubble, yes. But other shadows, too, darkened his face.

Beth and Alex were probably right.

"Listen, Marsh, I'm sorry if—"

He gave his locker a shove. Refused to look at his partner and friend. "You just *had* to remind him."

The lack of sleep, the headache on its way to a migraine, the thought of three months without even the shallow solace of work—all of it churned in his empty stomach. He had to get out of here.

He turned but Alex blocked his path. "Cap needed to know. The way you've been cutting corners, storming around for weeks . . . and arresting the Price kid? I was legit scared he was going to fire you." Alex threw up his hands in a show of exasperation. "So yeah, I reminded him of the anniversary. Maybe I overstepped."

Two years. Two years to the day since Laney's eyes closed, since his little girl . . .

"Maybe you overstepped? *Maybe?*" His voice was too close to a snarl.

"Beth is worried. I'm worried. You aren't yourself, man. What would Laney think if she could see you—"

He snapped, his last scrap of self-control demolished in one fell swoop as he dropped his bag and lurched at his brother-in-law, both hands snagging Alex's collar. Lockers rattled at the force of his push, Alex flinching as Marshall raised one fist.

"If it's what you need to do, go ahead."

Alex's calm tone, the way he met Marshall's eyes—it was a wound all its own. For one tortured moment, he couldn't move. Couldn't do anything other than wince at the pain in his head and the guilt punching through him.

Finally, lungs heaving, he dropped his balled hand. Backed away. What had he almost done?

Alex slumped against the locker. "Let us help—Beth and me. Or the captain. You know he'd do anything for you."

Marshall picked up his bag, slung it over one shoulder. He placed his firearm and badge on the bench running the length of the lockers. "Turn 'em in for me, would you?"

"Marsh—"

Legs brick-heavy but pace brisk, he escaped down the hallway.

2

"*P*lease don't do this, Marshall."

Marshall plunked his suitcase onto his unmade bed. Before he could use his foot to nudge away the navy blue comforter he'd thrown off in the middle of the night, his sister snatched it from the floor, folding it without breaking a beat.

"Don't leave. Not like this. I know yesterday was rough—"

"Try brutal." He surveyed the empty luggage. What exactly did a man pack for a road trip with no set destination?

"Okay, fine." Beth dropped the neatly folded blanket next to his suitcase. "I know yesterday was brutal—"

"Try the past two years." No, make that three. His world had turned upside down the day Laney died. But it had started tilting dangerously long before.

First there'd been the fever that started the day after her sixth birthday and didn't go away. One visit to the clinic. Then another. Blood work. Test results. A diagnosis without a cure.

Brutal didn't begin to cover it.

Marshall lumbered across his sparse bedroom. No wall shelves, knickknacks, throw pillows—Penny had taken all of those when she'd moved out. He yanked open one dresser drawer. A few pairs of jeans, a handful of shirts, boxers and socks. That should do it, right?

"Would you just stop for a second?"

The frustration in Beth's voice halted his movement. Honestly, he didn't mean to exasperate his sister. Nor Captain Wagner nor Alex. *Alex.* He should've at least texted an apology last night. Just like he should've apologized to his exhausted coworkers before stalking out of the station yesterday.

But the temptation to flee to his townhouse and drift into a haze aided by some heavy-duty painkillers had been too much to resist.

He'd awakened early this morning in yesterday's clothes, with only a dull headache in place of last night's migraine and the first inkling of a plan. By the time he'd downed half a pot of coffee and trudged in and out of the shower, he'd made his decision.

He stood in front of Beth now. His six-foot-four frame towered over her, but as usual, his height did nothing to deter her air of older sister authority—a perfect storm of love and bossiness. She had Mom's eyes, blue and unflinching.

Whereas he'd gotten the Hawkins murky gray. *"Like that eerie color in the sky right before a thunderstorm,"* Penny had said once before they were married. She'd assured him it was a compliment. A weird compliment, he'd countered. She'd replied with a kiss.

Life had really been that simple once. That happy.

Beth's stare bore into him. If she hadn't become a doctor, she'd have made a good cop. Maybe he should've brought her in to question the Price kid. Probably could've wheedled a confession from him. "I need to do this. I need to go."

"Go where?" A streak of something purple stained her shirt. Jam? One of the twins, surely.

"I don't know."

"To do what?"

"I don't know."

"Marsh."

"Beth." He wished he were the kind of brother who could place his palms on his sister's shoulders. Find the words to assure her . . . of what? That he was going to be okay? That, sure, as of yesterday, he'd officially lost everything but he could troop on.

"You're really going to leave. Just like that? What about the townhouse?"

He'd loved this place once. He'd renovated almost every room over the years, transforming it from a bachelor pad into a perfect first home for a young family.

But it didn't hold any importance to him anymore. Not with that empty bedroom across the hall. The empty space on the other side of the bed.

"I'd ask you to water the plants while I'm gone, but . . . " He shrugged.

Beth's fists landed on her waist. "A joke? You're making a joke about my penchant for killing houseplants at a time like this?"

He patted her head before moving to the dresser once more. "We aren't all born with a green thumb, Bethany Lou. It's all right."

"You can be the most maddening little brother, you know that?"

"I'm thirty-five and have eight inches on you. Isn't it about time you dispense with the 'little'?"

He lifted a handful of clothing from a drawer. Eventually Beth would see he was doing this as much for the rest of them as for himself. He was too much of a mess. Too . . . broken.

A wad of shirts tucked under his arm, he closed his top drawer and opened the next. "Don't worry, Beth. This is exactly what I need. I'm just going to get in the truck and drive and see where I end up. The townhouse will be fine. I'll stop by the post office on my way out of town to have them hold my mail. Money-wise, I'm good." The life insurance had seen to that.

Before Laney's death, he hadn't even realized there was a children's rider attached to his policy. Penny had always taken care of anything involving paperwork.

Until she hadn't anymore. Until she walked away, one last piece of paperwork left behind. Divorce papers.

He dropped his clothing into the suitcase.

"You've thought of everything then." Beth tipped her head to look up at him from where she now sat on the bed.

He rubbed his fingers over his unshaven jaw. "Glad you came over, though. I ordered a backyard playhouse online a few weeks ago. Figured I'd put it together for Ethan and Makena when the weather gets nice. But now . . . did you drive the truck today? If so, I can help you load it and maybe Alex can build it for them."

Beth just studied him for a moment, indecision blending with compassion in her gaze. He lowered to the foot of the bed—he on one side of the suitcase, his sister on the other. For a fleeting second, he almost considered staying. He could bring the playhouse over to her house himself, enjoy the twins' squeals, have dinner at Beth's big dining room table. Maybe they could even Skype Mom and Dad, who were still in Florida at their winter home. And all the while,

Marshall could let his family's company convince him for a few hours that life was okay. That *he* was okay.

But eventually he'd have to come back to this bare townhouse. And in his aloneness, he'd remember how Laney used to wish for a backyard and a dog. He'd remember house shopping with Penny and their promises to Laney that eventually they'd find just the right one. Maybe even one like the home in that magazine ad she'd shown them. The one with the blue door and matching shutters.

Truth was, he'd lied to his sister just now. He hadn't ordered that playhouse a few weeks ago. It'd been sitting in the garage for years. A Christmas present he never got to give.

"By the way, Marsh, I, um . . . I ran into Penny at the grocery store the other day. She had her baby with her."

Any lingering thought of abandoning his plan vanished. He jerked to his feet, flipped closed the lid of his suitcase. "There are about a thousand things I'd rather talk about right now than my ex-wife." Or her new family. The man she'd met mere months after walking away from Marshall. The baby she'd been pregnant with before the divorce was even finalized.

"She asked about you."

His palms flattened atop the luggage. "You talked to her?"

"She's as worried about you as the rest of us. You were married to her for ten years. She still cares—"

"Well, I don't."

"You don't mean that. Maybe it'd help if you talked to her. You could get some closure."

Closure. Right. As if all the gaping holes in his life could be filled with one conversation. No, he didn't need to talk to Penny. He needed to take a cue from her. She'd moved on. He could too.

And if he couldn't, if this trip, wherever it took him, wasn't enough to fix him . . .

He couldn't let his thoughts tow him there. Not to such a dark place. Not when his sister, who always read him too easily, watched him still.

"Tell Alex I'm sorry about yesterday, will you? And give the twins a hug for me."

"Marsh—"

"Please, Beth, just let me go. I'll call, all right?"

She stood. "Once a week or else I'll have Alex put out a statewide APB for you."

Probably wouldn't help to tell her he'd be across the state line by noon.

"One more thing."

"Yeah?" He surveyed his room. Was one pair of shoes good enough? Should he throw in his work boots?

"The pills." Beth held out her hand. "I want every bottle."

"What?"

"I'm not letting you hit the road under the influence of anything stronger than an aspirin."

"I can't sleep without the Ambien, Beth. You know that."

"And you wake up drowsy, so you over-caffeinate, which gives you a headache. And on the days when the headache turns into a migraine, you gulp down a few Fioricet. Or more than a few. Which makes you so dizzy you can barely stand up straight."

"What, do you have a hidden camera watching me?"

"You're over-medicating and it's making everything worse. I'm a doctor. I know the signs."

He stomped into the master bathroom. "You're a pediatrician."

"And you're acting like a child at the moment, so it's rather fitting, don't you think?"

Her face appeared behind his in the medicine cabinet mirror over the sink. Stern, stalwart. Had she been hanging around Captain Wagner or something? He heaved open the cabinet, waved a hand in front of it. "Fine. Have at it."

"I want to see inside your sock drawer, your closet, your kitchen cupboards—"

"Should I pull out every pocket of every pair of pants too?"

"Be as sarcastic as you want but this is for your own good. I know the migraines are awful. Keep one bottle of painkillers if you need to but promise me—please—that you won't take them unless you truly need to. If you're going to take a road trip to who knows where, you need to be clear-headed."

She might be annoying, but she had a point. And he wasn't stupid. He'd been walking a tightrope between necessity and addiction for longer than he cared to admit. And with the threatening place his mind had gone to only minutes ago . . .

Beth was right. This was for his own good. He'd give her every bottle, even the migraine meds. If he couldn't function the next time one hit, so be it. It's not like he'd be on the job.

He walked to his nightstand, rummaged around for the half-full bottle of sleeping pills.

"Marsh?"

"Huh?" He found another bottle—prescription painkillers—under the bed. Already empty.

"We'll wait on the playhouse. The kids will love helping you build it." She waited until he rose and faced her to finish. "When you get back."

When. Such assurance in the word. That he'd return and

when he did, he wouldn't be this same shadow of a man anymore. He was glad Beth believed it possible.

Maybe someday he'd believe it too. Until then . . .

He'd drive. Just . . . drive. And try to convince himself he cared where he ended up.

Mara had given herself twenty-four hours to digest the letter from the bank that could ruin everything. But now she was done waiting and worrying. It was time to take action.

That's what she'd told herself while she drove the two miles into Maple Valley. As she walked into the First State Bank. And out again.

And now, as she neared the Sugar Lane Bakery, the same determination coaxed her onward. *For Lenora.* Wherever she was.

A gentle rain pattered atop the bakery's yellow awning and the mingling scents of coffee and cinnamon curled in the damp air. A chatty customer at the bank had told Mara to come here when she'd overheard her asking to speak with the bank's senior loan officer.

"Everybody knows Jonas takes a midmorning coffee break at the bakery."

Another customer had nodded his agreement. *"Even on rainy days he walks. Take Elm Street then turn onto Main. If he's on his way back, you'll run into him."*

Apparently Maple Valley fit the small town stereotype of everyone knowing everyone. Mara gave her soggy umbrella a shake before closing it and reached for the bakery's door.

But the scene inside stopped her cold even as the bell

overhead jangled and the door bumped into her backside, nudging her over the threshold. *Sooo* many people. Nearly every seat in the place was occupied. Chatter cluttered the air.

Huh. Were the pastries that good?

And why hadn't she thought to ask that lady at the bank for a description of Jonas Clancy?

Mara swallowed as she dropped her umbrella into her tote bag. It was a stylish bakery with dark walnut flooring, shiplap on the walls, glass display cases up front. Maybe she could ask the person working behind the counter to point out Mr. Clancy.

Minutes later, peppermint tea in hand, she had her target. Gray coat on the back of his chair and a newspaper on the table in front of him. He was seated near a lanky window—alone, thankfully, with one of the only vacant chairs in the place across from him.

She squeezed past the last table between her and the banker. "Excuse me, Mr. Clancy? I'm sorry to interrupt, but I was wondering if I could talk to you."

"Of course. Have a seat." Thinning hair and lines etched into the man's face bespoke his age. Despite the curiosity in his expression, his grandfatherly gaze almost put her at ease.

She lowered into the empty chair. Pulling the foreclosure letter from her bag, she willed a grin into place. *Confidence. Determination.* "My name's Mara. I'd like to talk to you about the Everwood." She lifted the letter.

"Oh. I . . . I see."

"This says the mortgage hasn't been paid in three months. That doesn't make sense. Lenora wouldn't have skipped payments."

Mr. Clancy scooted his newspaper off to the side. "That letter is addressed to Lenora Worthington. Are you a family member or an employee? I don't think I caught your last name."

She took a drink of her tea, barely tasting it for all her swirling anxiety. She wasn't off to a good start here. She'd practically pounced on him. *There's no reason not to tell him your name. He's not going to blast your identity and whereabouts to the world . . . to Garrett.*

She reached one palm across the table for a handshake. "My name's Mara Bristol. I've been staying at the Everwood since last summer—about eight months now. I help Lenora run the place in exchange for room and board. I guess you could say Lenora gave me sort of an unofficial job."

It was a paltry description of what Lenora had truly done for Mara. From Mara's first day at the B&B, Lenora had offered rest and kindness and security. Eventually she'd invited Mara to stay and help run the inn—no matter the shoestring budget or slowing business as winter set in.

Peaceful days had unfolded, one into another, until eventually Dad, Mom, Garrett, and all her lonely years bouncing from family to family as a nanny had started to fade as if from a different lifetime altogether.

The plain truth was, Lenora Worthington was the sole reason Mara was still here. Here in Maple Valley at the Everwood. But also *here.* Alive and closer to whole than she'd been in so long.

She'll come back. She has to.

Mara could see Jonas Clancy's churning questions, but a bump from the chair behind her—along with an unfamiliar voice—interrupted. "You're staying at the Everwood? That old haunted house?"

Mara angled around. The voice belonged to a woman, probably about Mara's age, with raven hair pulled into a sleek bun. Her bright red lips spread into a friendly grin.

"Uh, yes."

Intrigue lit the woman's face, but before she could say anything more, another voice cut in.

"Huh, so you're Mara."

Mara stiffened against a pang of dread, her gaze darting past the woman to the man sitting across from her. He wore a uniform, his badge glistening despite the lack of sunlight. A hint of silver at his temples tapered into dark hair that matched his deep-set eyes.

Why would a cop know her name? Nobody here should recognize hers as a familiar face. She'd been so careful . . .

"You know her?" the woman asked.

The police officer pushed away an empty mug. "No, but I know Lenora."

The woman tipped her head, one of her large hoop earrings brushing her shoulder. "Who?"

"The owner of the Everwood B&B. Bought the place, oh, about nine or ten months ago, I'd guess." The cop glanced at Mara as if seeking confirmation.

She gave a slight nod. Lenora had bought the Everwood last June. Mara had arrived in July.

"Sam Ross," the man said. "Police chief. I used to run into Lenora all the time at the library. She mentioned you."

"She . . . she did?"

He didn't have a chance to answer before the woman across from him spoke again. "I didn't even realize the Everwood was under new management. Some newspaperwoman I am." She shook her head, laughter in her eyes as she looked to Mara again. "I'm Jenessa Belville, editor of the local paper. Well, editor, reporter, and photographer all in one. My BFF here is—"

"Not your BFF, Jen." Sam leaned back in his chair, arms folded.

Jenessa's dimpled grin deepened. "Sam's always grumpy. Ignore him."

Mara would love to, but his dark-eyed study of her was too unsettling. It reminded her of Mr. and Mrs. Lyman's stares when she'd finally gotten brave—or maybe desperate —enough to complain about their college-aged son, Garrett.

She'd nannied the Lyman family's younger children for more than two years by that point. She'd been reliable, responsible, well-loved by the kids. Shouldn't that have been enough for her employers to trust her? To know she wouldn't make up stories?

And what reason could the local police chief have for looking at her with the same sort of skepticism now?

"Uh, nice to meet you both," Mara finally said.

Jenessa's fingers tapped against her covered cup. "So tell me all about the Everwood. I haven't been there since I was a kid. Is it still as creepy as it used to be? Do you live there? Does it get much business anymore?"

"Sheesh, Jen, give her break," Sam broke in. "She's here to talk to Jonas, not get interrogated."

Great. Just how much of her conversation with Jonas Clancy had they overheard?

Jenessa flashed an exaggerated pout toward Sam before turning to Mara again. "He's right, I totally interrupted. But don't be surprised if I show up at the Everwood one of these days. My curiosity is piqued."

"Maybe I'll come with." Sam balled a napkin in his hand, gaze unmoving.

The bakery's front door opened, ushering in a gust of cool air. Oh, *why* hadn't Mara just stayed back at the Everwood today like she had every other day?

And what? Clean all its empty rooms all over again for guests who wouldn't show? Sit around wondering when Lenora would return? Wondering why she'd gone so suddenly and where . . . and if she was coming back at all?

"How long has she been gone, Ms. Bristol?"

The banker's soft question drew her back around in her seat. Too much was happening at once. That police chief's disquieting stare. Jenessa's disarming chatter. The banker reading her situation far too well.

"About five weeks." Lenora had taken off on an early February morning, all casual and cheery, with every indication she'd be back soon.

If only Mara had asked more questions. Insisted on contact information.

"And you're staying at the Everwood? Alone?"

Why did she get the feeling the police chief was still listening? She offered only a bare nod.

"I'm not sure how appropriate it is to discuss Lenora Worthington's business with . . . as you said, an 'unofficial' employee." He laced his fingers atop his newspaper. "But since you've already read the letter, I can tell you it's accurate. Three months' worth of mortgage installments have gone unpaid. And unless they're paid in full in thirty days, we'll have to begin foreclosure proceedings."

There it was. The dreaded truth.

Mara's dejected gaze drifted to the window. A lone ray of sun had finally pushed through woolen clouds to settle over the quaint town square. Old-fashioned brass lampposts lined puddled walkways. This really was a cute little town, complete with a picturesque riverfront, antique shops, and tourist spots. Mara had read all the brochures in the display case in the Everwood lobby—the one for the Maple Valley Scenic Railroad, the apple orchard, the old mansion that'd been turned in to a library.

For a while there, she'd thought this could be . . . it. Her place. For good. Finally.

Mr. Clancy leaned forward. "If Lenora has abandoned the property—"

"She wouldn't. She loves it."

The argument was too familiar, conjuring feeble, youthful words from twenty years ago. *"Dad wouldn't just leave. He loves us."*

Then again, love wasn't always enough.

But Lenora wasn't Dad—never mind that Jonas Clancy's look of doubt could've been Mom's. Lenora had made plans for the Everwood—all kinds of plans for fixing it up, breathing new life into it. And in the weeks-turned-to-months Mara had spent helping run the B&B, Lenora's vision for the old house had become Mara's. She'd convinced herself Lenora needed her as much as she needed Lenora.

And yet, a memory trickled in—of Lenora talking about her years as a travel photographer, trekking the world with her husband. *"We didn't have kids, so we could do that—take off on a whim. One day we'd be in church or at a coffee shop or sitting in front of the TV at home and we'd look at each other and just know...it was time. We'd call one of our magazine contacts and a day or two later, we'd be on a plane."*

What if Lenora had gotten one of her whims?

No. *No.* "She'll be back soon."

Mr. Clancy flattened his palms on the tabletop. "I do hope so. For everyone's sake. The Everwood is the only lodging in Maple Valley. We're no Atlantic City, but we have enough fairs and festivals year round to draw visitors. I wish I could do more to help."

He was a kind man. Understanding. Which might've made her feel a little better if not for those words knocking around in her brain. *Thirty days.*

Thirty days and she might find herself without an anchor all over again.

"Thank you, Mr. Clancy." She stood, gathered her cup of lukewarm tea, umbrella, tote bag. "I appreciate your ti—"

The bakery door opened again, robbing her attention—a hiss of wind, jangling bells, and . . .

She dropped her cup.

A silhouette moved through the doorway. Broad shoulders, longish hair, swaggering gait.

Shock clawed its way from her lungs, scraping her throat and escaping in a gasp.

Garrett.

No. There was no way. No possible way . . .

A happy shriek—the newspaper editor's—jarred Mara's already tumbling nerves. "Lucas!"

The form zigzagged around tables, his features coming into focus as Jenessa bounded toward him, and Mara's racing pulse refused to slow. *Not Garrett. Look at his face. It's not Garrett. Jenessa called him Lucas.*

But the scare was enough. She moved so swiftly that the chair behind her tipped. She ignored the puddle of tea at her feet. Ignored Mr. Clancy—or maybe the police chief—calling her name.

Pricks of rain stung her face the moment she stepped outside. She gulped for air, for relief.

It didn't come.

3

---

*M*ara awoke to a crash of thunder and the feel of something moving in the bed. Her pillow muffled her yelp, the sudden hammering of her heartbeat nearly drowning the squall outside.

Until the soft movement stole closer and an unwelcome paw batted her hair. *Not Garrett.*

She flipped onto her back. The cat that had chased away Mrs. Jenkins stared at her from fawn-colored eyes, his back stiffening when a flash of lightning stirred the room.

"Scared, are you? Serves you right for barging into my bedroom."

A stormy gale thrust itself against the side of the house. It was the second time she'd awoken this night. The first had been to the sound of sheets of rain and the eerie keening of the old elm tree out front.

She'd spent the next hour hunting for a flashlight and buckets, searching out leaks all over the house. No small feat considering the Everwood's rambling square footage —three floors counting the spacious attic. She swung her legs over the side of the bed, resigned to being awake while the storm continued. Might as well check her rain pails.

Although why she'd bothered with them, she really didn't know. *Thirty days.*

Which was worse? The reality that in a month, she might be forced out of this place, find herself unmoored and on the move again, or the realization that Lenora hadn't been making her mortgage payments since *before* she'd left.

Mara didn't even want to consider what that might mean.

She collected her pink fleece robe from the foot of the bed, hard floor chilled underneath her bare feet, and pulled it over her striped flannel pajamas. That rascal of a feline brushed up against her leg. She scowled. "How many times do I have to tell you I'm not a cat person?"

She could've sworn he shrugged his bony shoulders before sidling past her and out the bedroom door.

At a shaking boom of thunder, Mara grabbed the flashlight from her nightstand and padded from the room. The electricity had gone off hours ago. Her thin beam of light cut through the darkness pervading the corridor, the storm's fury threatening to reach inside. More thunder, pounding rain surely bruising the already beaten down slate roof, and somewhere a tree branch rapped against a window. Moving shadows splayed over pinstriped wallpaper.

Mara's fingers tightened around the flashlight as she moved down the hallway. *It's just a spring rain, that's all. Just a little thunderstorm.* The shadows were just shadows—hers and the cat's—and all the noise came from outside not inside.

It'll be over soon and—

A thump sounded.

Mara froze. *That* came from inside. First floor. Too heavy to be the cat.

She flung open the door that led to the closed-off attic stairway, clambered up its steps, heart thudding. She burst into the attic, the light of her flashlight frantically roving the space as she listened for more noise from below . . .

Nothing. Only the racket outside and the moaning of the house as it stood its ground.

A nervous giggle slipped past her lips. So she'd spooked. An entirely reasonable reaction considering—the darkness, the storm, the leftover fear from this morning when she'd made a fool of herself in the bakery.

Something swished against her robe. She didn't even have to look. "Just can't stay away, can you?"

The cat bounced onto a box, one of dozens scattered across the attic.

"Or maybe you're just a scaredy-cat looking to the only human around for protection. Hate to tell you, but you picked the wrong girl."

She'd thought she was being brave this morning— venturing into town, pleading the Everwood's case. But if those minutes in the bakery had proven anything, it's that she was still the jumpy girl who'd arrived on the Everwood's doorstep last summer.

She moved around the attic, checking her buckets, employing a spare to empty a few that were already half full. Trickling water joined the sound of her soft footsteps. The cat followed her from corner to corner, climbing over boxes, covered furniture, who knew what else. According to Lenora, all of this, like the cat, had come part and parcel with the house when she'd purchased it. Lenora had spent quite a lot of time up here sorting through boxes. How many nights had Mara lain in bed, listening to her padding around overhead?

What were you searching for, Lenora?

Why hadn't Mara ever thought to ask Lenora more about her own life? She knew about Lenora's photography and that she was a widow as of a couple years ago.

She knew too that the older woman had actually spent some of her childhood in this house. Lenora's parents had run the Everwood for a time decades ago. Lenora said she'd always looked back fondly on those years. After her husband had died, she'd come back to visit the place only to end up buying it.

Another whim.

Mara had never thought to question the feasibility of it all. She'd just assumed that if Lenora had plans to fix up the place, then she also had the finances and long-term strategy to make them happen. Clearly that wasn't the case.

The cat's slanting eyes glowed through the darkness and the truth hovered in the quiet. "She's not coming back, is she?"

The thought had wriggled in off and on over the past five weeks, but every time she'd swatted it away. Now, though, she couldn't hold it at bay any longer.

Lenora hadn't been paying her mortgage. She hadn't moved forward with any renovations after the kitchen. And though it was strange that she would've left without packing all her belongings and giving Mara some kind of notice, it was in keeping with the nomadic lifestyle she and her husband had once lived.

Lenora wasn't coming back. It was time for Mara to accept it. With a sigh, she hauled her nearly full bucket to the stairs, careful not to let the rainwater slosh over the edge.

Back on the second floor, she treaded over the worn narrow rug that stretched to the top of the open staircase leading to the first floor. Her steps slowed as a chill wound its way up to her. A draft? Coming from downstairs?

And another thump.

Except, no, that wasn't a thump. More of a slap . . .

She gulped, the bucket's weight like an anchor, her toes curling in the cold. She inched down one step, then another. The flashlight under her arm had ceased to be useful, dangling as it was toward the floor, her precarious grip on it waning. "Cat?" she whispered. "I can't believe I'm saying this, but I could use some company about now."

Slap.

Halfway down the steps, she craned her neck to peer past the check-in desk, and a relieved breath whooshed past her lips. It was only the front door, thrust open by the wind, apparently. Had she forgotten to lock it? She never forgot. Maybe she'd been distracted by the storm.

She crept down a few more steps. She'd survived her second scare of the night. Soon she'd be back in bed and—

A moan. Not the wind but a real moan. A man's moan.

And then she saw it, the clump at the bottom of the stairs. The moan was coming from the clump and the clump was beginning to move and—

Mara reacted before she could stop herself, both arms lifting her bucket, her flashlight dropping free. The man had barely risen to a crouch when the shower of water splashed over him.

His gasp gave way to a deep-throated groan as rainwater puddled around him. Mara's flashlight plunked step-by-step to the floor, and by the time it rolled to a stop in front of him, the hulk of a man was standing to his feet with only a slight sway, his white shirt clinging to his skin and clashing with the dark.

Mara couldn't make herself move as he slowly lifted his head, water slicking down his cheeks.

"Was that . . . entirely . . . necessary?" He rasped the words, fatigue clinging to his tone, showing in the way he gripped the banister with one hand.

"I . . . you . . ."

He flicked wet hair out of his eyes with a shake of his head. "You gonna chuck that empty bucket at me too?"

"If I have to." Her own words surprised her, and a flash of lightning lit the man's profile just long enough for her to catch the faintest dash of amusement in his tired eyes. It vanished as quickly as the storm's crackling light.

Thunder boomed and the front door thwacked against the wall. "This place have a cellar?"

"A cellar?"

"A basement. We need to take cover." He picked up her flashlight, shined it around the entryway.

"It's just a thunderstorm."

"You're the only one here?"

"How do you know—"

He pointed the flashlight at her gaping robe. "Don't think you'd be wearing those old-man pajamas around if you thought you were going to have company."

"Old-man paj—"

"But seriously, is anybody else here? If so, we need to wake them up and get down to the basement. If there's no basement, we at least need to get away from the front portion of the house."

"It's just a thunderstorm. It'll pass." She descended the rest of the stairs and slipped past the towering man, intent on closing the front door.

"I'm telling you, that wind is no joke. Could be a tornado on the way. And you've got a tree out front that looks like it could—"

The holler of the wind cut him off, blowing the bucket

from her hands and billowing her robe. And a dreadful crack split the air. *That's not lightning.*

It was her sole coherent thought before the single crack splintered into a thousand whining blows. She heard the shattering of glass and something crashing—

And the man's yell from behind as strong arms lifted her from her feet.

How Marshall had gone from passed out on the front lawn of a dilapidated B&B to stalking down its hallway with a flailing woman in his arms, he honestly didn't know. Everything was a muddled blur.

He'd been driving—one highway to another. He vaguely remembered crossing into Iowa. At some point, he'd felt his daily headache morphing into a migraine. Daylight had unraveled into dark. He'd pulled onto a side road and . . . oh yeah, he'd stopped at a gas station in some dinky town to ask about lodging.

That's how he'd ended up at the B&B. Was it the migraine that'd knocked him out before he'd made it inside? Or some kind of medication withdrawal?

All he knew was he'd woken up soaking wet to the incessant creaking of that tree that leaned way too close to the house. He was coherent enough to know danger when he saw it. But he'd been so dizzy when he rose to his feet that by the time he burst into the house, he'd passed out all over again. *Pathetic.*

"Put me down!"

He had one arm around the woman's back and the other under the crook of her bent knees. Her bare toes bounced as he thudded through the house. "I just saved you from being walloped by a tree crashing through your front door. You could show a little more appreciation."

He got a mouthful of her hair as she whipped her head to look over his shoulder. Did she realize how tightly her arms gripped his neck? Dang woman was going to strangle him.

"Where's the basement door?"

"Put me down and I'll tell you."

"And have you run back up front to survey the damage? I don't think so."

"But—"

Thunder shook the house. "Lady, this is no great treat for me either. I've been on the road since noon. I've got a headache like you wouldn't believe." Why hadn't he saved just one bottle of painkillers from Beth's raid? "I'm tired. I'm wet. All I want is a bed—"

"Door's right there."

"—and instead I'm hauling a stubborn woman . . . what?"

"I said the basement door is right there."

Her breath was warm on his face and the fleece of her robe tickled his skin. And for one fragile, foolish moment, his hazy brain let down its defenses. Like a fog, the memory curled in—of carrying Penny just like this. Of her arms knotted around his neck as he stepped over the threshold into their first—and as it turned out—only Milwaukee home. He could almost smell that coconut lotion she always used to wear.

"The door?"

He closed his eyes, warding off the memory, and when he opened them again, it wasn't Penny's face only inches from his. And it wasn't coconut he smelled, but something subtle and soft. Like apples or—

"Are you okay?" The bundle in his arms had stilled even as the storm raged.

He managed a gruff nod before lowering her to her feet then reached for the doorknob and yanked. Too hard. He heard a screw hit the floor and the woman's sharp intake.

"Did you just rip that door off its hinges?"

"Only the bottom hinge. Must've already been loose." He shuffled down one step and waited for his sight to adjust to a new layer of darkness. At least he still had the woman's flashlight. He'd tucked it into a belt loop before hoisting her from her feet. He pulled it loose now.

"What's your name?"

He flicked on the flashlight. "Marshall. Yours?" Stairs creaked behind him as she followed.

"Mara. You're not a serial killer or anything, are you?"

"If I was, wouldn't I have let that tree do its job instead of rescuing you?"

"No, because serial killers have routines. There's always a method to their madness. You wouldn't have let the tree take me out because it would've ruined your master plan to kill me yourself."

Well, wasn't she a morbid one.

He reached the bottom of the steps. Damp dust and the musty scent of mothballs clogged the air. He lifted the flashlight to survey their surroundings—sagging shelving, a few paint cans, empty crates, filmy cobwebs in every corner. Charming.

"These aren't old-man pajamas, by the way."

He swung the light back to the woman—Mara. It landed on her bare feet first, traveled the length of those striped pajamas, and settled on her face. Freckles and blue-green eyes. Red hair skimmed her shoulders and—

Wait. He darted the flashlight to her head once more. That wasn't just red hair.

"Your forehead." He stepped closer.

She backed away. "What about it?"

Another step forward for him. Another step backward for her. "You're bleeding."

Puzzlement clouded her eyes as she lifted one hand to where a tangle of hair slanted over her forehead. "Guess you didn't save me from that walloping after all."

It was all he could do not to flinch when she brushed her hair away.

"It's that bad?"

"It's a head wound. They always seem a lot worse than they are. They bleed a lot."

She held her red-splotched hand out in front of her. "Yeah, I'm kind of getting that." Her rattled tone defied her calm words.

He swung his flashlight around the room again. Surely there was a towel down here or a rag or something.

"Marshall?"

He turned in time to see her begin to sway. From the wound or the sight of the blood? He reached out to steady her with his free hand, guiding her toward a tipped-over crate. "Take a seat."

Up close the wound looked even worse, matting her hair to the side of her face. His weariness warred with his concern as he sighed, tucked the flashlight through his belt loop again, and snagged the hem of his shirt with both hands.

"Wait, what are you—"

The rest of her words were muted by the tussle of his damp shirt coming over his head. He ignored her wide eyes and the sudden cold scraping his skin, instead reaching for her hand. He placed his wadded up shirt into her palm then lifted it to her head.

"Hold it firm." He whirled toward the staircase.

"Where are you going?"

43

That was panic in her voice, plain and simple. "To get something to clean up that wound."

"Can't that wait?"

He started up the stairs. "Don't close your eyes or drift off. You could have a concussion." Must've been a branch that hit her before he'd pulled her out of the way.

"Marshall?"

He stopped halfway up the stairs.

"There's a first-aid kit in the kitchen. Drawer closest to the fridge."

He started up again.

"Marshall?"

"Yes?" His voice was tight around his impatience. Maybe he should've just climbed into his truck to wait out the storm. Better yet, he should've skipped Iowa altogether. He could've driven north from Milwaukee instead. Crossed into Canada.

"There's a cat. I don't even like him, but if you happen to see him . . ."

He allowed himself a glance over his shoulder. She looked so small down there, hunched over that crate, his shirt hiding her wound. He let out breath. "I'll find your cat, Mara."

"Thanks. Though, technically, he's not my cat."

She really felt the need to correct him at a time like this? *Exasperating woman.*

He might've said it out loud—a fitting accompaniment for his rolling eyes—but who would've known with another boom of thunder vibrating the house? With the aid of the flashlight, it took all of thirty seconds to locate the kitchen. Huh. From what little he could see, it looked more modern than he would've expected. He discovered the first-aid kit exactly where Mara said he would.

But the cat? Could be anywhere. Was he going to have to

tour the whole house to find him? With the way Marshall's luck was going—

A searing hiss cut into the night. He turned, rain thrashing the window over the kitchen sink, and there stood the cat on the counter—back arched, tail ramrod straight. "All right, pal, let's go."

He reached one hand toward the feline. Got a scratch in return. Lovely.

"Suit yourself. She said she didn't even like you that much, so I doubt she'll cry too many tears if I show up without you."

He marched from the kitchen, not bothering to see if the cat followed. But as soon as he opened the basement door, the animal raced past his ankles. He bounded down the steps in time to see the cat jump onto the crate next to Mara.

Marshall crouched in front of her, lightly taking hold of her wrist to remove his wet shirt from her forehead. "Here, hold the flashlight for me. Tip it toward your face."

"Do I need stitches?" She bit her lip at the end of the question, the light glowing under her chin and highlighting the spray of tiny freckles over her cheeks and nose.

Pears. That's what he'd smelled earlier. "A little Neosporin and a bandage and I think you'll be fine." Though she might have a nice goose egg to show for it come morning.

He leaned closer but she tipped back. "Wait."

"Not a serial killer, remember? I'm just going to clean it. You don't want it to get infected."

"I know that." But she slipped past him, off the crate, and stood. She shrugged her robe from her shoulders and held it out. "Here."

"That's all right. Pink's not really my color."

Her focus flitted from his face to his bare chest and back again. "You're not wearing a shirt."

"I think we can weather the scandal." Was he actually teasing her? Here he was wet and cold and shirtless, a scratch stinging his hand, headache and all . . .

Except the headache seemed to have faded somewhat. And the scratch was nothing. And he honestly didn't know why, but he was suddenly glad he hadn't driven to Canada. "I don't need your robe. Wouldn't fit me anyway."

"You have to be cold."

"I'm fine."

"You have goose bumps."

He sighed.

He rolled his eyes. Again.

He put on the robe.

The sleeves barely made it past his elbows and he'd have caused a seam to split if he forced it to close in front. So he ignored the belt and let the robe hang open. Which was apparently enough for Mara because she gave him a satisfied nod and reclaimed her spot on the crate.

"Now can I clean your wound?"

"Now you can clean my wound."

He flipped open the first-aid kit and bent in front of her again.

"Marshall?"

With a light touch, he brushed her hair away from the gash marring her forehead. Made no sense, none at all, the way his pulse picked up in that moment. And she was wrong about those goose bumps. He wasn't cold. "Yeah?"

"How long do you think we need to stay down here?"

"Until the storm stops, I guess."

He finished cleaning the wound and stuck a bandage in place, then lowered to the floor.

"How'd you end up here anyway?"

"Got directions at a gas station." A fuzzy memory slid into focus. Pulling up in front of the house. The sign under the tree with its stenciled letters. Laney's magazine ad . . . had he let it blow away? His empty stomach twisted at the loss.

"I'm sorry I threw that bucket of water on you."

"No matter. I was already rain-soaked." How long had he lain out there on the lawn anyway? Felled by his own weakness. He really was pitiful.

But he'd made it through a day. One day. No pills. No work. No stubborn, reckless decisions that made anyone else's life difficult.

He closed his eyes and leaned back against the damp wall. One day. It was something.

4

LENORA

*M*ara showed up on my doorstep looking like a wounded bird. On a summer night when I was already grieving my own clipped wings.

I'd bought the Everwood only a few months earlier and though I knew it was where I needed to be—even wanted to be—I missed George so terribly that day. Missed our adventures. Wondered if it would take longer than planned to learn how to settle.

But then Mara knocked and it was as if God said, "Here, Lenora, receive this reminder as the gift it is. Your grounding has more of a purpose than you think."

And so I did.

I opened my door to a woman with beautiful red hair and I saw her bruises, both inside and out. My heart did that thing George used to tease me about . . . reach for the closest hurting soul and hold on tight. In fact, it's what I'd prayed for after George died—that God would give me someone to focus on rather than myself and my newfound solitude. A new family.

I like to think that if I'd ever had children of my own,

once in a while even as adults they'd need me the way Mara Bristol needed me that night.

The way I wish I'd let myself need my parents. Instead, George became my world the day we married. Why didn't I think there was room for both? Or maybe it's not fair to blame our romance and the carefree lives we lived—all that travel—for the distance between me and my parents.

Maybe it was always there.

There's so much I've never understood about them, you see. Why we left Maple Valley so suddenly when I was six. Why I had no grandparents or cousins or aunts and uncles. Why Dad never talked of his past and why we only ever heard the same few stories about Mom's childhood.

George teased me about that too—my wonderings. He used to say I could find a mystery in anything. And I would laugh and allow my questions to retreat, huddle up and wait, tucked away for another day.

But George is gone now. And "another day" finally became "today."

My questions led me to the Everwood, once my childhood home.

And the answers ripped me away all over again.

But first . . . there was Mara. My wounded bird.

I learned some things about her right away that first night. For starters, no one had ever made that girl a proper cup of tea before. I saw the way she accepted the saucer when I handed it to her—that pinched expression that said she'd never liked the stuff but would drink it out of politeness. And then, surprise of all surprises, she discovered she liked it. That's what a suitable steeping and just the right amount of milk and honey will do.

I learned she hailed from Arizona. Then Texas, Ohio, Illinois. I'm not sure she ever meant Iowa to be a stopping point. But she was out of money by the time she arrived at the Everwood.

Oh, and she didn't like cats.

It took longer to learn the rest. I'd known she was running but it was weeks before I'd discover why. Months before she'd share all of it . . .

Many days I knew it was best to keep things light. So I'd tell her about George's and my travels. Or chuckle at the strange delight she took in mixing her own cleaning products and dusting one room after another. Or I'd ply her with questions about the children she nannied.

"What made you decide to become a nanny?" I asked her one afternoon as we sat in the two dining room chairs we'd dragged into the kitchen. Yellowed linoleum still covered the kitchen floor, though it'd started curling up in one corner. The cabinets were an outdated shade of walnut, three of their doors and one drawer missing their handles. Rust stained the sink.

I'd always planned to update the kitchen first. But before Mara's arrival, it'd seemed too hefty a task for a lone, old woman. Realization had begun to settle in, as well—the financial kind. I had enough money to redo this kitchen but only just. Until Mara joined me, many was the morning I'd awoken with the same first thought: *What have I gotten myself into?*

But that afternoon, myself reinvigorated and Mara more at peace than I'd seen her since that first July night, we had decided to make a list of all that needed to happen to modernize and beautify the kitchen.

She considered my question for a few quiet moments then shrugged. "I don't know if I ever really decided to become a nanny at all. I'd been working as a housekeeper at a hotel in Phoenix for almost a year after graduating high school. I heard some guests talking about needing a nanny for the summer. Just drifted into it, I guess."

She smoothed her hand over the notebook in her lap as she spoke, its open page displaying her crinkled hand-writing—notes about keeping and painting the existing cupboards, replacing doors, flooring, curtains, appliances.

"It's kind of funny, really. I don't know that I ever really thought of myself as someone who loves kids. I don't *not* love them, but I don't think I've ever had a strong maternal instinct like other girls."

I pulled a dripping teabag from my mug. "I think probably what you have is a caretaking instinct. A gift, really."

"I'm not a gifted person, Lenora. Never have been." She said it with all the nonchalance in the world.

I felt the same old compassionate twitch of my heart-strings and was sure—just sure—that somewhere George was smiling. "Mara, my dear, I have watched you run a rag over woodwork with more care than I used to take cleaning my camera lenses."

"Because I'm weird and I like cleaning."

"No, because you take care of things that matter to you. You're a born caretaker. You've even taken care of me."

"You've got that completely backward, Lenora. If anything, you've taken care of me."

"Yes, well, you don't know how many times before you showed up here, I was ready to give up on this old place. It's been hard to keep seeing its hidden beauty amid all the work of it. In helping me care for it, you *are* caring for me."

She gave a little laugh and said something about how helping around the Everwood was the least she could do. And then, we went back to our list-making.

So many conversations followed in the weeks after that while we sanded and painted the old kitchen cupboards. Pulled out that ugly linoleum floor. Perused appliances and countertops in magazines and online. Although it didn't escape me, not in the slightest, the way Mara hid herself away when the deliverymen happened by.

A person can't hide forever. This, I know. But we all need a safe haven now and then.

The Everwood had been that once to my family, though I hadn't known it at the time. I was only beginning to untangle the unknown strands of my childhood when Mara landed in my life.

But the Everwood was meant to be her refuge too. I felt it deep in my bones . . . deeper than the brittle cold of an Iowa winter.

So I let her stay. And I loved her. I loved her in every way I knew how. Like a mother and a friend. Both in silence and in words. In home-cooked meals and a room of her own and occasional efforts to open up her eyes to her own inner qualities, her strengths.

Such a gift it was. To watch a hungry spirit begin to heal right in front of me. She might very well discover her wings again one of these days. Just thinking about it brings me joy.

There might be little hope left for me, but I have all the hope in the world for her.

And maybe that, I tell myself now in this strained haze where the light can't seem to get in, is enough.

5

There was a man asleep in the basement. Wearing Mara's bathrobe. Nearly six hours he'd been slumbering in that dank cellar, up against a cinder block wall. Exactly where he'd dozed off not long after bandaging her head.

She had about as much of an idea what to do with him as she did the toppled tree crowding the Everwood's battered porch.

Or the police chief standing in her storm-wrecked entryway.

Sam Ross didn't wear a uniform today and his badge was nowhere in sight. But his furrowed brow and dark eyes said what his attire didn't—there was more to his visit than mere friendliness. So she hadn't been imagining his misgivings at the bakery yesterday.

"I'm sorry if you drove all the way out here to see Lenora." Did her voice sound as groggy as she felt? "She's . . . not here."

The police chief rubbed his clean-shaven chin. "I see.

Does she know about all of this? The tree? The porch? The missing front door?"

Mara hadn't even noticed that yet—the fact that the door wasn't just open but gone entirely. The tree must've taken it out. It was probably splintered among the mess on the porch. She cupped her hands around her warm mug, willing the hazelnut brew to give her what a few fitful hours of sleep and a hasty shower hadn't—the energy to face the wreckage around her.

She hadn't been able to make herself survey the damage last night when the storm had finally settled. She'd crept up the back stairway instead, the one that curved around Lenora's living quarters, too tired to deal with the fallen tree or figure out what to do with the stranger still sound asleep below.

But now . . .

Oh Lenora, what in the world am I supposed to do about this?

The tree trunk lay in a fractured slant, porch boards and roof tiles scattered in heaps around it. One roughhewn limb had fallen through the picture window into the sitting room. Guess that accounted for the shattering glass she'd heard just before Marshall wrenched her away from the front door in time to avoid being knocked off her feet by the branch reaching into the entryway.

"Well, does she? I heard you tell Jonas Clancy that Lenora left you in charge of the place. You do have some way of getting ahold of her, don't you?"

Irritation added a tick to his square jaw when she didn't answer—but, too, concern. For Lenora?

"Look, ten years on the force have taught me to trust my instincts. My instinct says something isn't right here."

"Mr. . . Chief Ross—"

"Sam." Sunlight invaded the space around him. "Are you squatting here?"

She almost spit out her coffee. "*What?*"

His drilling stare didn't so much as flicker. "You hesitated to give Jonas your last name yesterday. You tampered with someone else's mail."

"I didn't . . ." Well, she did.

"Your explanation about what you're doing here was flimsy at best. Unofficial employee?" He folded his arms. "And most perplexing of all, you told Jonas you've been in town for eight months, yet I haven't heard so much as a single choo-choo from the local gossip train about you. So you're either one heck of a hermit or you've gone to great lengths to remain anonymous."

Or both. "I didn't know eavesdropping was such a big part of a police chief's job."

Was she seeing things or did he almost free a grin? "The point is, despite all that, I'm trying real hard to give you a chance to explain yourself before I jump to conclusions, but you're not making it easy."

She set her coffee mug on the check-in desk with a clunk. "Well, I'm not squatting. Lenora asked me to take care of the place. That's what I'm doing."

His dark eyebrows lifted but instead of arguing, he inclined his head and considered her for a moment. "I told you yesterday that I ran into Lenora a few times at the library. The time she mentioned you, she was carrying this stack of children's books. I happened to ask her if they were for grandkids and she said no, they were for Mara. Only she clammed up real quick after that, like she hadn't meant to say your name."

"I don't know what you want from me, Chief—Sam."

"I thought I was pretty clear on that. A little forthrightness."

"Then I'll be forthright. I'm managing the Everwood as

best I can in Lenora's absence. I don't know where she is. I don't know how to get in touch with her. I wish I did."

He sidestepped a branch and looked around the debris-filled lobby. "When I first met Lenora, I was surprised that anyone would want to take on this old place. I wonder if she just got in over her head. Maybe she knew what was coming and decided to jump ship rather than stick around to watch the bank repossess."

Mara wanted to argue but hadn't she come to the same unwilling belief last night? That Lenora wasn't coming back. She'd abandoned the Everwood, abandoned Mara.

Like too many others before her.

Just like that, Mara was eleven again, almost twelve. It was the eve of her birthday. There was a set table. A roast in the slow cooker. A pretty dress. A rehearsed speech.

Dad had walked away a year earlier, but he was coming back for her birthday. And Mara had a plan. She'd convinced Mom to make Dad's favorite meal while she'd cleaned the whole house. They'd eat together, the three of them, just like they used to. Dad would realize how much he'd missed them.

But the plan hadn't worked, hadn't won Dad back. Instead, it was as if she'd lost Mom too. *"He was never going to stay, Mara. I wish you hadn't talked me into this."*

Sometimes she honestly wasn't sure which was worse—Dad abandoning his family for a music career in Nashville or Mom so steeped in her own anger and grief that she just stopped seeing Mara. Stopped caring.

Sam cleared his throat, tugging Mara back to the present. He stared at her bandaged forehead. "You didn't have that yesterday. The tree?"

She nodded. "Just a scrape." She swallowed a long gulp of her coffee, prayed he didn't notice the shaking of her hand.

"So what's your plan? Just hang out here until the bank forces you out? Or are you actually trying to run this place?"

Again she used her coffee mug like a shield, drinking instead of answering.

Sam expelled a sigh. "Fine. I'll help you deal with the tree then—"

"No. I mean, that's okay. I can handle it."

"I really don't think you can."

"Please . . . just . . . leave."

He shifted his weight from foot to foot. But finally, with a nod and another sigh, he turned.

Before relief could set in, though, he faced her again. "Look, Maple Valley has an emergency relief fund for local businesses. We had a tornado a few years ago, followed by a flood only months later. Lots of businesses needed help getting back on their feet. So the city council started a grant program."

"I'm not sure why you're telling me this."

"Neither am I. But if you've got some thought of keeping this place afloat . . . well, there's a fund, there's money available." He shrugged. "Do with that what you will."

He turned and strode across the wrecked porch, down what was left of the steps. He crossed the lawn, pausing near her car before pacing to his own.

"Hope you know he just took down your license plate number."

Mara jumped at the voice, coffee mug jerking, liquid splashing over her shirt. She turned. The man from the basement—still shirtless, still wearing her pink bathrobe.

Marshall shouldn't laugh. He really, really shouldn't laugh. But the sight of her was too much. Coffee all over her shirt, wet hair windblown from the open door, cheeks tinted red from the cold. Bare feet again. Weren't her toes frozen?

While he tried and failed to stifle his chuckles, Mara plunked her mug onto the counter nearby, her gaze traveling the length of him. His brown hair undoubtedly resembled a lion's mane, and yesterday's bristle was likely today's beard. Between the grass-stained jeans, the too-small robe, and the lack of a shirt underneath, he had to look ridiculous.

But however he looked, he *felt* like a new man this morning. He'd *slept* last night. Five—maybe even six—hours in a row. For once, he hadn't awakened in a medicine-induced fog either. No headache, not even a single twinge in a single muscle from sleeping in a sitting position.

Which was probably why he truly laughed now. Because he was in his first good mood in two years. "This seems fitting, doesn't it? You doused me with rainwater last night. Now I scare you into spilling coffee on yourself this morning."

"I could have third degree burns and here you are laughing."

If she'd burned herself she'd be running for cold water right now, not standing there with her hands on her hips, glaring at him. "I hope you at least appreciate that I hung back in the dining room until your friend left. Figured I wasn't dressed for company."

"He's not my friend, and if you're trying to be funny, I'm not in the mood." Her eyes flashed with annoyance. Call him batty, but he was caught between the urge to keep teasing—because, frankly, there was something charming about her cross temperament—and the desire to somehow make her feel better. Help her out. She did have a tree intruding on her house, after all.

The distant sound of a motor faded and Mara gave a heavy sigh before reaching for her cup once more and lifting it to her lips, only to find it empty.

"Surprised I didn't hear you leave the basement," he said. "Not exactly how I expected to spend last night—sleeping on a cement floor in a woman's robe."

"I'd like it back eventually, if you don't mind."

"Fine." Didn't take him more than a second to slip it off, hold it out. And wow, if her cheeks were red before . . .

"I didn't mean *now*."

"You are one hard woman to please, you know that? How's your head, by the way?"

She blinked. Opened her mouth. Clamped it closed again.

"Don't be mad. I saved you from the tree, remember?" No smile. Nothing. Fine, no more teasing. "I can see your day is not off to the best start. Is there anything I can do to—"

She snatched her robe from his outstretched hand. "What do you mean he took down my license plate number?"

Okay. "He stopped by your car. He took out a little notebook. Pretty blatant." He shrugged. "Why? Does that bother you? Are you a criminal, Mara?" So much for no more teasing. What was with him this morning?

Mara's freckles bunched and those aqua eyes of hers shot arrows. "Thank you for the help last night. Thank you for returning my robe. And, yes, thank you for waiting to make an appearance until he left. It's bad enough the local police chief thinks I'm squatting. The last thing I need is him seeing you—like that—and wondering if any other funny business is going on here."

Don't say it, Marsh. Don't even open your mouth. "Care to elaborate on what you mean by funny business?"

Could her eyes get any narrower? "But as there's a tree in the lobby and foreclosure on the horizon, which I'm sure you've figured out from your eavesdropping—"

"Hey, I wasn't—"

"—it's probably best that you leave." She spun away from Marshall again, trudging to what he assumed was the bed and breakfast's check-in desk—a long counter dusty with storm debris. Rays of blue and green sunlight poured through the row of stained glass overhead, somehow unharmed by the storm.

He hadn't noticed that last night, the stained glass. Hadn't noticed much of any of it, really. Certainly not the ornate crown molding that matched the fancy banister of the open staircase. Nor the pillars that added a majestic air where this room opened into what looked like some kind of parlor or something. The floors needed a good sanding and fresh staining. But rip out the kaleidoscope of wallpaper, paint and polish and clean up the storm's mess, and this bed and breakfast—this Everwood—could be something pretty nice.

Of course, he hadn't seen the upstairs yet. If every room up there needed the kind of makeover this first floor did, the project would take more than a few weeks' time. And more than a little money too.

"Marshall? Did you hear me?"

He'd moseyed away from Mara but turned to face her now. She was biting her lip again, all vexation toward him gone and replaced with an uncertainty painted into every feature of her pale face. Right, she'd asked him to leave.

"I'm sorry to be rude. It's just . . . I have enough to deal with as it is." A breeze cascaded through the open front door, a nearby broken window, riffling through her hair.

"I wish I had red hair, Daddy. Like Anne of Green Gables."

For once, the memory of Laney's voice didn't feel like torture. And it hit him—that, yes, he would've liked to stay here. A day, maybe two. He could help move that tree off the porch. Maybe he should offer.

But there was pleading in Mara's eyes and it wasn't for his continued presence. "I guess I'll take off then."

She only nodded.

An unspoken goodbye balancing between them, he mirrored her nod and turned.

Despite the dazzling sun and the clear blue sky, cold needled his bare skin as he picked his way across the ruined porch. The scent of rain still lingered in the air and the grass underfoot was damp. He reached his truck in seconds, rounding to the passenger side first. He nabbed a long-sleeved shirt from his suitcase and pulled it over his head.

He couldn't help another glance at the house. It was as in need of some heavy TLC outside as in—a good scraping, fresh paint, new shutters. Still, there was something regal about the Everwood. Something winsome and beckoning. He almost wished the foreclosure had already taken place. Then there'd be a FOR SALE sign in the yard and . . .

You would've loved it, Laney. We'd have had a heck of a time talking your mom into it, but with enough begging from you and bribing from me, we could've done it.

His slow release of breath expelled the usual sharpness of his pain. The ache was still there. But for the first time in a long time, he didn't sink with it nor run from it nor beat against it until it changed shapes, morphing into anger or blame or guilt. Anything to spare him from the force of his grief.

Instead, he simply dragged his gaze from the house and walked on steady legs to the other side of the truck. He would've piled into the driver's seat then. He would've turned the keys in the ignition, steered the truck onto the gravel lane that led away from the house, and navigated his way back to the highway . . .

If not for the glint of gloss-print that caught his eye just as his hand gripped the door handle.

No way.

Before his disbelief could gain hold, he bent to retrieve the wrinkled paper near a back wheel. The moment sunlight landed on the image, his heart constricted. Laney's house. How on God's green earth had that magazine page survived the storm?

He honestly could've cried. He could've plunked down on wet grass and bawled his eyes out and—

The blare of his phone lanced into the quiet. He dug it from the back pocket of his stained jeans, one hand still gripping the paper, and glanced at the screen. *Alex.*

He lifted the phone. "Hey, Alex." He couldn't stop looking at it—Laney's house. That blue door she thought was so pretty. The porch swing. The tree. "Let me guess—Beth told you to call."

His brother-in-law laughed. "She didn't want to be over-bearing by calling herself."

"My sister? Overbearing? I can't possibly imagine it. Listen, man, about the other day—"

"You don't have to say it, Marsh."

He let himself wander away from the car, toward the arched arbor at the side of the house, a sprinkle of violets pushing through the damp, brown earth around it. "I do, though. I have to apologize. Not just for the other day, but—"

He stepped under the arbor and gasped at the sight of the Everwood's back yard. It stretched to where a line of trees stood guard around the property. Sunlight glowed over a low fog that rolled into the grove. To the west, rope and stakes cordoned off a garden in need of attention.

A man could live a good life on land like this. The air smelled of spring—loamy and fresh—and the March breeze, though weighted with a chill, was a hopeful whisper.

"Marshall? You stopped talking mid-sentence. Where are you, anyway?"

"The middle of nowhere. Iowa." Laney could've run to her heart's content here. Oh, how she used to love running, even in their cramped townhouse, pumping her legs and swinging her arms.

"Iowa. Huh. Well, just tell me you're doing good so I can tell Beth you're doing good." Alex paused. "Tell me you're doing okay so *I* can know you're okay." He said it like the partner and friend he was.

Marshall looked again at the picture of Laney's house before lifting his gaze to the weather-beaten B&B. "I'm doing okay, Alex." *Maybe even more than okay.*

He pocketed his keys and strode toward the porch. He couldn't leave yet. Once upon a time, he'd been a likable, dependable guy. Surely he could conjure up the old Marshall long enough to convince Mara to let him stay—at least to help with the tree, if nothing else.

The sharp *thwack* of Marshall's axe sliced into the otherwise quiet of an unfolding twilight—the sky a swirl of pastels, the peeking western sun a pale sliver.

Mara dropped an armful of chopped wood onto the pile at the side of the house. She turned in time to see Marshall once again lift the rusty axe up and swing it down with forceful precision. A chill niggled down her spine, as packed with awe as it was the frosty cold.

What on earth had possessed her to tell Marshall he could stick around for the day?

And why wasn't he wearing a coat? Hints of spring might have hovered over the dewy ground earlier this morning, but on the cusp of night, the air had turned crisp. Winter hadn't gone into hibernation just yet. Nevertheless, Marshall wore only an unbuttoned flannel over the gray shirt underneath. The layers weren't enough to hide the strain of his muscles as the axe came up again.

Hours and hours he'd worked, hacking away at the fallen tree and wrestling it from the porch while Mara cleaned up inside, sweeping glass and debris, taping a quilt into place over the broken sitting room window, emptying buckets of rainwater. Marshall had barely stopped long enough to gulp down the peanut butter and jelly sandwich Mara brought him around lunchtime before getting back to work.

Once he'd finally cleared the porch, he'd started axing the tree into firewood. A chainsaw would've made the job easier, but all he'd been able to find in the garden shed out back was the axe. For the past hour and a half, he'd chopped while Mara gathered and piled the pieces.

And over and over, she'd replayed this morning. *"I'd like to stay and help clean up, if you'll let me. I know you turned down that cop when he offered, but . . . it's a tree, Mara. You can't move it by yourself."* He'd paused, looked down at her, as much of a giant of a man in the light of day as he'd seemed last night.

Handsome too, even with that wild, windblown hair and an untrimmed beard. Not that it unnerved her or anything. It was just a fact.

Okay, fine, it completely unnerved her. So why, then,

had she just stood there, mute, staring back at him until he finally spoke again? *"Besides, I don't have anywhere else I need to be."*

"Mara?"

She blinked. Marshall faced her now, the axe hanging loosely from one hand. Great, she'd been staring again. "It's almost suppertime," she blurted.

He glanced into the distance, at the fading colors of the horizon. "Guess it is."

She patted her work gloves together, dirt dusting the air. "I don't have much in the way of groceries. I've been eating boxed mac 'n' cheese for days."

His lips tugged upward and she noticed for the first time the creases that bracketed his mouth underneath his whiskers. More lines than dimples, but the effect was the same. The edges of his flannel shirt lifted in the breeze. "I haven't had that stuff in forever."

"I eat it all the time. Lenora says I have the taste buds of a five-year-old. Funny thing is, I can cook. I'm totally not useless in the kitchen. Yet I could happily eat mac 'n' cheese and tater tots and sugary cereal every day of the week." All day they'd worked in silence, and *now* she was rambling?

"Five-year-olds get all the good food. I should know, I had my—" He stopped, seemed to catch his breath. "I have a niece and nephew." He turned away long enough to stick the axe into the stump at his feet before facing her again and nudging his head toward the house. "Lenora. She's the owner?"

Mara nodded.

"And she's . . ."

"Not here."

"Kinda picked up on that." Another smile. Not the brief smirk from this morning when he'd teased her about the spilled coffee or even the half-grin of seconds ago over a conversation about mac 'n' cheese of all things. But the real thing—a smile that reached all the way into his gray eyes and spoke of a newfound something that hadn't been there last night or even earlier today when he'd first come up from the basement.

A measure of peace. She recognized it like it was her reflection in a mirror eight months ago, her first day at the Everwood...

When she'd prayed her first prayer in years. *Thank you, God, for bringing me here.*

In general, she wasn't convinced the prayers of a girl who'd never done all that much with her life mattered to God. But the gratitude had spilled from her all the same. She'd almost believed in that moment that God had led her here. Lenora, with her strong faith, certainly would've said that was the case.

Is that why Marshall had come back to the house this morning—because it beckoned to him as it had her back in July? Just how long was he planning to stay? Overnight? Why hadn't she asked him this morning? Or this afternoon?

Why didn't she ask him now instead of just standing here, mute all over again, while the cold reached through her jacket?

Enough. She snapped on her heel and started back for the house. She needed to come up with a plan. Figure out what to do about that mortgage and the bank and Lenora. Although, really, what could she do about any of it? What she really needed to do was get this bed and breakfast some paying guests. They'd had a steady enough stream of visitors in the fall months, all the way until Christmas actually.

Since the holidays, however, business had slowed considerably. And since Lenora left, nothing.

Until Marshall.

Maybe she'd be better off looking for a job, putting her

resume out on career websites. But if she did that, she'd officially become traceable. And if by some insane chance, Garrett *was* still looking . . .

"I've found you twice now, Mara. I can find you again. You don't get to ignore me."

Her fists balled inside her work gloves, the first traces of panic quickening her breath, her steps.

"Hey, Mara?"

She spun then wished she hadn't because the puffs of white air around her face were coming too fast and Marshall would see and— "Yes?"

"Why children's books?"

The question caught her off guard enough to slow her breathing. "Just how much of that conversation this morning did you overhear?"

"Some of it." He leaned on the protruding axe handle, tipped his head to one side, pretend innocence sliding into his expression. "Possibly all of it."

She pulled off her work gloves, set them on top of the firewood piled up against the shed, and stuffed her hands in her pockets. "Lenora asked me several times what I dreamed of doing when I was a kid. She knew I had to go to work right after high school. I guess she wanted to know what I might have done if I'd had more options."

It'd seemed sweet at the time, as if Lenora cared about her hopes and dreams. But had she really just been trying to get Mara to think about what might come next? Life beyond the Everwood? Perhaps because, as Sam had said this morning, she knew what was coming?

"Anyway, I never had an answer for her. I don't recall having some big dream as a kid. So one day she came home from the library with this stack of children's books and said perhaps if I could remember what it felt like to be a kid, I'd remember having a dream, too." They'd lounged in the den all afternoon, thumbing through picture books and eating M&Ms in front of the fireplace.

The memory made her want to laugh and cry all at the same time. And when she chanced a look at Marshall, this stranger who had spent all night in the cellar and worked all day as if he had as much at stake in the Everwood as she, all she saw in his eyes was compassion.

And maybe determination. "I'd like to help, Mara."

The breeze scraped over her cheeks. "You already have. I don't know what I would have done about the tree—"

"No, I mean, I want to stay and help fix this place up. I know I haven't seen all of it, but I don't think it's so rundown that it's beyond hope. Do some work, do some advertising, and we can fill those empty guestrooms. Fresh paint inside and out, some new furniture, landscaping—"

"What . . . I can't . . . Marshall, this isn't my property."

"And yet, here you are." He rushed on. "I know foreclosure is a possibility. But what bank wants to deal with a rundown old B&B? If they repossess, they're stuck with trying to offload it on someone else. They'll have to do an auction or a short sale. Plus, the owner being AWOL just adds to the mess. If you ask me, they're not going to care *who* rescues the Everwood as long as someone does."

He was forgetting one awfully large detail. "But paint and furniture and landscaping and advertising . . . all of that takes dollars. Lots of dollars."

"So look into that emergency business fund the cop mentioned. And if that doesn't pan out, well . . . I've got a little money."

Who *was* this man? "I can't take your money. I don't know you from Adam. I don't know a single thing about you." Except that he was a hard worker.

And that he'd had a soft touch last night when he'd

cleaned her wound. That he'd picked her up as if she weighed no more than a stuffed animal.

And that once, just before they'd headed down to the basement, her face mere inches from his, a flash of lightning had given a glimpse of such deep pain in his eyes she could almost feel it. Like the shuddering of the house against the storm.

But now he was all ease as he took a step closer and held out his hand. "Marshall Hawkins. Thirty-five. Born and raised in Milwaukee. And funnily enough, my middle name's Adam."

"Be serious."

When she didn't accept his handshake, he reached to tug her hand from her side. His palm was callused and his grip secure. "I *am* being serious. I've been thinking about it all day. I'd like to stay, Mara. I'd like to help. Please."

There was something earnest and vulnerable in his tone, in the way he seemed to hold his breath now as Mara stalled. Trying to find an argument or excuse, a reason not to accept the lifeline he offered.

Finally, as if he couldn't stand the wait, he released her hand and let out his breath. "If it's too weird for me to stay here, both of us sleeping in the same house without any other guests, I could find a hotel."

He was smiling again and actually, maybe she was too. It was a crazy thought, illogical and probably impossible. But what if Marshall was right? What if, together, they could save the Everwood?

She *had* promised Lenora she'd take care of it.

"There aren't any hotels in Maple Valley." That's what Jonas from the bank had said yesterday. And it was all the more reason to do whatever she could to turn the B&B into a successful business.

Her reply was a crack in her resistance and Marshall

knew it, those creases around his mouth deepening. "Then maybe I can lug a mattress out to the garden shed and camp out there."

She bit her lip, burrowed her chin into the warmth of her jacket, and made her decision. "I have a better idea."

6

The stale breath, hot on her cheek, sent alarm spearing through Mara's entire body. But the fear robbed her ability to move.

"You told them, Mara? You tattled to my parents? Like you're my nanny?"

How had Garrett gotten into her bedroom? She'd locked it, diligently, every night since the day she'd found her clothes pilfered through and the blankets on her bed disturbed. And that note on top of the dresser . . .

Her mattress shifted with Garrett's weight. He was supposed to be at college right now. Midterm break wasn't for another two weeks. She'd purposely made plans to take off those days and stay at a hotel for as long as Garrett was home.

But here he was, looming over her from his seated perch beside her. "How could you do that to me?"

"Get out of my room, Garrett." She pulled her sheet around her shoulders, willing her trembles to stay trapped underneath her skin.

"You shouldn't have told them."

He was right about that. Mrs. Lyman had, at least, appeared uncomfortable when Mara had finally summoned the courage to talk to her employers. But Mr. Lyman's response had dripped with bitter condescension. Garrett, Mr. Lyman's oldest son from a previous marriage, wasn't a saint, the man had acknowledged. But harassing the younger children's nanny?

The way he'd looked Mara up and down in that moment, the utter disbelief in his expression . . . His dismissal was almost as shriveling as Garrett's constant attention.

She should've given her notice right then and there.

Mara inched to the far edge of her mattress. "Garrett, I wasn't trying to be hurtful. But you—"

Skinny fingers clamped over her mouth, hard and bruising, muffling her words and her breathing until . . .

Mara awoke, lurching from her pile of pillows, skin slicked with sweat despite the chill of her room.

Except, no, this wasn't her room and it wasn't her faded patchwork quilt tangled around her legs. Lavender and vanilla clung to the air and muted sunlight filtered through sheer curtains. *Lenora's room.*

Her labored breaths slowed. Just a dream—a nightmare. She wasn't in Ohio or even Illinois. Nor was she alone.

A rhythm of thumps echoed through the house. *Marshall.* She swung her feet to the cold floor as the pieces of last night dropped in. He'd asked to stay. She'd said yes. And she'd moved into Lenora's living quarters at the back of the first floor.

Funny thing was, Marshall thought she'd moved down here for the sake of space or privacy. But truthfully, she'd fallen asleep easier last night than any of the nights since Lenora left—and it didn't have a thing to do with what bedroom she was in.

Marshall Hawkins's presence in the house probably

should've made her feel uneasy, especially after everything with Garrett. But instead, hearing Marshall's footsteps overhead as he'd settled in to a guestroom upstairs, knowing she wasn't all alone in this big old house, had been oddly comforting. She'd felt . . . safe.

So, no, she hadn't switched rooms out of propriety. Instead, it had been a symbolic move more than anything else. She was claiming the place Lenora had abandoned.

Which now, in the morning's bright light, seemed far nervier than it had nine hours ago.

At another thump from the other end of the house, she rose, her gaze landing on the framed photo on Lenora's bedside table. A man with gray hair whose straight nose, high cheekbones, and warm smile gave him a Jimmy Stewart appearance. George, Lenora's husband.

Other details she'd missed in the fatigue of the previous evening caught her attention. A cardigan hanging from the closet doorknob. The white sneakers Lenora always wore around the house lined up near the door.

It sure didn't look like the space of someone who didn't intend to return.

Then again, from the stories Lenora had told Mara about her life as a travel photographer, this wouldn't have been the first time she'd abruptly picked up and left. Traded in one season of life for another without so much as a backward glance.

But shouldn't Mara and the friendship they'd developed have been worth a backward glance? Or maybe she'd imagined their closeness. Maybe, considering Dad and Mom and the Lymans and every other family she'd nannied for, she should've been prepared for Lenora's eventual departure from her life.

Her stomach growled and she shook off her gloomy thoughts. She made quick work of a shower and threw on a pair of jeans and a light sweater. She let her damp hair hang free as she made Lenora's bed.

She would've stopped in the kitchen then to start a pot of coffee brewing, but more noise from the front of the house sent her that direction instead. She padded, still barefoot, through the dining room, into the sitting room . . . and froze between pillars.

Marshall stood on a ladder in the lobby, reaching over its top to pull an already-peeling section of wallpaper loose. It ripped all the way to the floor until he released it into a wrinkled pile at the foot of the ladder. Half the lobby wall was already uncovered, plaster cracks and chipped paint exposed.

"What are you doing?"

He jerked at the sound of her voice. The ladder jostled and he quickly hooked one arm through a rung to keep himself from falling. He wore jeans and another plaid flannel shirt and when he turned, she could see that he'd once again not bothered with a razor.

Wonderful. She had a lumberjack tearing up her lobby.

"*What* are you doing?" And now she was repeating herself.

The tarp she'd hung where the front door was supposed to be whipped in the wind, cold wedging its way in. Marshall jumped to the floor. "Isn't it obvious? I'm getting a head start on the day. This wallpaper—" he gestured around the room "—is enough to give a person vertigo. So it's the first to go."

There were those grooves around his mouth again, along with a lightness in his gray eyes. He seemed eager and energetic, ready to plow forward and . . .

Oh dear. The anxiety she'd felt in her dream chafed its way back in. "What are we doing, Marshall? W-what was I thinking?"

Marshall stuffed his hands into his back pockets. "Huh? You sleep okay?"

She could feel it—the panic—gurgling in her stomach and climbing up her throat. And what was that vinegary smell? Had he used a solvent on the walls?

"This is crazy. We can't do this. Seriously, what was I thinking?" Repeating herself again. "We can't just start ripping down wallpaper. I don't own this property. I don't have money. This is probably against the law. Oh my goodness, could we be arrested for this?"

Now he was laughing. A deep baritone laugh that under any other circumstances she might find startlingly irresistible.

"This isn't funny, Marshall. This . . . you . . . I don't even know you."

He opened his mouth but she spoke again first.

"And don't say Marshall Hawkins, thirty-five, Madison or whatever."

"Milwaukee."

"What?"

He ambled forward, scooting a pile of wrinkled wallpaper out of the way with his work boot. "I'm from Milwaukee, not Madison."

"Where you're from is not going to matter when we get in trouble for damaging someone else's property." Coffee. She needed coffee and breakfast and a return of her common sense. She whirled, moving in a half-trance, half-march toward the kitchen.

Marshall's steps hurried behind her. "We're not damaging the property. These walls are going to look a hundred times better when we're done. And I'm not sure why you're so upset right now. Didn't we talk about this last night? You said I could stay and help."

"I wasn't thinking clearly. Or maybe I wasn't thinking at

all." In the kitchen, she crossed to the cupboard near the sink, flung open its door and reached for a box of Lucky Charms. "What makes me think I have any right to . . . to do anything around here, much less start remodeling rooms? And even if I had all the right in the world, you can't just tear down wallpaper willy-nilly. We need a plan, a list. We need to talk about what's feasible and what's not and make a budget and a supply list a-and . . ." She dug her hand into the cereal box and stuffed a handful into her mouth just to cut herself off.

Marshall had stopped in the kitchen doorway. "Wow, you weren't kidding about sugary cereal." He wandered over to the coffee pot, opened the cupboard above it, and found a bag of grounds. "I think I'll skip laughing about the phrase 'willy-nilly' and instead assure you there was logic to my decision to start where I did. The lobby is the first thing people see when they come inside. It makes sense to give it priority."

She gulped down another bite, watching Marshall's back as he moved around the kitchen as if entirely comfortable in the space. As if he hadn't just landed in her world a mere thirty-six hours ago and turned it inside out.

She'd gone from isolated and alone to . . . to having a guest and companion and helper all rolled into one confident, somewhat mysterious, all the way rugged man. But though last night she'd convinced herself there was solid rationale to accepting Marshall's help, seeing him on that ladder minutes ago had shredded her confidence.

Something that didn't seem to bother him in the least. Within minutes, he had the coffeepot gurgling. He turned to face her again. "So, you're having second thoughts."

She nodded, mouth full.

"Because you don't own the Everwood and because you don't know me."

Another nod. Another bite of cereal.

"Well, second problem first—I understand being weirded out that I'm a complete stranger. And that I'm a man probably doesn't help." Marshall rubbed his whiskered chin. "Actually, the cop in me would tell you you're smart to distrust me."

She hugged the cereal box to her chest. Another police officer? So that's why he'd known exactly what Sam Ross was doing when he'd stopped by her car yesterday and scribbled her license plate number.

As nonsensical as it was, though, she didn't distrust Marshall. The same instinct that'd warned her Garrett Lyman's seemingly innocent infatuation with her wasn't innocent at all told her Marshall Hawkins, thirty-five, from Milwaukee-not-Madison was harmless. He didn't intimidate her. He confused her.

"You're a cop?"

"Thirteen years on the force, six as a lead detective for the Milwaukee PD." He crossed one leg over the other, leaning backward against the counter. "I've never committed a crime. Never had so much as a speeding ticket. And I'm actually pretty good at house projects. I've done all kinds of repairs and updates in my own townhouse and my sister's place, too."

If he was telling her the truth—which her gut insisted he was—he was making a pretty good case for himself.

"As for not owning the Everwood," he went on, "frankly, I don't think that's an issue. The owner isn't here. You are."

She dropped into a chair at the kitchen table. "It's not that simple."

"No, it's not that complicated."

"Marshall." She said it like a scolding.

He dropped into the seat across from her. "Mara."

She set the cereal box in front of her, though it did little to hide him from view. And the question she really wanted to ask slipped out. "*Why?* Why are you even here?"

He scooted the box out of the way, looked her straight in the eye. "Because I want to be. And that *is* the simple, uncomplicated truth."

"Don't you have a life to get back to?"

His expression turned into a blank slate. "I have time. My job and my life right now . . . it's all flexible. But if you want me to leave, I can go."

He hadn't answered her question, but he'd played his hand all the same. He had a past he didn't want to talk about. Same as Mara. "You'd leave just like that? After destroying the entryway?"

Sunlight streamed through the window over the sink and whatever shutter had closed over Marshall's eyes seconds ago lifted. She might not know this man, but she could see the pull of his shadows and feel his need for light. It was as if he teetered between desperation and desire. And that . . . that she knew.

"You can't tell me you'll miss that wallpaper, Mara. It was horrible."

It *was* horrible. A complete eyesore. "Why does the lobby smell like vinegar?"

"Homemade wallpaper removal solvent. Water and white vinegar. Vinegar can do all kinds of things."

A man who knew the hidden talents of vinegar. Had her heart just fluttered? "I know. Cleaning is my hobby. I make homemade cleaning products all the time."

"Cleaning isn't a hobby."

"Anything can be a hobby. Some people read. Some people run. I like to make things pretty and shiny. What's wrong with that?"

He nabbed the cereal box and reached inside. "This stuff will rot your teeth, you know."

"That's what Lenora always says." *Said.* Lenora, who wasn't here. Who hadn't paid her bills and had left Mara to face the impending foreclosure.

Who'd asked her to take care of the Everwood.

"Tell me this," Marshall said. "Why does this kitchen look like it belongs in an entirely different house?"

"*That* was Lenora's top priority. Guests may not see much of it, but Lenora said the kitchen is the most important room in any home and especially at a B&B. We worked on it all through the fall."

"You did good. It looks fantastic." Marshall leaned forward. "You made it pretty and shiny."

Smooth, using her own words to compliment her.

"How about this?" he said. "I haven't seen the whole place yet. Why don't you give me a tour? Then we can sit down and do what you said—make a list and a plan and a budget. While we're at it, we'll figure out how you're going to get that emergency grant from the city too."

Right, the grant. Money. The only way this crazy undertaking would even be possible. "Cereal."

He handed her the box. Grinned. Folded his arms and tipped his chair back until it leaned against the wall behind him. "Cereal. Coffee. Tour."

"You're humoring me, aren't you?"

"It's working, isn't it?" His chair plunked to the floor and he stood. "But if you're going to eat straight sugar in the form of dehydrated marshmallows for breakfast, at least do it the right way—with a bowl, a spoon, and some milk."

"I'll eat my cereal the way I want, Marshall Adam Hawkins."

And there was that low, rich laugh again.

It was the fireplace in the den that took Marshall's breath away.

He stopped two strides into the room, captured by the hum of the wind in the chimney and the sight of the rugged, uneven stone fixture that reached to the ceiling. Never mind the soot stains or the nicks in the wood mantel, the fireplace—big enough for a grown man to hunch inside —made the room.

And then there were the exposed wooden beams over-head, the built-in bookshelves, the picture window over-looking the rambling yard, and the tangle of trees at the edge of the grove.

He turned back to Mara. She stood in the doorway, her face alight with anticipation.

"So this is why you saved the den for last."

She broke into a smile that spoke of relief and delight. "It's wonderful, isn't it? The original house was built in the late eighteen hundreds, but we're pretty sure this back part of it—the den and the attached bedroom and en suite I'm using now—was added on sometime in the forties or fifties. Lenora could never quite decide whether she wanted the den to be open to guests or kept as a private living space."

Gone was the panicked Mara of an hour ago. Throughout their tour of the massive bed and breakfast— including the eight bedrooms and four bathrooms upstairs —her tension had unwound so palpably that Marshall could feel it. It had given way to an enthusiasm that added a bounce to her steps.

Mara loved this house. She loved this room.

From what he could tell, she'd loved the Everwood's owner too. Curious, that whole situation.

Though truthfully, as Mara had led him around the house, he'd begun to understand why the owner might've given up on the place. Creaky floors, leaky attic roof, bathroom fixtures stained with lime and rust. It was entirely possible that in offering to stay and help fix up the house, Marshall had bitten off far more than he could chew.

Yet he couldn't bring himself to freak out the way Mara had earlier. He simply felt too . . . good. Purposeful, even. Yesterday as he'd chopped up that tree—the physical labor, the distraction—it'd been a gift, a reprieve. He'd slept like a baby again last night, dreamless and content.

The amount of work to be done here was staggering, but it was so much better than aimlessly roaming the country. He hadn't had a plan when he'd set out from Wisconsin. Hadn't cared about anything other than going.

But everything had changed when he'd seen this house. When he'd stood out in the rain that first night and traced the lines of its windows and shutters and eaves. When he'd found Laney's magazine ad in the grass yesterday morning.

When he'd settled into his guestroom last night, almost forgetting his years-long standoff with God and nearly uttering a silent prayer of thanks. That he'd stumbled onto this house. That Mara had agreed to let him stay.

That he *wanted* to stay. How long had it been since he'd been able to name a single desire other than to rewind time and return to a day when he could still look in the mirror and see a father? A husband?

Mara stood in front of him now. Her coppery hair had dried into soft waves. Did she ever wear socks? "I'm glad you like this room. It's my favorite one in the house."

"I do like it. It may even make up for that terrifying doll room." Marshall pulled one arm across his body, stretching muscle that ached along with everything else in his body. A good kind of ache, the remnant of yesterday's hard, satisfying work.

Mara rolled her eyes even as she laughed. "Terrifying?

Aren't you being a little dramatic? I mean, they're peculiar, yes, but—"

"Peculiar? No. The outdated pastel tile in every bathroom—that's peculiar. The guestroom with all the clocks? Weird and unsettling. The one with three wooden rocking horses—why?" He stretched his other arm. "But the dolls? Mara, their eyes follow you around the room. I'm pretty sure I got goose bumps."

She arranged the throw pillows on a faded blue sofa. "I'll have you know that room almost had a tenant the other day. Some author was looking for a place to stay and that doll room was her favorite in the whole place. If not for that silly cat, she'd be occupying it right now."

"I can't believe it. I don't believe it."

She laughed again, folding a blanket over the edge of a chair before turning back to him and tucking her hair behind her ears. They stuck out just a little, her ears, just enough to be both noticeable and . . . well, cute. That is, if he were still the kind of man who noticed that kind of thing.

Instead of a man who hadn't noticed a pretty woman in, hmm, he didn't know how long.

He hadn't even been all that aware of Penny in what had turned out to be the sunset years of their marriage. In those eleven wretched months of Laney's sickness, he'd spent every spare moment researching treatments and calling specialists and gathering second, third, twentieth opinions. Investigating like the cop he was.

Not realizing his marriage was withering away as horribly and entirely as . . .

As a neglected house, he supposed.

But unlike his marriage, this house wasn't beyond saving. Crazy as it sounded, just being here felt like a second chance. A last-minute lifeboat when he'd been all but ready to let the stormy ocean have him.

Save the Everwood, save himself.

Maybe Mara was right—maybe he was being dramatic. But then, today was his second day without a headache. If that wasn't a sign, he didn't know what was.

He clapped his hands and nodded. "All right. Let's make that list of yours. I'd say this room doesn't really need much work at all." Although the furniture could use an upgrade and if a person were going for perfection, an electric sander and some varnish might work wonders on the floor. But there were definitely more important repairs to focus on.

"There is one thing." Mara pointed at the fireplace. "The damper's stuck. A couple of weeks ago I pulled on the chain and it wouldn't open. I decided I'd rather not smoke myself out, so I haven't lit a fire since."

"That should be an easy fix. I'll take a look."

The sooty odor of the chimney clouded around him as he crouched under the opening. He fiddled with the damper chain and reached one hand into the darkness.

He sensed Mara bending near him. "I didn't mean you had to deal with this right now, Marsh."

Did she realize she'd used a shortened version of his name? Penny used to call him Marsh.

"You're Marsh when I'm distracted. Marshall when I'm serious. And when I'm feeling flirty . . . Marshmallow."

He shook his head against the memory, flecks of ash floating all around. He coughed as his fingers connected with a metal closure. Bingo. A little more fiddling, another tug on the chain and—

Metal scraped against stone and a shower of ash fell over his head. Dust swelled and filled his lungs. He hit his head on the stone interior trying to escape the falling debris.

"Marshall!"

He swiped the back of one arm over his eyelids. Turned his sleeve black.

"Well, the damper's open."

The man had spent an entire day hauling a tree from her porch. He'd slept on a mattress Mara knew was lumpy. He'd started working this morning before she'd even woken up. And now he'd injured himself fixing the fireplace at her request.

And here she was laughing at him. "You look like Dick Van Dyke in *Mary Poppins*."

"I think what you mean is, 'Thank you, Marshall, for fixing the fireplace to the detriment of your own safety.'" He wiped his face again, this time with the other sleeve.

"Yes, of course, thank you." Still laughing.

He straightened, narrowing his eyes despite the upward tilt of his lips. "Remember two nights ago when *you* were the one with a head injury. I was so nice and helpful. You could learn something from me, Mara."

"I'm sorry. I'll get you an ice pack."

"I don't need an ice pack."

Another stray giggle. "A chimney sweep brush then?"

His pretend grimace turned into a full grin behind his ash-flecked beard.

"Seriously, though, are you okay?"

"Now she asks."

"I said I was sorry." If he started glaring again, she'd start laughing again. "For real, thank you for fixing the damper."

"For real, you're welcome." He shook the soot from his

shirt then used his foot to scoot the black debris from the hearth into the fireplace.

"Marshall?"

"Yep?"

"This is going to work." She needed to say the words out loud. She'd felt it as they'd walked through the house—the exhilarating and heady sense that this was all going to work out. As if these old walls were whispering a promise and offering a purpose. She felt it again now.

Marshall cast her a glance over his shoulder, understanding in his expression. "It's going to work." He went back to cleaning up the mess around the hearth.

"Are you sure you don't need an ice pack?"

He didn't answer, his shoulders stiffening as he stared into the fireplace.

"Marsh?"

He waved her toward him. "What do you think that is?" He pointed toward a glint of metal. It was hidden down low against one of the fireplace's side walls, only visible from a certain angle, and even then barely noticeable under layers of soot and ash.

"Looks like a handle."

Before the words were out of her mouth, he was already stepping over the pile of logs, grasping the handle. He pulled then pushed . . .

And disappeared through a sudden opening.

Shock propelled Mara after him. She hunched under the mantel, avoided the pilot light, and tumbled through the hatch into the dark, the scent of burnt wood sending her into a fit of coughing even as she rose to her feet.

What in the world?

A sharp light cut into the hollow blackness—Marshall's cell phone.

"It's a room. A whole other room."

That was pure delight in Marshall's voice. He cast his phone's flashlight around the space—plain walls, no windows or furniture—before shining it toward Mara. "Did you know this was here?"

"No." And did it really count as a room? Though long and narrow, if she lifted her arms, she could likely touch two walls at once. It wasn't much bigger than a closet. Why build a closet onto the side of a fireplace? One apparently only accessible *through* the fireplace. It was the stuff of mystery books. And claustrophobia. Her breathing tightened.

"Do you think Lenora knew about this?" Marshall brushed past Mara and it wasn't only the odor of the fireplace she smelled anymore. Clinging hints of coffee, along with something musky and masculine and subtle . . .

Definitely close quarters. She took a deep breath, backing up until she felt a wall behind her. "If she did know about it, she never mentioned it. But then again, she did grow up here and she'd say things sometimes . . . "

"This old house and its secrets . . . the stories these walls could tell . . ."

Marshall's light shone in her eyes again. "She grew up here?"

Mara nodded. "Her parents ran the Everwood for a while when she was a kid. After her husband died, she decided to come visit and lo and behold, the place was up for sale." She slipped her phone from her pocket and tapped on its flashlight. "I'd hear her sometimes at night, padding around the attic. Like she was looking for something."

"You never asked what?"

"We aren't all detectives, Marshall." Except here she was, mimicking a detective's movements as she moved her light from corner to corner—looking for what, she didn't know. But there had to be a reason for this space. "I guess I assumed if she ever wanted to tell me what she was searching for—or anything more about her past—she would. In her own time."

Or perhaps, more truthfully, Mara had been so wrapped up in her own turmoil, she hadn't been able to look past Lenora's kind and welcoming exterior.

Guilt bullied her at the thought. How many times through her teenage years had she wished Mom could see through her anger and grief to the hurting daughter in front of her? Had Mara turned her own blind eye to Lenora?

Marshall must have heard her piercing inhale. He studied her now instead of the room's blank walls. "What? You remember something?"

"No. I . . . I just . . ." She pointed her light to his face. Despite his obvious exhilaration at finding this room, she could still see just enough of the faint circles under his eyes to remember the way he'd looked that first night—physically exhausted, but even more so, heart weary.

Finally, one corner of his mouth quirked. "You know, it strikes me that you know a lot more about me than I do you. You're almost a little mysterious, you know that?"

"It's the house that's mysterious, Marshall." More than she'd realized. "Not me."

"Yes, well, I don't even know your last name."

"Mara Bristol. Thirty. Born in Arizona, raised all over."

"Army brat?"

"No, just restless parents." A father searching for a dream his family couldn't fulfill. And later, a mom never content for long in one place.

"And before you wound up here?"

"I was a nanny. Four families in nine years. Anything else you want to know?"

"A detective always has questions, Mara."

Even in the dark, she could see the gleam in his eyes—teasing but also curious. The skittish Mara who'd shown up on the Everwood's doorstep months ago would've shrunk back.

But now, in the dim and the mystery of this space, all she felt was the first hint of a thrill.

Because of the hidden room, of course.

Because of the thought of bringing the Everwood back to life.

Because . . .

"Hello?"

At the muffled voice, Mara jumped. At once, Marshall's hands were on her arms, steadying her. Had he been standing this close to her all along or did the tight quarters of the little room suddenly feel even smaller? Could he hear the deafening thud of her heartbeat?

And who was in the house?

She pulled away and crawled through the hatch, feeling the ash under her hands and knees. Marshall was still squeezing through behind her when she rose just in time to see a familiar face entering the den.

That woman from the bakery the other day—the newspaper reporter. Jess, Jen—Jenessa. Right. Every inch of her sleek and stylish, from her tall boots to her all-black ensemble to her high ponytail. Only the shock on her face—her wide eyes, her open mouth—looked out of place. Her focus darted from Mara to Marshall to the fireplace and back again.

Until her bright red lips broke into a smile. "Well, I have about a thousand and one questions. But first, if he'll ever stop lollygagging, I brought you a surprise."

Another set of footsteps. Another familiar face.

Too familiar.

Not Garrett.

But the man who appeared around the corner—the same one who'd sent her scrambling from the bakery two days ago—could've walked straight out of this morning's nightmare.

"Lucas Danby," Jenessa declared. "A guest. So that tonight when you stand up during the town meeting and ask for a grant—Sam told you about the grant fund, right? —well, you can say you have at least one B&B room filled." She cast a curious glance to Marshall. "Or maybe two, as it were."

Mara couldn't take her eyes off the man—Lucas—as he came to stand beside Jenessa. Up close, the resemblance to Garrett wasn't nearly as strong. He was older, certainly, and where Garrett's cheeks still held a youthful fullness, this man's face was leaner, cheekbones higher and more pronounced.

Still, they could've been relatives. His lanky height, his hawkish nose, the dusty brown hair that almost reached the man's shoulders—all of it similar enough to Garrett that it sent another chill quaking through her, jumbling her thoughts . . .

Until finally the rest of what Jenessa had said pushed past the fog.

"Wait, a town meeting? *Tonight?*"

ow in the world was Mara supposed to stand up in front of Maple Valley's town leaders and make an eloquent speech asking for grant funds if she couldn't, well, stand?

"I can't wear these shoes, Jenessa." She closed the passenger-side door of the newspaperwoman's classic convertible and took a wobbled step onto the curb. "High heels and I—we don't go together."

No matter if they did look perfect with the gray pencil skirt she wore—also on loan from Jenessa—and her own blue scoop-necked sweater.

Jenessa moved around the car to join Mara on the sidewalk under the glow of a brass streetlamp. "Trust me, you'll thank me for the shoes. They're a hundred times better than those canvas things you were wearing earlier, and they'll give you confidence when you're up in front of half the town."

"Heels only give confidence to women who can actually walk in them." And were that many people really going to be here this evening? Was that why they'd had to park almost two blocks from the restaurant hosting tonight's gathering? Someplace called The Red Door—probably the lit-up building down on the corner. The one surrounded by vehicles.

"I didn't realize there'd be a crowd."

"There's not much for weeknight entertainment around here." Jenessa shrugged. "Town meetings are basically social hour."

A breeze danced through the quaint town center, swaying the nimble limbs of the saplings that dotted the square and twirling an empty flower basket that hung from a lamppost. The white, burnished light of a full moon backlit the wispiest of clouds in a midnight sky.

A gorgeous night after a frenzied day.

It'd been eight hours since Jenessa had swept into the Everwood and announced that she'd secured Mara a spot on tonight's agenda. Mara still hadn't caught her breath. She'd gone from getting Lucas, Jenessa's friend, checked in to preparing a presentation for the meeting. She'd reread all the Maple Valley brochures in the lobby display case, practically memorized the town's event calendar, and practiced at least a dozen different introductions.

But what would a well-worded introduction matter when she didn't have an operating budget or business plan yet?

"I'm not prepared for this," she said, teetering as she stopped midway down the sidewalk. "Shouldn't I wait until the next town meeting? How can I get up there and ask for ten or twenty or thirty thousand dollars when I can't provide a revenue and expense chart or—"

Jenessa laced her arm through Mara's to steady her. "I'm telling you, Mara, these people—the mayor and all the rest of them—they aren't going to care about charts or spreadsheets. Facts, numbers, and logic aren't the key to winning this crowd over. It's all about your *joie de vivre* and town spirit."

And her shoes, apparently.

Jenessa had insisted on accompanying Mara to the meeting. She'd stopped at the Everwood an hour ago to pick up Mara, but when she'd seen the basic khakis and button-down Mara had been wearing, she'd insisted on a wardrobe change. And she'd just happened to have the skirt and heels with her.

Just happened. Right.

They drew closer to the lights of The Red Door. From the outside, it was obvious the historic building had once been a bank, with its white block cement walls and the words FIRST NATIONAL BANK etched in stone above the bright entrance. The inside must have been renovated.

"Come on," Jenessa said, tugging her along. "I told Sam to save us a couple seats, but we're going to be late if we don't pick up the pace. We spent too much time dawdling at the B&B."

Because Mara had been stalling . . . hoping Marshall would show up.

She'd barely seen the man since their little adventure in the den this morning. He'd spent most of the day working in the lobby.

This afternoon, though, he'd slipped a paper underneath her bedroom door. A to-do list, just like he'd promised, with a scribbled note at the bottom. *"See? No willy-nilly-ness. Going into town to take care of Item #3 now."*

Item #3: Replacing the front door the storm had ruined.

It'd made her laugh at the time, but that was hours ago. She would've thought he'd have returned in time for the meeting.

That is, if he meant to return at all. Maybe the enormity of what they'd set out to do had finally dawned on him, and he'd hightailed it. The thought stung more than it should. It wasn't like they were dear friends. And the Everwood wasn't his responsibility, after all.

"Now, you'll remember everything I said?" Jenessa's voice cut in, her purse bumping against her hip as she power-walked down the sidewalk. "About all the fairs and festivals and other town events Maple Valley hosts every summer that bring visitors to town? Actually, make that spring, summer, and fall. We even have a few winter shenanigans. We had an ice maze a couple of years ago, and there's always a Christmas festival too."

"I'll remember."

"And remind them how much we need the Everwood. We have antique stores and cute landmarks coming out of our ears but not one hotel."

Her feet ached as she tried to match Jenessa's pace. "I know."

"And—"

"If we don't slow down, I'm going to twist an ankle, and you'll be stuck carrying me to that meeting."

Jenessa laughed as she halted. "It'd be a grand entrance, at least."

Mara slipped free of the shoes and bent to pick them up. "Ah, freedom." Though the sidewalk felt like ice under her bare feet. But at least her leggings kept her calves from freezing, too. She caught up to Jenessa, and they hurried to the restaurant. "You know, I still don't understand why you're helping me."

"Eh, I could use a good front-page story for next week's edition of the *Maple Valley News*. A town newcomer out to save the spooky old B&B should do the trick."

"Hmm, not as altruistic as I thought."

Jenessa laughed and took the steps up to the restaurant entrance two at a time. But she paused at the top, fingers wrapped around the door handle. "Actually, if you want to know the truth, the day we met at the bakery, I saw you through the window before you came in. You looked lost. And lonely. And like you could use a friend. So here I am."

Jenessa pulled open the door, but instead of the sound of voices and clinking dishes, it was the warmth of Jenessa's honesty that drifted over Mara. Her kindness.

It reminded her of Lenora.

And it made Mara wish she hadn't spent so much time living on the edge of Maple Valley without really being a part of the town. If she'd ventured in more often, maybe those five weeks without Lenora wouldn't have felt so bleak. She might've found friends. Could've visited one of those cute little tourist spots she read about in the brochures.

Well, it wasn't too late for that. As long as she could save the Everwood, that is, and secure her place here.

"I should've known you'd be barefoot."

Mara dropped a shoe as she spun on the middle stair to see Marshall strolling toward The Red Door.

"I'll go in and find our seats," Jenessa said from the doorway.

Mara nodded and as the door closed and the restaurant chatter faded, relief skittered through her, as buoyant as the muted strains of music that floated from inside. "They're Jenessa's shoes," she blurted when Marshall reached her. "Well, not so much shoes as deathtraps."

Marshall crouched to retrieve the lone heel, a smirk pulling at the corner of his mouth as he rose. "Your death-trap, ma'am," he said with a gallant drawl.

The tips of his hair were damp and he smelled of cedar and soap. The slant of light from the restaurant angled over his bristled face, illuminating long eyelashes, the slope of his nose, and the faintest lines at the corners of his eyes.

And maybe too a hovering hint of tiredness.

"You're here," she finally said.

"The local hardware store didn't have everything I was looking for, so I ended up going to Ames. Took longer than I thought. I would've called but I don't have your number. I ran back to the Everwood to clean up, but you were already gone." He rubbed his fingers against his temple as he spoke.

"You all right?"

"Just a headache."

He must've raced if he'd managed to jump in the shower before catching up with them here. "You didn't have to come, Marshall."

"Of course I did. I'm your moral support. Your cheerleader."

"Where are your pom-poms?"

"It's more of a mental, internal cheerleading style."

"I'm glad."

"That I don't have pom-poms?" He reached for the restaurant door behind her and held it open.

"No, that you're here." She ducked inside without looking back at him, half-embarrassed at just how much she'd meant those words.

But there wasn't time now to think about it—the embarrassment or the fact that in just forty-eight hours Marshall Hawkins had somehow become a regular in her life, a source of stability. She had to focus on this meeting, which was apparently just about to get going. The music had cut off and the room was quieting.

She caught sight of Jenessa waving from a seat up front. But where would Marshall sit? The place was packed.

"Go on, Mara," he whispered from behind her. "I'll find a spot to stand."

She looked over her shoulder. "But—"

"Good luck." His voice was low and close to her ear.

"And if you want my advice, skip the heels. Give the presentation barefoot. It'll charm the audience."

Marshall pressed through the throng of people packed into the restaurant, finding a spot along one wall, wishing he'd thought to grab something to eat back at the Everwood.

Every once in a while he'd get just lucky enough to fend off a migraine with food. Not often, but sometimes.

Maybe he could order a burger. This was a restaurant, after all.

Though it didn't look much like any restaurant he'd seen before—not considering the exterior. While a man behind a podium up front welcomed folks to the meeting, Marshall looked around. The place was remarkable—an inviting mix of exposed brick and wood, eclectic light fixtures, and long, yawning windows that overlooked the river on one side and the town square on the other. In one corner, a fire crackled behind a marble hearth.

"Used to be a bank."

Marshall swung a glance to the man standing next to him. Oh, the cop who'd come to talk to Mara the other day. Was that really only yesterday? He fought the urge to rub his temple again. "Must've been gutted down to its studs."

The man nodded, the look in his eyes one Marshall knew well—the practiced study of a policeman. Inquisitive with an edge of distrust. But his low voice was friendly enough. "Local guy named Seth Walker bought the place a few years ago. Shocked us all when we saw it for the first time after it opened."

Up front, a man with white hair and matching bushy

brows spoke in a booming voice. "Before we dive in tonight, I just want to remind everyone about the pet fashion show coming up next week. Every pet is welcome. Even that iguana of yours, Haddie Young."

Somewhere near the front, a squeal rang out.

"A pet fashion show?" Oops, had he said that out loud?

The cop grunted. "Mayor Milt's latest addition to the community event calendar. Nothing I love more than watching town newbies discover what a whackadoo place they've landed in."

Whackadoo seemed about right. Earlier today when Marshall had been at Klassen's Hardware in downtown Maple Valley, no fewer than four people had walked up to him to introduce themselves. Two of them had already known his name and all four knew that he was staying at the Everwood.

He might've done some investigating right then to figure out how news spread so lightning fast around these parts if not for the need to drive over to Ames. He'd ended up spending far too many hours roaming the aisles of a big box store . . . and before he'd comprehended what he was doing, he'd not only picked out a new front door but new shutters too. Then he'd gone and loaded his cart with primer and rollers and paint.

It wasn't until he was halfway back to Maple Valley that he'd felt it—the first hint of a dull throbbing. And the sudden awareness of what he'd done. *Blue paint. Deep blue.* Like the shutters and door of Laney's house.

"We'll have a house just like Green Gables sometime, Daddy. Only I want a blue door."

"Will we call it Blue Gables? Should I start calling you Laney of Blue Gables?"

His insides churned even now. He'd taken four ibuprofen an hour ago on an empty stomach. Stupid idea.

But at least he was here. He hadn't given in to the oncoming migraine. Yet.

". . . happy to introduce Mara, uh . . . Mara?"

Marshall blinked. Mara was first up on the agenda?

The man—the mayor, according to the cop—turned to where Mara had only just lowered onto a chair. "Hmm. I don't know your last name, young lady."

Even from here Marshall could see the flicker of hesitation in her eyes. Reminded him of the way she'd startled when their new guest first showed himself into the den this morning—Lucas Somebody-or-other. A flash of fear, then and now. There and gone in a moment.

He barely heard her soft response to the mayor.

Awkward seconds passed as Mara left her seat, her steps uncertain in those silly heels. Guess she hadn't taken his advice. But she made it to the podium, opened her folder, shuffled its pages. Looked up. "Uh, hi, everyone."

"Louder," came a call from the back of the room.

Come on, Mara. You can do this.

Mara coughed, her knuckles white where she gripped the podium's edge. "Hi, um, I'm Mara. I'm . . . that is, I . . . " She swallowed. "I currently manage the Everwood Bed & Breakfast. I'm here to formally apply for funding from the Maple Valley Emergency Business Fund."

At least she was speaking louder now. But she seemed stiff, unsure. He tugged at his collar. Was anyone else overheating in here? And was he just imagining it or was Mara scanning the crowd as if looking for someone? Looking for him?

"I know many of you probably haven't been inside the Everwood's doors in years. And to be honest, I don't blame you." The slight lilt in her tone did its job, drawing a smattering of chuckles from the townspeople. "But I don't think the Everwood's best days are behind it. I want to restore it and fill it with guests. I have a plan. And . . . and a partner too."

Finally, Mara's gaze landed on Marshall. And for one bewildering moment, everything else faded—his headache, the crowd, the simmering frustration that had begun on his drive back to Maple Valley when he'd realized how foolish he'd been to think the migraines and memories wouldn't find him here.

What had Mara just called him?

Partner.

With patient deliberation, she closed her folder and toed off her heels. And the way she was smiling, looking at him like . . .

Like he wasn't the fractured man he knew he was. A man who, at the merest hint of a headache, had already begun craving the numbing fog of a sleeping pill. Or, better yet, a few painkillers and a dark room.

He swiped at a bead of sweat on his forehead. Forced an encouraging smile and nodded at her.

She went on, a new confidence backing her voice. "I never meant to end up in Iowa. I'd never even heard of Maple Valley. But the first day I walked into the Everwood, I knew I'd found something special."

On she continued, barefooted and poised. Telling of the Everwood's potential, its unique allure and picturesque surroundings. She described the fiery colors of the grove last autumn, the snow-blanketed hills in the winter, the roses she couldn't wait to see bloom around the arbor this spring.

And he was . . . entranced. Was this truly the same woman who'd panicked when she'd found him ripping out wallpaper this morning?

"Underneath its outdated trappings, the Everwood has a beating heart of hospitality and history in this community.

It's been a haven to me, and I'd like the chance to make it so for others."

Soon, the questions began: Did she have any reservations booked for coming months? Could she get the Everwood fixed up in time for the Maple Valley Scenic Railway's spring opening? How did she intend to compete with the Peony Inn in Dixon or the hotels in Ames or even Des Moines?

Every question she addressed with composure and calm. But each time her glance returned to him, he heard that word again. *Partner.* With every thud in his head, he thought of that blue paint out in his truck.

And no matter how many times he blinked, swallowed, or rubbed clammy palms over his torso, he couldn't stop it from happening. The memory, banishing him from the present until he was back there again . . .

In Laney's silent bedroom with her book in his hands. A paperback, cover creased and pages yellowed. His voice as ragged as his heart. *"We started reading this during her first stint in the hospital. I wish we'd had a chance to get to the end before . . . "*

And Penny, from the doorway, *"We did get to the end, Marsh. Then we moved on to* Anne of Avonlea. *You just . . . weren't there for it. You were too busy calling other doctors and researching fringe medical trials and experiments."*

He'd never forget the look on Penny's face when he turned—a ceaseless swirl of pity. And worse, accusation.

Partner. Penny was supposed to be his partner. For better or for worse. Instead, she'd left him at his worst. Found someone else who could be her better.

He jolted from his perch by the wall, pushed through the crowd and made his way outside. Cold air tinged with moisture hit his perspiring skin. One deep breath after another, one step after another . . .

He turned away from the lights of the town square, moving instead toward the river he'd crossed over on his way to the restaurant.

"Marshall Hawkins."

He halted, lungs still heaving and head pounding. Footsteps caught up with him. He blinked, grasping for control, and gripped the hand stretched toward him before taking in the face it belonged to.

Of course. The cop. And he knew Marshall's name. Had he taken down Marshall's plate number yesterday too? Or maybe he'd just been hanging around the hardware store.

"Name's Sam Ross. I'd like to have a word with you, if you don't mind."

Marshall started walking again. "About what?"

The man strode beside him. He was nearly as tall as Marshall, and he didn't so much as flinch at Marshall's blunt tone. "Skipping small talk. Fine by me. I have some questions about you, the Everwood, Mara. Mostly, Lenora Worthington."

"Doubt I'll have answers. Is there a twenty-four-hour pharmacy in this town?"

"Come on, Hawkins, you're a cop, a detective."

"And you obviously did your homework."

Gone was any hint of the friendliness from earlier at the restaurant. "Yeah, I did, so don't tell me you don't also have a sense that something's up at that house. I met Lenora Worthington. I'm finding it hard to accept she'd just leave her business in the hands of a woman with no experience, who's apparently taking it over and—"

Marshall stopped again. "Aren't you the one who just yesterday told Mara the owner had most likely cut ties when she realized she was going to lose the Everwood to the bank? Now you're trying to tell me . . . what?"

"That I've started looking into this. That I think there's

more to it. And if you don't want to talk now, fine." Sam Ross's eyes hardened. "You can come see me at the station tomorrow."

Marshall gave a curt nod. "Time?" He was being rude and moody and needlessly uncooperative—everything that drove him crazy when he was the one on the job. But his empty stomach roiled and he was too close to feeling too much.

"How's 10 a.m.?"

"Fine."

"There's a pharmacy on the corner of Main and Betsy Lane," Sam called after him.

But Marshall was already moving again toward the fingers of moonlight combing the ripples of the river. As if they promised any escape.

The headlights of Jenessa's convertible revealed a tall form at work on the Everwood's porch. Marshall's back was rigid, his arms clutching the edges of a front door as he crossed the porch.

"Well, I guess you know where he disappeared to," Jenessa said.

Mara unbuckled her seatbelt, Jenessa's idling vehicle vibrating under her bare feet. This is why Marshall had walked out in the middle of her presentation? Because he couldn't wait to install the new door?

"Thanks for the ride. And the heels and the skirt. I'll make sure to get them back to you." She slid on the shoes and refused to let herself wince. "And thanks for making that presentation happen. I can't believe . . . " That she'd done it. That it'd turned out the way it had.

That the plan Marshall had concocted last night had become even more of a reality.

"You did amazing tonight," Jenessa said. "Seriously, I don't know why you were nervous. Everybody loved you. And you have a check coming your way."

Yes. Yes, she did. Except she'd had to make some steep promises. That's the part that scared her.

"By the way, I'm free tomorrow morning. A perk of running the newspaper practically on my own—flexible hours. I'll come out and help paint or clean or something."

Mara shook her head. "You've already done so much. You don't need—"

"Hey, I was serious about being a friend. And don't worry, there's plenty in it for me, too. All I've got for best buds right now are Sam and Lucas. Don't get me wrong, I love 'em both. But a girl needs at least one good female kindred spirit, right?"

"And that's what I am?"

Jenessa tipped her head. "I think you could be. We can test it out." She grinned.

A kindred spirit. Mara liked the sound of that.

With a quick goodbye, she slipped from Jenessa's car, zipping up the hoodie she'd shrugged into once she'd escaped The Red Door's crowd. She'd heard someone talking tonight about coming snow. She could believe it, with the way the nighttime chill cloaked her as she made her way across the lawn.

Muscles in Marshall's back strained as he held the new door under its frame as if assessing the fit. An electric drill propped near the threshold looked brand new. Had he bought it just so he could install those hinges for the door? How much of his own money had he spent today?

Questions that had plagued her ever since last night hobbled in all over again. What kind of man dropped everything to stick around and help a stranger fix up a rundown B&B? Didn't he have a job to get back to? Where'd he been on his way to when he'd stopped at the Everwood in the first place?

And why had he ditched the meeting so abruptly?

He didn't turn at the sound of Jen's car rumbling away. Nor at Mara's careful steps over the porch's damaged stairs.

"You could give a girl a complex, you know," she said to his turned back. "Walking out in the middle of my presentation. Pretending you don't hear me now."

He gave something of a grunt. Set the door down. Angled to face her.

And she saw what she hadn't before the meeting. The shadows in and around his eyes were back.

But apology hovered there too. "Sorry about that."

"Was my speech too boring?"

He pulled one arm across his chest, stretching muscle or maybe simply stalling. "You weren't boring. You were great. You really were."

She could see that he meant it, and she had the sudden desire to tell him everything. Not just how the meeting had turned out, but what had happened inside of her as she'd presented.

She'd discovered something tonight as she stood up in front of all those people. She'd finally figured out the answer to that question Lenora had asked her so many months ago, the one about what she used to dream of as a kid. As she'd talked about the Everwood and its place in the community, her own buried desire had come out of hiding.

She hadn't dreamed of a career as a kid. She'd dreamed of a *place*. In those childhood years of moving from town to town, she'd longed for belonging. In her young adult years of nannying, sleeping in beds and rooms and houses that weren't truly her own, she'd wished for a home.

Now she had the opportunity to stop wishing and start doing.

No, it wasn't her name on the deed to the Everwood. But it was just like Marshall said—Mara was here, Lenora wasn't. Nobody at tonight's meeting had questioned Mara's role at the B&B. Nor had they treated her as a stranger.

The Everwood could be her home. Maple Valley could be her place to belong.

But she couldn't tell all that to a man she barely knew. Even if she had begun to feel an uncanny connection to him. In just a couple of days, he'd slid into life at the Everwood as if he too had belonged here all along.

"Aren't you at least going to ask how it turned out?" she finally asked.

He opened his mouth but nothing came out. He turned away, combing his fingers through his hair, and when he faced her again, all the angles of his face seemed at once sharp and downcast. "I'm not a hero, Mara," he blurted.

"What?" For the third or fourth time tonight, she kicked off Jen's heels.

"You said it yourself last night and again this morning. You don't know me at all."

"You're Marshall Hawkins. Thirty-five. Milwaukee."

No reply.

"I thought you'd be slightly more impressed that I got the city right this time."

"I'm sorry I left the meeting early. I had a headache. I needed air." He hefted the door with a frown. "But Mara, you don't know the kind of person I am. I don't want you to think . . . " He struggled to fit the door into place as the hinges refused to line up. He gave a frustrated push.

Where was this coming from? She leaned one hand on the wall. "That you're a hero? Okay. Done. You're being bested by an inanimate object at the moment, so it's not the hardest thing to believe."

He didn't so much as crack a grin.

"If you're not going to ask, fine, I'll just tell you. The city council approved us for twenty thousand dollars. It'll take over a fourth of it to get caught up on the mortgage, but that's still almost fifteen grand left for paint and furniture and carpet and repairing this porch and paying you back for whatever you spent today and—"

"You don't have to pay me back."

"Yes, I do."

"Why are you arguing?"

She huffed. "Why are you?"

"I'm not—"

"And why aren't you wearing a coat? It's freezing out here."

He'd finally fit the door into place, and now he turned, the lights from inside tracing his profile. She could see a hint of those lines etched around his mouth—the ones until now buried under his frustration. "I'm glad the meeting turned out well, Mara. Congratulations on getting the grant."

At least he sounded sincere. "Yeah, well, I had to agree to some stipulations. For one thing, it's not a straight-up grant. It's more of a forgivable loan. I have to submit a business plan with specific project outcomes. The city council wants to review our progress"—and the clincher—"at an open house in three weeks."

"Three weeks." To his credit, he didn't flinch.

"The depot and scenic railroad opens in April. Business at the antique stores picks up this time of year. There's some spring festival coming up too. Basically, they want the Everwood ready for tourist season, I guess."

"So we wow their socks off at an open house. In three weeks. And just like that, they forgive the loan?"

She nodded. Waited. Wished he'd assure her it was doable. Instead, his gray eyes strayed past her toward the sound of tires over gravel.

Moments later, a car door slammed and a form emerged. She didn't gasp this time at the sight of Lucas Danby. No shudder, no instant fear of Garrett. Jenessa's friend had left this morning soon after checking in, but it'd been enough time for Mara to get over his resemblance to Garrett.

And yet, she must've had some reaction just now because Marshall picked up on it. He took a step closer to her, a spark of concern filling his otherwise empty gaze.

"He just looks like someone I used to know," she said, answering his unasked question. "That's all."

Lucas climbed the porch steps. He wore a stocking cap and a fatigue that seemed to weigh down his movements. Jenessa had told Mara this morning that he worked at the local apple orchard his sister owned.

He gave a simple greeting as he passed them, thanked Mara for the room, and disappeared into the house.

Marshall bent to retrieve his drill. "He's a quiet one."

"I don't know if I remembered to tell him breakfast hours."

Marshall pulled open the door then shut it, testing his work. "You're not just going to serve him Lucky Charms?"

"I'll have you know I make amazing blueberry muffins. With a lemon glaze and everything." Wind rattled through branches and off in the distance, a squirrel's climb pattered into the hush of the night. "Guess I'll get inside. Thanks for the front door."

Marshall nodded and she stepped inside, Jenessa's shoes dangling from one hand. Just when she thought he meant to let her leave without anything further, she heard his voice behind her. "I'm sorry again, Mara. For . . . disappearing."

She turned. "Well, you missed a riveting second half of the agenda. After voting on the grant, there was a huge debate about whether to plant pansies or anemones in the town square's flowerpots this year."

He closed the front door and turned its lock.

"And Marshall?"

He set his drill on the check-in counter and faced her.

"For the record, if you hadn't shown up here, I might still be sitting around waiting for Lenora to return. There might still be a tree in the entryway. And I certainly wouldn't have found the gumption on my own to start making things happen. You're putting your life on hold to help me out."

"Maybe I don't have much of a life to put on hold."

"I'm just saying, kindness is its own shade of heroism. And whatever else you are, Marshall, you are that—kind. And I'm grateful." Without waiting to see how he took in her words, she turned and headed toward Lenora's room.

Her room.

8

_____

"*I* was wondering whether you'd show."

Marshall had one hand on the police station entrance. He used the other to shield his eyes from the sun as he angled his gaze behind him. Sam Ross stood at the curb next to a squad car.

"Come on." The man motioned to the car, sunglasses tipped up over his forehead. "Get in."

Okay. Despite the glare of the midmorning sun, a thin sheen of frost still reflected off the sidewalk and covered grass yet withered by winter's cold. A near-white sky looked primed for snow, never mind that April was only a week away.

He dropped into the vehicle, impressed at the smell of new leather and the shine of the dashboard. Instead of a traditional mounting bracket and laptop, the vehicle boasted an in-dash camera and touchscreen with consolidated communication controls. "Pretty nice for a small-town department."

Sam flipped down his sun visor. "I'll try not to be offended that you sound surprised." He started the engine, flicking at the radio control as soon as the first beats of a song rang out. "Maple Valley's no Milwaukee, of course."

"I wasn't trying to go 'town cop, country cop' on you. Didn't mean anything by it." But he couldn't blame the guy for having his guard up. Last night Marshall had been mulish and difficult. He'd taken out his black mood on Sam Ross for no other reason than the man had picked a lousy time to approach him.

If not for the fact that his headache hadn't turned into a migraine, he might still be brooding.

Sam pulled away from the curb. "You ever find that pharmacy last night?"

"Uh, no."

Because anything that would've given him what he truly wanted—a dulling of his memories, a blunting of the pain he'd failed to leave behind in Wisconsin—required a prescription. And because there was just enough of Beth's voice in his mind or maybe his own conscience persisting to hold him firm.

Instead, he'd walked to the river in an aching daze, stood at its edge and traced the rise and fall of its bank until the cold had numbed his hands and chapped his cheeks.

Then he'd found his truck, intent on returning to the Everwood, though he'd taken a longer route back. He'd followed the river for a stretch, passed a well-lit arched iron bridge and an ensemble of storefronts decorated with awnings and flowerboxes. He'd circled the town center with its spacious lawn, trees wrapped in twinkle lights, and a band shell in the corner. Eventually, as he turned the truck from town, the city lights faded, replaced by a star-studded sky.

The drive had helped clear at least a little of the fog.

Mara had finished the job. "*Kindness is its own shade of*

heroism. And whatever else you are, Marshall, you are that—kind. And I'm grateful."

How many times had he replayed her voice in his head in the ten hours since? Was he really so hollow inside that such simple but earnest words could fill him so poignantly?

And how the heck were they going to pull off everything that needed to be done around the Everwood in three weeks? All the more reason to get this meeting with the local police chief over. He rubbed his palms over his jeans. "Where are we headed anyway?"

"Dispatch got a 9-1-1 call from Eunice Hathaway. Apparently she was near-frantic, kept talking about Frank Roosevelt. She asked for me specifically." Sam gave Marshall a sidelong glance before tipping his sunglasses into place. "Frank is her parakeet. He's gotta be something like 120 years old."

"I . . . see." Marshall shook his head. "Nope. Nope, I don't see."

"Like I said, this is Maple Valley, not Milwaukee." He made another turn. "I wasn't sure you'd actually show up, so I figured I'd deal with Eunice and Frank real quick. And you'd either be waiting for me when I got back or you wouldn't."

No lights or siren, so Sam must not have been that worried about the woman and her bird. "You said you have questions. You mentioned the Everwood's owner. I've only been here a few days, so I'm not sure how much help I can be."

Sam waved at a letter carrier before turning off Main Avenue, steering the squad car toward a residential area. "Well, first off, you can assure me you don't have anything to do with the woman's—Lenora's—disappearance."

"I've never even met her. And since when did we get

from thinking she abandoned the property because of an impending foreclosure to 'disappearance'?"

"Since my gut kept me up all night after meeting Mara Bristol."

"Some Pepto-Bismol may help with that."

Sam's eyebrows lifted above his sunglasses as he pulled in front of a small ranch-style house. "Put yourself in my shoes, Hawkins. You meet a sweet, older woman who seems like she has her heart set on settling down in this community and running the local B&B. Later, you come to find out she's left town with, apparently, no word on where she's going."

"People pick up and move all the time."

Sam pocketed his keys and stepped out of the car, waiting until Marshall followed to go on. "But now, a woman who by all accounts has been hiding out at said B&B and a stranger—that'd be you—with no discernable connection to this town, are making like they own the place."

Marshall rubbed one hand over his grizzled jaw. "Okay, when you put it that way—"

He was stopped by the sight of a woman in a tangerine pantsuit half-jogging, half-waddling from the house. "It took you long enough, Sheriff Ross."

It was all Marshall could do not to laugh at Sam's blink-and-you'd-miss-it grimace. "I'm the chief of police, Eunice, remember?"

"Does your title really matter at a time like this? When Frank Roosevelt's life hangs in the balance?"

They followed the woman into a house that smelled of potpourri and felt overly warm. Practically balmy. She rushed them through a cramped living room and into the kitchen.

Where her parakeet lay in a nest of blankets atop a table. Dead as its namesake.

And Sam, for all his nonchalance earlier, seemed completely stumped. "Uh, Eunice, I assumed Frank had escaped his cage again. This looks a little more . . . serious."

"Maybe it'd be better to call a vet," Marshall offered.

Eunice appeared to notice him for the first time. "I don't know who you are, but I'll thank you not to interfere." She waggled a finger at Sam. "Well, do something."

"I'm just not sure what it is you're wanting me to do, Eunice. Bury him?"

"Of course not. I'm starting to wonder how you got elected."

Sam took a long breath and Marshall barely quelled another chuckle. "Ma'am, I wasn't elected. Again, I'm the police chief, not the county sheriff."

"Then act like it. Why do you think I called you?"

"That's exactly what I'm trying to figure out."

She threw up her hands. "Your taser. I want you to try reviving Frank with your taser."

And that was it. Marshall pitched from the room before the laughter clogging his throat could make it out. He burst outside and let his amusement free. Oh, this was worth giving up an hour of work at the house.

By the time he reached Sam's squad car, he had his phone out, ready to text Beth. She'd love this. Alex would get a kick out of it, too. He'd probably tell the rest of the precinct and Captain Wagner's laughter would boom the loudest.

But with one glance at his screen, his mirth ground to a halt. A missed call. *Penny.*

He stared at her name, at the little photo underneath it. Russet hair in tight curls just like Laney's. The shape of her lips, her wide-set eyes—also Laney's.

But she had my chin. Everyone said so.

He pressed his eyes closed, but when he opened them, Penny's name still looked back at him.

No voicemail and he might not have listened even if there was. What could she possibly want? It's not as if they'd left any dangling threads between them. Everything had been divided, all the papers signed. The divorce lawyer had declared theirs one of the swiftest he'd ever wrapped up.

Penny had found herself a whole new life. A new baby with a new man. They'd probably even finalize things one of these days, get married.

The driver's-side-door opened. "Welp, if I *were* an elected official, I'd have just lost Eunice's vote."

Marshall turned over his phone, screen hidden against his knee. "That's . . . too bad."

Sam tipped his head. "Kind of expected you to be out here busting a gut."

"I was. I just . . . " He turned off his phone entirely and stuck it into his pocket. "So what happened? You weren't in there long."

"When I wouldn't tase Frank, Eunice kicked me out. I asked her if there was anybody I could call, told her how sorry I was, but she wouldn't have any of it." He started the car.

"Tough day on the job."

Sam snorted. "Not as bad as Frank's day."

Laughter found him again, and he pushed away Penny's intrusion. Sam started the car and in seconds, Eunice's house disappeared from the sideview mirror. "Listen, I actually do need to get back to the B&B soon. And I still need to stop at the hardware store." In other words, time to pick up where they'd left off.

Eyes on the road, Sam nodded. "All right, then. Look,

Hawkins, I'm not above admitting that maybe I'm just hankering for some real police work. But I can't kick it—the sense that there's more to Lenora Worthington's disappearance than first appears."

That word again—disappearance. "Mara knew her, though, and she seems to believe the woman capable of skipping town."

"How much do you know about Mara Bristol?" Sam propped one elbow on his door's armrest.

"You don't think *she* had something to do with Lenora's leaving?"

"I don't know what to think. Other than something feels off. I trust my gut. Maybe there's a simple answer. Maybe not. But I aim to find out. Hard to know exactly where to start. It's not like anyone's filed a missing person's report."

Which likely meant he hadn't gone as far as checking cellphone records, street cameras, or credit card activity yet.

But from the look on his face—lips pressed into a thin line, expression grim—he wanted to. "So." Sam pushed his sunglasses out of the way and glanced over at Marshall. "Feel like a little detective work?"

The dining room table didn't feel nearly sturdy enough under Mara's feet. Both arms strained around the glass bowl of the tarnished brass chandelier. If her position was precarious, Jenessa's was shakier still. She perched on a stepladder atop the table, reaching over her head to fiddle with the chandelier's chain.

"I'm really starting to think we should wait for Marshall's help with this, Jen."

The knees of Jenessa's cropped jeans were eye level with Mara. How did she manage to make denim and a long-sleeved plaid shirt tied at the waist over a white tee look fashionable?

Mara had barely finished cleaning up the muffins and scrambled eggs she'd thrown together for breakfast this morning when she'd heard Jenessa's knock on the B&B's new front door.

Marshall had gone in to town a while ago and promised to return with a paint sprayer. The first-floor ceilings were in for a makeover today. Mara's job in the meantime was to move or cover furniture, lay tarp over the floors, and attempt to remove this beast of a light fixture.

"How very un-feminist of you, Mara. We don't need a man to get this job done."

"Hey, if there were any brawny females around, I would happily accept their help, too, but—" The chandelier's weight dropped into her as Jenessa loosened the chain. "Whoa. Give me some warning."

Jenessa clasped the chain with her fists, leaning from the stepladder. "I've still got it. Kind of."

"Yeah, well, my arms are about to give out, so—"

"What in the blazes?"

Both women jerked. Lucas stood in the dining room doorway—something between a glower and a smirk on his bronzed face, a backpack slung over one shoulder. Jen wobbled on her ladder, one hand abandoning the chandelier to steady herself.

Leaving Mara with even more of the weight. Oh dear. She felt her legs bend, her arms weaken. "Oh no, oh no, oh—"

The whole table shook as Lucas jumped up to help, his arms shooting out to rescue the bobbing bowl, its dangling glass trinkets clinking against one another.

Jenessa let out an exasperated sigh. "And here I was just saying we didn't need a man's help."

Muscles bunched underneath Lucas's long-sleeved T-shirt. "Well, you needed something." His voice was taut as he helped Mara lower the chandelier to the tabletop. "You could say thank you."

Mara wiped dusty hands over her faded overalls. Had the light fixture ever been cleaned? And—gross—were those dead bugs inside the bowl? "Well, *I'll* say thank you. I would not have loved for my obituary to declare death by chandelier crushing. I appreciate the help."

Lucas had pulled his long hair back today—half-pony-tail, half-knot. He looked even less like Garrett when he allowed himself to grin. "That makes one of you."

Jenessa gave him a mock glare. He returned it and hopped off the table, pushing up his sleeves as he landed on the floor. Then, with a hurried jerk, he yanked them back down.

But he hadn't been quick enough. Mara could barely stifle her gasp at the sight of the red, mottled skin of his arms. Scars that could only have been produced from horrific burns.

He looked away and retrieved his backpack. "I'm heading over to the orchard, but if it snows, we won't get far on pruning. I'll probably be back early. Um, if you're still painting or whatever, I can help."

Mara slid off the table. "Oh, you don't have to do that. I feel bad enough that you're a paying guest here and the place is in disarray."

"Doesn't bother me. I like staying busy."

Jenessa eased off the stepladder then jumped to the floor. "I'm covering a school board meeting, so I won't be here later. Coming for Sunday dinner, Luke?"

"Don't I always?" He turned and moments later the sound of the front door closing echoed through the house.

Jenessa was quiet for a long moment. "Afghanistan," she finally said, low and meaningfully. "He doesn't like to talk about it."

"Do they go all the way up his arms? The scars?"

Jenessa nodded, her gaze on the window that overlooked the parking lot, compassion or maybe concern filling her eyes as she watched Lucas toss his backpack into his truck.

"How do you know him?" Mara stacked one dining room chair on top of another. "And Sam too. You seem like an unlikely trio."

Jenessa turned, blinking away her emotion. She pulled the stepladder from the table, folded it up, and leaned it next to the stacked chairs Mara had slid over to one wall. "We're friends because we're three single adults in our 30s in a town full of minivans. People don't realize what it's like being single when almost every community and church event is set up for families. It's a bummer sometimes. But it's less of a bummer when you've got a group. Sam and Luke are much more than my friends. They're my . . . my family, I guess. Maybe it sounds silly."

"I don't think it sounds silly at all."

Because hadn't Mara gone half her life wishing for the same thing? Someone to fill in the gaps left by Dad's physical absence and Mom's emotional abandonment. But she didn't have siblings and, pathetic as it sounded, she'd never really had friends either. At least, not the kind who stayed with her from one season of life to another. There'd been too many moves, never enough time in one place.

And though some of the families she'd nannied for had been plenty kind and welcoming, she'd never truly felt a part of their circles.

"You're lucky to have them, Jen. And they're lucky to have you."

"I really am. And they really are. Especially considering I'm making lasagna this Sunday. It's already assembled and in the freezer." She dragged the last dining room chair to the edge of the room. "Sam and Lucas come over every Sunday after church. Well, Sam comes over every Sunday. Luke spends half the year working on a fruit farm in Mexico. But when he's in town helping his sister with the orchard, he never misses dinner. Though he usually skips the church part." She turned to Mara. "You should come too. To Sunday dinner. And church, if you like."

Church. Huh. It'd been, what, seven or eight years since she'd attended a service? She'd always felt a little out of place. Her faith, a little too flimsy. Her life, a little too unimpressive. She believed in God, though. Uttered a prayer now and then—like on the night she'd arrived at the Everwood.

"No pressure, of course," Jen added quickly. "If church isn't your thing, I hope you'll still come to dinner. You can even bring Marshall. I'll play reporter, and we can uncover all his secrets."

"How do you know he has secrets?"

"A handsome man with mysterious gray eyes arrives in town during a thunderstorm . . . He *has* to have secrets. Otherwise, it kills his whole vibe."

"Well, I'm pretty sure it'd take more than lasagna and a round of Twenty Questions to get him to spill them." She'd never even gotten a straight answer out of Marshall as to why he'd left that meeting last night. The man was a hundred kinds of helpful, but so far, he didn't seem at all inclined to talk about his life prior to blustering into her world.

She knew his profession, though. And from a couple of

comments over breakfast this morning, she'd picked up that he was on some kind of extended leave of absence from his job. Though she got the feeling if she ever asked why, he wouldn't be eager to share.

Mara inched the chandelier to the edge of the table. What were the chances she and Jenessa could heft it out of the dining room?

Jenessa leaned the stepladder against the wall. "Speaking of secrets and mysteries, did you know your friend Lenora isn't the first Everwood owner to up and vanish?"

Mara abandoned the light fixture. "What?"

"I wasn't joking last night about doing a story on your quest to save the B&B. I was doing a little fact-checking, looking through some newspaper archives. Turns out back in the early sixties, this young couple who'd run the place for about seven years simply disappeared. It's Maple Valley's own little cold case."

"You're kidding."

"The police tried to track them down, but they never got a single lead."

Mara gripped the straps of her overalls. "Why were the police involved? I mean, it's not a crime to leave town."

"Yeah, but it was the way they left—one night they were here, the next morning they weren't. They didn't tell a soul and it didn't make sense. They'd made a home here. They had a whole life. They had friends."

That hadn't stopped Dad. He'd had friends. He'd had a whole life. Mara's hands slid from her overall straps to her pockets. Two decades and still the hurt found ways to resurrect itself. It's why she never listened to the radio anymore. The chances were just too high she'd hear one of Dad's songs and feel the old ache.

"Not to mention they had a thriving local business," Jenessa went on. "Guests were staying at the Everwood when they vanished. Police wouldn't let the guests leave town until they'd been questioned, but they didn't get any leads."

Two sets of disappearing B&B owners. Nearly sixty years apart.

Except Lenora hadn't vanished. She hadn't disappeared in the middle of the night. She'd packed a suitcase and walked out the front door in the light of day.

Wait, Lenora . . .

"Did the articles you read mention a kid?"

Jenessa's forehead wrinkled. "Hmm . . . I dunno. I was skimming pretty quickly. Why?"

"Lenora's parents ran the Everwood for a while when she was young. I don't know the specifics of the timing, but what if her parents were the owners who disappeared?"

Jenessa's eyes lit with intrigue. "Forget uncovering Marshall's secrets. I'm beginning to think this house has a few of its own."

The image arose of that little room behind the fireplace. "You have no idea."

Marshall found Mara in the attic, surrounded by boxes and cloth-covered furniture. A burning sunset streamed through the lone circle window, casting an orange-ish hue over the room. Dust clung to the air, along with the stuffy scent of old cardboard.

He climbed the rest of the way into the unfinished space, tufts of insulation peeking through the attic's wood walls and ceiling. He made a mental note to look at the roof tomorrow, see what he could do about patching leaks. "I wondered where you'd disappeared to."

Mara piled one box onto another, the window's light adding golden hues to her red hair, which was currently laced in two haphazard braids. He'd showered after a full day's work, but clearly she hadn't allowed herself the same luxury. She still wore those overalls from earlier, now splattered with paint, and her arms were covered in tiny flecks of white thanks to the sprayer he'd used on the ceiling all afternoon.

"She was looking for something up here." Mara bumped into an ornate standing mirror. An antique? Why was it stuffed away in the attic? A little polish and it'd make a nice fixture downstairs.

"You're talking about Lenora?" If so, it was handy timing. He'd been meaning to broach the subject all day, talk to Mara about Sam's concerns, confess his growing interest. He'd tread lightly, of course, but the more he thought on it, the less he was able to dismiss the strangeness of it all.

But Jenessa had been around when he'd first returned to the Everwood and, later, Lucas Danby.

Mara huffed and the strands of hair that'd escaped her braids fanned around her face. "I heard her puttering around in the attic all the time. Why didn't I ever ask what she was looking for? Or better still, offer to help her go through all this stuff? Was I just that wrapped up in my own mess?"

There was a trace of something frantic in her eyes. If it'd been there earlier in the day, he'd missed it. But it was there now, as obvious as it was troubling. He wanted to ask what had brought this on, but even more, he wanted to ask about her "mess."

"How much do you know about Mara Bristol?"

He'd bristled earlier at Sam's question and whatever it

might imply. Yet he'd be lying if he denied his own curiosity.

But prying into Mara's life was not the reason he'd followed the sound of her thumping footsteps to find her here. "You never ate supper, Mara."

She finally looked at him—more than a spared glance this time—and noticed the bowl in his hands. "You brought me cereal."

"In a bowl. With milk. And a spoon. The way it's meant to be eaten."

"I'm so hungry I can't even think of a good retort."

He sidestepped an old dresser and handed her the bowl. "Are *you* looking for something up here?"

She shook her head. "Thank you. And no. I just had the silly idea that if I came up here and took a look around, something would click into place and I'd suddenly understand . . ."

"Why she left?" he finished for her.

"Or why she bought this house in the first place." She dropped onto a plastic tub, folded her legs.

And he had the instant and foolish but irresistible thought that she was just plain endearing in this moment. Maybe it was the braids. The overalls. The paint smudge on her cheek. Made him think of the cover of Laney's beloved *Anne of Green Gables*. All Mara was missing was a straw hat.

She'd looked pretty in that skirt and sweater last night. But this Mara charmed him to his core.

And that . . . was a problem.

Because he hadn't come here for this—here to the attic or here to the Everwood. Last night had proven that the darkness could still reach him here. A few good nights of sleep, a few days without the numbing effects of pills didn't mean he'd suddenly transformed into the Marshall Hawkins of a decade ago.

Someone healthy and whole. He'd even been a man of deep faith at one time.

But that was then. He might find solace here in Iowa. Temporary relief. But healing? The kind of happiness and sturdy trust in God he used to know? Those things didn't happen in a few days' time. And if there was one thing Penny had made clear when she'd left, it was that the broken man he'd become in the wake of Laney's death wasn't fit for sharing a life with anyone else.

Which meant he had no business whatsoever being attracted to a woman in any way, shape, or form.

Never mind that her way, shape, and form tugged on strings inside him he hadn't acknowledged for years.

"So have you found anything cool up here?"

She gulped down a bite of cereal. "Not much. Ratty furniture. Mothballs. There's a box of old film reels. I recognized some of the titles. *His Girl Friday. My Man Godfrey. Hands Across the Table.* They're classic movies. I guess that counts as cool." She pointed toward the box.

"You guess? That's definitely a sweet find." He towed over a wingback chair with torn fabric then sat across from her. He glanced inside the box she'd gestured toward, pulled out a reel, and read the title. *Love Before Breakfast.* Next to the title, a set of initials scribbled in white marker. *J.S.* "If you come across a projector and screen, that'd be even better."

"Not so far, but I can't guarantee they aren't around here somewhere under a sheet." Mara set her bowl down beside her. "Oh, and I found this."

She pulled a small photo from the front pocket of her overalls and handed it to him. A man and woman in sepia tones—the man leaning against a fireplace mantel and the woman grinning up at him. It'd been taken in the den downstairs, that much was clear. He flipped it over to see their names scribbled in blue ink. *Arnold and Jeane.*

"Do you know who they are?"

"No, I just love the photo. They look so sweet and innocent. Young and in love."

He passed it back to her. "So, Mara Bristol is a romantic."

Her smile was too small and too brief. She returned to her cereal, but only a couple bites in, she set it aside again. "I've felt so guilty all day."

"Guilty? Why?"

"I've been assuming Lenora abandoned the Everwood." Mara stood. "But today Jen told me about this cold case, other missing B&B owners, a police investigation and . . . I never thought to talk to the police, Marsh."

She paced a few feet away. "What if Lenora was in a horrible car accident? What if she was mugged or . . . or hurt? What if she left because she was in some kind of danger?"

He rose. "You're freaking yourself out—"

"That's the point. Why wasn't I freaked out *earlier*? I was a little worried, sure, but if I'd been thinking . . ." She shook her head, dropped her hands into the pockets of her overalls. "But I *was* thinking. I was thinking she's just like Dad. Another person who chose to walk away. Once again it was all about my pain, about me. Just like it was with Mom—"

"Mara." He said it softly but firmly.

She bit her lip, hands in her pockets, one strap of her overalls falling down over her shoulder.

And the urge was almost too much—to close the distance and pull her into a hug of comfort. Like he would've Laney.

No. Like he would've Penny.

Instead, he sat on the tub she'd abandoned, moved her

cereal bowl, touched her elbow—enough of a gesture to prompt her to lower next to him. He rummaged around for words, for the right question to ask.

But she made it easy on him. "My dad left when I was eleven. You may have heard of him, actually. Stephen Bristol. Ring any bells?"

"Sounds a little familiar."

"He put out a few albums over the years, but his real success was in songwriting. Turn on any country station for more than ten minutes and you'll probably hear a Stephen Bristol song, even if he's not the one singing it."

Her dad had traded in his family for a stint in the spotlight. Marshall curled his fingers over his knees to keep from forming them into fists. "I can't fathom leaving my . . . a father leaving like that."

"He came back once, around my twelfth birthday. I had this childish thought that if we cleaned the house and made his favorite dinner and dressed up, maybe he'd stay. I talked my mom into going all out." She looked up to the ceiling, cobwebs clinging to cedar beams. "Of course, he didn't stay. Mom was upset we'd even tried. She never got over it and we were never close after that." Her gaze lowered then. "She died right after my high school graduation. A heart attack. She was only forty-three."

He couldn't help it then. He reached over, gripped her hand. "I'm so sorry."

"It was a long time ago." She shifted, her knees bumping his, her palm still encased in his. "I always told myself I wouldn't be like Mom—bitter, assuming everyone else would let me down just like Dad. But that's what I did when Lenora didn't come back. I should've—"

He squeezed her hand. "Mara, you're human. You're entitled to your pain." He said it with a conviction born of experience. Because isn't it what he'd told himself over and over since Laney's death? The pills, the desperation, the recklessness at work . . . He had a *right* to be a mess of a person.

Because God or fate or maybe just circumstance had made a wreck of his life.

"But I don't want to spend my life letting my pain be the lens through which I see the world."

"I'm just saying, it's not your fault if the things that hurt you affect how you react to the events in your life now."

Mara looked up at him. "But we always have a choice, don't we? To let our hurts forever weaken us or . . . or instead find some way to draw strength from what we've been through."

His gaze moved from their clasped hands to her face, tracing the pattern of her freckles. "I guess so." It sounded nice, anyway. But he wasn't sure he could ever look at all he'd lost in the past two years and see any of it as a chance to grow stronger.

But then, this was about Mara. Her past. Her pain. Her desire to choose hope over bitterness. He could admire her for that.

The orange light of dusk had faded; the attic, dimmed. Silence idled between them, neither one, it seemed, in a hurry to move.

Until, finally, Mara cleared her throat, slipped her hand from his. "Sorry, I, um . . . I'm not sure why I told you all that."

"I'm a natural listener." It's what Penny would've said once upon a time.

"That's how Lenora was too." She sighed.

He wasn't going to get a better opening. "About Lenora. I met with Sam Ross today. He, uh, he wants to look into her whereabouts."

"He does?"

"And that means coming out here. He'll want to look at her computer, go through anything she may have left behind. I think it's a good idea and from the sound of things, maybe you do too?"

He could see her resolve as she stood, nodded, shook the dust from her overalls. "Yes. I should've talked to him weeks ago."

"Hey, no more 'should'ves,' all right? Be a little nicer to yourself, Mara." He bent to retrieve her cereal bowl, then rose. "You gonna stay up here for a while?"

"No. I didn't know what I was looking for anyway. Maybe Sam will find something." She rubbed her palms over her bare arms. "What I should be doing is working on that business plan for the city council. Figuring out how I'm going to fill up this place with guests."

They started toward the stairs that led to the second floor, the creaks and moans of old floorboards a chorus underfoot. "For what it's worth, Mara, I hate country music."

He thought she might laugh. Instead, she stopped him in his tracks when she lunged into him—arms around his waist, head against his chest, the leftover milk spilling from the bowl in his hand. He felt the warmth of her voice through his shirt. "Thanks, Marsh."

Not two seconds later, she'd broken away and started down the stairs. Leaving him stunned. Frozen in place. Happy.

Yes, he definitely had a problem.

9

LENORA

We ran. And I've never understood why.

I've searched what few memories I still own from my youth, and I've combed through moments and images and snippets of conversation. I've wondered why it took me so long to question it all. Why didn't I beg for answers when I had the chance—as a teenager, a young adult?

And would Mom, would Dad have even answered if I'd tried?

I remember it was summer and I was eight years old. The window in my bedroom—the room Mara chose her first night at the Everwood—was open. I remember the low hum of the cicadas the night before we ran and the reach of a full moon ringing all the edges in my room—my bed and dresser and closet door—with thin light.

I remember that I forgot to brush my teeth. That I could still taste on my lips the salt of popcorn from our weekly family movie night in the den. Another black-and-white film to which I'd fallen asleep. Only to awaken an hour later, or maybe two, nestled against Dad as he carried me upstairs.

I remember the happiness.

And then the shock. Awakening in the morning to Mom flinging open my dresser drawer and Dad calling my name in a frenzy as he shook my shoulders.

I remember clothes stuffed into an old leather suitcase and toys left behind.

They argued, Mom and Dad, as we piled into our 1952 Crosley station wagon. There was something Mom didn't want to leave, though Dad insisted. But there, my recollection fades.

But I know we ran.

Away from the Everwood.

Away from Maple Valley.

Away from home.

Enchanting.

It's the word I breathed upon my return to the house in the grove. I'd forgotten the smell of summer and soil, the tiny sounds that formed the great choir of nature—the chirp of birds, the far-off chortle of frogs and crickets, the hypnotizing hum of cicadas. I'd forgotten how far the fields stretched, how they reached into a golden horizon.

The same word came to Mara's lips months later. It was Thanksgiving and there was just enough autumn left in the air to justify a morning walk through the grove. But winter had begun to awaken too—its hovering presence draping tree branches in ribbons of frost and glistening over the hard ground.

"If you think the countryside is enchanting now," I said, "wait until it snows."

"I can't wait. I love snow.

Sunlight glimmered in Mara's eyes that morning. It reminded me of a Bible verse somewhere in the Psalms. *"Restore the sparkle to my eyes . . ."*

I would wonder, later, if she'd still say the same about snow considering it was a blizzard that kept me from making it back to the Everwood by Christmas. I'd left a few days earlier—chasing my first lead, hoping to gift myself with answers to questions that grew with intensity the longer I lived at the Everwood, fruitlessly searching decades' worth of items abandoned by past owners.

It'd killed me, waiting out that snowstorm in a Minneapolis Marriott, knowing Mara was spending Christmas alone in that drafty house.

But Thanksgiving.

"You know what, Lenora?" Mara's tone matched her jaunty steps. She'd seemed to age backward while living with me. Her freckles had deepened in the last month of summer and hair that'd barely skimmed her chin now brushed past her shoulders. Gone was the anxiety that'd too often turned her knuckles white and shown itself in bruise-colored circles around her eyes.

Maybe she no longer fears Garrett showing up.

Though I knew by then that Garrett wasn't the only tender spot in her past. Her parents had left their own indelible marks on her life.

"What?" I finally answered.

"This is my first holiday in a decade spent exactly where I want to be."

If not for a crisp wind drying my eyes, the remark might've drawn tears. Joyful tears at the contentment I heard in her voice. But also tears of sadness for all her lonely years.

"I liked being a nanny. I really did. But I hated holidays. The families always assumed I had a place to go. Or, almost worse, if they knew I didn't, they'd give me a pity invite." Mara had wiggled on her gloves. "That's not fair, I guess. They were well-intentioned invitations. But the couple times I took up my employers on spending holidays with their family, I felt awkward and out of place."

"Well, you're not out of place here, Mara."

"And I'm grateful for it."

My limbs were tired and my breath tight, but the hallowed set to Mara's profile kept me from complaining. "You know, I think maybe God led you here, Mara."

"Actually, it was a random brochure in a rest stop."

"Don't underestimate God's ability to use even the things we label as 'random.'"

"Maybe. But I always got the feeling I wasn't quite impressive enough to warrant that much notice from Him." She bit her lip in that way of hers.

"Far be it from me to speak for the Almighty, but I feel fairly confident saying God isn't looking for impressive people. He's looking for people who are willing to be impressed by Him."

Mara took a long, deep breath and looked around. We'd reached the far end of the grove, where the space between trees widened and the countryside unrolled into hilly meadows and farmland. "I don't know if I have the kind of faith you do, Lenora. But I know God created all this—and that's impressive. I can't get over how beautiful it is out here. I don't know if it's the quiet or the frost or what but it almost seems . . . sacred. Like church or something."

And surely it was.

For months I searched the attic, hoping to find clues, hoping the boxes I dug through might spark memories or return to me forgotten snatches of conversation. We left something behind the day we fled the Everwood. If I could only find it, remember it . . .

This is why I bought the old house, after all. Though, as time passed, I started to think maybe God brought me here not to expose my past but to pave the way for Mara's future.

George's brother—one of my few relatives left—is an accountant. Wise with money but not always with a widow's heart.

On the day I bought the Everwood, he scoffed. And can I blame him, really? To use what little was left of his brother's life insurance on a ramshackle house in a grove on the edge of a tiny town. He called it foolish and I suppose he wasn't all wrong.

For if I hadn't bought the Everwood, I might not be here now. Without sight and sound. Other than a beeping that every now and then severs the quiet.

And maybe, strangely, a voice I once knew.

10

"That was incredibly unhelpful."

Sam Ross jabbed his phone into the pocket of his navy blue police uniform. Mara tried not to let his scowl intimidate her. Just as she'd been attempting for the past forty-five minutes not to let the three other officers currently tromping through the Everwood morph her unease into straight-up intimidation.

They'd already carried out the computer behind the registration desk, hauled boxes from the attic, combed through Lenora's room.

And just now, Sam had finished a short and apparently futile conversation with the only living relative of Lenora's he'd been able to find so far.

Mara paced the sitting room while waiting for him to continue the uncomfortable questioning he'd been in the middle of before his phone had rung. When exactly did Lenora leave? Had she given any indication of her destination? Was Mara sure she didn't have a cell phone?

Why hadn't Mara reached out to anyone when three,

four, five weeks went by and Lenora didn't return? Hadn't she been worried?

The pungent smell of fresh paint clung to the air. She was redoing the room in a pleasant, airy yellow—so different from the striped burgundy wallpaper that had darkened the room before. Mara had covered two walls this morning before Sam and his officers arrived.

If only her mood were as sunny as those two walls.

If only Marshall were here.

But he was in the dining room, taping around the baseboards and crown molding. Which is exactly where he should be. Because they couldn't let a police investigation slow down their progress on the renovation—not with an open house less than three weeks away.

And because it was silly to think she needed him by her side just to answer a few questions. She felt ridiculous enough as it was considering last night—that impulsive hug in the attic. He had to think . . .

Well, she didn't know what he thought. But she knew what *she* thought—that she was as much embarrassed by that hug as she was touched by the time Marshall had spent listening to her. That while laying in bed last night, all she'd been able to think about was how he'd brought her that bowl of cereal. How he'd held her hand.

How an embrace that hadn't lasted more than a couple of seconds—one he hadn't even returned—could so wholly and abundantly fill her senses. The solid warmth of his chest. The subtle woodsy smell of his soap. The sound of his thumping heart.

The echoes of warning in her own, cautioning that she'd known him less than a week. Not nearly enough time to have begun forming the kind of attachment that led to spontaneous hugs and spilled secrets. It'd taken her a good month, maybe more, to share as much with Lenora as she had last night with Marshall.

Yes, it was a good thing he was working a room over. She could deal with Sam Ross's questions on her own.

She squared her shoulders. "So, Lenora's brother-in-law hasn't heard from her?"

Sam turned from the broken window at the front of the room, still half-covered with tarp. "No, and he wasn't bothered by it either. From the sound of things, he was used to going months without hearing from his brother and Lenora. Said they traveled a lot."

Mara nodded. "They were freelance photographers."

Sam rubbed his chin. "The crazy thing is, there's hardly anyone else to reach out to. Lenora and her husband never had kids. The brother-in-law never married, so there aren't any nieces or nephews. George Worthington had some extended family, but if the brother-in-law doesn't know anything, it's hard to believe anybody else will. Though I'll do my due diligence and reach out to each of them."

"Other than that, where do you go from here?"

"Hopefully the computer and papers we've pulled from her desk will give us a running start. We'll check credit card and phone records, bank account activity. Freelance work makes it a little harder to check with past employers, but we'll try to identify some publications she shot for regularly, see if someone hired her for a job. I realize you said she'd retired but you never know." He flipped open the little notebook he'd been scribbling in all morning. "Otherwise, you're our best and only lead for the moment."

There was a gravity to his tone and something of a warning in his raised brow, discomfiting enough that she couldn't help looking away. She crouched beside an open can of paint, reached for a stir stick, and swirled it into the yellow liquid. "I've told you everything I can think of.

Believe me, I wish I knew more. I feel guilty enough for not doing something earlier."

"So why didn't you?"

"I told you already, I didn't think of it as a disappearance. At first, I thought she was coming back. And then later, I assumed . . ." The remorse she'd felt all day yesterday punched its way in again. Marshall had told her to give herself a break, but that was easier said than done. She looked up to meet Sam's eyes, unspoken but undeniable allegation in his expression. "Am I a suspect?"

"Suspect? We don't even know there's been a crime yet."

Yet.

"But since you brought it up, if there were a crime . . ." He tapped his pen against his notebook. "You're the last person we know of to see and talk to Lenora Worthington. And from what I can tell, you're the only one who stands to gain anything by her disappearance."

She shot to her feet. "Gain anything? What could I have—"

"You're staying free of charge in a house you don't own. You're running an establishment you don't own. You were granted twenty thousand dollars from Maple Valley to fix up a property that, once again, you don't own."

"I think you've made your point. No, the Everwood isn't mine. But Lenora left me in charge. She asked me to take care of it. That's what I'm doing." She crossed her arms. "As for the money, I wouldn't have even known about the city's business fund if not for you. I don't know why you'd try to help me if you think I'm up to something fishy here. Maybe you could do us all a favor and make up your mind."

A slow clap ricocheted throughout the room, followed by a hearty "Hear, hear!"

Jenessa strode in the room, upbeat as always, back to full fashion in another all-black ensemble. Only her turquoise feather earrings added a splash of color. "Sam, you're crazy if you think Mara has anything to do with Lenora's disappearance."

Sam glared at her. "No one asked for your opinion, Jen."

"Since when have I waited to be asked?" She pushed her hair over her shoulders and came to stand beside Mara.

"Why are you even here?"

Her blue eyes gleamed. "I have information for our investigation."

"*Our* investigation?" Sam closed his notebook. "Nope, not happening. I don't need you interfering—"

"Fine. I'll talk to Mara." She turned her impish grin on Mara. "I'll tell *you* what I've discovered about Lenora's parents and their disappearance. All it took was peeking at some county records, running some names and birthdates through a few databases."

Sam had started moving across the room, but his footsteps slowed as Jenessa went on.

Her dimples deepened. "I'm pretty sure it *was* Lenora's parents who vanished from Maple Valley in the sixties. The County Assessor's Office helped me out there. A Kenneth and Sherrie Rayleen owned the Everwood from late 1956 to 1962. I did a search in our digital archives and found an article about them from fifty-six—just a short piece about the new inn owners and it mentions a daughter." She glanced over her shoulder at Sam. "You're still here?"

He gave a puff of annoyance. "Just go on, Jen."

Her expression turned smug. "The crazy thing is, I can't find any record of a Kenneth and Sherrie Rayleen, with the same birthdates, *anywhere* after 1962. Or a Lenora Rayleen either. At least not one whose age matches."

Sam cut in. "If all you did was a Google search—"

"Of course I went deeper than that, Sam. I may not have the same resources you do but give me a little credit. And it gets stranger." She turned to Mara again. "Not only could I find no record of them after 1962, I couldn't find anything before the mid-1950s either. No marriage license, no past addresses."

Sam had given up any pretense of disinterest and he stood with them now. Mara chewed on the new information. What could this mean? Could Lenora's parents simply have passed away at young ages? But if that were the case, wouldn't Jenessa have found obituaries?

Jenessa pulled a piece of paper from her purse and handed it to Sam. "Here you go. Names, birthdates, what records I could find from the fifties and early sixties. Do your own search, Sam, but I'll be sincerely stunned if you find anything."

That was as begrudging a look of acceptance on Sam's face as Mara had ever seen. And maybe a smidge of pride. "You're kind of annoying, you know that, Jen?"

"Yep. And you love me for it." She refocused on Mara. "Hey, is Lucas around?"

"Uh, no. He left for the orchard at the crack of dawn."

"Bummer. I was hoping . . . "

Sam pocketed his notebook and the paper Jen had given him. "Give him space," he said softly.

"He was in Mexico for months. That doesn't count as space?"

"Jen."

Mara watched the exchange, clueless yet curious.

Sam started toward the lobby but stopped halfway across the room. "Oh, Mara. Right before that return call from Lenora's brother-in-law, you'd started telling me about a trip Lenora took around Christmas. We never got back to it."

"Oh. Right." She bent to pour yellow paint in a metal tray. "A trip up to Minnesota. She left on December twenty-second and only expected to be gone a couple of days. But a blizzard hit." She dipped her roller into the paint. "She ended up not making it back until the twenty-seventh."

"Did she mention a reason for the trip?"

Mara shook her head. Once again, she hadn't asked. *Why* hadn't she asked?

Sam pressed his lips into a thin line and soon Jen was talking again, asking Sam about Sunday dinner, bugging him about giving Mara a hard time.

"You spent Christmas all alone here? No guests?"

Mara whipped her gaze behind her. When had Marshall come in? "There were a few guests before and after Christmas, but none were around on Christmas Day. I pretended it wasn't a holiday, treated it like a normal day. It wasn't that bad."

Marshall looked doubtful. He also looked . . . tired. His hair stuck out as if he'd combed his fingers through it one too many times and those circles were back under his eyes. And he was leaning against the wall. The wet wall she'd been painting just before Sam arrived.

"You okay, Marsh?"

"What? Oh, yeah. Just a headache. I'm fine."

"Too bad you can't say the same about your shirt."

He straightened, looking down and over to where a streak of yellow climbed the side of his back. "Oh. Lovely."

She turned away to hide her smile. The one that was surely too big and gave away too much.

A cold wind bellowed, curling its way under the roof of the Everwood's porch and rattling what little remained of the lattice climbing one side.

"Yep, definitely snow on the way." Drew Renwycke observed the bundle of cotton-white clouds overhead before hopping off one corner of the porch, easy enough to do now that the railing had collapsed. "That's March in Iowa for you."

It was the most the man had spoken since Marshall met him on the front lawn minutes ago. He'd gotten Renwycke's name from the owner of the hardware store downtown. A local who'd returned to town a couple of years ago and opened his own carpentry business.

"Used to be in construction too," the store's owner, Sunny Klassen, had said. *"He does everything from putting up buildings to home renovation to custom woodworking."*

But could he repair a porch that'd taken the brunt of a fallen tree's damage? Preferably in just a couple of weeks' time?

Drew had already picked his way from one end of the porch to the other, inspecting rattling floorboards and the half-demolished stairs. He dropped to his knees now and peered underneath.

Marshall unrolled the sleeves of his flannel shirt, wishing for a coat and quick answers from the guy.

Wishing even more that the hazy beginning of a headache he'd awoken with this morning would make itself scarce. He blamed another phone call late last night from Penny. Unanswered, of course. Probably didn't help that he'd been up on the rooftop at the crack of dawn, patching leaky spots.

"So what do you think?" he asked Drew, jumping down to the grass, still brittle from an overnight frost. "Is it salvageable?"

Drew straightened, cheeks ruddy from the wintry bite in the air and the knees of his Levi's now smudged with dirt. "Honestly, no."

Marshall kept a groan at bay, but frustration clamored all the same. Ever since Mara had returned from the town meeting, he'd been trying not to let it show—his uncertainty that they could really get this whole place in top form before the open house she'd agreed to. And now they had the local police trailing through the house, slowing down today's work. At least they'd moved down to the basement at this point and Mara was back to painting. He would be too as soon as Drew finished his assessment. Not a positive one, apparently.

The man shook the dirt from his hands. "Sorry it's not better news, but even if that tree hadn't destroyed half the porch, it probably should've been ripped out years ago. A lot of the wood is rotting and I don't like the way things look down there." He signaled toward the underside of the porch. "You may have bigger problems than a ruined porch."

No stopping his groan this time. "Termites?"

"Or maybe carpenter ants. Which wouldn't be as bad but it's still a hassle to deal with. In either case, they tend to be dormant during winter, but evidence of past damage is obvious. I'd get a pest control guy out here ASAP."

He hated the thought of telling Mara. Between the renovations, planning for the open house, and trying to figure out how to advertise and book rooms on a miniscule budget, she had enough to deal with. Not to mention that grilling she'd just received from Sam Ross.

He'd overheard all of it and it'd been all he could do not to march into the next room and tell Ross to take it easy. But the closeness of last night had carved an awkward distance between them this morning. And, really, it might be for the best.

He glanced up to a sky bleached of color, expecting a

swirl of flurries any minute. "So what do we do about the porch?"

Drew eyed the marred structure. "Your best bet is to do away with all of this and build a brand new one."

Resigned, Marshall sighed. "I've never built a porch before."

"You'd be surprised at how quick of a project it can be. Heck, you can buy pre-fab stuff that makes it a cinch. Although, I'm probably betraying my woodworking trade in saying so."

Marshall's phone cut in then. A text that he spared only the briefest glance. Penny.

I'm gonna bug you until you call me, Marsh.

With a puff of white air, he stuffed his phone into his pocket and refocused. Tried to blink past the throbbing in his head.

Probably futile to ask but he might as well try. "Any chance you're up for the project? I mean, it's Mara's call, obviously, but she'd probably be happy to hand it off to an expert. Problem is, we're on a time crunch." And even if they had all the time in the world, money might be an issue. Which meant the pre-fab option was probably the way to go. Unless Drew could give them a good deal on a custom build.

"Business picks up for me in the spring, but I might be able to squeeze it in." Drew gave the porch another once-over. "Tell you what—you get pest control out here, figure out what you're looking at, and give me a call. I'll see what I can do."

Marshall's relief was instant.

But short-lived. A car had rambled down the lane and

parked out by the police vehicles while he and Drew were speaking. Out came a woman . . . and a young girl.

Before they even crossed the lawn, Sam Ross appeared at the top of the porch stairs. "Well, hey there, you two. You got here fast."

The girl came flying toward Sam. "Hi, Dad!"

Dad.

How could one tiny word slice so deep?

"Sorry to spring this on you, Sam," the woman said. "I couldn't say no to the extra hours. Thanks for letting me drop her off."

"Are you kidding? An extra day with my Mackenzie Lee?" Sam crouched and opened his arms to the girl. She was seven, maybe eight years old . . .

Marshall's stomach lurched.

It took all of a few seconds for him to swing himself onto the porch, ignoring the steps, and launch into the house. All of a few seconds more to find himself upstairs . . .

Wrenching open the medicine cabinet in his bathroom, the one at the far end of the second-floor corridor. Small but adequate. Old but clean. Aqua tiles, rusty faucet . . . empty cabinet. He closed it with a bang.

He jabbed his fingers through his hair. What about the cupboard under the sink? He'd settle for anything—aspirin, ibuprofen.

Anything to ward off what he knew was coming. Already the familiar pain stabbed—so much more than the headache. Penny's repeated calls. The little girl on the lawn. He hadn't even looked at her long enough to take in many of her features, but it didn't matter because all he'd seen was Laney.

Fraught need had him crouching on the floor, wrinkling his nose at the musty smell wafting from the cabinet under the sink, searching. Nothing. Just an old box of tissues, some cleaning products, and a few spare rolls of toilet paper.

The slam of the cupboard door joined his frustrated groan before he dropped into a sitting position.

How many times had he cowered on his own bathroom floor back home just like this? There'd been a time or two when he'd battled the urge to down every pill in the place. Would heaven still welcome him if that were his choice? Would he find Laney waiting?

It'd be worth it. It'd be worth it to see her again. Alive and whole instead of silent and still like the last time.

They shouldn't have had an open casket. There was nothing healing or peaceful about it.

Marshall dragged his palms over his cheeks. *Stand up, Marshall.*

It was a whisper. A prodding. A conviction.

In another life, in his old one where he was still a man of deep faith, he might've believed that was a divine murmur. God's voice. Saying his name. Letting him know someone saw and heard and cared.

But if it was God, why pick now to finally step in? After all He'd taken, why would God expect anything other than this version of Marshall—this shriveled, broken version? Mara said they always had a choice, but how was a man supposed to choose anything when all he wanted was to feel nothing?

If it is you, God, then help me. Please.

Because he couldn't keep living like this. One step forward, two steps back. Always waiting for the next attack of grief. Trying to move on but never quite believing it was possible.

I need you to take the pain away, God.

Or if nothing else, he needed God to help him stand up

and go downstairs. He had work to do. He had someone counting on him.

But the headache, the roiling in his stomach, and . . . Why was it so warm in here?

"Marshall?"

Surprise knocked into him. Mara?

"I saw you run up the stairs. Is everything okay?"

"Everything's fine." It took way too much effort to stand, pat down his hair, open the door. His vision blurred and the room around him spun.

And then . . . nothing.

"I hate tea."

Marshall's voice was raspy, but gone was the feverish glaze in his eyes and though pale, his skin was no longer slicked with sweat.

Mara perched at the edge of the mattress far too small for the man half sitting, half laying against the mountain of pillows behind him. If not for the weariness tugging at her inside and out, she might laugh at the obstinate set to his jaw. "Just drink the tea, Marshall. It'll help you sleep."

She pressed the back of her palm to his forehead—blessedly cool. Unlike earlier when his temperature had spiked to 102 degrees. He'd been half incoherent, mumbling while Sam helped drag him to his bed. He'd tossed and turned for hours, tangled in sheets damp from his perspiration.

Mara had lost track of how many times he'd uttered the name. *Laney.* She'd never heard such anguish in a man's voice.

Marshall let out an exasperated breath and reached behind him. "Why are there so many pillows on this thing?"

Was it his amusing aggravation or the way his hair stuck out every which way that gave him such a boyish look just now? "Careful. You're going to make me spill your tea."

"Good. Then I don't have to drink it." He pulled a pillow free and lobbed it onto the floor.

"You're an awfully stubborn patient."

"I'm not sick, Mara. It was a migraine."

"With a fever."

"I get fevers with the migraines sometimes. It's not that big of a deal."

"You passed out on the bathroom floor!" And it'd scared her more than she was willing to admit. She held a dainty teacup toward him. "Now drink up. It's chamomile."

"Can't I just have a glass of water?"

"Yes. After the tea."

He accepted the cup with a roll of his eyes, the handle much too small for his hand. "And you call me stubborn." He downed the whole thing in two long swallows. "There. Happy now?"

She plucked the cup from his fingers and set it onto the bedside table. "Tea is the best remedy around. That's what Lenora always used to say. I used to hate tea too, but if someone keeps pouring it down your throat, eventually your taste buds adjust."

"If you think you're going to pour any more of that stuff down my throat, you've got another thing coming, Miss Bristol." He closed his eyes again, his long lashes resting against his cheek as he leaned against the pillows.

This close to him, she could make out the faint lines of his face—tiny etches near his eyes she'd found herself memorizing while he slept, albeit fitfully. There was a scar near his hairline, hidden, save for when she'd swept his damp, disheveled hair from his forehead while his fever raged.

The man needed a haircut.

A shiver trickled through her, and she wished for one of the blankets off Marshall's bed. Moonlight filtered through lacy patches of frost over the room's lone window and beyond, snow whirled in the wind. The flurries had started hours ago, eventually turning to a thick blanket of snowfall. Such wintry weather this far into spring.

"Hey, Marsh?"

"Hmm?" His chest moved up and down now, slowly, peacefully.

"This happens regularly? Migraines that make you this sick? I've never heard of people getting fevers with migraines." They weren't the questions she'd wanted to ask, and really, she should let him sleep.

"They're not usually this bad. And fevers aren't a common symptom for most people with migraines. But lucky me, once every few years I get the full shebang."

"Is there medicine—"

"No." His eyes had snapped open and one fist curled at his side.

Okay.

"Sorry. I just mean . . ." He ran his tongue across his lips. She should get him that glass of water he'd asked for. "No need for medicine. The worst of it is over."

Maybe this was why he was on leave from his job. *Let him sleep.* But she had to ask. Not about the job but . . . "Who's Laney?"

Though he didn't move a muscle, the question had barely slipped free before the tempest in his gray eyes rose to match the blustering snow outside.

"You said her name a few times."

Seconds dragged before he tore his gaze from the window. He reached behind to rearrange his pillows again. "Laney was my daughter."

It was all he said, but oh, it told her so very much. *Was.* "Laney—what a pretty name."

"Nickname for Elaine. She was named after her grandmother—Penny's mom."

That almost answered another question. Marshall's phone had blared twice in the hours he'd wrestled with his fever. Both times, Mara had seen the name on the screen. After the second time, she'd stuffed the phone into a dresser drawer.

So Penny must be . . . an ex-wife? Current wife? Although, he didn't wear a ring.

Marshall turned away from Mara. A line of pale skin circled one wrist. Where he'd worn a watch while out in the sun? The span of his shoulders took up much of the bed.

The same man who'd pulled a door off its hinges that first night, who'd carved up a tree and chopped it into enough firewood to last a winter, had uttered his daughter's name with such a gentle love, even in the throes of a fever. A father's love, she knew now.

Had she ever once heard her father say her name in such a way?

"How long has it been?" Would he know what she meant?

"Two years. Six days."

She'd felt his pain burrow under her skin seconds ago, and it bled into the marrow of her bones now. She didn't even have to ask her next question.

"Leukemia." As if the word snuffed the last vestige of energy from him, he sunk into the mattress, closed his eyes.

A tree branch rapped against the window and the creaks of aging floors cut into the silence. Reminded her of nights awake in her own room, listening to Lenora move about the attic.

It must've been the thought of the attic that made her do it, reach for Marshall's hand the way he had hers last night.

She didn't know how much time passed as she sat there, holding Marshall's limp hand, muscles cramping from her refusal to move. Eventually his breathing settled into a rhythm. She glanced at the clock on the bedside table—1:24 a.m. Gently, she slid her hand free and rose, bending to retrieve the teacup from his nightstand. But her focus hooked on a paper sticking out from underneath the saucer.

She lifted the page. A magazine ad for a construction company? It was old and faded, lines of white evidence of how many times it'd been unfolded and folded again. The company it advertised was out of Maine. So why . . .

The house.

She held the page closer to her face, tilted into the light of the alarm clock. The house on the full-page ad wasn't the Everwood, but it could've been. Decades ago, before so many weathering seasons, so many years of neglect. Blue door, blue shutters . . .

It felt somehow telling, this piece of paper. Something he'd saved, kept near on the nightstand.

She looked to the man in the bed again, to the slow rise and fall of his chest. *Marshall Hawkins. Thirty-five. Milwaukee.*

A father with a broken heart.

11

He should've awoken feeling half-dead. His body should ache from the fever and his head still throb. His mind should be a dark room, windowless and empty except for the memories that had propelled him there in the first place.

Instead, he was upright. Freshly showered and shaved. And his mind felt as crystal clear as the icicles hanging from a tree branch just outside his window.

"Say something, Beth."

Marshall buttoned up his plaid shirt, stopping at the second one from the top, watching himself in the mirror. His cell phone lay on the dresser in front of him, set to speakerphone—pointless considering his sister's extended silence.

Until finally, "I don't get it. You had a migraine so bad you passed out. You had a fever on and off all night. Yet you're 'doing fine.'"

That's what he'd said. That's what he'd meant.

And if anyone should understand, shouldn't it be Beth? She'd been on his case about the sleeping pills and painkillers for months. He'd made it through his first migraine since she'd declared war on his dependence on the meds. She should be proud.

He plucked his phone from the dresser and tapped out of the speakerphone before lifting it to his ear. "I didn't take anything. I didn't throw up. Twenty-four hours later I'm on my feet again."

To be fair, it'd been a little longer than that. It was past noon now, the sun mounted high in the sky and the landscape completely transformed since he'd blacked out in the bathroom. Had it snowed all night? White blanketed the hills and entwined tree branches.

"This is good, Beth. This is progress. You were right about the pills. "

"I'd feel a lot better if you were here."

"Yeah, but if I hadn't left Milwaukee when I did . . ." His reflection stared at him still. He looked for the storm in his eyes and couldn't find it. "I was losing myself. A little more every day."

"And now you're finding yourself?" Beth asked. "In Iowa, of all places? At a B&B you're helping fix up?"

"I'm finding . . . something." He turned from the mirror and reached for the glass of water on his bedside table.

What would his sister say if he told her he'd sort of, well, prayed last night? She'd long ago given up trying to talk him into joining her family for church. Alex hadn't asked him to come to the precinct Bible study in forever—the one Marshall used to lead.

Since the day Laney died, he'd done all he could to shun the faith he'd once depended upon. But last night on the bathroom floor, he'd called out to God. Maybe it was nothing more than impulse on his part. But what if God was still listening?

What else could account for the fact that today, for the

first time in so long, when he'd woken up from dreams of Laney, it wasn't anguish he'd felt but instead something warm and honey-sweet? In those first lucid moments, laying on his back, gaze on the whirring ceiling fan, he'd let himself remember his little girl. Let his memory wander to a day not so different from this, the two of them stretched out on Laney's daybed, his arm behind her shoulder and a book propped against his bent knee.

Yesterday, all it had taken was a glimpse of a girl—Sam's daughter, apparently—and he'd nearly fallen apart.

But it was different today. He didn't know why but it was. And maybe, *maybe* he could allow himself to at least consider that God hadn't entirely left him to his own mess. That He'd heard Marshall's desperate prayer last night. That perhaps He'd even led Marshall to the Everwood in the first place.

"Beth, do you think . . . if something ever happened to one of your kids, do you think you'd still hold on to your faith?"

"Marsh—"

"I know it's horrible to even think about it. I shouldn't have asked."

"Yes, it's awful to think about. I don't think I can even let my mind go there. And I can't pretend to know what it must feel like to try to keep believing, to keep having faith in God's love when facing the kind of loss you have. But what I do know is that if you're asking a question like that, then probably somewhere deep down there's still a piece of you that wants to believe."

He lowered his water glass to the bedside table. An untouched cup of cold tea sat next to it. He vaguely remembered downing one cup of the stuff. Had Mara brought another sometime in the night?

They'd talked at some point too, hadn't they? She'd

asked about Laney. Maybe the biggest miracle of the night was that he'd answered.

"Did I say too much?" Beth's voice had softened.

"No."

"God cares, Marshall. You can trust Him with your broken pieces." When he didn't respond, she went on. "Are you sure you're feeling better?"

"I'm feeling better. Promise." He swallowed a long gulp of water and moved into the hallway. Huh, it was lunchtime but it smelled like breakfast. "Can I let you go? I missed out on most of a day's work yesterday and it's already noon."

"I have to ask you something first. And please don't bite my head off."

It didn't take a genius to know what was coming. "On second thought, maybe I'm not feeling better. Maybe it's best to spare me from whatever it is you're about to say about Penny." He'd found his phone in a drawer—Mara's doing? He'd seen the missed calls.

"She texted me. She still has friends on the force. She heard through the grapevine."

About his administrative leave? "Glad to know the Milwaukee PD's ongoing effort to keep criminals off the street isn't impeding the spread of gossip."

"She said she tried to call you. Is it that hard to believe she might still care about you? Can't you at least—"

"Penny walked out of my life when I was at my lowest. She doesn't get to play the concerned partner now." End of subject. His steps pounded on the stairs until he hit the landing.

"Marsh—"

"Gotta go, Beth. Love ya." Not nice, perhaps, to end the call so abruptly, but this day had started out so good. Why ruin it with talk of Penny? Besides, he smelled food and heard voices and . . .

He paused with his hand on the banister, the truth sailing through him: He was happy. Plain and simple and surprising as that. He'd forgotten what it felt like to wake up eager for the day.

Tantalizing scents—maple and cinnamon and coffee—filled his nostrils, and a contentment he couldn't explain filled all the rest of him.

He reached the kitchen in time to see Mara plop a platter of pancakes onto the center of the table, where Lucas, Jenessa, and Sam all sat with plates and steaming mugs of coffee in front of them. Mara wore a frilly pink and white apron with streaks of batter on the front. Not the tidiest cook, it seemed.

Was it his growling stomach that alerted her to his presence? "Marshall, you're up?"

Everyone else was looking up now too, and it struck him that he should probably feel embarrassed. Sam and Jenessa had been at the house yesterday when he'd blacked out. Lucas had surely heard about it. But he couldn't seem to muster up the chagrin. Not with such foreign gratitude grabbing hold of him.

Nearly all of it directed at Mara. "I thought it was about time. I can't remember the last time I slept so late." Not without the aid of a couple capsules of Ambien, anyway.

Mara was staring at him. Trying to figure out if he was well enough to be up? Or maybe shocked that he'd actually shaved, combed his too-long hair over to the side.

"Do you want some pancakes?" she finally asked.

"Sure, I'm starving."

"Breakfast," Lucas said. "It's what's for lunch." Might be the very first time Marshall had seen the guy smile.

"With a side of mystery," Jenessa added. That's when Marshall noticed the papers spread out in front of them.

Yellowed newspapers, faxed sheets he recognized as background check returns, old photos of the Everwood.

Mara was already turning back to the cupboards, probably to grab Marshall a plate. He angled around the table to step up beside her. "I've got it."

"Thanks. 'Cause I need to flip more pancakes."

He found a plate, retrieved a mug from the dishwasher full of clean dishes, plucked a fork from the silverware drawer. Mara flipped her pancakes, the sizzle and smell enticing his appetite all the more. "No cereal?" he asked.

"Don't be crazy. I had a bowl hours ago." She turned to him, scrutinizing him all over again. "Are you feeling okay? You look okay. You look great. I mean, better. You look . . ."

"Go on." That pretty blush of hers could warm a man clear through. Seriously, he could probably go stand out in the fresh snow and be just fine and dandy. "You were saying?"

She reached for the nearest hot pad and chucked it at him. "Sit down, Marsh."

"Um, first." He lowered his voice. "Thank you. For last night. For everything."

Simple words and probably not enough to convey the depth of what he felt right now. But they needed to be said and so he'd said them.

"You're welcome." Her soft whisper was nearly as entrancing as her radiant cerulean eyes. But then she lightened, her freckles bunching the way they did whenever she grinned. "But I don't think you're thankful for *everything*."

"No?"

"You were a big baby about drinking that tea. Like a five-year-old refusing to swallow his cough syrup." She pointed him to a chair across from Sam. He obeyed and a moment later, a stack of pancakes sat in front of him.

And instantly, the memories flooded in. Sunday mornings before church. Laney standing on a stool beside him. Pancakes in the shape of a smiley face, a Christmas stocking, a puppy. Her giggles, her sticky hands, syrup always somehow winding up in her hair or on her dress, and Penny's good-natured griping about how they'd be late for Sunday school again . . .

"Marshall?" Mara stood at his side with a syrup bottle in her hand. It was a collision—his old happiness with his new. Still tentative. Perhaps still fragile. Because those might actually be tears he felt at the backs of his eyes.

He blinked, accepted the syrup from Mara, smothered his pancakes.

And thankfully, when that distraction ended, Sam provided another. "So, here's what you missed, Hawkins. We're still waiting on phone records and such, but we did a computer sweep yesterday. Turns out Lenora was in contact with an art history professor in Minneapolis late last year. We know she took a trip to Minnesota in December, so logic says maybe she went to talk to this dude."

He swallowed a gulp then reached for the mug Mara had set in front of him. "I assume you've contacted him?"

"Voicemail. Waiting on a return call." Sam gestured to the mess of papers in front of him. "In the meantime, we're trying to dissect the mystery of Kenneth and Sherrie Rayleen. Jen had it right. No record of them before the mid-fifties. Nothing after 1962."

"Everybody take note of this day," Jenessa said, spreading butter over her pancakes. "Sam Ross just said I was right."

"And here's something extra interesting." Sam slid a copy of a newspaper to Marshall. "Lenora Worthington's wedding announcement from 1973. No picture, but look at her maiden name—Fry. And her parents' names—Aric and Alice Fry. Same people, new names."

"Wait, what makes you think they *are* the same people?"

Jen jumped in before Sam could. "Because there's no record of an Aric and Alice Fry that matches up to these people before 1962." Her eyes were alight with intrigue. "And because I looked up every single owner of the Everwood from way back when to now. Most of the others didn't have kids and if they did, none of them matched Lenora's age."

Marshall looked at Sam. "So. Witness protection?"

"Yeah, my mind went there too, but federal authorities are more thorough than that. When they give you a new identity, they go all the way. We would've found medical and dental records, employment history from before they bought the Everwood, degrees, you name it for Kenneth and Sherrie." Sam scraped his plate clean. "My best guess? We're looking at a couple who had just enough money and resources to start over when they needed to, but it all happened under the table."

Mara finally joined them, sitting in a chair beside Marshall. "What I don't understand is why they would need to start over. Lenora used to talk about her childhood years at the Everwood as idyllic. And what does an art history prof have to do with it—or does he at all?"

"Your guess is as good as mine," Sam said.

It was an echo of Marshall's internal reply. They'd stumbled upon multiple mysteries at once. Whether or not any of them were connected, it was too soon to tell.

But he'd solved plenty of puzzles before without all the pieces turned over. He'd thought he left his detective hat in Wisconsin, but no. He was a part of this now.

"I cannot believe I'm doing this." Mara huddled into the warmth of her coat and the striped scarf around her neck. She should be back at the house pulling down curtains in the guestrooms or making sure Marshall didn't work too hard after having a fever just last night.

Instead she was freezing her tail off at the town square with Jenessa. Holding a borrowed pet carrier. Waiting for her turn to waltz across the band shell stage as part of the Maple Valley Pet Fashion Show.

A hiss sounded from the carrier.

"Pretty sure my nameless cat doesn't want to be here any more than I do."

Jenessa tied the strings of her fur-lined hood underneath her chin. "You're going to have to do something about that nameless thing in the next ten minutes, my friend. You're supposed to give your pet's name to Mayor Milt when you walk past so he can announce it."

Music drifted over the square, and despite the wintry late afternoon cold, the place was abuzz with people and activity. The line from the bandshell stretched half a block long. "I can't name this cat. I don't even know if it's a boy or girl."

Jenessa laughed. "Pick a gender-neutral name. Whiskers."

"Too generic."

"Jamie. Taylor. Pat."

"I'm weirded out by animals with human names."

The line inched forward and Jenessa nudged Mara to move with it. "For it not being your cat, you're sure picky about the name."

"Why am I doing this again?"

"Because in a few weeks, you need to tell the city council you have a bunch of reservations for the B&B. So you should be out and about in the community, reminding people that you're here and that the Everwood's doors are still open. Word-of-mouth is the best advertising there is." Jenessa moved her camera bag from one shoulder to the other then pulled out her Nikon. "There are probably people right here in town who would love a weekend getaway that's close by."

Right. Yes. She'd gone searching for the cat and lured him-or-her into the carrier with a trail of tuna, all for the sake of the Everwood. Of course, that had turned out to be the easy part. Coaxing the feline into the pirate costume had been another story. They'd lost the captain's hat somewhere between their parking spot and the square.

A woman with a poodle wearing what looked like a trench coat and a newsboy cap strutted across the stage. Jenessa lifted her camera to snap a photo. Apparently this thing was worthy of a headline.

The line moved again, bringing them closer to one of the portable heaters set up on the lawn. Cold as it was out here, this quirky little town knew how to throw an event. Between the music, the refreshments, and the pastel bulbs hanging from trees, the square was festive and bustling. Shoveled paths crisscrossed the area.

Mara had to admit coming here might've been a good idea considering the number of people who'd stopped to say hello to her as she waited for her turn to take the stage.

"One thing I don't get—why wasn't this thing moved inside? It's supposed to snow again this evening." Next up, a dalmatian in a tuxedo.

"This is Maple Valley, Mara. We've held snowman-building contests when there was barely any snow. We've gone forward with a live nativity after one of the wise men burned the roof of our makeshift stable. We had a parade once just a couple of days after a tornado. Live around here long enough and eventually you stop asking why and just go with it."

Jen's twinkling laughter fit the mood of their surroundings—carefree delight. It reminded her, surprisingly, of Marshall. Of the way he'd appeared walking into the kitchen this morning, looking hale and hearty and not at all like a man who'd spent half the night battling a migraine and a fever. Without the beard, those grooves around his mouth looked more like dimples. Without the hair flopping over his forehead, she could see the crinkles at the corners of his eyes.

Without the heaviness weighing down his shoulders, he was almost lighthearted. Which, now knowing what she did about the tragedy he'd faced, was a wonder. Yet there hadn't been a hint of grief in his expression when he'd thanked her in low, husky tones before sitting down to eat.

"Choose a name yet?" Jenessa asked. "Four more people and you're up."

Inspiration struck. "How about Lenny? That could work for a boy or girl, couldn't it?" She handed her hot chocolate to Jenessa so she could kneel and open the carrier. Snow seeped through the knees of her jeans as she reached in for the cat. He-or-she came straight to her, not even a hiss or a scratch.

When Mara straightened again, Jenessa was smiling.

"Lenny. After Lenora. I like it." She reached into her pocket. "One more thing." She held up a black band.

"I am not wearing an eye patch, Jenessa Bellville."

"Oh, come on, it completes the look." She fit it on over Mara's hair, leaving the patch on her forehead for now.

"Where'd you even get this thing?"

"My mother used to direct the community theater. My basement is full of costumes and—" She cut off. "Oh my gosh, is that Logan Walker?" She spilled half of Mara's cocoa as she jumped and waved. "Logan! Charlie!"

A man with a young girl sitting on his shoulders, her legs bumping against his collarbone, tromped over in the snow.

"Jenessa Bellville, I was hoping we'd run into you," the man said. He crouched to let the girl slide down his back then popped up to give Jen a big hug. "Amelia's going to be bummed she missed you. She's back at Dad's house with Kate and my new nephew."

"Don't tell me you guys are in town just to see the pet show."

Logan laughed. "Hardly. We're back for Dad's birthday. Plus"—he leaned in and lowered his voice—"don't tell anyone, but we're thinking of moving back."

"What?" There went the rest of Mara's cocoa. "Seriously? It feels like you just moved away."

"It's been almost two years," Logan said. "Chicago's great but we miss Maple Valley. We miss family even more."

Mara was straightening Lenny's baggy pirate pants when Jenessa tugged on her. "Oh, Logan, this is my new friend, Mara. Mara, this is Logan Walker and his daughter Charlie. One of Maple Valley's famous Walkers. His cousin, Seth, owns The Red Door. His brother, Beckett, is married to Lucas's sister. Logan inherited the newspaper a few years ago and ended up selling it to me." She bent to kiss Charlie's cheek. "You're as adorable as ever, Miss Charlie."

"I'm Charlotte," the girl said.

Logan grinned. "It's her new thing. Going by her full name."

They chatted for another minute as a young boy led a goat wearing a bowtie across the stage. Logan promised to give his wife a hug for Jenessa before moving away.

Jenessa turned to Mara, a new sheen of gratefulness in

her eyes. "Man, I did not expect to see him here today. I don't think he has any idea how much he changed my life when he sold me the newspaper. If not for that, I could still be . . ."

Lenny purred against Mara's chest. "Could still be?"

Jenessa shook her head as if freeing whatever serious thoughts had huddled there. "Eye patch in place. You're up."

Moments later, Mara was climbing the steps of the bandshell stage, the sound of her name reverberating over the square, eye patch covering one eye. "Come on, Lenny. All we have to do is strut our stuff and this will be over with."

Somewhere in the line a dog barked and Lenny wriggled in Mara's arms.

"It appears Captain Lenny is eager to get back his pirate ship," the mayor quipped.

Laughter fanned through the crowd, and Mara found herself giggling along with them. Who would've thought that after eight months of solitude at the Everwood, she'd be up in front of these townspeople for a second time.

On a whim, she leaned over to the mayor's microphone, held out Lenny, and gave a playful "arrrgh."

The audience clapped and Mayor Milt beamed. "Way to get into the spirit of the day, Mara." His white mustache twitched. "Although, it seems you may have misunderstood the purpose of this event. This is a *fashion* show. Not a costume show."

Mara gaped, her focus flipping to Jenessa, who shrugged and laughed from the side of the stage.

"And for anyone who doesn't recognize Miss Bristol with her eye patch on," the mayor continued, "this is the intrepid young lady who's currently intent on reviving our Everwood. You can read all about it on the front of this week's *Maple Valley News*."

Wait. What?

Lenny meowed, the crowd clapped once more, and Mara moved to the edge of the stage. She pushed up the eye patch as soon as she reached Jenessa.

Jenessa lowered her camera. "I'm *soooo* sorry. I didn't realize this was about fashion, not costumes—"

"The front page?"

Jenessa's grin turned sheepish. "So, I guess you didn't see yesterday's paper."

"You're mad." Jenessa spoke over the rasping heater of Lucas's truck, snow crunching under the tires and splaying past the window. Lucas had insisted they take his truck into town earlier rather than Jenessa's little car since the roads had still been half-covered from last night's snow.

Now it was snowing again and the wind had picked up.

"I'm not mad." Mara's fingertips were smudged with black from the newsprint, her toes were still numb from the cold, and she dearly wished Jenessa would drive a little slower considering the near white-out surrounding them. But she wasn't mad.

"I thought you'd be excited about the article. We need to drum up interest however we can. Plus, it's such a sweet underdog story."

A stack of newspapers sat in Mara's lap—courtesy copies, Jenessa had said. Because, yes, that was Mara's photo splashed on the front page under the headline, "Everwood B&B Gets its Second Wind." The photo was from her presentation at the town meeting. She hadn't even noticed Jen's camera with her that night.

But it wasn't the photo or the headline or even the

article itself that bothered Mara. It was her name in print—and probably online since surely the *Maple Valley News* had a digital edition. It was the possibility, however slim, of Garrett still looking for her.

"I've found you twice now, Mara. I can find you again."

And all it'd take now was one little Google search. *If* he was still looking.

Which was just an irrational fear, right? He had to have given it up by now. Recognized his absurd attachment to her for what it was. He'd just been an infatuated college kid who'd gone too far.

"I really am sorry if the article bothers you, Mara. I should've run it by you. I thought it'd be a fun surprise. I'd hate to . . . to lose your friendship or—"

"You're not going to lose my friendship." Lenny meowed from the carrier at Mara's feet.

"I wouldn't blame you. I steamrolled into your life. I got you on that town meeting agenda without asking. I dragged you to this pet thing. I keep showing up at the B&B. I'm clingy, that's what Sam says. And I know he's joking, but sometimes I wonder . . ." Jenessa's brow was pinched, her grip tight on the steering wheel, her usual perk as subdued as the lights of the Everwood up ahead. Barely visible through the snowstorm.

"You and me, we're good, Jen. I promise." Mara leaned toward the warmth of the truck's heater. "Hey, can I ask you something? Back in town, you made a comment about where you'd be if Logan Walker hadn't sold the newspaper to you. What did you mean?"

Jenessa was unusually silent for a moment. "I spent a lot of years . . ." She started, stopped, tried again. "Let's just say, Lucas isn't the only one with scars. His are just a little more visible."

This was a whole new side of Jenessa—a new layer

underneath her bubbly surface. *Jen. Lucas. Marshall. Me. We all have our wounds.*

"Jen—" Mara began, but the skidding of the truck stole her next words.

Jenessa's knuckles whitened on the steering wheel. "I thought the chains on Luke's tires were supposed to—"

The vehicle lurched over a patch of ice and suddenly they were swerving, veering off the road. The newspapers flew from Mara's lap, plopping to the floor and she was yelping, Jenessa squealing—

Until a snowdrift caught the front end of the truck. They stopped with a jerk, the clatter of Lucas's orchard equipment colliding with their panted breaths. "Lucas is going to kill me."

Mara's seatbelt lanced into her chest. She unstrapped herself and reached down for Lenny's carrier. "That could've been worse."

"Way worse. But Lucas is still going to kill me." Jenessa shifted in her seat, the engine still growling and, thankfully, the heater still chugging. She shifted the gear into reverse, but despite its spinning wheels, the truck didn't move. "We're stuck."

Yes, and considering they were caught in a snow bank and the wind was picking up more every minute, they either needed to get out and try to free the truck or ditch the vehicle and make a run for the Everwood.

Or the guys were about to make the decision for them. Because that had to be them, appearing like dark silhouettes through the snowfall and hurrying toward the truck. The driver's-side door flung open only seconds later and Lucas reached in to twist the keys free from the ignition and haul Jenessa from the truck.

And there was Marshall on Mara's side of the truck,

kicking snow out of the way and yanking her door open. "Are you all right?"

She nodded, glancing over to where Lucas had pulled Jen into a hug. "Huh. I don't think he's going to kill her."

"What?" Marshall helped her out, taking hold of the carrier, steadying Mara when her boots sunk into the snow.

"Nothing."

"You sure you're okay? We saw the headlights coming down the lane. Lucas had been pacing for like half an hour, worrying about you guys driving in this. I thought he was going to have an aneurysm when you started swerving. Sam wasn't much better."

She looked over again—Lucas had finally released Jen, but he still had one arm slung over her shoulder as they tramped through the snow toward the house. Sam was on her other side, the wind carrying his disgruntled voice across the distance. *A little family.*

"We had no idea the roads were this bad in the country." Marshall helped her up the ditch and onto the lane—or what she assumed was the lane. Hard to tell with fresh layers of snow and gusting wind. "Are we just leaving the truck?"

"Doesn't look damaged, only stuck. We'll deal with it later when the blizzard dies down. Let's get inside." With his free hand, Marshall reached for hers and tugged her forward. "How was the pet show?"

His long strides had her nearly jogging to keep up. "Zany. Hilarious. I wore an eye patch. I still can't figure out if there was a point to the whole thing."

"Bet Eunice is sad Frank missed out."

"Huh?"

He whisked her up the porch steps without answering and into the welcoming light of the house. Marshall lowered Lenny's carrier and the cat bounded free, disappearing up the steps. Snow clung to Mara's hair and her coat and tracks where Jen and the others had barreled in before them covered the floor. And, oh, the warmth. She might even stop shivering eventually and—

Wait. Something was different.

Marshall stepped behind her to help her out of her coat. "You'll have to forgive us if we went overboard."

Her gaze swept through the lobby. Why were there twinkle lights hanging around the window and tracing the edge of the check-in desk? Was that garland twisting around the staircase banister?

She shot a glance to Marshall. He grinned. "Check out the den."

She made quick work of yanking off her boots then trailed through the sitting room and dining room and . . .

She stopped at the opening to the den. *What?* Unlike the dining room, lit by the tawny glow of sconces Marshall must have replaced after the second coat of paint dried, none of the den's lamps were on. Instead, more twinkle lights—tons of them. Around the fireplace, the picture window, the built-in shelves. A Christmas tree too? Complete with ornaments and candy canes hanging from its branches. Stockings over the fireplace. A red and green blanket draped over the couch.

Marshall joined her in the doorway. "Like it?"

"I'm so confused."

"You said Lenora was gone at Christmas. You said you spent the holiday alone here. That you tried to pretend it wasn't Christmas at all."

They'd even set up a Nativity on the fireplace mantel. "But . . . this . . . I don't understand."

He looked adorably exasperated. "We're giving you Christmas, Mara. I thought that was kind of clear. We found a bunch of stuff in the attic. I know it's cheesy, but—"

"Are you kidding? Cheesy? No, Marshall, it's wonderful. It's . . ." She couldn't decide whether to cry or laugh or throw her arms around him. "It's by far the best Christmas I've had in years."

"You haven't even been to the kitchen yet. We're making homemade pizzas. Not a very fancy Christmas feast but—"

"I love pizza." The kitchen—that must be where Jen and the others were. And they'd turned on music. She could hear it drifting through the house.

"Do you love it as much as cereal?"

"Probably a tie."

"By the way, don't eat the candy canes. They were in a box in the attic, so who knows how old they are."

Marshall started to turn away but she reached for his arm. He paused. The thought snuck up on her—a surprising one—that he must've been an amazing father. If he'd do something like this for a friend he'd barely known for a week, think of how much he must've poured out his love for his daughter.

And . . . Penny?

She cast the thought away, focusing instead on the way Marshall's gray eyes danced in the dim light of the dining room sconces. A shadow of stubble covered his cheeks and chin. And oh, she might want to do a whole lot more than give him a grateful hug right at this moment.

And yes, yes she'd definitely warmed up.

"Merry Christmas," she finally squeaked.

He reached down to slowly unwind her scarf from her neck until it dropped to the floor. "Merry Christmas, Mara."

Everything—*everything* was perfect. The crackling fire. The pizza they'd almost finished. The laughter that filled the den.

Mara's delight. It was everything he'd wanted when he'd found those boxes of ornaments in the attic this afternoon, when the idea had first taken hold.

She sat cross-legged on the floor in front of the fire, with the cat she supposedly didn't like curled in her lap. She was intent on the black-and-white Christmas movie on the TV, their second in a row. This wasn't one he recognized— something about a lady who was pretending to be married and a soldier and a baby and he didn't even know what else.

Because he couldn't pay attention. Because all he could keep thinking about was earlier, in the den doorway. About the very real possibility that if Mara had waited one more drawn-out second to eke out that "Merry Christmas," he would've done something crazy. Or maybe stupid.

But possibly awesome.

He would've kissed her.

Definitely crazy.

He glanced around the room. Jen and Lucas were crowded onto the faded blue loveseat and a sprawling Sam took up half the couch next to Marshall. They realized they were good and snowed in for the night, right?

I wonder if Mara will make Jen and Sam pay for their rooms.

The thought made him laugh and Mara shot him a glance with her eyebrows slanted. Oops, guess it wasn't a funny part of the movie. But he grinned all the same and she grinned back and . . .

And apparently thirty-five wasn't so old a man couldn't feel like a dopey teenager again. He turned his eyes back to the TV, but a moment later, a knock echoed. Someone was at the front door? In a blizzard?

Mara started to rise but he beat her to it. After all, he

was the only one not paying a speck of attention to the movie. "I've got it."

He trekked through the house toward the lobby with long strides, tarp crinkling underfoot in the dining room and sitting room. They could roll that up now that the first-floor painting was done. It'd probably take most of the day tomorrow to haul furniture out of the guestrooms so they could start painting upstairs.

A mess of boots and shoes littered the floor around a coat tree loaded with winter wear. He reached for the front door.

And the cold yanked the breath from his lungs as the woman waiting on the porch lifted her gaze. "I guess I found the right place."

Penny.

Everything was *not* perfect.

12

He was being a coward.

Marshall paced from one end of his bedroom to the other, the shock from last night nowhere even close to having worn off. Had he slept more than an hour? Two?

He'd heard everyone else—minus Penny, of course—leave earlier this morning. Guess the roads had been plowed. Someone had said something last night about church. He'd barely listened. While the guys had cleaned up the kitchen and Mara and Jen had gone upstairs to prepare rooms for their guests, he'd just stood there in the lobby, staring at his ex-wife.

Glaring, according to her.

"I drove six hours to get here, Marshall. The last two of them in a blizzard. The least you could do is stop glaring at me."

"What. Were. You. Thinking?" Each word had been its own bullet.

"You know I'm a good winter driver—"

"You know what I mean, Penn. What the heck are you doing here?"

172

She'd just plain refused to give an answer. It was late, she'd said. She was exhausted, he was clearly agitated, and they might as well wait to talk until morning.

Agitated, though? That didn't even begin to cover his state of mind last night. Or this morning.

Or when he heard her knock on his door just now. She didn't wait for permission to enter. If she thought that extra cup of coffee she carried was enough to smooth things over—

"Still a bear this morning, huh, Marsh?"

Her tight curls were held back from her face by a headband. She always wore headbands—all different colors and sizes and patterns. She still had that old University of Wisconsin sweatshirt, too. It was so faded its letters were barely readable anymore despite the morning light filling the room.

"Most people wait after knocking to enter a room."

"Well, you're up and dressed, aren't you?" She plunked the extra mug on the dresser, then wrapped both hands around hers.

He turned away, facing the window where waves of cold rolled off the glass. "I don't know why you're here, Penn. I don't know what wasn't clear in me not answering any of your calls or texts."

"Oh, you were plenty clear." He heard the mattress creak as she sat. "But I can be stubborn too. And by the way, because I know you're going to ask—yes, I got your whereabouts from Beth. Don't get mad at her for it. You know how good I was at my job."

An expert interrogator, his ex-wife. It was how they'd met a decade and a half ago. Penny had been a couple of years ahead of him on the force. Stunned the whole precinct when she'd agreed to a first date with a rookie as green as grass.

She'd given up her job after Laney was born, but apparently she still had her interrogation skills and she'd turned them on his sister. But no, he wouldn't get mad at Beth. Because he was darn sure his anger was all used up on the woman now sipping coffee on his bed.

He spun around. "Fine, let's just get it over with. What do you want? Why the phone calls? And *why* are you here?" He stalked to the dresser, grabbed the mug, didn't even sputter when the brew burned his throat.

"Because no matter how obstinate you are, I care about you. We were married for ten years, Marshall. We went through . . ." Her voice shook but he refused to look at her. "We went through one of the hardest things a couple can ever go through. So go ahead and be as irritated as you want, but I was worried when I heard you'd been put on leave. An arrest without an ounce of evidence? That's not like you."

Except it was exactly like him. Looking back, he'd grown so reckless on the job that he was surprised Captain Wagner hadn't cut him loose months ago. Missed court dates. Unfiled paperwork. Stakeouts when he'd been so distracted—or worse, overmedicated to the point of dazed —he was next to useless.

"How would you know what I'm like?" He heard the darkness in his tone. More bitter than the coffee he continued to choke down. He'd forgotten how strong Penny always made it.

"Marshall—"

"It's not your place to worry about me anymore. I'm fine. Actually, I'm great. Or was until you barged in."

"Wow. Harsh."

Well, sometimes that's exactly what the truth was— harsh. Laney's diagnosis—harsh. All those months in the hospital—horribly, horribly harsh. The day Laney had closed her eyes and he'd known, even before her chest stilled and the machine buzzed and Penny wept, that they wouldn't open again—a kind of harsh he still didn't know how he'd lived through.

He gripped the handle of his coffee mug so tightly that the muscles in his hand cramped. When had Penny come up behind him? Her reflection felt like a taunting.

"You were supposed to be my partner." He said it murky and low. "Partners don't abandon each other. When one of them is at his lowest, the other *stays* and fights and honors the commitment."

She didn't so much as flinch. "You can tell yourself all you want that I'm the one who abandoned you. But you weren't there for me either. It's like you disappeared into yourself, Marsh. You were drowning yourself in sleeping pills. You wouldn't talk to anybody, not even me. And even before Laney died, you spent more time treating her illness like one of your cases than—"

He lost it. Lost his grip on his anger. Lost any ability to hold himself back. He flung the coffee mug across the room. It slammed into the wall, coffee splattering, running in streams down to the floor. "Get out."

Penny stood her ground. "No."

Surely any minute now a headache would begin throbbing. His lungs heaved and his eyes stung. No, no he would not give her the satisfaction. "*Why* are you here?" he asked again, hating the desperation he heard in every forced syllable.

Penny stared at him, hard and unbending.

"It's not because you're worried about me. Beth knew I was fine. That's what she would've told you. So what do you want?"

He thought she would argue, but instead her shoulders dropped. "Jason and I are getting married. Soon."

He swallowed, still trying to breathe like he hadn't just run a sprint through a dark tunnel of his worst memories. "What does that have to do with me? Don't tell me you want my blessing."

She released an exasperated breath. "No, I don't want your blessing. I want . . . I just want to tell you how sorry I am. For everything. I can't go into a new marriage without saying that." The hard edge in her voice was gone, replaced with a shaky vulnerability.

Almost worse.

"Fine. You said it. We're good." He couldn't look at her. Or himself. He turned away from the mirror atop the dresser, moved to the closet, reached for a different shirt and changed into it just to have something to do.

"We're nowhere close to good and you know it. Jason said it would be like this. He wasn't excited about me coming here. Noah's only been taking bottles for a few weeks now and . . ."

Noah. A boy. In a fit of self-torture awhile back, he'd figured out that the baby had probably been born about seven months ago. Two months after the divorce was finalized. But he'd stopped himself from going so far as to find out the gender, the name, anything else.

Penny sat on the bed again. Head down, coffee cup propped on her knee, her remorse so vivid he could almost taste it.

Somewhere under the weighted cloak of his resentment, he felt the barest prick of understanding. "Jason . . . he's a good guy?" A good father?

She looked up but didn't answer the question. "I was so angry, Marsh. When I left you, I was such a mess. And when I started seeing Jason . . . you had the pills, I had him. I was self-medicating too." She shook her head. "I want you to know that even when I was first seeing him, I knew what I was doing was wrong. It was only making things worse. I thought about coming back so many times."

But she hadn't.

Nor had he gone after her. A better man would've tried. A better man would've at least attempted to claw his way out of the grief and anger, for the sake of his wife if not himself. But even if he had, in the end, would it have mattered? She'd wound up pregnant. If the deal hadn't been sealed before, it had been then.

She lifted her eyes to his now. "Marsh, I am truly, truly sorry for the way I walked away from our marriage. I was unfaithful. I was rebellious. Thankfully, the pregnancy ended up being a reality check—emotionally, spiritually, all the way around. God has given me a second chance at life and I'm so grateful, but that doesn't change the fact that I hurt you. Deeply. I hope someday you can forgive me. That's what I came here to say."

Marshall didn't know why but he sat. With plenty of distance between them, he sat and he actually looked at her and he tried to listen. Forgive her? He wasn't ready for that. Wasn't even sure what it looked like. But maybe he could at least try . . . talking.

He could try to hear what she said not as words spoken by his ex-wife, the woman he used to think would be by his side forever, but words spoken by the one person in the world who'd loved and lost the same treasure as he.

"Do you ever still . . ." It took everything in him to breathe out the question. "Don't you ever just break down about losing her?"

"Of course I do." She inched closer. "I still fall apart sometimes. Now and then, yes, of course."

He finally met her eyes. "It's not now and then for me, Penn. It's *always*. It's always with me. I'm always broken."

That's what he'd believed, anyway, before coming to Iowa. He'd started to think differently yesterday.

But then the past had elbowed in.

It would always elbow in. There might be a good day from time to time. A day when the memories comforted instead of tormented. But there'd always be another bad day around the corner. Another crash of grief and heartache and helplessness and . . .

And *this* was why he'd needed the pills. He had to find something to take their place. A new numbing. Something.

He wrenched to his feet. "Got work to do."

"Marsh—"

"Sorry about throwing the cup."

She stood and moved across the room as if to finally leave him be. But he knew her well enough to know she had more to say. Which is why he wasn't surprised when she stopped and turned near the doorway.

"For the record, Marshall, I didn't leave you because you were broken. I left because I was. I had to find a way out of the darkness."

And she hadn't been able to do it with him. It hurt, even after all this time.

"I made a mess of things along the way, but God met me there. He did. He forgave me and He's been working on my heart ever since. I just want to make sure you find your way out too. Better yet, take God's hand and let Him lead you out."

Mara never would've believed the state of Jenessa's house if she hadn't seen it with her own eyes. From the outside, it was clear the brick, two-story structure had once been a stately home. The yard, surrounded by a wrought-iron gate, was neatly kept. But inside?

Inside the house could almost pass as a hoarder's domain. Books, newspapers, and all manner of knick-knacks cluttered the worn furniture in the entryway and living room. The hutch in the dining room was so over-crowded with dishes, picture frames, and who knew what else, it looked like it might collapse any minute. Mara had only peeked into the galley kitchen, but it appeared much the same as the other rooms.

The disarray was nearly enough to distract her from the thought of Marshall back at the Everwood with the woman he'd introduced last night as his ex-wife. Or the lingering impact of that church service she'd just sat through.

Actually, it wasn't the service itself that had embedded itself into her anxious thoughts. It was Mayor Milton Briggs coming up to her afterward, his flock of friends all tittering with excitement over the Everwood and the upcoming open house. She'd envisioned a simple reception with refreshments, maybe a couple dozen guests. But now the mayor talked as if half the town might show up. He'd mentioned entertainment, tours, extra parking.

And worse, he'd sprung a surprise on her.

"I'm truly sorry about this, Miss Bristol," he'd said, "but I should've consulted the calendar. We already have an event on the second Saturday in April. How does April sixth sound instead? I'd like to keep it on a weekend, but so many of our weekends later in the spring are already booked."

A whole week earlier? "I really don't think we can have everything finished that quickly."

"Oh posh." He'd waved his hand. "You don't have to have the whole place fixed up. Just show us your business plan and give us a peek at the work you've done so far. We just need to see enough to have confidence in the Everwood's future."

She'd have to start by building her own confidence. April sixth was only two weeks from yesterday.

Which meant she really should've hurried back to the Everwood after church rather than take up Jenessa's invitation to join her, Sam, and Lucas for Sunday dinner. But Jenessa had insisted and Sam had assured her she wouldn't want to miss Jen's lasagna.

Turned out to be the truth. Mara had polished off two helpings already.

"I still can't believe you came to church with us, Luke," Jenessa said, lifting her water glass, ice clinking. "Kit was happy to see you there too."

Kit—Lucas's sister. Married to Beckett Walker—brother to Logan, who Mara had met yesterday. That is, if Mara had correctly understood Jenessa as she'd whispered a whole recitation of "Who's Who in Maple Valley" as church began.

"It's not a big deal, Jen. It's not like I've never been to church before." Lucas's long hair was pulled back but not as haphazardly as usual. Unlike Sam, he didn't wear a tie and starched shirt, but his dark jeans and sweater were the dressiest Mara had seen him wear.

"It is so a big deal. Sam and I wish you'd come with us every week, don't we, Sam?" Jenessa gave him a pointed look. "Maybe you could stick around town for more than a few months this time, too. I'm sure Kit would welcome the help through the summer and fall. What's Mexico got that Maple Valley doesn't?"

"Lay off him, Jen." Sam leaned back in his chair, arms folded over his chest.

"I'm just saying—"

Lucas pushed his plate away and stood. "You said something about dessert, right?" As quickly as that, he disappeared into the kitchen. Jenessa promptly followed.

Whatever tension had begun to simmer just now apparently eased quickly. Within seconds their laughter drifted from the kitchen into the dining room. From her seat, Mara caught sight of the pair of them—Jen pulling dessert plates from a cupboard and Lucas lowering a stack of dirty dishes into the sink, sleeves pushed to his elbows. He must not mind if Jen saw his scars.

"If she'd ever stop mothering him, she might figure it out."

Mara's attention darted to Sam. He'd said it with an air of irritation—and maybe a little amusement too. She pulled her napkin from her lap and bunched it on her plate. "Figure out what?"

Sam didn't answer. But maybe he didn't have to. She glanced into the kitchen again. Now Lucas was holding plates while Jen dished out dessert, laughing at whatever she said. Mara thought of how he'd run out to the truck last night, pulled Jen into a relieved hug. How, later, he'd plopped down beside her onto the loveseat in the den before anyone else could. Capitulated when Jen had asked him to come to church today.

She looked back to Sam. "Jen doesn't have any idea?"

"That Luke is a lovesick puppy? Not a chance, though he's getting worse and worse at hiding it. Why does she think he came home from Mexico a month earlier than planned?" Sam pressed his palms to the table. "Jen pampers him. Heckles him. Constantly asks him to permanently move back. Even flirts with him now and then. But the guy could finally cut his hair, put on a suit, and show up on her doorstep with a rose in hand and she still wouldn't realize there's a lot more going on."

Or she did but was scared of messing up a friendship.

Mara glanced around the dining room. The four chairs at the unoccupied other half of the table were piled with books and magazines. It just didn't fit at all—Jenessa, who always seemed so put together, living in a house that felt not just cluttered but almost stiflingly crowded.

Sam must've read her mind. "It was her parents' house. Luke and I have been trying to get her to put it on the market for a year now. She says she will eventually but I think she just doesn't want to deal with all the stuff. Junk, most of it."

"Her parents?"

"Her dad died almost two years ago—emphysema. Her mom passed a year later from liver failure. She struggled with alcohol for years." He turned his head toward the kitchen, but not quickly enough for Mara to miss the compassion in his eyes. "Jen had a pretty rough go of it there at the end. She stays busy these days."

He talked about Jenessa with the same tone of care and empathy in his voice that Jenessa had when talking about Lucas's scars. Maybe this was why Mara had really stayed for dinner—because this small group of friends had something she wanted. They were knit together. They knew each other's wounds. They saw deeper and held tighter.

Lenora had said once that she believed God had led Mara to the Everwood. If that was true, could He have led Mara here too? To this band of friends who'd so quickly adopted her into their circle?

She could almost hear Lenora's affirming answer. *He knows what our hearts need, Mara.*

"The three of you have something special," she said.

Sam gave a nonchalant shrug, but it didn't hide the caring man she was beginning to discover underneath. Come to think of it, this was the most congenial conversation she'd had with the police chief.

"Well, there's more than one kind of family," he finally said.

She wanted to ask Sam about his daughter. About the woman who'd dropped her off at the Everwood a couple of afternoons ago. In all the fuss of Marshall passing out in the bathroom, she'd never had a chance to ask that day. But Jenessa and Lucas were returning with plates of blueberry pie now.

And Mara's phone dinged with a text. She slipped it free and glanced down. Marshall.

Coming home soon?
I'm about to start boxing up the creepy dolls.

She read it once. Twice. No mention of Penny. And he'd called the Everwood home.

"I hope you're not thinking about trying to sell those on eBay or anything. Technically, Lenora owns them, remember."

Mara was back. He'd known it when he'd heard her steps over groaning floorboards, but it was her voice from the guestroom doorway that sent relief spooling through his tired body.

Penny's intrusion had entirely upended him, shattering whatever tranquility he'd found at the Everwood. But maybe now that Mara was here, he'd find his equilibrium again. He turned from the cardboard box half-filled with porcelain dolls bundled in bubble wrap. "Even if I did post them on eBay, who would buy them?"

Mara moved into the room. She wore a long gray

sweater over a pink shirt and leggings—and a grin. "Some people collect stuff like this."

"Some people aren't creeped out by ghost-white faces and glass eyes, I guess." He lifted a doll with a green dress. "But don't worry. All I'm doing is packing them up."

Except for a few of them. A few that Mara just might find waiting for her in her bedroom whenever she ventured down there. One under her sheet. Another atop her dresser. The last one hiding behind her shower curtain.

A silly prank, for sure, but it'd distracted him from Penny for a little while at least. She'd stuck around for a few hours this morning, but by lunchtime she'd given up on reviving their earlier conversation. She'd hit the road after an awkward goodbye in the entryway. No hug or physical touch of any kind, the few feet between them feeling like a stretching cavern.

She'd tried to bridge the distance one last time. *"I know why you're staying here, Marshall. I saw the magazine ad on your nightstand. Even if I hadn't, it would've clicked eventually. You're staying here for Laney, and if it's healing something inside of you, then I'm glad."*

He'd opened the door for her, but she wasn't done.

"You can't spend the rest of your life living solely for her memory, though. You just can't. Remember her, yes. Treasure the years we had with her, of course. But if all this"—she'd gestured to the freshly painted entryway, the new light fixture overhead, the tarp still covering the floor—*"is merely keeping you locked in the past or distracted in the present, then it's only a Band-Aid."*

He hadn't been able to find the words to argue. Because there weren't any to find. They might not be married anymore, but Penny still knew him better than anyone.

And as he'd stood on the porch and watched her drive away, for the first time since their divorce, he'd let himself acknowledge the piercing truth—he missed that. Missed having someone who *knew* him. Someone who didn't just see past his damaged surface but who was willing to walk into the deep waters.

Beth and Alex, Mom and Dad, Captain Wagner—they were all supportive. But it wasn't the same as having a true partner in every sense of the word. Would he ever have that again?

Mara picked up a piece of bubble wrap and started swaddling one of the larger dolls.

"How was church?" he asked.

"I thought it might feel weird—going back to church after so long. But I felt strangely at home." She cast him a curious glance and he braced himself for the questions he knew were coming. "Marshall, we're, um, we're friends, aren't we? I know you've barely been here a week now but it feels like longer."

"We're living in close quarters. I've seen you in your pajamas. You've seen me passed out on a bathroom floor. I think we can safely say we've passed the stage of mere acquaintances."

"So then, as your friend, is it okay if I ask . . . why was she here?"

"She's getting remarried." He stuffed his doll into the box. "I guess she wanted to clear the air first or something."

Mara's pause communicated as much as any sympathetic words would've. "That's quite the effort to go to," she finally said, "tracking you all the way to Iowa."

"Well, I wouldn't answer her calls, so . . ." He shrugged. "She's as stubborn as me. Probably why we ended up together in the first place."

"Were you married long?"

"Ten years. Actually, want to know how we met? I'd just joined the precinct and there was this reception during my first week. A fancy little shindig for a long-time officer's retirement. She's there. I'm there, in uniform, feeling like a fish out of water. At some point I look over at the food table and see this woman sneaking a napkin filled with canapés into her gun holster." He'd laughed at the time. Almost laughed now. "She's got this thing for fancy appetizers. Caviar, mushroom puffs, shrimp. It's weird."

No, what was weird was how that'd just slipped out. As if it was completely normal to discuss his ex-wife in everyday conversation. "I have no idea why I just told you that."

Mara set her wrapped doll next to the one he'd laid down. "I'm a natural listener."

His words from the other night in the attic.

Penny's words from long ago.

"Well, we ended up a statistic." At Mara's raised brow, he went on, picking up another doll. "Couples who lose a child —they're that much more likely to separate. When she first left, I didn't realize it was for good, but then . . ." He shook his head.

"It's like you disappeared into yourself, Marsh. You were drowning yourself in sleeping pills. You wouldn't talk to anybody, not even me."

His lungs squeezed at the remembrance of her words. They'd felt like an accusation hours ago, but she was just being honest, wasn't she?

And if he was honest, too, he could admit that in those first months after Laney died, Penny had tried. She'd asked him to go to counseling with her, to find a grief support group, return to church. But instead of being willing to traverse their loss together, when she'd waded in, he'd only pulled her under until they were both sinking.

She'd had to break free to save herself. He was the partner who'd failed first.

"Marshall?"

He was staring at the doll in his hand, locked on its glass eyes and empty expression. "Anyway, Penny's on her way home now."

"Already? That's a long drive to make back-to-back. She could've stayed."

"She has a baby to get back to." He set down the doll. "And I don't know about you, but I'm ready for things to get back to normal around here." That is, if a never-ending list of repairs and to-dos plus a couple of mysteries to solve counted as normal. He'd already taken too long of a break yesterday, spending time Christmas-ifying the house. Speaking of which . . .

"Hey, we never got around to presents last night."

Mara was popping plastic bubbles now instead of wrapping dolls. "What?"

"Christmas in March. There were presents." Or, at least, one present. He'd thought it was a good idea at the time, but then, with everyone else around, he'd felt too dumb or embarrassed—*something*—to give it to Mara.

He latched on to the welcome diversion. "Downstairs."

Mara followed him down to the den where the tree was still lit and the room still smelled of spice and pine. Probably from the Christmas candles he and Sam and Lucas had dug out from the boxes of decorations.

And under the tree, the gift he'd wrapped. He grabbed it and held it out to Mara. "Sorry it's wrapped in newspaper. You'd think with everything else we found in the attic, we'd have come across wrapping paper, too. But no such luck."

"You got me a Christmas gift?"

"Trust me, it's nothing that exciting. Open it."

She had the package open in seconds. The spread of her smile was slow and filled with wonder. "Photos of the Everwood?"

When she looked up at him, her eyes were so lit with delight, he could almost forget Penny had ever been here. Almost.

They were old black-and-white and sepia photos—a few five by sevens, some eight by tens, all framed. All it'd taken was a little dusting, Windex on the glass, and he was pretty sure they'd make a cool wall decoration somewhere downstairs.

More than that, he was pretty sure Mara would like them.

"I assume a past owner framed them and had them on display at some point," he said.

"I love them." She held the whole stack in her arms, struggling to look at them, one after another.

"Here, let me help." He reached for the frames, handing her one at a time. Honestly, he hadn't looked that closely at any of them yesterday. Only enough to see that two of them showed the Everwood's exterior—one taken during winter, as snow covered the lawn and the bushes that lined the porch, and the other likely in the spring or summer, the mass of leaves on the giant elm filling the corner of the photo.

The other four showed rooms inside the house. The kitchen, the dining room, a guestroom, and the den.

Now, as Mara handed each photo back to him, he looked closer. "I wouldn't know when these are from, except that one of the photos has a scribble on back. It says 1965."

"Not long after Lenora's parents disappeared." She handed him the photo that featured the den. It showed the fireplace, stone reaching all the way to the ceiling, a wing-back chair in the corner—possibly the same ripped one he'd sat on in the attic the other night. And . . . huh. There was a faint square on the wall above the chair and an end table. As if a piece of artwork once hung there, the rest of the wall around it faded by the sun.

"Hey, Mara, you know that photo you found in the attic? The couple—Arnold and Jeane. Do you still have it?"

"Yeah, it's in Lenora's—uh, my room."

"Can you get it?"

She cast him a curious glance, but she handed him the last frame and crossed the room to the door leading into hers. A second later, her squeal rang out.

She appeared in the doorway, a doll in hand. "Really, Marshall?"

He chuckled as he set down the frames. That was the doll from the dresser. Just wait until she got in bed tonight. "Couldn't help myself. Sorry."

"Something tells me that apology was not entirely sincere."

"Not entirely, no."

She marched across the room, doll tucked under her arm, and held out the photo. And . . . yep. That's what he'd thought.

"What is it, Marsh?"

"This may be the loosest, flimsiest hunch ever, but I have an idea why Lenora wanted to talk to that art history expert."

13

LENORA

*S*ometimes in my dreams, they call me Eleanor.
Mom and Dad, that is. They call me Eleanor,
and they remind of the little room—the one hidden behind
the fireplace. Dad shows me where to step behind the pile
of logs and find the handle. And Mom's hushed words
repeat the instructions I've heard before.

*"Eleanor, if ever anything bad should happen, climb into the
secret room and wait for us. Don't come out until one of us comes
for you."*

In one particular dream, I obey. It's a dark, snowy night
and one of our guests has twin sons. I don't see their faces
nor know their names or ages, but I know they aren't nice.

So I find a flashlight in a drawer in the kitchen, wait
until the den is empty, and I face the open mouth of the
cold fireplace. I ruin my frock in the ash and soot until I
find the metal handle. I tumble into the room and click on
the flashlight.

That's when I see the painting leaned up against a
corner. I wander to it, shining the flashlight over the bright
colors of the scenic landscape—a tree with deep pink blos-

soms that remind me of one of Mom's dresses. I wonder how it got here and why I didn't notice it missing from the den wall before.

But it's not enough to hold my interest, not when I'm bravely hiding in a secret room and the flashlight isn't the only thing I found in the kitchen. I reach into my pocket for a cookie and nestle against one wall.

Hours later, Dad finds me in the secret room. I've had my nap in here, it seems, and he finds it hilarious. Though he scolds me soundly for giving him and Mom a scare. He whisks me from my hiding place, and I forget to ever ask about the painting.

He calls me Eleanor.

"Is there such a thing as a tree doctor?"

It was the first day of December and I'd grown wonderfully accustomed to Mara's voice echoing about the house. She came loping into the den where I sat staring at the fireplace, remembering only in blurry scraps. As if my memory were a photo album of pictures so faded and yellowed I couldn't quite make out the images.

Just before she entered the room, I'd had the thought that maybe it was time to give up my quest. After all, I still didn't know what I was searching for. The room behind the fireplace was as void of answers as the attic. And I needed to focus on the present. The kitchen renovation had ended up far more expensive than I'd planned, and I was beginning to worry about paying January's mortgage installment.

Mara dropped onto the window seat. She was barefoot, of course, and wearing an overly large sweatshirt. I could tell by the brown smudges on her hands she'd been polishing woodwork again.

"A tree doctor?"

"The way that old elm tree out front leans and groans worries me. Plus, have you noticed the faint reddish tinge to the bark of that tree in back by the garden shed? I think it may be a magnolia tree. We should ensure it's healthy because those things can be beautiful. Who do you think we should call?"

I looked away. "I don't know."

"I'll Google it. And maybe whoever we get out here can give us some ideas for planting some bushes and maybe a few more trees. Just two or three. Don't you think it'd be pretty in the spring to have some flowering trees up front? I'm thinking of pink and purple blossoms."

I dragged my gaze from a blank space on the wall—unsure why I was staring at it in the first place—and noticed the way she was leaning forward, legs crossed and hands on her knees. Mara Bristol had come alive. It didn't matter if she was sweeping snarled leaves from the porch or clipping stray threads from a rug or dusting furniture in too many unused rooms—she'd found such joy in taking care of this old house.

And I didn't know how to tell her there wasn't money for a botanist or horticulturist or whoever it was that doctored trees.

"I'm so happy you're happy here," I began, thinking to broach the topic. But something else came out instead. "If you hadn't come to the Everwood, Mara, where do you think you might be now?"

She looked puzzled at the question. "I don't know, really. I think even if Garrett hadn't happened, I was ready to be done nannying, but I didn't know what would come next. A lot of my life's been that way."

We sat quietly for a moment, like we did often. When we could feel the atmosphere changing. When there was a heart conversation to be had.

Finally, she spoke up again. "If I'm really honest with myself, I think when I was running from Garrett, I may have been running from myself, too—from disappointment at nothing in my life turning out the way I'd ever envisioned. I never really had this big career ambition or anything, but I thought eventually I'd develop one. Or at least . . . I'd have a family. Marriage, kids, a house. I thought I'd get to a point where I felt settled. Instead, it's like I've been out in the hallway all this time, waiting for . . . for some feeling of *this is it*."

"Life's hallways can be good, Mara. That's where we're prepped and stretched and matured into the people we need to be for whatever comes next." I leaned forward in the loveseat. "There are good things in the hallway."

"But what if it feels like the hallway is just stretching on and on forever. And none of the doors you expected to open actually do?"

I couldn't help but smile. I loved it when she asked me these questions. "Then maybe you start looking for another door. And if it's not open yet, maybe you push it open. There comes a point, my girl, when you have to just stand up and move and take the next step even if it's the only step you see."

"What if you take a wrong step?"

"That's where faith and trust in God comes in. If you're walking with Him, He's not going to let you wander through a trapdoor."

She gave me a sidelong glance. "Except I don't know that I have as deep of a faith as you."

I lifted my eyebrows. "So, maybe that's the first door you choose. Choose to look for Him, Mara. When you do, I think you'll see He's been with you all along . . . even in the hallway. His love is an *always and everywhere* kind of love."

Mara's pensive expression reminded me of George's in that moment. Thoughtful, reflective George. Sometimes I think if not for me, he would've chosen to settle down and raise a passel of kids. I was the impulsive one but he loved me enough to come along for the ride.

He would've come with me to the Everwood, I'm sure of it. He would've loved the den. He would've been just as concerned as Mara was about the trees. He would've—

Trees.

Mara had said something about trees with vibrant blossoms and . . .

Pillows tumbled to the floor as I bounded to my feet.

"What is it, Lenora?"

The lines of a fuzzy image in my mind had begun to sharpen. A flowering tree on a scenic landscape. The painting in the fireplace room. The one that used to hang on the wall. And my parents' hurled arguments over something left behind on the day we fled the Everwood . . .

I had a lead.

14

*T*hey'd waited all day Monday for the art professor to call back or email. Then Tuesday. Finally this morning, Marshall had gone into full police mode, deciding enough was enough and declaring his plan to make the four-hour drive up to Minneapolis and get answers.

So here Mara was, sitting beside him in a cramped office on the campus of the University of Minnesota. It smelled of stale coffee and leather. A series of framed watercolors ornamented one wall, and the shelves lining another were crammed with textbooks and sculptures.

Professor Anthony Hodgkins had yet to return after showing them into the space and promising he'd return soon.

"He probably thinks we're crazy, landing on his doorstep out of the blue like this," she whispered.

Marshall had his chin on his fist and a faraway look in his eyes. The vinyl-covered chair he sat in was way too small for him and he shifted. His height and breadth made the few college kids they'd passed in the art department hallway look like gangly teens. "It's not exactly out of the blue considering how many times we tried to contact him." His tone held the gruffness of a police officer on the trail of a suspect.

But then he lightened just enough to cast her a teasing look. "I showed up on your doorstep unexpectedly and that turned out all well and good, yeah?"

It simply wasn't fair that such a brief dimpled grin—yes, she'd finally decided those lines under his stubble *were* dimples—and a wink could turn her palms sweaty and her cheeks warm. "I don't know if finding a porcelain doll in my bed at night and my shower the next morning counts as 'well and good.'"

"Sure does to me." It was practically a drawl.

It'd been like this ever since Sunday. One minute he seemed lost in his own thoughts, distant, focused on work around the Everwood or putting the pieces of Lenora and her parents' disappearances together. The next, he was lighthearted, even playful. He'd mused endlessly about that hidden room behind the fireplace while they worked—coming up with one entertaining story after another as to why it might be there.

Honestly, he'd begun to remind her a little of Jenessa, a busy bee intent on staying distracted. And it was clear enough now what he was trying to keep from thinking about—a wife who'd walked away, a child who'd died. How did a man ever recover from that?

Maybe he didn't.

Once or twice on the way to Minnesota she'd started to ask about Laney, but like the intuitive detective he was, he'd seen her questions coming and deflected them with ease.

"I hope we get something out of this trip," she said now. "We're giving up a whole day of work."

"Yeah, but the pest control people are taking care of the

carpenter ants today. It's probably easier to do that without us underfoot anyway."

He wasn't wrong. And at least it was only carpenter ants they were dealing with, not termites. With that good news, they'd been able to hire Drew Renwycke to come out later this week to work on the new porch. Mara was pretty sure the man had quoted them a ridiculously low price for the project, but even so, her grant dollars were beginning to dwindle dangerously low.

As were the number of days left before the open house and the city council's review of their progress. But they *were* making progress. In just two days, they'd painted all eight guestrooms. Mara had ordered new mattresses and bedding. She'd stuck with neutral colors and simple décor rather than coming up with themes for each room. The house already had plenty of unique features as well as large windows that displayed the outdoor beauty all around. She'd rather skip the kitsch and keep things simple so the Everwood's natural charm could shine.

Still, for every task they'd accomplished, another three or four popped up. And now that Jenessa's newspaper article had drummed up local interest, they'd booked a few rooms for early May. Which made everything seem all the more real.

But with the computer from the front desk still in police custody, Mara had been forced to take down reservations by hand and have people mail their deposit checks. Not an effective way to do business. She'd likely need to dip into what meager funds were left to buy a new computer, and she might as well upgrade the system they were using while she was at it and—

"Mara, I can hear the wheels in your brain spinning." Marshall reached over and squeezed her hand. "Stop worrying. We still have a week and a half until the open house."

"I should've stayed back at the Everwood today. I could've gone to the library and worked on our website and Facebook page."

He gave her a look she couldn't read. "You said 'our.'"

Heat traveled up her neck. "I didn't mean to imply . . . I know you're not staying indefinitely. But you've done so much work. None of it would be possible without you. We're partners. It's *our* project. That's all I meant. Not, you know, anything else." Where was the mental spigot to turn off her sputtering words?

"Partners," he repeated, expression still indecipherable. Still holding her hand.

Which he released a moment later when Anthony Hodgkins reentered the room. The professor looked to be barely thirty, if that. He wore a faded jean jacket over his tee and tan pants. Only the flecks of gray in his goatee kept him from fully fitting in with the students they'd seen spilling from his classroom a few minutes ago.

"Sorry for the wait. I've got office hours on Wednesdays after class, so I needed to make sure my TA could cover for me." He flopped into the chair behind his desk, its wheels spinning him backward until he hit the wall.

"Sorry to show up unannounced—" Mara began.

"But if you'd returned any of our calls, this wouldn't be necessary," Marshall finished.

Okay, so they were playing polite cop, crotchety cop.

But the professor was unfazed. "Dude, I haven't listened to a voicemail in probably five years."

Mara put her palm on Marshall's knee before his rolled eyes could lead to a curt retort. "We have some questions about a painting. And a woman who we think may have come to you asking about the same painting."

He rolled forward. "No way. The Jameson piece?" He slapped the top of his desk with his palms. "Has to be. Only other time someone has randomly shown up at my office to ask about a painting, she wanted to know about *The Crabapple Tree*, too."

Mara's hope rose. "So you did see Lenora."

"Sweet older lady with silver hair and glasses? Looks like a grandma? I don't remember her name, but that's only 'cause I've got sixty-some kids in Art History 101 this term and my brain is maxed."

Marshall leaned forward. "But she was here around Christmas?"

The professor nodded. "She must've found my name online somewhere. I did my thesis on Henry Jameson. Early 1900s artist. Never very widely known outside art critic circles, but he had a few renowned pieces, including a two-piece painting called *The Crabapple Tree*. She told me this crazy story about remembering the Jameson from when she was a kid. Well, the story itself isn't crazy—all it consisted of is a faint memory of seeing the painting on the wall of her childhood home. Which, I mean, come on. She looked like she could be seventy. She probably just remembers seeing a picture of it somewhere."

Now Marshall was the one restraining Mara. He'd placed his hand over hers on top of his knee. He spoke through gritted teeth. "And why is it so crazy to think she'd have a memory like that?"

"Because that painting's been missing since the 1940s. It was one half of a pair, both part of a prized collection belonging to Argo Spinelli. Think Al Capone, but just slightly less machine-gun-happy." The professor reached for a mini-fridge near his desk and pulled out an energy drink. "Thirsty?"

They both shook their heads.

"Spinelli's an interesting guy. He's worth a thesis of his own. Got his start during Prohibition, like a lot of mob types. And like a lot of them, he had his fingers into Hollywood too. His daughter was even an actress for a short while." He shrugged. "Anyhow, when both canvasses went missing, Spinelli took out ads in newspapers across the country, pleading for the return of the Jameson, bemoaning the loss of his 'greatest treasure.'"

He took a swig of his drink before continuing. "One canvas turned up in 1960. Some art collector in Europe got his hands on it. And then, crazily enough, he was found dead in an alley. Police were eventually able to link the murder back to Spinelli, which is how he finally ended up behind bars. But apparently, even from prison he continued his quest for the other half of the painting. Never found it, though. Died in the late eighties."

Mara dropped back in her chair. She couldn't have imagined such a wild story. But Marshall's hunch had proven correct. Lenora *had* been looking for the painting. Surely that's what accounted for all those nighttime searches in the attic. It hadn't been some fanciful, impulsive hunt either. She'd gone far enough to research, to travel and consult with an expert.

Which begged the question—had Lenora purchased the Everwood solely because of the possibility of finding the painting?

If so, then why all the talk about bringing it back to life? Why go through with a kitchen renovation or let Mara fill a notebook full of ideas for the rest of the house if she planned to leave once she found what she came for? If nothing else, why hadn't she asked Mara to help search the house if she thought the painting might be there?

"It's a great little mystery, that missing painting," the professor said. "But trust me, neither half of *The Crabapple*

Tree was ever tucked away at a bed and breakfast in Iowa. It would've taken a first-class criminal to get that thing away from Argo Spinelli."

He leaned back, propping his feet on his desk. "And what kind of criminal hangs up a stolen piece of artwork worth millions in a rural bed and breakfast, anyway?"

"She found the painting, didn't she?"

Marshall plucked his sunglasses from the cup holder in between his seat and Mara's and dropped them over his eyes. Vivid sunlight reflected off pastures quilted in white. The sky was a stunning blue today, the rolling landscape of farmland making the drive back to Maple Valley a pleasant one.

If not for the tension radiating from the seat next to him.

The professor had told a riveting story, and it'd seemed to settle things in Mara's mind: Lenora Worthington had never intended to stay at the Everwood. She'd come searching for something specific and when she'd found it, she'd left.

If she'd found it.

So Mara conjectured, anyway.

Didn't feel exactly right to Marshall, though. He couldn't put his finger on it, but something didn't line up. "Mara, we don't know—"

"It makes sense. It explains why she was always puttering around in the attic. It explains why she'd just up and leave. She knew the painting was worth a boatload of money and she didn't want to wait around to offload it and make a fortune." She reached forward to turn up the heater.

It still wasn't toasty enough in here for her? He'd started overheating twenty minutes into the drive. "But she bought the B&B last June, right? It wouldn't take more than half a year to search the attic or even the whole house."

Mara shrugged. "Okay, then maybe she didn't find it and she was just sick of looking and gave up. Or after talking to Hodgkins, she got another lead that took her away from the Everwood and it was simply too much bother to let anyone know where she was going or that, oh, by the way, she wasn't coming back."

Marshall closed the vents nearest him. "Or you're not being fair."

She twisted in her seat to pin him with a glare.

"I'm just saying, you're assigning motives to her that could be way off mark. You told me that when you came to the Everwood last summer, Lenora made you feel safe and welcome. You said she took you under her wing and gave you a home. Does that really sound like a woman who has tunnel vision over a piece of artwork to the point that she cares more about it than someone she spent months building a friendship with?"

He could see his argument take effect in the way she slumped against her seat.

"I never met Lenora, so maybe I don't know what I'm talking about," he conceded. "But last week you felt bad for assuming she'd abandoned the Everwood. I'm just trying to save you from another round of guilt if it turns out her disappearance has nothing to do with this painting."

"Do you really think that's the case?"

He didn't know what he thought yet. Only that his gut protested the idea that a woman Mara and Sam had described as sweet and gentle would be hardened enough to leave someone worrying about her indefinitely, painting or no. And that even if this whole thing was about some missing painting, they still should've been able to track her down.

But the last activity on her credit card was a gas station in Davenport and she could've gone anywhere from there. Sam had an officer looking through camera footage from tollbooths in a six-state radius, on the lookout for her license plate number, but so far . . . nothing. Gruesome as it sounded, a serious car accident would make sense, especially one that landed her in a hospital and unable to communicate. But they'd scoured accident reports with no leads.

Now their only lead was a canvas that'd been missing for almost eighty years and a high-profile criminal family that'd surely scattered and died out decades ago.

Mara propped her feet on the dash and leaned against the headrest, eyes closed, lashes curling against her cheek. She looked peaceful despite the questions he was sure still swarmed inside her mind.

"Hey, Mara? Random question. I've never really asked how you ended up at the Everwood."

She opened her eyes and rolled her head his direction. "I was on the road. I saw a brochure in a rest stop. An *old* brochure, as it turns out. Made the Everwood look pristine and new. I thought it looked pretty, and I needed a place to stay for awhile, so I sought it out."

"But weren't you on your way somewhere? Were you looking for a new job at the time? Waiting to start a new nannying position?"

She visibly shuddered. Which made him both curious and concerned. And worried she'd turn the heat up even higher.

"Uh, no. I was done nannying. Actually, I'd wanted to be done for a long time." She dropped her feet from the dash-board and sat up straighter. "I love kids and some of the families I worked for were really nice. But I was sick of feeling like an add-on, you know? It would've been different if I'd had family to go home to on holidays or days off. Or if I'd stayed in one place long enough to make close friends."

He passed a dawdling RV. "So you gave it up and hit the road."

He could feel her watching him, and he glanced away from the interstate to see the uncertainty in her eyes. There was more to the story, and she was trying to decide whether to share it.

The cop in him wanted to prod her on. Instead, he gave her time to decide as he shrugged out of his coat.

"Are you hot?"

"Uh, more like boiling."

She laughed and reached for the controls. "Why didn't you say something?"

"Because you were still cold."

And that, it seemed, made her decision for her. She let out a long breath before speaking. "My second-to-last family was in Ohio. I was in charge of a couple of younger kids, but there was an older sibling—a half-brother from the father's first marriage."

His grip tightened on the wheel. She'd barely explained a thing, but already the air between them shifted as he began to sense the direction her story might be going.

"Garrett was in college, so I didn't meet him until I'd been with the family for several months. And I didn't think much of it when I did." Her gloved hands were knotted in her lap. "But then he found me on social media and messaged me—repeatedly. Started coming home for visits more often too."

Yes, he definitely knew where this was going. His foot pressed harder on the pedal.

"He asked me out and I said no. That should've been the end of it. I was ten years older than him, for heaven's sake. But he kept asking and the asking turned into harassing. I began asking for days off when I knew he'd be home." She yanked off her gloves. "It was never violent or anything. But when he started leaving notes in my room, I decided to talk to his parents about it. Except they didn't believe me. Just a silly crush, his dad said."

"Idiots." He growled the word.

But Mara didn't appear to hear him. "Then Garrett came into my room one night while I was sleeping."

"We gotta pull over if this is going where it sounds like it's going, Mar."

"It's not. He just scared me, that's all. He was mad that I'd talked to his parents, and he was trying to intimidate me."

"There's no 'just' and there's no 'that's all.' Harassment is harassment."

"Well, anyway, I packed and left the next day. Didn't even give two weeks' notice. It was easy to get another job. There was a family who knew the Lymans. They were in the same social circle, made all the same rounds of galas and fundraisers and such, and they'd told me once if I ever needed a new position . . . " She took another breath, pausing as if filtering past details. "I hadn't even been there two weeks when Garrett showed up at their house. I was packing my bags again by the end of the day. The family didn't want any drama."

It was all Marshall could do not to hit the steering wheel.

"I knew I couldn't stay in the same town. So I hit the road. A couple months later, I was still sort of floundering. I was staying in a hotel in this suburb outside of Chicago. And he found me there."

"He *followed* you?"

"I'd posted my resume on a job site online and it had my cell number on it. Somehow that led him straight to me."

Marshall's tires squealed as he yanked the wheel and veered onto the exit ramp they'd nearly passed.

"Why are you—"

"Mara, you're describing a stalker." He pulled onto a side road. "What did you do when he showed up?"

"He barged into my room and tried to talk me into going back to Ohio. I told him he was crazy and to leave me alone. He backed me into a corner. There was a . . . struggle. But it was short."

"Did he hurt you?"

"I wound up with some bruises. But I kicked him, uh, strategically and got out of there. I heard him yelling after me. 'I've found you twice now. I can find you again.'" She had the door handle in a vise grip. "I knew he was a creep before, but this time . . . I guess I took it more seriously. I deleted all my social media accounts, took down that resume. I started driving and . . . You know the rest."

She wasn't shuddering now. Her voice didn't even quiver.

But things were beginning to make sense. The way she triple checked the Everwood's locks at night. How upset she'd been about that newspaper article of Jenessa's. She hadn't even told him about the article until a couple of days ago, and he hadn't been able to figure out at the time why she wasn't pleased about it. He understood now.

There were so many questions he wanted to ask now. Had she filed a police report? Were the kid's parents aware that he'd followed her across state lines? What if there were other women?

And how—how had she held it together all alone like that?

Even in his worst, most grief-stricken and lonely moments, somewhere in the back of his clouded mind he'd known he wasn't truly alone. He'd had Mom and Dad, Beth and Alex, Captain Wagner, other friends on the force. He might've done all he could to push them away. He might've been inarguably convinced none of them could understand the depth of his pain.

But still . . . he'd had them.

Mara hadn't had anyone.

He steered onto a gravel lane at the foot of a snowy hill and parked. "Mara, have you . . ." No. He swallowed his questions. They could wait. All of it could wait. He leaned toward her, his elbow propped on his armrest. "You are an incredibly strong person. You amaze me. Thank you for sharing something so difficult with me."

The engine grumbled and outside, a breeze skimmed a dusting of snow from the hill.

She bunched her gloves between her clasped hands, meeting his gaze without a hint of the leftover fear or anger or hurt he might've expected to be there. "Thank *you*."

"For what?" Saying she was strong? It was only the truth.

"For not getting us into a car accident when you thought that story was going an even worse direction."

She was smiling. After all she'd just told him, she was smiling and easing against her armrest. How? She'd just shared something awful and vulnerable.

Without the hum of the heater, the silence should be awkward and uncomfortable. Instead, the air between them felt somehow both taut and cozy at once, the console separating them like the thinnest barrier. He should ask one of those questions rolling about in his brain. He should pull back onto the road and make his way to the interstate.

He should definitely stop staring at her mouth.

Get a grip, man.

"Hey." He squawked the word. Mara jumped. "How do you feel about sledding?"

Mara was cold and wet and tired and happy. It'd been two hours since she and Marshall had piled back into the truck after sledding down that countryside hill, and still her damp jeans clung to her skin and soggy socks chilled her feet. But oh, she was happy.

As the nighttime lights of Maple Valley glittered through the dark up ahead, she leaned against her headrest and closed her eyes.

She'd been startled when Marshall asked about sledding then convinced he was joking. But he'd hopped down from the truck, grabbing the coat he'd shrugged out of earlier. He'd reached into the cab behind and, wouldn't you know it, he'd come up with a sled.

"Do you always drive around with a sled underneath your back seat?"

"Like the Boy Scouts say, 'Be prepared.'"

"I think they mean survival supplies. Food and water."

He'd met her on the passenger side of the truck. "Laney loved sledding." A simple explanation saturated with meaning. "Couldn't ever bring myself to take it out of the truck."

She'd had the irresistible desire to reach up and cup his cheeks, already ruddy from the cold, and tell him . . .

That she wasn't the only strong one.

That if he didn't feel like being strong, though, she was here.

But he'd tromped into the ditch toward the rise of a hill before she could find the words, his boots sinking into feet of snow. "C'mon. It'll be fun."

"But this could be private property."

"We're currently in the process of renovating private property, aren't we? A little rural trespassing should be nothing to us."

"I'm not dressed for sledding."

"Not a good enough argument." He was already halfway up the hill. "Let's go, Mara Bristol."

So she'd followed, breathing hard by the time she made it up the steep hill. Maybe she'd better start exercising one of these days.

Or maybe it wasn't the jaunt stealing her breath. Maybe it was tucking herself into the plastic sled, right in front of Marshall, his long legs on either side of her and his arms wrapping around her middle. Maybe it was his voice in her ear. "Hold on."

"To what?" But her question was lost to the wind and a squeal as they hurdled down the snowy hill, picking up speed and more speed and more—

Until the ditch loomed and spraying snow gargled her laughter and they hit a rut, spilling into the cushiony ground below. Cold, wet, happy, she'd stood. "Again?"

Over and over they'd zoomed on the sled—sometimes together, sometimes one at a time—leaving tracks up and down the snowy hillside.

And now she was still cold and wet and happy, no matter how furiously the heater panted. At least Marshall didn't seem to be overheating this time. He still wore his coat and a relaxed expression as he pointed the truck to the road that led to the Everwood.

They'd spoken hardly at all on the way home. They hadn't needed to.

Within minutes, the shadow of the Everwood rose up ahead. A lone lamp glowed yellow in one window. Marshall parked next to her car and soon they were climbing the porch steps.

She finally breached the quiet. "I can't wait to get out of these clothes." She stumbled over a step. "And into dry ones, I mean."

"I know what you meant."

And yet, she heard the rich undertone of teasing words he didn't say. She unlocked the door. He followed her in. Coat, scarf, gloves, shoes—one by one she shed her layers. The subdued light from the lamp in the sitting room barely reached into the lobby.

She heard the click of the front door's lock, and she glanced behind her. "Lucas isn't back yet."

Marshall hung his jacket on the coat tree. "He can knock. I'll let him in."

The house smelled of paint and at a gust of wind, little taps and brushes sounded all around—twigs, snow hitting windows and eaves.

She turned to Marshall. "Well, I know it's not that late, but I think I may call it a night."

"You're not hungry or anything?"

"Maybe I'll grab a Pop-Tart on my way through the kitchen."

One dark eyebrow rose. "Not a bowl of cereal?"

"We're out of milk."

And now one corner of his mouth. "You like it with milk now?"

"I always liked it with milk." Why was she still standing here, rooted to the cold floor? "Anyway . . . goodnight."

"Goodnight."

She turned but only took one step before whipping back around. "But if you're hungry, don't let me stop you. Help yourself to anything in the kitchen."

"I've been helping myself to anything in the kitchen for over a week now."

"Right." She turned again. Made it three or four steps this time. When she angled back, he was still standing in the same spot. "I feel like I should hug you goodnight." Oh, she was absurd. Just plain ridiculous and awkward and if the creaky floorboards chose now to open up and swallow her, that'd be just fine.

But all Marshall did was shrug. "You can hug me goodnight. I'm not stopping you."

Well, she couldn't turn and run away now, could she? *Stupid. Stupid. Stupid.* But there was nothing else to do other than close the distance between them and circle her arms around his waist. There, she'd done it and now she could turn around and get out of here before he could see how her cheeks burned.

But then he lifted his arms and tucked her against his chest. And the awkwardness slid away until she was pretty sure she could happily—even wet but no longer cold—stay here forever. Because he was warm and he smelled like cinnamon and nutmeg. Right, because they'd stopped to get apple cider and she'd said something that made him laugh, and he'd tipped his cup, and then complained the cider had dripped into his coat and down his shirt. The same shirt that didn't come close to muffling the sound of his heartbeat now and—

She looked up to see him looking down.

"Mara Bristol," he said low and husky, "if you want me to kiss you right now, I will. But you're going to have to make it really clear. After what you told me about that creep, no way am I about to make any assumptions, let alone a single move without—"

She was on her tiptoes in an instant, cutting him off with a kiss—impulsive and unpracticed. For one horrid moment, she thought that rumble in his chest might be laughter.

But no, it was the sound of a man relieved. His arms tightened and one hand moved into her damp, tangled hair as he kissed her back. Seconds—minutes?—blurred, until finally, still crushed to his chest, she leaned back just enough for the breathless words to slip out. "I guess I made it really clear."

And then he did laugh.

And he kissed her again.

15

Marshall stood on a section of rooftop that jutted over the front of the Everwood, a sun-warmed breeze sweeping over his skin as he took in the grove's budding trees and the rolling hills beyond. Almost hard to believe that just days ago this landscape had been painted in wintry white.

Spring had come to Maple Valley. Maybe for good this time.

And it might've even found its way into his soul.

He took a deep, cleansing breath, not at all bothered by the sounds of Drew Renwycke's three-man crew pushing in from below. They'd torn out what remained of the damaged porch yesterday and expected to have a new one well on its way by the end of today.

Marshall had high hopes of his own for the day. They'd finally begin painting the exterior of the house. He wanted to remove all the second-floor shutters before getting started, though, thus his climb onto the roof.

But first . . . first he just wanted to stand here and breathe. Take in the view. Count the days since his last headache, his last pill. Marvel at how strangely wonderful it felt to wake up with muscles sore from hard but rewarding labor.

For the past two days, he'd worked on scraping away the Everwood's old, peeling paint. Spent so many hours with a scraper in hand that he'd gone to sleep last night still hearing the rhythm of blunt metal against wood siding. It was a tedious job but he'd had help. Lucas, Jen, Sam—they'd all pitched in.

And Mara. Sweet, beautiful Mara who'd turned out to be her own kind of warm front, thawing his heart in ways that should've been impossible. Those kisses Wednesday night—whew, a man stranded in a frozen tundra could survive on that memory alone. How many times was he allowed to mentally relive them before it got just plain ridiculous?

And how long was he supposed to wait before he did it again? Thankful as he was for the friends who were helping, lately there were a few too many people constantly around this place for his liking. Jen had even stayed overnight last night.

He hadn't had a single moment alone with Mara since two nights ago. Not to kiss her again *or* to ask her the questions that'd badgered him ever since she'd shared her past on the way home from Minneapolis.

He crossed the slanted roof on careful footing. As long as he was up here, he should check his patchwork from last week too. Make sure that late round of snow hadn't undone his repairs.

"Marshall Hawkins!"

With a grin, he crept to the edge of the roof and peered over. Mara stood barefoot in dewy grass. She was wearing those baggy overalls again and she waved a porcelain doll in the air, her other hand on her waist.

He heard chuckles from the men working on the porch below. "Something wrong, Miss Bristol?"

"In the coffee mug cupboard? Seriously?"

"Made you laugh, didn't it?"

"It made me jump and knock a mug out of the cabinet is what it did. It fell to the floor and broke."

"Don't you know you shouldn't walk around barefoot when there's broken glass around?"

She was pretty always but when she flashed that glower of hers—the one she tried so hard to keep in place and failed at so badly—she was downright captivating.

"I'm coming up there."

Be my guest. She disappeared from view and seconds later, the ladder rattled against the side of the porch roof. He dropped the tool belt from his waist and ambled to the edge. "Careful, Mara."

Her red hair tumbled over her shoulders as she looked up at him. "I'm perfectly capable of climbing a ladder."

"Yeah, but your feet are probably wet from the grass and the ladder will be slick." He reached down as she neared the top, stretched out his hand. "Why don't you ever wear socks and shoes like a normal person?" He pulled her over the edge, bringing her to her feet with mere inches of space between them.

She didn't step back. "What's wrong with bare feet?"

Her toes peeked out from under those silly old overalls. *Adorable.* "As it turns out, nothing at all." He shuffled closer and hooked one arm around her waist. "It's not so bad a coffee mug broke, you know. That cupboard was crammed way too full anyway."

"Wouldn't have been so full if you hadn't stuffed a doll in it."

"Touché." The word was barely past his lips before they met hers. *Finally.* She leaned into his kiss without even a trace of hesitation, her hands coming up to his chest. Only when the sound of men talking below somehow pushed in did he make himself stop. "Good morning, by the way."

"Good morning." She fiddled with the button of his shirt pocket. "That was . . . quite the greeting."

He'd never seen her smile so widely or blush so deeply. Wouldn't be the last time if he had anything to say about it. Although right at the moment, it'd probably be smart to take another step back and get some distance. Otherwise he'd just keep on kissing her and never get a thing done today. He slid his hand from Mara's waist, but his feet refused to budge.

What had he come up here for anyway?

Right. The shutters.

"We've got a lot to do today," he said lamely. And yet, he finally had her all to himself. He hated to ruin such a perfect moment, but the cop in him could only wait so long. "Mara? There's something we need to talk about."

She still stood close enough that he could smell whatever pear-scented lotion or perfume it was she always wore. But gone was her dazed look from his kiss and in its place, a sigh. "I knew we'd have to talk about it eventually. For two days I've been walking around wondering when we'd finally grow up and talk like adults."

"Huh?"

"I kissed you. And you kissed me. That's kind of a big deal. I mean, people talk about that kind of thing. Right? I don't have much of a dating history, but you've been married, so I figured you'd be the one to—"

He was shaking his head, chuckling, fighting the desire to skip the talk and kiss her all over again. "That's not what I meant."

"No? So we're just never going to acknowledge that something has massively changed here?"

"Not what I said, Miss Bristol." This would be a whole lot easier if she wasn't so cute when she was exasperated. "Of course we should talk about . . . this. At some point. But I need to ask you about Garrett."

She turned away and he immediately missed her closeness. "There's really nothing more to say."

"There is. I want to make sure you're safe. If you give me a last name and a street address—"

"There's no point, Marsh. It was months and months ago."

"Lucas looks like him, right? That's why you jumped when you first saw him here last week. You were upset about your name and location being in the newspaper. You're still dealing with the after-effects of Garrett now."

She ran her palms up and down her bare arms. He pulled off the flannel shirt he wore over his tee and held it out. She accepted it without hesitation. Great, she looked even cuter swallowed up in it.

"Did you call his parents? Let them know what he'd done?"

She gave a bare shake of her head. "They didn't believe me before, so—"

"Did you file a police report?"

"I didn't think—"

"Mara, he threatened you. He followed you to another state. He hurt you."

She lifted her hand to comb her fingers through tangled hair, the sleeves of his shirt flopping over her wrist. "I'm sorry I didn't handle this to your exacting standards, Marshall, but I'd never been in that kind of situation before. And I was alone. I didn't have anyone to lean on. I just wanted to get away."

He stepped closer to her, but she stepped backward. Just like that first night in the cellar. He'd handled this all wrong, throwing questions like darts at her. Especially when she'd been expecting a discussion of an entirely different nature. "I wasn't trying to accuse you in any way. I'm sorry. Really. I'm only trying to help here."

"It's just hard to talk about."

"Sometimes it's worth talking about the hard things." This time when he took a step toward her, she didn't move away.

"And yet . . . you don't talk about Laney."

The space between them cooled in an instant. He bristled even as he told himself not to. Even as he watched the regret slide into Mara's blue-green eyes the moment the words were out.

"I shouldn't have said that, Marsh. They're drastically different situations. I would never compare—"

"It's okay." She'd only spoken the truth, after all. But even so, he could sense it—his wall going up. And he hated it.

Because he was ready to admit he felt things for this woman he hadn't felt in so, so long. He was ready to acknowledge that for the first time in years, he could almost imagine a new life. He'd put Penny's visit out of his head. He hadn't given a thought to how many days were left of his administrative leave. Since kissing Mara on Wednesday night, he'd let his mind and his heart fill to the brim with desire he'd not even known he was still capable of.

He was ready for whatever might be blooming between them.

But he was not ready to talk about Laney. Not even with her.

"Marshall—" she began, but something past him caught her attention and she broke off, her eyes widening. He turned. What in the world? Cars—a whole line of them—

moving down the gravel lane in a cloud of dust under tires.

"What's going on?" Mara bit her lip as she turned to Marshall.

The first cars were parking now, people piling out with brushes and rollers, ladders and buckets. "I think they're here to help."

Mara still wore Marshall's shirt.

All these hours later, she still wore his shirt, and she still regretted bringing up his daughter the way she had. Surely it wasn't wrong of her to be curious about his past, especially with all that had happened between them in such a short time.

But it'd been insensitive to toss his great loss into the middle of an already tense conversation. They'd hardly exchanged two words the rest of the morning and into the afternoon. He didn't seem angry. Only . . . distant.

Or maybe he was just busy acting as team captain for the townspeople who'd surprised them by showing up ready to be put to work.

"Hey, you going to help or just perch up there motion-less with your brush dripping paint on me?"

Mara's gaze swooped down from where she balanced near the top of the ladder she'd been sharing with Jenessa for the past hour. A drop of white paint had landed on Jen's shoulder. "Sorry."

Jen hopped off a rung near the bottom. "I need more paint."

Mara did too. She made her way down and abandoned her roller long enough to re-knot Marshall's shirt at her waist. Laughter, voices, and the clatter of people at work rose in every direction around the Everwood.

After the group from town had descended on them this morning, Marshall had taken charge while Mara ran inside to grab shoes. By the time she'd returned outside, at least two dozen people were at work, prying open cans of paint and setting up ladders. A few had been assigned to help Drew and his crew with the porch.

Jenessa knelt near a paint can and used a screwdriver to lever open its lid. Mara carried over their empty can and found a spare brush to scrape out any remaining paint.

"Are you ever going to admit that you're the one who got all these people to give up their Saturday to come out here?"

Jenessa's stylish straw hat blocked her eyes. "Nope. 'Cause I didn't."

"Someone had to have spread the word that we were painting today."

Jenessa propped her stir stick on the upturned lid of the paint can then poured a smooth pool of white into her tray. *White house, blue door.* Such a deep blue it was almost purple. Just like that magazine ad she'd seen on Marshall's nightstand.

Another thing she wanted to ask him about. Would he clam up about that too?

Maybe she should just ignore her questions. But ever since that first kiss, she'd found herself wanting to know *everything* about him. Not just about his past, but his thoughts on the future. He had a job to return to, didn't he? A whole life back in Wisconsin.

Slow down, Mara. It was one *kiss.*

And another this morning. And two days' worth of exchanged looks and shared smiles and . . .

And she had it bad. For a man she'd only known two weeks.

A man she hoped she hadn't pushed away this morning.

The thing was, when he'd asked those questions about Garrett, about whether she'd called his parents or notified the police, a heavy weight had thunked through her, landing in her stomach. She hadn't done either of those things. She'd done . . . nothing.

Just like she'd done nothing when Lenora hadn't returned one week after another.

"You're staring again, Mara. Do you need a break?" Jenessa stood at the ready, paint tray in one hand and roller in the other.

Mara shook her head. "Nah, I've got hours left in me." She moved the ladder down the wall a few feet then grabbed her roller and started climbing. "I still can't believe all these people came out to help today."

"By the way, if you want to thank someone for all this help, you should talk to Sam."

Mara paused halfway up the ladder. "Sam? Gruff Sam?" Who'd only just a week ago had suspicions about Mara's presence here?

"The man has a heart of gold, Mara. The minute he decided you weren't, in fact, a squatter or somehow involved in Lenora's disappearance, he became your ally." Jen streaked white paint over the wall below. "He'd be here himself, except Harper got called in to work and asked him to watch Mackenzie. I'm sure he'll come later, though."

Mackenzie. Sam's daughter. There was a mystery all its own. "So Harper is . . ."

"His story to tell."

"Oh."

Jenessa held on to the back of her hat as she tipped her head to look up at Mara. "Fine. Only the bare facts. Sam and Harper were never a thing. It was a one-night stand on the day he was left at the altar."

"Sam was left at the altar?"

"By Lucas's sister."

"*What?*"

Jenessa went back to painting. "That's all you're getting from me. Other than Sam's an amazing father and it stinks that he doesn't have Mackenzie with him more often. I'm pretty sure he would've married Harper as soon as he found out she was pregnant if she'd been willing. Sometimes I think that hurt him—maybe still hurts him—almost more than being jilted did."

Mara would never look at Sam the same again. Every day she spent with these friends, she glimpsed another piece of their family-like puzzle. They cared so intently for each other.

And now they'd turned that care upon her. Even Sam.

Mara lowered her roller and Jen grabbed it, dipped it into the paint and lifted it back up. The smell of hamburgers, courtesy of Seth Walker and The Red Door, wafted from the grill, and music drifted from speakers that'd come from who knew where.

"You know what I think?" Jen said. "I think there must be something magical about this house. Even Lucas seems happier since he's come here. I used to think it'd make a perfect haunted house. But now, the whole atmosphere has changed."

Yes, and Mara was changing with it. With every week that passed, her roots grew deeper—not just at the Everwood, but here in Maple Valley. For eight months she'd lived on the edge of this little town without having any idea what she was missing out on. Now that she knew, there was so much more at stake than simply saving the Everwood. This is where she wanted to stay.

If Lenora were to show up and ask her again about her dreams, this would be her answer—this place and these people.

And that man across the way currently helping Logan Walker carry a stack of two-by-fours. A strong, ridiculously handsome man who'd burrowed his way into her heart. Maybe the only man she'd ever known who looked just as attractive with a beard or without or especially with an in-between shadow. He was kind and funny and protective and . . .

And oh, how she wished she could take back this morning.

Not all of it. Not the kiss. Just the careless way she'd brought up his daughter.

Mara rolled paint across the wall as far as she could stretch. Then froze.

A song, a voice she hadn't heard—hadn't let herself hear—in years floated from the speakers.

> *You're my forever girl*
> *The one my heart adores*
> *You're my always girl*
> *I could never ask for more*

"All right. Another drip. We're going to have to switch —" Jenessa cut off, head tipped to Mara. "What's wrong with you?"

Mara clambered down the ladder. "That's one of my dad's songs. Not just one of his songs. That's *him* singing." She'd told Jenessa while they'd scrubbed the lime stains from one of the upstairs bathtubs earlier this week about Dad leaving.

She started to march toward the speaker now but

paused and returned to Jen. What was she going to do? Demand someone turn off the radio?

> *When you're right here*
> *And I'm far away*
> *You're the one I'll think of*
> *And when we're back together, this is what I'll say*
> *You're my forever girl . . .*

"They're horrible, cheesy lyrics, right?"

Jen took the roller out of Mara's hand and propped it near the can. "I don't know. They're kind of—" At Mara's slanted brows, she started over. "Yep. Horrible. Cheesy."

"Country music is the worst."

"The worst." Jen nodded.

"Marshall thinks so."

"He's a smart man."

"Of course he is." Unlike some. Unlike a man who left home then rubbed salt in the wound by turning a little chorus he used to sing at his daughter's bedside into a commercial hit.

If only he didn't sound so much like he meant the words as he crooned them in a slow, acoustic melody.

Her attention caught on Marshall once more. He was still with Logan Walker, but now the man's daughter was with them, jumping at her father's side until he reached down to swing her onto his hip. Was that hard for Marshall to watch? If it was, he didn't give anything away. In fact, he reached into his pocket and pulled out a packet of Tic Tacs, offering the girl one.

There. Those two men—that's what fathers looked like. Logan Walker clearly besotted with his kid. Marshall Hawkins carrying around a broken heart out of undying love for his.

And with what she'd just learned about Sam . . .

She wasn't bitter and she wasn't mad, but oh, she was lying to herself if she pretended it didn't still hurt.

Jenessa came up beside her, draped one arm around her back. "Have you ever tried to reach out to your dad, Mara?"

"I emailed him a few times when I was a teenager." And she'd called him once. After Mom's heart attack. She'd found a phone number in Mom's things and left a message for him when he didn't answer.

He hadn't even shown up for the funeral.

"Maybe it would help if you did. Maybe it'd give you closure."

Or it'd only open a door in her heart she'd closed long ago.

Except have I really? If hearing his voice still stings this much?

"I hate to say it, guys. I really do."

Marshall looked up from the mess of papers spread across the coffee shop table, knowing what Sam Ross was going to say before he said it. He knew that mixed look of frustration and resignation.

"We've hit a dead end."

He didn't have to look at Mara to sense her deflating next to him. On her other side, Jenessa gave a dramatic sigh while across the table, Lucas finished off his beverage.

They'd been sitting in this coffee shop for almost an hour discussing Lenora, reviewing what they knew.

Spirits had been high when they first arrived. They'd decided to celebrate the long, successful day of work by driving in to Maple Valley for ice cream. But by the time they'd arrived in town, it was already after 9:30 p.m. and the only place left open was the coffee shop on the riverfront—Coffee Coffee. It was an eclectic little spot with a mishmash of brightly colored furniture and mosaic-topped tables.

They sat at a table edged up to one of the shop's large front windows. No peering moonlight tonight—not with those downy clouds filling the near-black sky. But the light of the lampposts dotting the walking path around the riverfront reflected over the water's ripples.

Sam folded his arms on the tabletop. "We know Lenora was in Davenport, so we could start calling hospitals in the area, but how far out do we go? We might have a grainy pic from I-80 in eastern Illinois but still no credit or debit card activity. Her name and license don't show up in any accident reports."

"She can't have just disappeared." Mara sagged in her chair. From disappointment at their stalled case or simply fatigue from so many hours in the sun?

Probably both. Marshall fought the urge to drape his arm around the back of her chair. Before their talk on the roof this morning, he might've, even with their friends looking on.

But there was a strain between them now. He itched to make things right. Apologize for bulleting so many Garrett-related questions at her. For prickling the moment she'd mentioned Laney.

Then again, what if a little distance was a good thing? There was still so much Mara didn't know about him. She didn't know about the pills, about the mistakes he'd made on the job that had forced him into administrative leave. If she had any idea how low he'd sunk in the past couple of years—

"Marshall?"

He blinked to attention. Had Sam just asked him something?

"You're the big-city detective. You see anything here we're missing?"

He scanned the documents on the table—information on *The Crabapple Tree*, a Wikipedia entry on Argo Spinelli, notes on Lenora's vehicle. "You're checking art dealers?"

Sam nodded.

He hated to think what the lack of bank activity or failure to locate Lenora's car might signal. Probably nothing good. If she *had* found the painting, maybe she'd also found a buyer. Maybe it was a sketchy buyer.

Sometimes he hated having a policeman's mind.

He picked up the printout on the painting. "It goes back to this. I know it. Either she found it. Or she's still looking for it. Or—"

Sam stole his next words. "Or someone else is still looking."

Lucas sat up straighter. "If this Spinelli guy was some kind of mob boss, he may still have living relatives or associates out there. Even though he died in prison a few decades ago, maybe they're out to make good on an old grudge. Could be dangerous."

"And if Lenora was making inquiries about the painting—"

Mara bolted from her chair and without a word crossed the coffee shop and disappeared out the door.

An awkward hush fell over the table.

Jenessa cleared her throat. "I could go . . ." It was a half-hearted offer considering the look she gave Marshall. A perfect match for Sam's and Lucas's expectant glances.

Marshall pushed away from the table. He reached for Mara's empty travel cup. She'd gone for the decaf house blend, hadn't she? He stopped at the counter for a refill.

"Take her on a walk over the Archway Bridge."

His attention darted to the woman with jet-black hair behind the counter. The owner, according to Jenessa. Megan, according to her nametag. She hardly looked twenty-five. Awfully young to be a business owner. "Say what?"

"Mara looked upset. Walking across the Archway Bridge always makes me feel better. It's the big white one."

"You know Mara?"

She flicked her hair over her shoulder with a roll of her eyes. "This is Maple Valley. I've got the caffeine. So I hear things. All the things."

All the gossip, she meant. "Well, thanks for the suggestion."

"If you're smart, you'll take it." She gave him a wave of her hand, shooing him out the door.

He found Mara on the walking path, gaze on the river, arms hugged to her waist. The breeze lifted strands of her hair. He handed her the coffee. "You all right?"

She shook her head.

Down the path he saw the bridge the barista had mentioned. An arching iron structure. Picturesque even without the glow of moonlight. He pointed. "Want to walk?"

Not until they reached the bridge did she finally speak up. "Marshall, about this morning—"

"I'm sorry about that, Mara. I really am. I just threw those questions at you—"

"No, I'm sorry. The way I brought up . . ."

Did she think he'd get upset all over again if she said Laney's name? They stopped halfway across the bridge. The sound of the wind brushing over the river, water lapping at its bank, the twinkling lights of the riverfront businesses . . .

228

that barista was right to suggest this. It was peaceful, calming.

Mara leaned against the railing, one arm dangling over, the other hand lifting her cup for a drink. He traced her profile with his gaze. He wished . . .

He wished what?

I wish I could stay.

Here in this little town with its quirky events and friendly people. Here where his life brimmed with new possibilities.

Here with Mara.

But what about Beth and Alex and the kids? What about his job—Captain Wagner and his coworkers? As much as he liked his new friends here, he *did* have people he cared about in Wisconsin, even if he'd done a lousy job of showing it in recent years.

He closed his eyes. Inhaled the scent of Mara's coffee, heard the distant motor of a car, the swish of tall grass along the riverbank. Longed for a regretful moment for the kind of faith he used to have. The old Marshall would've prayed about his competing desires. Would've asked God for guidance.

"*Somewhere deep down there's still a piece of you that wants to believe.*" Beth had said that. Maybe it was the truth.

When he opened his eyes, Mara was watching him. "Why'd you leave just now, Mara?"

She looked away. "I'm just . . . I'm so annoyed with myself. Sam and Luke were talking about people looking for the painting, people who could be dangerous, and all I could think was, if I'd just done something . . . if I'd asked Lenora what she was looking for or gone to the police station when she didn't come back . . ."

"Didn't we already talk about this that night in the attic?"

"It's not just Lenora. I should've called Garrett's parents. I should've filed a report."

He could kick himself. "Mara, I never meant to make you feel—"

"And my dad. I called him one time as a teenager. *One* time. I heard one of his songs today, and it's a song he wrote for me. And I know it's crazy to think, but what if . . . what if he was trying to reach out through his music and I never paid attention? For almost twenty years, I've lived with the thought that he gave up on his family. But didn't I give up on him too?"

Marshall turned to face Mara, planted his hands on her shoulders. "He left you. You're not the one who should feel guilty."

She set her coffee cup on the railing. "It's not guilt. It's disappointment. I'm disappointed in myself for being so . . . so passive. I don't want to be someone who gives up too soon or runs away too fast or misses out because I'm too passive to *do* something."

"Would a passive person stand up in front of a city council and make a presentation to secure a grant? Or pour herself into fixing up a B&B that everyone else assumed was a lost cause? And you're not just saving the Everwood, Mara. Every day that I've spent here—with you—I've felt a little more whole. You *are* doing something. And it matters. You matter."

Her eyes filled with tears. He slid his hands from her shoulders to her back and pulled her close. He held her for a long, quiet moment. Felt her heart beat against his. Heard his soul whisper once more. *Stay.*

Could it be that simple?

You've only known her two weeks. You have a life back in Wisconsin. There are a hundred things she doesn't know about you. And probably just as many you don't know about her.

Well, maybe that's where he should start. Take a step back—emotionally, physically, and otherwise—and give it some time.

"Hey, Mara?"

From the cocoon of his arms, she looked up at him. Her eyes no longer glistened. "Hmm?"

"I was wondering . . ." He swallowed. "Do you think . . . is there any chance . . ." Man, it'd been a long time since he'd done this. "Could we go on a date? After the open house is over and things settle down. I feel like maybe we've gotten ahead of ourselves in some ways and . . ." Her breathtaking smile messed with his train of thought.

"By 'some ways' you mean those couple little kisses, right?"

He was thankful for the dark that masked his flush. "Not gonna lie, Mara. If you count those as 'little' kisses, I'm pretty eager to see what you consider a not-so-little kiss."

"And here you said we shouldn't get ahead of ourselves."

"That's not exactly what I said, and for the record, if memory serves, you're the one who started the kissing thing." If they kept talking about kissing, he was going to have to forget about taking a step back. "By the way, you haven't answered me."

"Yes, Marshall, I would love to go on a date with you." She eased away from him, retrieved her coffee cup, and started across the bridge. "In the meantime, I'm going to learn every little thing I can about Argo Spinelli and his crime ring. Because if this all ties back to the painting and the painting ties back to him then it's *not* a dead end. Surely we can learn more about him. That prof said he had a daughter, right? We should find out if he has living relatives, known partners—"

Marshall halted, his mental cogs spinning, a thought—a

hunch—coming in to focus. It was there, right at the edge of his brain . . . "*Oh.*"

"Marsh?"

"The photo. Those film reels we found in the attic. We need to get back to the Everwood."

"Marshall, slow down. It's not worth getting your very first speeding ticket." Mara gripped the seatbelt over her shoulder. Less because of concern over Marshall's driving and more because her own jitters.

If Marshall's hunch was correct, would it finally give them a solid lead?

"When did I tell you I've never had a speeding ticket?"

"Your second morning at the Everwood. I was eating Lucky Charms. You were trying to convince me I wasn't crazy to let you stay."

"Good memory."

Yeah, well, he was a memorable guy.

The headlights of Lucas's truck behind them shone in the rearview mirror.

"I still don't understand how you put it all together." Mara's leg bounced on the floor. She had ordered decaf tonight, right?

Marshall turned onto the gravel lane that led to the house. "You mentioned Spinelli's daughter, and I suddenly remembered that professor saying his daughter was an actress. And then I remembered those film reels in the attic. I think they had initials on them. J.S."

And back at the bridge Marshall had pulled out his phone and Googled until he'd discovered the name of Argo

Spinelli's daughter. *Jeane.* Like the Jeane in the photo Mara had found. *Jeane Spinelli. J.S.*

"I'm tracking with you, but what's the daughter of a mob boss doing at a B&B in Iowa?"

Marshall lifted one eyebrow. "Running it? Think about it. Lenora's parents—who we already know went by at least two different names—had a painting that belonged to Spinelli. Maybe they were art thieves or maybe—"

"Maybe Arnold and Jeane are Lenora's parents." Which made Lenora the granddaughter of a high-profile career criminal.

"I want to look at those film reels to see if I'm remembering the initials right. It's just a hunch at this point."

Marshall pulled up in front of the house. The first coat of fresh white paint stood out against the night's shadows. But wait . . .

"We should keep digging online and see if we can find a photo of Jeane Spinelli too. And—"

"Marsh." His name came out in a sharp gasp as her attention snagged on the Everwood's open front door.

And the figure running toward the grove.

Marshall saw the racing form only a moment after Mara. He thrust the vehicle into park. "Tell Lucas."

He was out the door in seconds, his scrambling gaze locking on the intruder, but it was far too dark to make out any details.

Soon he heard Lucas sprinting behind him. Grass, leaves, twigs snapped and crunched as they ran. He entered the grove, dodging trees . . . but whoever they chased had too much of a head start. He cleared the grove and reached a parked car. The intruder sped away before Marshall could get so much as a glimpse of the license plate.

Marshall slowed, lungs heaving. He bent over his knees, breathing hard, looking up when Lucas reached him.

"Get a look at him?"

He shook his head.

"A burglar? Or . . ." Lucas looked into the distance where the car had disappeared. "What are the odds we're not the only ones looking for Lenora?"

Frankly, Marshall would rather entertain that thought than the other one that'd immediately entered his brain. *Garrett.*

16

LENORA

$\mathcal{I}$t was February eighth—the day I almost told Mara.

The credits of an old movie rolled to the upbeat tune of a brassy orchestra number. Mara's eyes drifted closed where she curled in her nest of blanket and pillows on the couch.

Guests were few and far between, especially since Christmastime. Could Mara see how much it worried me? I'd deleted two messages from the answering machine—warnings from the bank—already.

I watched her fight sleep, and I knew she deserved some warning about what was to come. I'd rehearsed the words all day.

I'm leaving in the morning, Mara. There's someone I need to see. A . . . a family member. That is, if the information from the private investigator I'd hired was correct.

Information I'd paid for dearly with money that should've paid the mortgage.

I'd let it consume me, this need for answers. But every answer only led to more questions. Why would my parents

have had a stolen painting? Is that why we ran? Were we . . .
criminals? And where was the painting now?

I'd used the computer at the public library to find the
investigator because the Everwood's Wi-Fi had gone down
again. I'd compensated him in cash because he insisted.

I wondered if I was chasing one dead end after another.

But on February sixth, he called me with a name and an
address. And I'd held off the whim as long as I could.

*I'm not sure how long I'll be gone, Mara. Take care of the
Everwood for me, though, please. When I come back, we'll figure
out the rest—the money, the mortgage, the lack of reservations. I
promise.*

But instead of telling her, I'd let her sleep.

And in the morning, I was simply too keyed up and
anxious to explain. Or perhaps worried that once I told her
about my search, I'd have to admit the rest—that my need
to solve a mystery had endangered the Everwood.

And if I tarried too long, she might tell me not to go.
She'd noticed my fatigue of late. Just a day or two before,
she'd witnessed a dizzy moment as I'd stood from the
loveseat too quickly.

So all I did was extract a promise and take my leave and
tell myself everything would be okay.

It wasn't the house I expected.

Although, I'm not sure what I did expect. An imposing
mansion with grand pillars? Or perhaps a glitzy downtown
apartment. Something that hinted at wealthy, if criminal,
roots.

But this was nothing of the sort. It was a quaint little
cottage in the country. Yellow with white shutters and

flowers lining the walkway to the front door. Just to be sure, I looked at the address on my scrap of paper again. I had to squint to read the words, my eyesight bothering me as it had off and on for a day or two—or maybe a week, come to think of it.

But I made out the words and, yes, I was in the right place. At the right house. *Davis Saddler.*

My limbs felt numb but surely I'd simply been in the car too long.

I'd imagined this meeting so very many ways. Smiles of joy. Frowns of contempt. Most likely, my common sense told me, it would be something in between. I'd thought once or twice that perhaps this Davis Saddler would be dangerous.

But I'd come too far to turn back.

All of this I thought as I walked that flower-lined path. Until the door opened.

And then I thought nothing at all.

I'm so sure I've heard this voice before. He speaks in low murmurs. There are other voices too, but his is the one I latch on to in my confusion.

It's not George's. Oh, no. If it were George's, there would be dancing and laughing and no more of this wretched darkness. Though I can't hear George, there are moments when I can feel him beckoning. There are moments I long to answer his call.

But what of Mara? What of the Everwood?

The voice speaks again, louder this time. Does he know Mara, I wonder? Does Mara know I'm here?

And where—Lord, help me—is here?

17

*M*ara should've been more nervous. She had thousands of dollars riding on tonight. More importantly, the future of the Everwood.

Yet as she descended the open staircase, Mayor Milt and the rest of the city council trailing after her, a strange sort of confidence bubbled inside of her. Maybe it was the fact that they'd oohed and ahhed every step of the way through this tour so far. Maybe it was the pretty, navy blue sundress swishing over her knees and her cute yellow flats.

Or it was the comfort of knowing her friends were scattered about the place helping with the open house. Sam and Lucas were manning the parking lot. Jenessa was welcoming guests in the lobby. Marshall was taking care of final details out in the back yard—the surprise centerpiece of tonight's open house.

Whatever it was accounting for her unexpected assurance, nearly everything about tonight felt *right*.

Everything but Lenora's continued absence.

They still hadn't made progress on finding any

remaining relatives of the Spinelli family. Nor had they figured out who it was who'd intruded in the Everwood last week.

But nothing had been missing and there hadn't been any repeat incidents.

"I have to admit, Miss Bristol, I had my doubts about this whole venture, but I'm impressed with the work you've done. And in so little time too."

It was Sarita Rodriguez who spoke as they reached the first floor. The youngest city councilperson and from what Mara could tell, the most in tune with matters of business. The others had asked plenty of questions about the renovation and her plans for the future, but Sarita's inquiries were much more detailed. Though most of the changes they'd made were cosmetic, were structural renovations needed as well? What factors had determined the Everwood's room rates? Were they competitive with other B&Bs? Would she be hiring additional staff?

Mara gave Sarita a grateful smile. "I didn't do it on my own, that's for sure."

Not even close. In this past week, the Everwood had been a buzzing hive of activity. Anytime they weren't at their jobs, Jenessa and Sam and Lucas had been here. Marshall had pulled thirteen- or fourteen-hour days every day this week.

Even people from town had stopped out now and then to offer their help. Mara had met more of the Walker family, and though Drew Renwycke had finished the new porch last weekend, he'd come by with his brother one morning to help Marshall replace shutters and install flowerboxes underneath the front windows.

It was almost as if now that they remembered the Everwood was here, the people of Maple Valley were drawn to this place—to this tucked-away, once-forgotten house that'd slowly come alive again.

And never in her life had Mara felt more a part of something. More like she belonged. Like someone had carved out a space here in this town, in this house, with these people, just for her.

Maybe . . . maybe Someone had. At least, that's what Lenora believed. To Lenora, God wasn't just a distant creator, interested only in the people who impressed Him most. She believed God guided her steps and gave her life meaning and purpose.

What if Lenora was right and God had led Mara here? What if He'd never been waiting for her to impress Him, but just to . . . notice Him? Active and at work in her life?

Mara led the council members through the dining room where a lacy cloth and place settings covered the nicks in the long table and a new light fixture hung overhead. She pointed out the framed historical photographs Marshall had given her that decorated the walls.

Hopefully Marshall was ready out in the back yard because it was time for the final stop on her tour. The council members followed her through the kitchen, out the back door and . . .

Mara gasped as she stepped onto the small patio. She'd known what Marshall was planning out here, but she'd been so busy inside that she'd hardly glanced out the windows. The sight of it took her breath away.

Lanterns dangled from tree branches and sat atop each round table that dotted the freshly mowed lawn. Light ropes traced both sides of the walkway that led from the house. The magnolia tree near the garden shed was in full bloom, some of its snow-white blossoms falling with the breeze and dusting the grass underneath. In one corner of the yard, near the roped-off garden, Marshall had set up a movie screen where they planned to show one of the old films they'd found in the attic.

Lenora would've loved this.

"You, Mara Bristol, are a miracle worker," Mayor Milt said, his gaze sweeping over the sprawling yard and the townspeople beginning to gather. "I think we can safely say this is a rousing success."

"I really can't take all the credit. So many people helped and the weather cooperated too."

The April sky was painted in gorgeous shades of pink and violet, and a warmth that could almost pass for summer hovered in the air. Even the trees had seemed to anticipate this event—buds opening into leaves practically overnight.

Marshall had a few heaters and a portable generator on hand just in case it cooled down too much in the evening, but so far, it didn't feel like they'd even need them.

The mayor reached up to pat her cheek—a gesture that from anyone else might seem overly familiar but felt merely sweet and grandfatherly coming from the older man. "You're being modest and it only makes me appreciate you more. I hope you're planning to stay in Maple Valley. You fit in here well, Mara."

The words couldn't have more fully warmed her heart if they'd come complete with a key to the town. "I sure hope to stay."

"I am a little surprised, though, that the owner isn't here. I've gathered she's somewhat of a silent proprietor, but I would've thought she'd want to see this."

Why did she get the sense the mayor might understand a little more than he let on about Lenora's absence? So far, no one had bothered to question whether Mara belonged at the helm of the Everwood. Well, except for Sam in those initial days. But now, not for the first time, her conscience pricked. Other than her friends and that loan officer from the bank, no one else knew how long Lenora had been gone.

Or that she hadn't okayed any of the improvements they'd made here.

If Mara confessed the truth, would it undo the good impression she'd made tonight? Would the mayor see her as an imposter?

Suddenly, it didn't matter. He'd been so kind and welcoming. Everyone had. She owed them honesty. "Actually, I need to tell you something about the owner."

The mayor held up his hands to stop her confession. "I don't need to know any more than what I can see with my own two eyes. And what I see is that you have the Everwood's best interest in mind, and you've made good use of the city's funds. For now, that's good enough for me." He patted his stomach. "Now, I heard someone mention refreshments and I want to get a good seat for the movie."

"You'll take a look at my business plan later?"

"Oh, don't you worry. Sarita will go over it with a fine-toothed comb." He leaned toward her. "But I feel fairly confident in saying you don't have a thing to worry about, Miss Bristol."

He moved off into the yard, stopping at the first table he came across to chat with its occupants.

And what had been confidence before now unfolded into unadulterated delight. All their hard work was paying off. Perhaps some of their guests tonight would be so impressed they'd tell their out-of-town friends or even book their own future stay. In hopes of that, she was offering a special deal for open house guests who made spring or summer reservations. She should head inside and ask Jenessa if anyone had taken them up on the offer so far.

But just for a moment, she wanted to stay out here and let herself breathe it all in—the anticipation in the air, the loveliness of the spring night, the scent of lilacs mingling with the sweet aroma of the magnolia tree's blossoms.

This all felt . . . it felt like she'd finally done what Lenora had said all those months ago. Opened a door. Stepped out of the hallway and into a world of new possibilities.

Yes, Lenora, wherever she was, would've loved this.

Her gaze drifted to where Marshall chatted with the man running the projector. As if sensing her attention, he glanced up. Flashed her a grin that made her heart dance.

"The dress is pretty, Mara. But you're *beautiful."*

That's what he'd said an hour and a half ago when she'd first emerged from her room. The same gooey warmth that had filled every inch of her then curled over her now.

It'd been like this all week. One look from the man could scorch her in the very best of ways. Yet it seemed he'd meant what he'd said about taking a step back. No more kisses and they hadn't had much time to talk—really talk— either. But maybe tomorrow they'd go on that date.

Maybe she could ask him about his life back in Wisconsin . . . and whether or not he felt the pull to return. Maybe he'd finally open up about his daughter.

"Whatcha thinking about?"

Jenessa's voice in her ear made her jump.

"Whoa, how in the world did you manage to sneak up on me while wearing heels? I should've heard you coming."

"Oh, I think you were a little distracted." Jenessa's knowing expression matched her saucy tone.

"Don't know what you're talking about. I was just admiring the gorgeous night."

"That and something else. Or should I say some*one* else?"

Mara elbowed her friend and turned. "How's it going at the front desk?"

"Perfect. We have five reservations already. One couple wants to book a room for an entire week in June. They have relatives coming into town. But there's a man at the desk now who wants to talk to you."

Mara glanced over her shoulder once more before following Jenessa inside. Marshall winked at her. *Gorgeous night, indeed.*

She trailed her friend, pausing for a moment when she caught sight of the man at the desk. He wore a long trench coat and carried a briefcase. Who brought a briefcase to an evening open house?

He glanced her way. "Mara Bristol?"

"Yes, that's me."

He held out an arm so lanky the sleeve of his coat stopped short at his wrist. "Jim Morse. Sorry to draw you away from your guests but I was hoping I could talk to you for a minute."

She shook his hand and stepped behind the desk. "How can I help you?"

"I'm interested in the Everwood." He plunked his brief-case onto the counter. "That is, I'm interested in buying it."

Marshall strode across the Everwood's parking lot to where Sam perched against a black SUV. The movie was just about to begin out back, but Mara hadn't returned outside yet. He planned to find her as soon as he checked in with Sam.

"Any sign of last weekend's intruder?"

Sam wasn't in uniform, but he might as well have been. There was a reason he was stationed at the parking lot—surveillance. "So far, I recognize every person here tonight, save for a guy who showed up driving a rental car. But I did the casual chit-chat thing. Found out he's a businessman from Des Moines, in real estate."

"You believe him?"

"No reason not to, but I've got Lucas inside keeping an eye on him."

Surely they were being overly cautious. But ever since last week's intrusion, Marshall couldn't shake his need to be on high alert. Never mind that there'd been nothing suspicious since Saturday. No other shadowy figures lurking outside the Everwood.

"I'm inclined to think whoever that was last weekend was just a teen making trouble," Sam said. "There's not a whole lot for entertainment in Maple Valley. Actually, I take that back—there's plenty of entertainment, just not of the variety that appeals to teens."

Marshall scanned the length of the packed parking lot. Tonight's turnout was impressive. He just wished he could get his mind off police matters enough to enjoy it.

"We're missing something, Sam. I've got that feeling."

Sam nodded. "The one that keeps you up at night."

"Makes your food tasteless until you've figured out where it's coming from."

"Turns you into the worst date ever." Sam coughed uncomfortably. "Not that I've been there or anything."

On a different day, Marshall might have been tempted to parse that comment for clues into Sam Ross's life outside his role as police chief. They'd developed something of a working relationship in these past weeks—a friendship, even. Yet the man's personal life was as much of a mystery as Lenora's current whereabouts.

But Marshall's focus was laser-beam straight tonight.

One good thing—Marshall was fairly certain that Saturday night's incident didn't have anything to do with Garrett. Mara had finally given him the kid's full name as well as permission to look into his whereabouts. Sam had been the one to contact the guy's parents, Mara's former employers—mostly because Marshall knew if he made the call himself, he wouldn't be able to hold back from reaming them out for not taking Mara seriously when she'd originally come to them with concerns about their son.

But Sam had gotten the information they needed. Garrett was studying abroad in France this semester. A fact his college had confirmed.

So the creep was out of the picture.

"I was about to come looking for you, though," Sam said. "Your buddy Alex came through for us. Just got the call. Apparently, he's been trying to call you all day. You lose your phone or something?"

Or something. The truth was, Beth had texted yesterday to ask if he'd be home in time for the twins' birthday party in a couple of weeks. And two days ago, Captain Wagner had called, ostensibly to ask a question about a case Marshall had closed weeks ago. But he wasn't dense. Cap had called out of fatherly concern. He was checking in.

Which Marshall appreciated. Yet the less he thought about his life in Wisconsin, the more he was able to stave off the choking grief that used to be his constant companion. Well, constant, that is, whenever he wasn't gulping pills and escaping into the fog. Refusing to feel at all lest he feel too much.

But now he was feeling again. Feeling *good* things. He was a new man here. He'd taken off the blanket of his old, wrecked life, folded it up, and tucked it away in a closet. Like one of those breakable porcelain dolls.

And so, yes, today he'd left his phone on silent and kept it in his room.

He hadn't considered that Alex might be trying to get in touch with him. After Academy, Alex had spent a couple of years as a cop working for a unit that specialized in organized crime in the Great Lakes area. A handy connection, to be sure. Marshall had called him earlier in the week and asked if any of his past contacts might be able to provide information on whoever could be left of the old Spinelli family. He must've come up with something.

"What's the news?"

"Argo's son, Jeane's brother. Still alive. And get this— living in Springfield, Illinois."

Well, then. Marshall clapped his hands together. "Springfield. Okay, so we start—"

"Already on it. Got a man checking hospitals, contacting the Springfield PD. We'll review footage from every toll road in the vicinity."

He had to tell Mara. Nothing was concrete but it was a lead. More of one than they'd had in days. He should run up to his room and grab his phone so he could text Alex too and—

Sam's phone buzzed from his pocket.

Marshall paused.

A brief greeting, an "okay" and a "got it" later, Sam tapped out of the call. "That was fast."

Marshall's impatience itched. "What?"

Sam pocketed his phone. "Springfield Memorial Hospital. There's a Jane Doe."

Mara was reeling. "You want to buy the Everwood?"

Jim Morse had beady eyes and a nasally voice, and he'd finally seemed to realize Mara was still back on his initial point. He'd had other inquiries. How many guests were currently booked in the place? How long had she managed it? When could he speak to Lenora Worthington?

But Mara couldn't get past his first statement.

"*I* don't want to buy the Everwood," the man finally explained. "But I work for a firm that represents a small company that has a new plant up in Dixon. They'll be regularly flying in researchers, international investors, and other corporate leaders. They wish to purchase a house large enough to serve as a host site, and so far we haven't found anything suitable in Dixon."

So much information at once. "How'd you find out about the Everwood?"

The man adjusted his spectacles. "Saw an advertisement for the open house. Figured it couldn't hurt to take a look."

Out of habit, Mara toed off her shoes. Really, she shouldn't be so bothered by this man's questions. *Just tell him the owner doesn't plan to sell. End of story.*

It was the truth, right?

Or perhaps she was making assumptions. Lenora *had* missed those few months of mortgage payments. Even though Mara no longer believed Lenora had simply abandoned the Everwood, it didn't mean she hadn't started to rethink the B&B's future. For all Mara knew, Lenora might've put out feelers about a potential sale. Maybe she'd even talked to this man already. He did know her name.

"Mr. Morse, I really can't speak for the Everwood's owner. It's not presently for sale, but other than that—"

"Trust me, we'd offer a good price. Certainly much more than market value." He pulled a business card from his briefcase. "If you could have Lenora Worthington get in touch with me as soon as possible, I'd be most appreciative."

Easier said than done. The faint strains of orchestra music flitted through the house. The movie must be starting out back.

"I'll do my best."

As she was shaking his hand, Marshall and Sam came bursting into the house. "We found her, Mara." Marshall was grinning, his tie hanging loose and crooked, his gray eyes light with elation.

With no notice of the businessman, he swooped around the desk, gathering Mara into an impulsive hug then stepping back with his palms on her shoulders. "It's Lenora. We know where she is."

Her heart was pumping so fast it might race its way from her ribcage. "You're serious? Of course, you're serious. Where?"

Mr. Morse had left and Sam spoke from the other side of the desk. "A hospital in Springfield."

She couldn't believe it. She really couldn't. "You're sure?"

"A nurse confirmed it," Marshall said. "Well, technically she confirmed that there's a Jane Doe who matches Lenora's description."

Sam gave an amused grunt. "Probably broke confidentiality rules doing it. But Hawkins here is persuasive. Practically grabbed my phone out of my hand to do the questioning."

"That's not all." Marshall's palms were warm as they slid down her arms to take her hands. "She was checked into the hospital by a man named Davis Saddler. According to Alex, Davis Saddler is David Spinelli."

Mara watched her own eyes widen in the mirror behind Marshall. "It almost fits too perfectly."

"David is Jeane's brother."

Lenora's uncle then. How long had Lenora been in the hospital? Why hadn't she called? Or maybe she couldn't . . .

Had the nurse given Marshall any details about whatever it was that kept Lenora in the hospital? And why would Lenora's uncle check her in as a Jane Doe?

One question after another budged into each other. But only one made it out. "When do we leave?"

*I*t was all too familiar—the fluorescent lights of the hospital, the sterile smells. Doctors in white coats and nurses in scrubs, carrying files, conversing in hushed tones, walking with purpose.

Leaving Marshall only to wait, helpless to control the situation or the desperate slope of his own emotion.

But this wasn't Mayo and this wasn't two years ago.

Still, he couldn't help falling into the old rhythm—finding patterns on the ridges in the ceilings, tracing the lines of the hand railings along the wall. All while he tried to stay awake after the overnight drive.

Mara was tapping her foot on the waiting room carpet next to him. Just how many cups of gas station coffee had she gulped down since they'd left Maple Valley? He'd tried to convince her to wait to leave until after a good night's sleep. But she'd insisted on hitting the road soon after the open house ended. She was too keyed up to sleep anyway, she'd said.

Not entirely true. She'd dozed for a good three hours in the car before they'd switched places near the Iowa-Illinois border, giving him a chance to catch at least a couple hours of shut eye.

He'd found it hard to rest, though. Partially because he was just as eager as Mara to arrive at their destination and see the final pieces of this puzzle finally fit into place.

But also because for the first few hours of the drive, he could've sworn they were being followed. He hadn't been able to pinpoint the make or model of the car whose headlights were more of a dim blue than a normal yellow. It never got close enough.

But from midnight to one a.m. to two, it kept disappearing and then reappearing in his rearview mirror, up and down hills and around what few curves they took on I-80. He'd slowed down twice just to see if the car would get close enough to pass. When that didn't work, he'd sped up.

Which had finally done the trick. After no sign of the car for another half an hour, he'd mentally laughed off the whole thing, finally comfortable enough to give Mara the wheel for a while and let himself sink into a restless sleep.

"I don't understand why they don't let us in to see her. We drove all this way. We've been worried all this time." Now both of Mara's legs were bouncing. "You'd think someone would have a little mercy on us."

They still didn't have a clue what had landed Lenora in the hospital in the first place. The nurse Marshall had spoken to last night hadn't been willing to do anything more than confirm they had a patient matching Lenora's description, fitting the timeframe of her disappearance. He'd had to push hard to get the additional detail that she'd been checked in by a Davis Saddler, aka David Spinelli.

But whatever had caused Lenora's hospitalization, it must be serious. If she'd been missing for five weeks when Marshall had wound up on the scene then this would mark week eight. Two months in the hospital—two months in which she hadn't reached out to Mara.

He felt compelled to warn Mara somehow, to try to soften the blow before it came. He knew what it was like to walk into a patient's room and feel his heart splinter at the sight awaiting him. He knew what it was like to try to paste on a smile of strength and encouragement when all he wanted to do was escape into the hallway—or better yet a hollow stairwell—and let his trapped sorrow have its way.

Even now he could feel it. Suffocating and blistering. And, of course, a headache.

He pitched to his feet, feeling the ache of muscles all through his body that had been stuffed in a car for too long.

"Marshall?"

Why did Mara's voice sound so distant? He blinked. Hard. Rubbed his scratchy cheeks then his eyes. Turned. "Yeah?"

"Are you okay?"

Just thirty minutes ago he'd have been able to answer that question so easily. Never mind the lack of sleep, the long hours of work at the Everwood in recent days, the formerly unsolved mystery of Lenora's whereabouts. Before they'd walked into the hospital, he'd have said that yes, he was okay.

More than okay. He'd have said that he'd loved working at Mara's side. So much so that every day this past week, he'd entertained the thought of staying. Had even considered asking Sam about a job with the local department. *I want to stay.* What was keeping him from it?

Maybe this. The grief that always managed to find its way back in. Today it was a hospital waiting room. On another day, it might be a memory. An anniversary. Laney's birthday.

"Marshall, please sit down. You look ragged. Are you

getting another migraine?" Mara had come to stand in front of him, and she was the one with her hands on his cheeks now. "Maybe you should go out to the truck and try to sleep for a little bit. All we're doing is waiting anyway."

"I'm fine." The lie slipped off his tongue too easily. Like all those times he'd lied to Captain Wagner and Alex, assuring them he was up to whatever job the day demanded. Like all the times he'd lied to Beth and his parents during the funeral, after the funeral, and later when the divorce became a reality.

And perhaps like he'd been lying to himself in these past weeks. Maybe this hospital waiting room with its stark white walls and fake plants and muted TV was the harsh reminder he'd needed to pop the bubble he'd been living in.

Before he yanked Mara too deeply into the mess that he was.

But the compassion in her eyes was so tempting.

"Seriously, Marsh, why don't you rest for awhile? You could even check into one of the hotels around the hospital, get some actual sleep. I'll be okay here on my own."

The thought of that vehicle with the pale blue headlights flashed. He shook his head—overactive cop brain again.

Mara took the motion as a refusal to rest. "Well, at least sit down and drink some coffee. Eat some of the M&Ms." She led him to the chairs they'd vacated and held out the family-sized M&M bag he'd grabbed at a gas station hours ago. "Actually, what we really should do is find a cafeteria and get some real food. Who knows how long they'll leave us sitting here before anybody tells us anything? I still don't think it's too much to ask that someone at least give us a general idea of Lenora's condition."

"It's certainly not." The voice came from behind them.

Both Marshall and Mara shot to their feet.

The man was tall and slender, slightly bent at the shoulders, leaning on a cane. Could this be—

"I'm Davis Saddler," he said. "Come with me."

Davis Saddler had to be approaching ninety years old. Yet it was Mara whose limbs wobbled and hands trembled as she followed him down a hospital corridor that smelled of bleach. The recently mopped floor shined beneath their feet.

"I'm sorry the hospital personnel wouldn't give you any information when you first arrived." There was a slight croak to his voice. "The truth is, even if the hospital didn't have confidentiality procedures, I have my own reasons for being concerned with privacy."

"Is she okay? Is she conscious? What happened?" And what had he meant by his own privacy concerns?

The web of lines on his face deepened with what might have been a grin if not for the guarded mask that tempered it. "I'll answer as many of your questions as possible, Miss Bristol. But surely you want to see your friend first."

"How do you know her name?" Marshall barked the question.

"Same way I know yours, Mr. Hawkins." The man stopped outside a room. "Research." He grasped the door handle. "I need to warn you—she hasn't woken up. Not fully. But we've had some hopeful signs."

Marshall gripped Mara's hand. Without his anchoring, her impatience might have sent her careening through the door. Instead, she walked slowly into the room, only the sound of a machine's beeping and the tap of Davis Saddler's cane filling the hushed silence. The subtle scent of flowers floated on the air—carnations from a vase near Lenora's bed.

Lenora. Her thin frame was covered by a pale blue blanket, her silver hair splayed on the pillow behind her. If not for the IV stand, the tangle of wires and patches taped to her hand, she might look as if she were only sleeping.

The tapping of the cane stilled behind her. "It was a massive stroke." Davis Saddler spoke in low tones. "She woke up for just a few minutes in the ambulance before suffering a series of smaller strokes."

Mara heard shuffling and shifting, probably the man taking a seat behind her. But she couldn't make herself turn from Lenora's face—the peaceful curve of her lips, the utter stillness. Her skin didn't appear as ashen as Mara might have expected.

"At first the medical team kept her in a coma on purpose. Dr. Nichols will be able to explain it all to you. But for the past weeks, they've weaned her off every stabilizing medication and have tried to bring her out of the coma." The man paused. "Things are progressing. She's twitched her thumb, moved her toes. Yesterday I could swear I saw her eyelids flutter."

Marshall squeezed her hand. "What's her prognosis?" she asked softly.

"Unfortunately, that's uncertain at this point. Her organs are functioning on their own. She's not on life support. But it will be hard to know how the strokes affected her cognitive abilities or mental faculties until she wakes up."

Mara turned in time to see him sink back against his chair. "Which I pray she does," he finished.

He looked so . . . tired. As if whatever Lenora faced had been a battle for him too. And he looked like he cared . . . intensely.

But there was so much that didn't make sense. If he knew who Mara was, why hadn't he contacted her? She let go of Marshall's hand and placed herself in front of Davis Saddler. "I need an explanation."

"I know. Sit down."

She sat and Marshall's hand landed on her shoulder. He stood behind her as she fastened Davis with her stare.

With a sigh, he folded his hands in his lap. "Can I assume since you managed to find Eleanor, you've put together who I am?"

"Eleanor?" Mara and Marshall asked together.

"Forgive me. You know her as Lenora. I suppose I've let myself think of her as Eleanor because there have been so many times over the past decades when I wished to hear my real name spoken again . . ." A strand of wistfulness entered his gaze. "But then I don't know that Eleanor's her real name any more than Lenora is."

"Mr. Saddler," Marshall cut in, an edgy bite to his voice. "We drove six and a half hours overnight."

"Right." Davis straightened, cleared his throat. "I wasn't expecting Eleanor's—Lenora's—visit. I don't know how she identified me or located me or why she didn't call before showing up at my house. I never got to ask her. She had her first stroke on her way to my front door. I called 9-1-1 immediately and told the dispatcher I didn't know who she was, which was true enough at first. But when I got a good look at her face . . . she looks so much like Jeane."

He unclasped his hands, gripping armrests on either side of his chair. "Of course, I looked at her driver's license. Saw that her name was Lenora. But when she woke up in the ambulance, a paramedic asked her if she knew her name. Eleanor, she said. Over and over. And if I hadn't been sure before, I was then. The one time I met my niece, her parents called her Eleanor."

Mara glanced at the bed again, at Lenora's tranquil face. *What secrets did you harbor, Lenora?*

Or maybe she hadn't harbored them at all. Had she been hungry for answers about her own identity?

But why didn't you tell me? I could've gone with you. We could've searched together.

"Eleanor or Lenora—whatever her name, I was sure she was my niece. I was overjoyed and apprehensive at the same time." He looked to the bed and back again. "Jeane escaped, you see. She and Arnie got away. I don't know how they did it, but they managed to elude my father and his entire network of underlings and start over with new identities. But he never stopped looking for her. He talked about trying to find his greatest treasure up until the day he died, so doggedly that I was convinced he'd have cronies still looking even after his death."

His greatest treasure. "But . . . the painting? I thought . . ."

Davis shook his head as if reading the direction of her thoughts. "All those ads and newspaper articles talking about his lost painting, his lost treasure—*his* people, a whole criminal underground world spread across the country, knew it was code, a plea for information about his daughter."

"But Jeane and Arnold did have the painting."

One side of the man's mouth lifted. "Ingenious little plan of theirs. It was a two-piece painting. They sold one half to fund their initial getaway. That was easy enough to piece together when it turned up later."

And it'd led to the buyer's death, so that art professor had explained.

Davis ran his wrinkled hands up and down his armrests. "Jeane did what I couldn't. She figured out how to leave my father's world. Whereas I . . . in many ways, I'm still living in his shadow." He was looking down now, thoughtful, maybe remorseful. "Hard as I once tried to break free, new name and all, I'm still Argo Spinelli's son. All these decades later, my father's old connections—descendants, members of other crime families—still manage to find me now and then. I no longer try that hard to hide from them. Instead, I give any information I come by to state and federal authorities. But when my niece found me, all my old fears resurfaced. Was somebody still looking for Jeane? For the painting?"

He lifted his gaze and met Mara's eyes. "So, yes, I checked her in as a Jane Doe. I told hospital staff I would work with local law enforcement to identify her. I'm paying for her stay and all her care, so they haven't questioned it."

Mara stood and walked to the window, trying to digest everything the man had said. The sun's warmth reached through the glass. Exhaustion dragged through her even as her mind raced. There was still one thing that didn't add up. "But you know who I am . . . and Marshall too. How?"

The man's wrinkles deepened again. "At first I was too overwhelmed by the seriousness of Eleanor's condition to think about where she'd come from. I spent day after day at her bedside. I was hopeful eventually she'd wake up and explain everything for herself. But when that didn't happen, I got to work. Her license plate alone narrowed my research down to the span of a county. Once I'd connected her to the old house Jeane and Arnie used to own"—he leaned forward in his chair—"that's when I enlisted the help of a friend. I believe you had a visit from an S.B. Jenkins a few weeks ago."

Mara gasped. "The author looking for a place to stay and finish her book?"

Davis released a laugh. "Is that what she told you? I knew Sally would come up with a good enough story, but I wouldn't have guessed that." At Mara's continued look of shock, he went on. "She's a private investigator. Probably should've retired five years ago but I'm glad she didn't because she provided the information I needed."

Mara looked to Marshall. She'd almost forgotten about him, how haggard he'd looked out in the waiting room. What did he think of all this?

But he wasn't looking at her. He was looking at the bed, concentration in his gaze. She'd come to recognize that look—his detective expression. Were there more threads to the story she hadn't thought of yet?

"I hope you can forgive an old man for being too cautious to contact you," Davis said.

"Hey, Mara?" Marshall's voice was a whisper.

But it was Davis's kind blue eyes that drew her. "You must care deeply for Eleanor to go to such lengths to look for her. I've been praying every day for wisdom on how to handle this situation. Even more so, I've been praying that she'd wake up and—"

"Mara, look," Marshall's tone lifted. He pointed.

Her attention flew to the bed. Hadn't Lenora's right hand been at her side before? It was on her chest now. And were her eyelids fluttering?

Mara's breathing hitched.

Suddenly, a machine's shrill beeping clamored in and before Mara could so much as move, the hospital door flung open. One nurse then another. A doctor.

Mara found herself budged out of the way, heard the rapid patter of Davis's cane, and someone's commanding voice. "Hospital staff only. Everyone else out. Please."

Was it just being in a hospital again that had all of

Marshall's hackles raised? The incredulity of Davis Saddler's story?

Or something else?

They'd been shoved out of Lenora's room twenty minutes ago and Mara was still pacing the hallway, refusing to return to the waiting room. A nurse had found a chair for Davis, who sat hunched over his knees, his cane propped next to him.

Marshall merely stood with his back rigid, no matter the drowsiness threatening to overtake him. He shouldn't feel this limp. He'd gone through many a sleepless stretch longer than this. But at least the tiredness made sense.

His skittish nerves didn't. Despite Davis Saddler's explanation, something still felt off.

Or his senses were simply in disarray—too many thoughts of Laney jumbling his instincts. Memories of hospital stays, waits out in hallways just like this.

Except not like this. It seemed Lenora was on her way to waking up. There'd been no such happy ending for Laney.

He felt a hand on his back. Mara had halted her pacing, coming to stand beside him, slipping her arm around him. "You look like you could fall asleep standing up."

He kissed the top of her head. "I really hate hospitals."

"You must've spent a lot of time in them . . . with Laney."

He only nodded.

"I'd love to hear about her sometime."

His heart constricted.

"Did she have dimples like you?"

"I don't have dimples."

"You do. I didn't think so at first. I told myself they were just smile lines. Because it really wouldn't be fair for a man with such handsome features already to have dimples too. But they are definitely dimples." She squeezed in closer. "Did she look like you, Marsh?"

He pulled away so abruptly it had to have stunned her, but he didn't look behind to see. "We should text the others. Jen, Sam, Lucas . . . They'll be wondering."

"Marshall—"

"Good news for you folks."

Stark relief flooded in as the doctor emerged from Lenora's room.

"Is she awake?" Mara asked.

"She's awake and apparently she heard your voice before opening her eyes. That is, assuming you're Mara?"

She nodded.

"Good. Because she's asking for you. Give us a few minutes more and we'll have her ready for a visit—a brief one. Just one or two of you at a time." The doctor gave Mara a friendly pat on the shoulder. "It seems you were what we needed all along to coax her into fully awakening."

The second he slipped back into the room, Mara launched herself at Marshall. "I can't believe it!" She kissed his cheek and buried her face in his neck.

He allowed himself the luxury of holding her for a moment. She fit so perfectly in his arms, like she was made for a space that had been empty for so long. And he was happy for her. He was.

And he was happy for the older man he could see over her shoulder, clearly overcome. There were tears glistening in Davis Saddler's eyes.

If only he could shake his own melancholy. His unsettled intuition. And the flair of pain pinching at the backs of his eyes.

"Hey," he said softly into Mara's hair. "I've got a bit of a headache. I think I'll look for some aspirin. Maybe grab a bottle of water from a vending machine."

She leaned back. "Don't you want to come in?"

"He said only one or two visitors at a time. It should be you and Davis."

She nodded, stepping back and running her fingers through her hair. He leaned down to peck her cheek, gave Davis a nod and started down the hallway.

"Marshall?"

He looked back.

"You'll be here waiting afterward, right?"

"Right outside the door."

19

LENORA

*T*he tiniest sip of water is startling, trickling down my parched throat. I'm not sure I could move a single limb if I tried.

But there is light.

And there is more. A tone once distant is drawing nearer and as my cracked voice tries to say her name, her face comes into blurry view.

"It's okay, Lenora. Please don't try to talk if it hurts."

But I try again anyway. "Ma . . Mar . . ."

She cups my right hand in both of hers, and I'm not sure if it's the wetness of my tears or hers on my cheeks. "Yes, I'm here. I'm so glad you're awake. I've missed you so much."

It strikes me that I'm not in my own bed. I'm in a hospital. Nurses and doctors bustle about the space above me as the darkness surrenders to shapes, color, and the slow-burning certainty that George will have to keep waiting for a time.

I hear another woman's voice. A nurse? She picks up a

plastic cup from the bedside table. "I'll give you three a couple minutes alone, okay? But I'll be right outside at the nurse's station."

You three? Is someone else with Mara?

Mara reads the question in my eyes. "Your uncle's here too, Lenora. You found him. He's been at your bedside all these weeks making sure you got the best care."

Weeks? I try to speak again, but this time, the strain is too much.

"Would you like another drink, Elean—Lenora? I can get the cup back from the nurse."

This . . . this must be my uncle's voice. I heard it in the dark. There's something about it—the timbre, the way he stretches his vowels—that reminds me of Mom.

I barely move my head, just enough to see the shape of him, backlit by stripes of sunlight that edge through window blinds. There's something merry about the curve of his thin lips and all those lines on his face—even more than mine. I try to smile.

He takes my left hand. "I knew as soon as I saw you that you had to be Jeane's girl. I have so many questions for you. Right now I can't tell you what it means to me to be in the same room with you. Family."

Family.

If only George could see me now. I bet he'd never tease me again about seeing a mystery in everything.

And Mara—oh, there's much I want to say to her. I want to make sure she knows that even as I searched for my roots, hoping there might be something left of my old family, I was so very aware God had given me the gift of a new family. A daughter to stand in the place of all the children I never had.

Please, God, return my voice to me soon.

"Are you actually smiling, Lenora?" Mara leans closer to me, a plastic cup with a straw in her hands. "You are. Trust you to wake up after eight weeks of unconsciousness and flash a grin."

Eight weeks. Heavens.

My uncle is standing and I see he walks with a cane, its tap and drag slow across the floor. "I'll ask the nurse about that cup of water."

Mara only nods, still grasping my hand. "I have so much to tell you about the Everwood. And you have to meet Marshall. He's been staying there, but he's not exactly a guest. . . Well, it's hard to explain, but I think you'll like him."

I've seen moments of happiness pass over Mara's face in the months since I met her last summer. But this—this bright-eyed glaze of sheer joy—this is new. And I don't think my awakening is the only reason for it.

"There's something else." She leans in even closer. "Lenora, I emailed my dad. Just a couple days ago. I haven't told anyone else, not even Marsh. I'm not sure why I did it. But I opened the door and I took a step through it."

I see tears glistening in her eyes, and oh, I know what this means for her. I wish I could give her a hug. Make a cup of tea and talk for hours. *Soon.*

Mara blinks. "They said I could only stay in here for a few minutes, but I promise I'll be back as soon as they let me. Did they fill you in on why you're here before I came in? It was a horrible stroke—several actually—but you're going to recover. I'm sure of it."

I feel sure too. Down deep in these old bones. *Someday, George. But not now.*

I try to squeeze my fingers around Mara's.

But then I realize there's someone behind her. He

approaches slowly, softly, without a word. He isn't looking at me.

I swallow and try to whisper. "Who—"

But Mara's hand is yanked from mine. I hear a muffled squeal and I try—oh, I try so hard—to raise any sound at all.

And then . . . she's gone.

20

"Why did you take her away?"

Marshall stood in the center of the hushed hospital chapel, its backlit stained-glass cross sending beams of color to land on burgundy carpet around his planted feet. He hadn't meant to come here. Hadn't meant to pray—if his whispered question even counted as a prayer.

But here he was.

He stepped in between a row of chairs, fingers gripping the cloth back of a seat in front of him. "Other parents get to keep their kids. But you took mine." There'd been no miracle for Laney—not like for Lenora. There'd been no doctor striding from the room with a grin and good news.

That's why he was here in this chapel. Because with each step he'd taken away from Lenora's room, the unfairness of it all had begun its gong-like chiming.

When Davis Saddler had told that story about his father spending the rest of his life fruitlessly searching for "his greatest treasure," his daughter, Marshall had actually empathized with the criminal. Their circumstances might be different, but what if Marshall was destined for the same hopeless ending as Spinelli? Spinelli's prison bars were literal but wasn't Marshall trapped, too?

By anguish at all he'd lost. By his own inability to fix what was broken inside of him. By this endless cycle of one day thinking he was on the road to hope and healing and the next, feeling the stab of despair all over again.

Beth had said he could trust God with his broken pieces. He'd almost started to believe it. But how was he supposed to trust God to be careful with his broken pieces when He hadn't been careful with Laney.

You weren't careful then, no matter how much I prayed.

If he couldn't trust God to fix him, if he couldn't fix himself, then where did that leave him?

Impulse or maybe desperation surged through him and before he realized what he was doing, his phone was at his ear. One ring. Two rings. Did he actually want Penny to answer or—

"Hey, Marshall."

His head pounded and he could feel his pulse in his ears. "Hi, Penn. Um, sorry. I don't know why I'm calling." True. Yet not. "I'm . . . I'm in a hospital and—"

"Are you hurt? Sick? Beth told me you've stopped with the meds, but maybe you shouldn't have gone off them so fast or—"

"It's not that. It's . . . I don't know how . . ." He closed his eyes and sat. "Penny, I—"

The sound of a baby's cry rattled across the line. A sharp reminder. He shouldn't have called her. She had a whole new life. She wasn't his wife anymore.

And even if she were, he didn't know what he needed.

You need Me.

His gaze flew to the cross once more.

"Marsh?"

He ended the call, jabbed the phone into his pocket. His head pounded. "If you want me to believe," he said, his voice hard, "you're going to have to give me something. Anything."

He stared at the cross.

Nothing.

Enough of this. He jerked to his feet. He shouldn't have come in here. He'd told Mara he'd be waiting outside Lenora's room, so that's where he'd be. Never mind that he'd never found that bottle of water or aspirin.

He was halfway up the chapel aisle when its double doors flung open. Davis?

The man was breathing hard, leaning crooked against his cane. "You need to come. Mara."

"She's already done seeing Lenora? That was quick."

Davis was shaking his head before Marshall even finished. "She's gone."

Marshall's gut twisted. *Gone.* Lenora? As in, she'd passed away? "But the doctor said she was doing good. How . . . what happened?" His picked up his pace.

Davis was still shaking his head, so rapidly now that his cane wobbled too. "Not Eleanor."

He reached Davis just as the man's cane slipped from his grasp. Marshall caught it with one hand while reaching out to steady Davis with the other. "I'm confused. What are you say—"

"Mara." His voice had spilled over into a near yell. "She's gone and Eleanor is upset. We can't understand her. Something about a man—"

Marshall's pulse quickened.

And then he was running, feet carrying him down hallways and around corners until the commotion from Lenora's hospital room invaded his senses. A beeping machine, multiple voices. He skidded into the room.

Lenora was twisting against her pillows, her rasping voice pitiful and panicked. Unintelligible.

"You shouldn't be in here." A nurse touched his elbow and pointed to the door.

"The woman who was in here before, where is she?"

The nurse shook her head. "We don't know. We're trying to get our patient calmed right now."

"But—"

With surprising strength, the woman nearly pushed him from the room. He spilled into the hallway, headache raging now, but his policeman's reflex finally drove him past his panic. He scoured the space, gaze darting over every corner and doorway even as he jogged to the nurse's station.

Two women looked up from computers as he caught his ragged breath. "I'm looking for a woman. Red hair, about five foot eight." He combed his memory. "Jeans and a blue pullover."

"A patient?"

"No, no, a visitor. She was just here. She was in room 302."

He jabbed his fingers through his hair. Hadn't his instincts tried to warn him? Outside Lenora's room, earlier in the waiting room . . . on the drive. Those headlights.

He'd felt it in his gut, the knowing that something was off. But he'd let the hospital memories distract him. Let his pain and all his efforts to shove it down sidetrack him.

"I saw a woman with red hair." A third nurse moved toward him now. "She was walking down the hallway a few minutes ago. She was with a man."

Garrett.

Not Garrett.

Mara's sprinting heartbeat collided with her disbelief. For what felt like the hundredth time, she tried to yank free from the man's grip, but his hold only tightened, his fingers digging into her arm as he shoved her from the stairwell into the parking garage. Their steps tolled against the cement floor and their panting breaths echoed.

If not for the gun he'd flashed back in Lenora's room, she'd have yelled for help. Called for Marshall. Called for anyone.

Finally, he twisted her around to face him. And it smacked her all over again.

Not Garrett.

Her instant panic when the man had grabbed her in Lenora's room had morphed into terrified certainty. Garrett had finally come for her. She'd been sure of it.

But then the man had spoken into her ear and it hadn't been Garrett's voice. *"I've got a gun. Stay calm and walk with me. If you don't, I'll happily use it."*

And it wasn't Garrett's face in front of her now. But in her fear, she fumbled to remember his name. Morton . . . Morris . . . *Morse. Jim Morse.*

The man with the briefcase. From the open house.

"You wanted to buy the Everwood."

He flashed a menacing grin at her blurted words. "Seemed like a fine enough solution at the time but this will be much more expedient. Either you're going to tell me where the painting is or you'll make a nice little bit of leverage when I ask your friend Lenora where it is once she's talking again."

The painting? This was about the painting?

If only she'd been faster to act when he'd first edged into Lenora's room. But his threat in her ear had sent shards of ice down her spine. And without a doubt in her mind that he'd meant what he said about using the gun, she'd let him tow her into the hallway and out the door underneath an exit sign.

"Where's the painting?" he asked again.

"I have no idea." The whirr and rumble of engines and tires bellowed in the parking garage around them.

"Fine. Then you're coming with me." He jerked her arm again, sending a spasm into muscle already tight with alarm.

Even as she yelped, she put every ounce of her strength into planting her feet, pulling away. Were those footsteps she heard now? A flash of color darted behind the man. Marshall? Willing herself not to look at the gun, she ignored the slice of pain in her shoulder and tried wrenching away once more.

He grunted, yanking her back to him, lifting his gun—

Halting footsteps. A surprise thump.

Jim Morse crumpled to the cement, his gun sliding under a nearby car.

Marshall? Garbled emotion churned inside her. Gasping for breath against the shock, the stabbing pain in her arm, Mara lifted her relieved gaze.

Garrett.

Everything tipped off axis all over again. Garrett. Who was supposed to be in France.

It took only a moment for realization and adrenaline to kick in. She whirled, panicked attention darting to the stairwell door as she picked up her feet and—

It was one moment too many. An arm rippling with muscle shot out to pin her against Garrett's body. Garrett Lyman was no longer the lanky college kid she remembered. He radiated with ominous strength as he laughed into her hair then spun her back around to face him.

There was a glint of steel in his eyes. And a blade in his

hand. "Let's go." He shoved her forward. Just like that, she'd gone from one horrific situation to the next.

"This is crazy, Garrett. Aren't you supposed to be in France? How did you even find me?" And where was Marshall? What if Jim Morse roused and came after them?

"It was child's play, Mara. I had a Google alert set up for you. There was a newspaper article. I caught a flight."

So that fear had been well founded, after all. "It's been a year. Why were you still—"

He slammed her against a black Buick. "Because I told you I would. I said I'd find you and I did. Now get in." He wrenched the door open and thrust her inside. The lock clicked. She attempted to unlock it, but it clicked again. And again.

And Garrett was rounding the car. They'd be out of this garage within the next minute or two. And once he pulled out onto the open road, how would Marshall ever—

Phone!

She had it out of her pocket by the time the driver's side door opened. She fumbled to open a new text.

"What do you think you're doing?"

She heard Garrett's growl, felt the air move as he landed in his seat and his hand lunged toward her—

Black Bui—

His hand closed over hers, squeezing until she dropped the phone. Had it sent? Had she even finished the text? He reached over her to grab the phone and tossed it out his door. "Nice try."

"Why are you doing this?" Frustration poured out in her shrill words. "You can't possibly think you're going to get away with whatever it is you're trying to do."

"Stop talking to me like I'm a kid." He jammed his key

into the ignition. "You think I haven't thought this through? I've known where you were for over a week, Mara. I didn't go rushing in hot-headed and rash like last time. I waited." He looked over at her, malice and desire twisted together in his taut expression.

"So that was you last week at the Everwood?" *Stall. Keep him talking.*

The engine sputtered to life. "Plan A didn't work out. What of it?"

"And you've just been waiting around ever since? Lurking?"

"You're a hard woman to get alone." He peeled out of the parking space.

"You don't have to do this, Garrett. You haven't committed much of a crime yet, other than scaring me half to death." Pain blazed through her injured arm. If he made it out of the parking garage—

He pummeled the accelerator, his knife tucked against the wheel under his left hand. At least he hadn't gone after Morse's gun earlier.

Could she reach for the wheel fast enough? Manage to get his knife? She gripped her door handle.

"Don't bother trying again. Got the child lock on."

Fine. She'd go for the wheel. She shifted, reached—

His elbow slammed into her hurt arm and her shriek split her eardrums. He whipped around a curve, barely avoiding an SUV going the opposite direction. And suddenly, up ahead, jarring daylight gushed in. Another thirty seconds and he'd be free of the garage.

"Garrett, please."

He swore, gunning the accelerator.

Even if not for the half-finished text from Mara, Marshall would've known the Buick was his target. The moment he'd barreled out the door of the stairwell and into the garage, his focus had snagged on the fallen man's form in a heap on the floor.

Then the black vehicle that lurched from its parking space.

It'd taken less than a split second to plan his own course. No point chasing after the car on foot. Instead, realizing his truck was parked a level below, he'd sprung toward the stairwell once more, scrambling down clanging metal stairs and surging into open garage. The odor of cigarette smoke and gasoline clung to chilled air as he ran toward his truck.

He reached the truck just as a flash of black flew by in his periphery. The garage's exit was only one level down. If he didn't catch up in time—

No, he wouldn't even think of it. His tires squealed as he veered out of his parking space and swerved the direction the Buick had gone. One more curve and—There!

The Buick rushed toward the glare of sunlight that clashed with the shadows of the garage. For a moment, Marshall hoped for an easy resolution. There was a booth up by the exit, a long bar stretching across the ramp.

But no, instead of slowing, the vehicle in front of him only sped up.

Over the pounding of his headache, Marshall fought for a decisive calm. Okay, then. He knew what he had to do. At least there weren't any other moving vehicles around.

He pressed his pedal to the ground, heard the growl of his engine, the images outside his windshield blurring but for his moving target up ahead. He was gaining ground.

Wait until the last second . . .

He was nearly on top of the Buick.

Now.

He pounded the brake and jerked on his steering wheel and though his insides quaked, the truck did exactly as he'd hoped—curving off to the side as its back end swung around. "Please, God . . . Mara."

The prayer burst from his lips as his truck bed crashed into the back of the Buick, clanging, scraping metal and shattering glass . . .

He shot from his seat and out into the air, first angling toward the Buick's passenger side, but reversing course when he saw the driver's door open and a figure pitch forward.

Garrett.

"Stop!" He roared the word, long legs catching up to the kid in three easy strides.

But just as he reached him, Garret whirled around, wielding a blade and a holler of his own. "Get back."

Marshall slowed his steps. Garrett's blond hair was mussed and a trickle of blood ran down one side of his face. It was all Marshall could do not to turn back to the car, check to see if Mara had been injured too.

"Kid, I have chased down criminals holding far worse in their hands than a measly knife. You might as well—"

"I'm not a kid." Garrett charged at him with another howl.

Marshall braced himself for the impact, planting his feet but leaning enough to avoid the plunging of Garrett's knife. The blade merely nicked his torso as he latched onto Garrett, shoving him to the side.

With a grunt, the kid hit the back end of a jeep but he managed to stay on his feet. Before he could charge again, Marshall grabbed him from behind and stretched for the hand that grasped the knife.

"Marshall!"

Relief flooded him at the sound of Mara's voice but he

didn't turn. Garrett had surprising strength, butting against him, jutting an elbow into Marshall's ribs, refusing to loosen his hold on the knife. Marshall whipped him around and slammed Garrett's arm against the jeep once, twice.

Finally, the knife clattered to the ground.

Still, Garrett fought back, throwing a wild punch that barely brushed Marshall's cheekbone before Marshall wrestled him down. He pinned both of Garrett's arms to the cement floor as footsteps hurried toward him.

"Marsh, are you okay? You're bleeding."

"I'm fine," he panted. "Stay back, all right?"

More footsteps—security guards, thank goodness. By the time they reached him, he'd hauled Garrett to his feet.

The moment he handed off Garrett to a guard, he spun toward Mara. She stood motionless, face as ashen as the cement walls of the garage. If not for the way she cradled one arm, he'd have pulled her into his hold without another thought—and wouldn't have let go for anything.

The moving lights of a security vehicle flashed on the wall behind her and voices faded around him. He stopped in front of her. "I'm so sorry, Mara. I'm so—"

"Sorry? Marshall, you just . . . you're bleeding and . . . what in the world do you have to be sorry for?"

He cupped her cheeks in his hands. "Are you okay?"

"Mostly. Something's up with my shoulder. Might be dislocated."

"I'm sorry about the crash. I couldn't think of any other way to stop him. If he'd gotten out onto the open road, it would've turned into a car chase and—"

"I know. And it's not the crash that hurt my shoulder. Garrett did that. Or maybe that Morse guy. I don't know."

Because Marshall had left her alone. Because despite his gut instinct, he'd let down his guard. Let emotion distract him. He dropped his hands. And who was Morse? The crumpled man, obviously, but what did he have to do with this? "I'm sorry. I shouldn't have—"

"Marshall, would you stop apologizing?" She leaned into him, still supporting her arm and avoiding where Garrett's blade had ripped his shirt and cut into his side. "You just saved the day."

Garrett's raised voice sounded in the distance. Marshall and Mara would need to answer questions, probably go down to a police station and make statements. But he couldn't move from this spot. Couldn't let go of the guilt slamming through him, just as heady as the relief from only moments ago.

"I should've known. After the lurker last weekend . . . then on the way here, there were these headlights and . . . "

Mara shook her head against his chest. "I knew you'd come. I distracted him as long as I could. Because I *knew* you'd come."

And then, as if the shock had finally slid away, she succumbed to tears. As carefully as he could, he wrapped her in a tender embrace as her tears wetted his shirt. "It's okay, Mara. It's over now."

His head was leaden and his lungs still scraped and he was pretty sure Mara wasn't the only one shaking right now. She needed to see a doctor about her shoulder and his side could use a bandage. He needed to send officers to pick up the man she'd called Morse.

But for now he needed to hold her.

And to believe his own murmurs, even if only for a few feeble, fleeting seconds. "It's all okay."

21

"I have some very good news for you, Lenora."

The doctor whisked into Lenora's hospital room, steps as brisk as his voice was breezy. He'd become Mara's favorite of all the medical personnel she was now on a first-name basis with, after two weeks of days spent visiting at Lenora's bedside, accompanying her to physical therapy, slow walks up and down the corridor.

Mara sat on the ledge under the room's lone window, sunlight heating her back, hope warming her soul. "She gets to go home?"

Dr. Nichols held both ends of the stethoscope curved around his neck. "You're stealing my thunder, young lady."

"Sorry, doc." But oh, this is what they'd been waiting for. At first, they'd been told Lenora might be in the hospital for a month or more, but her progress in the past stretch of days had astounded everyone.

Lenora was sitting up in bed, her silver hair woven into a braid. Gone was the leash tethering her to an IV pole, the fog in her hazel eyes. There were still lingering effects of her stroke—the way one corner of her mouth tilted downward, the slowness of her speech, the need for a walker for the time being. But looking at her now, it was hard to believe she'd spent two whole months unconscious.

"But yes, Mara's got it right," Dr. Nichols said. "We'll need to talk about in-home care and get your physical therapy and rehabilitation plan into place. But by this evening, you'll be on your way home."

Home.

The word felt like spring. Like the peace of a gentle rainfall and the bright joy of a sun-kissed, green landscape all at once. Home to the Everwood.

Where Marshall waited.

He'd stayed in Illinois long enough to see Mara through all the chaos in that first week. They'd both made statements to the police. Garrett had been taken into custody. Between law enforcement, pending charges, and parents who could no longer deny his issues, Garrett wouldn't be crossing any more state lines.

As for Jim Morse, he was sitting in a jail cell on charges of attempted kidnapping as well as a slew of other criminal activities. And as expected, he had connections stemming back to Spinelli. From what they'd pieced together so far, he'd been keeping tabs on Davis for years. He'd eventually connected the dots and hoped they'd lead to the painting.

Just in case Morse wasn't alone, an officer was stationed outside Lenora's room at all hours. Another accompanied Mara back and forth between the hospital and the hotel.

So Marshall had returned to Iowa earlier this week, by way of a rental car since his truck had been totaled in the parking garage crash. Their first post-open house guests were due next weekend. Though Mara had considered canceling the reservations, Marshall had assured her he could get the place ready, even welcome guests and make breakfast if Mara wasn't back in time.

"I'll be the perfect host. Promise."

"You're the perfect superhero, that's what you are, Marshall Hawkins."

Though she'd said it with a playful grin, there'd been more sincerity in her words than she knew what to do with. He just kept doing it—showing up, providing exactly what she needed right when she needed it most.

He was the very definition of a hero. A rescuer.

She just wished he'd called more often in the past few days. Responded to her texts a little quicker. But surely he was just busy.

". . . so we'll schedule regular check-ups and monitor those things closely," Dr. Nichols was saying now. "Nurse Mendell will get appointments set up before you're discharged."

Mara hopped down from her perch at the window. How much had she just missed out on? "We'll be able to do those appointments and physical therapy at a hospital in Iowa, though, right? Ames is only about thirty minutes from Maple Valley and Des Moines is only an hour. I've already made some calls."

Dr. Nichols glanced at Lenora. "Well, yes. Certainly we can connect with your doctor in Iowa. But I wasn't aware that was the plan. I thought . . ."

Was he waiting for Lenora to jump in?

Lenora reached for the glass of water on her bedside table. She took a sip before her gaze sought out Mara. "We'll talk when Dr. Nichols is finished, dear."

"Actually, that's all I have right now." The doctor leaned down to pat Lenora's hand. "Don't tell anyone, but you're currently my favorite patient. I don't use the word 'miracle' often, but I don't think there's any other term that fits your case."

When he'd left the room, Mara lowered into the chair

beside Lenora's bed. She leaned over, grasping one of Lenora's hands. "We're going home."

"Mara—"

"I can't wait for you to see it, Lenora. The Everwood almost looks like a new house from the outside. I hope you're okay with the blue door and matching shutters. If you're not, blame Marshall, because it was his idea. The color is almost closer to purple than blue. Which I've tried telling Marsh, but he still insists it's blue. And you should see the lobby. Marshall made us start there and he was so right. Now it's light and airy and—"

"Mara, please."

The firmness in Lenora's tone finally cut through Mara's exuberance. "Sorry, I'm just really excited." To pack her bags and hit the road. To get back to Iowa.

To see Marshall.

A couple of phone calls, a few texts—they were no substitution for the man himself. She missed seeing him every day, working alongside him. She missed sharing breakfasts and going over renovation plans and all his teasing over her love of cereal and her tendency to go barefoot even on the coldest of days.

She missed finding those crazy porcelain dolls in so many crazy places.

She missed *him.*

Which was why she checked her phone a dozen times an hour for texts. Why she'd struggled to sleep last night when he'd never returned her evening call. Goodness, she might as well admit it—she was half in love with the man. Or maybe wholly.

Sunbeams washed the room in a warm glow. "Everything's going to be okay now, Lenora. More than okay." Of course, Dad still hadn't answered her email. Maybe never would. But his absence from her life was nothing new. She wouldn't let it derail the promising future unfolding before her.

Lenora sat up straighter, shifting against her pillows. "The thing is, I've had to make a hard decision."

Mara unzipped the hoodie she wore over a simple blue tee, the same outfit she'd worn time and again in the past two weeks. She'd packed too hastily the night she and Marshall left Maple Valley, never anticipating she'd end up staying in Illinois this long. "A hard decision about what?"

"About the Everwood."

A first barb of apprehension pricked her. She shrugged out of her hoodie. "Go on."

Lenora's hazel eyes were filled with compassion and concern. And regret. "I've decided to put up the Everwood for sale."

Mara stilled in her chair as her hoodie dropped to the floor. Cool air skimmed her bare arms, disbelief unraveling inside her. "What?"

"I know it's a surprise, dear—"

"A surprise?" Mara reeled from her chair, one foot snagging in her discarded hoodie. She kicked it free. "Surprises are supposed to be good things. Birthday parties. Unexpected gifts. But selling the Everwood?"

"This isn't a decision I've made lightly. I've agonized over it for days now."

"Yet you've let me talk about continued renovations and reservations and plans for the summer." She moved away from Lenora's bed, rubbing one hand over the opposite arm, willing her voice to steady and her mind to calm. "I thought you loved the Everwood."

"Of course I do. But you have to understand, I can't afford to keep it going."

"We've already talked about this. I took care of those outstanding mortgage payments. We have deposits now from the rooms we've booked so far. It's not a lot but it's enough to pay the bills for the next few months at least. And business is going to pick up even more come summer. We—"

"But I have hospital expenses. I can't let Davis, dear as he is, continue to pay for everything." Lenora gripped the edges of her bed's pale blue blanket. "Plus, I'd like to get to know Davis. He has children and grandchildren, Mara. I have cousins I've never met." She took a long, slow breath.

Mara turned away before Lenora could see the prick of tears in her eyes. Lenora wasn't only selling the house Mara loved. She was . . . leaving. Again.

Mara stared out the window, its paltry view no more than the beige and gray of the hospital's cement walls, the parking garage, other buildings squeezed in. She finally croaked the question she didn't want to ask, looking over her shoulder. "When? And is it okay if I stay until it's sold? I'll need to make some plans, update my resume—"

"Oh, dear girl, you don't think . . . I've made a mess of this. Mara, I want to ask you to stay here with me." Lenora attempted to scoot up against her wall of pillows. When she struggled, Mara hurried over to help her shift. "I should've led off with that. I'll need some in-home care, you see. And eventually help finding a home here—an apartment maybe or a townhouse—though Davis says he has plenty of room until I'm ready."

Mara sat down once more, idly reached for her hoodie, tried to make sense of Lenora's offer. She should find it comforting. Touching, really. One moment she'd felt cast out at sea and the next Lenora had tossed her a float.

But her sinking emotions couldn't find a firm grasp.

Marshall.

Of course her heart would tow her there. If she agreed to Lenora's plan, what of Marshall and his . . . their . . .

friendship . . . relationship? Or whatever it was. Whatever it could've been. They'd never even gone on that date.

Then again, for all she knew, Marshall might be readying to leave her too. Return to his life in Wisconsin.

"What do you think, Mara?"

Captain Wagner had shown up on the Everwood's front doorstep more than an hour ago, and Marshall still couldn't figure out why.

The man crouched as he climbed out of the fireplace after Marshall, his chuckles echoing off the stone interior. "Here I put you on administrative leave thinking you'd get some much-needed rest. Instead you take a road trip, remodel a house, and solve a mystery."

Soot stains marred the captain's shirt—starched and pressed as always, though the jeans and lack of tie gave him a considerably more low-key appearance than usual. Their venture into the secret room was the last stop on Marshall's tour of the bed and breakfast.

"It was a team effort," he said now.

"Which? The remodel or the mystery?"

"Both." He brushed the ash from his hands over the fireplace grate. "Best we can figure, this room didn't serve much purpose other than as a handy hiding spot for Jeane and Arnold. Davis—Jeane's brother—told us his father's house had a similar hidden room. He kept packed luggage stored there, complete with fake I.D.s, passports, whatever he needed to completely start over as someone new. Davis says Jeane probably took a cue from him."

Captain Wagner reached for the can of Diet Coke he'd abandoned on an end table before checking out the hidden room. He dropped onto the couch. "But you don't know why the couple fled the Everwood in the sixties?"

"Actually, we do now. We learned from Davis that while his father was searching for Jeane decades ago, Davis was conducting his own search. But he managed to do what his father didn't—he found them. Showed up on the Everwood's doorstep one night. Told his sister if he could locate her then their father wasn't far behind."

He plucked his own can of pop from the fireplace mantel and perched on the arm of the loveseat. "They said a final goodbye, and the next morning, Jeane and Arnold—who'd been living here as Sherrie and Kenneth—fled. Started over as Alice and Aric." And Eleanor had become Lenora. "Great story, huh?"

"Yup." Captain Wagner took a swig from his can, then rubbed his chin. "Though I'd like the ending better if you'd actually found the painting."

"We know it was in the secret room at one point. Lenora remembers seeing it there as a kid, though she also recalls it hanging in the den previously. Davis said it would've been just like his sister to display it for all to see—an act of defiance against their father. Apparently Jeane was gutsy like that. But we're guessing that when the buyer of the other canvas was murdered, they may have decided it wasn't such a good idea to keep it out in the open."

As for not finding the painting now, it wasn't for lack of trying. Since Marshall had returned last week, he'd scoured the place from the cellar to the attic. If Arnold and Jeane had left *The Crabapple Tree* behind, they were better hiders than he was a seeker.

It was probably silly to think he'd have had any more luck finding the thing in a week than Lenora had in months of searching. But it sure would've been the perfect "welcome home" surprise for Mara.

Or perhaps something to make their parting sting a little less.

The thought knotted inside him. For days he'd tussled with the conviction that he couldn't stay here. What he'd felt in the hospital when Mara had vanished—the kind of helplessness he'd hoped to never experience again—it was too much.

Too much emotion. Too much fear.

Too much . . . everything.

"I think I've lost you."

Captain Wagner's gravelly voice drew his attention and he slid from the arm of the loveseat onto the cushion. "Sorry. Just tired. Been pulling long days." Mostly outside. He'd weeded the garden, trimmed hedges in the back, and planted flowers and bushes all along the new porch. Even though temps were mild, the sun had reddened his cheeks and nose.

He glanced out the den's picture window. Sunlight spilled through the grove, dappling the lawn with light, and a chorus of birds chirped away. He wished he could find the right mood to match such a perfect spring day.

Especially with Captain Wagner so carefully watching him. "Captain, are you ever going to explain what you're doing here?"

"Already told you. Alex keeps complaining that your sister keeps complaining that you don't check in often enough. So I'm doing the checking-in myself. And consequently, saving you from one or both of them showing up here in that minivan of theirs."

"That's a long drive just to keep tabs on me. You could've called."

Captain Wagner leaned forward, elbows on his knees, fingers laced around his can. "I'm getting the feeling you aren't all that happy to see me."

"Of course I'm happy to see you. Gives me a chance to apologize for the way I left your office that day."

"I didn't come here for an apology."

"Still, I owe you one."

"Actually, I think what you owe me is a 'thank you.'"

"Say again?"

"You may be tired, Hawkins, but you look healthier than I've seen you in years. Don't I deserve a little credit for pushing you into this? I don't know if it's the physical labor or the sun or both, but something in this Iowa air is doing you some good." He took a measured pause. "Would I be right in thinking you've laid off the pills?"

Marshall's gaze shot from the new rug on the floor to his captain's face. "You, um . . . you knew about that?"

"I knew you came to work too often with your eyes glazed over." He took a drink. "My first thought was alcohol, 'til I saw you at your locker one day with a prescription bottle. Narcotics?"

Marshall set down his pop can, palms sweaty. He gave a stiff nod. "Some. But also sleeping aids. Sir, I'm really sorry. I get regular migraines, but still, I shouldn't—"

"I have three daughters, Hawkins. If I lost one of them, I'd fall apart at the seams. Might not be pills for me but it'd be something." He waited until Marshall looked him in the eye again. "Do you need help?"

Oh, that question could have all manner of layers. But at least he could honestly answer the one at the surface. He'd been dependent on the meds, yes, but not to the point of life-altering addiction. "I skirted a danger zone there. Beth cleaned me out before I left Milwaukee. Nothing since."

"Any withdrawal?"

"I passed out a couple of times the first night, but other than that . . ." He shrugged. "Got lucky, I guess."

"More likely, luck didn't have a thing to do with it. You have plenty of praying people in your life, son."

He slumped in his seat. "Yeah, well, I would've rather those prayers worked a little earlier. Before I had a reason to start . . ." He clamped his mouth closed. Captain Wagner didn't deserve his ire.

"A reason to start self-destructing?" The older man's tone was quiet, patient.

He thudded to his feet, moved to the fireplace and leaned on the mantel, head down. For once, there was no headache squeezing his thoughts. But there might as well have been. "I quit the pills, sir, but I don't think I can quit the grief. I don't think . . . it's never going to go away."

He didn't hear his captain stand. Didn't hear his steps. But he felt the warm hand on his shoulder, firm and gentle. "I can't speak to your grief, but I can promise you that you're not alone. You've got your family, you've got me, you've got friends on the force. If I'm not mistaken, you might have some friends here, too, correct?"

Marshall could only nod, the clogging in his throat too tight for words.

"You've tried pills, son, and that didn't work. You've tried pushing us away, isolating. That didn't work either." Captain Wagner squeezed his shoulder. "So try something different this time. Try leaning into the love and support of the people in your life. If not those of us back in Wisconsin, then here—though your sister would probably kill me for suggesting it. But I'm not blind. You seemed completely at home showing me around this place. Far more at ease than you've been around the bullpen in the past two years."

Marshall pushed away from the mantel, Captain Wagner's hand dropping from his shoulder. "I can't stay here."

"Why not?"

Because it wouldn't be fair to Mara. It'd become so clear

to him in this week away from her. He kept remembering back to what she'd told him about her parents. How her mom had never been able to get over her dad's abandonment. Had been so engulfed in her own despair she'd stopped seeing her daughter.

Marshall had already done that to Penny. In some ways, he'd even done it to Laney in those final, desperate months.

He wouldn't do it to Mara too.

Or maybe you're just a coward. Too scared of getting too close. Because the thought of losing another person . . .

Like he could've lost Mara in that hospital parking garage.

"Maybe I should catch a ride back with you," he said. Better than driving the rental all the way to Milwaukee.

"Not going to answer the question of why you can't stay here?"

"Are you trying to tell me I no longer have a job?"

"Of course not. But you still have several weeks of leave left. I'm not letting you come back early, if that's what you're thinking."

"Well, no, but—"

"Marshall!"

The call echoed through the house followed by the sound of the front door closing. *Mara?*

There hadn't been enough money to insulate the flooring—which meant he could hear every one of her steps as she hurried through the house. She was at the den's doorway in seconds. How had she known to look here first?

"Hey, Marsh." She set a packed grocery sack down.

"Hey yourself."

Her clothes were wrinkled from the drive and there was a slight frizz to her copper hair, but it was her tentative smile that held his gaze so long that he almost forgot—

"Oh, Captain Wagner." The words tumbled out. "Uh, Mara this is my boss. Cap, this is Mara. She runs this place." He glanced back at Mara in time to see a flicker of disquiet in her eyes. But she quickly blinked it away.

"Captain Wagner, nice to meet you."

The captain shook her hand. "It's only 'Captain' to my men in uniform. You can call me Eli."

Marshall swallowed, too many thoughts and questions twisting at once. Why hadn't she called or texted to let him know she was coming home today? Was Lenora with her? Why the groceries?

And did she have any idea what she did to him? He wanted to pull her to him and kiss her—forget Captain Wagner or the decision he was pretty sure he'd just made.

Instead, he jammed his hands into his pockets. "I didn't realize you were coming home. Why didn't—"

"We never went on that date, Marshall."

Was that a snort from the captain? He felt the back of his neck heat. "What?"

"I came back so we could."

"So we could go on a date."

Another snort and now a slap on the back too. "You heard her, son."

A gentle evening rain hadn't been a part of Mara's plan.

Yet its steady pattering against the metal roof of the train had a calming effect on Mara's nerves. Or maybe that was the dim light of the lantern. Or the view outside the freight car's open doors, the last sliver of subdued sunlight peeking over the horizon through thin rainclouds. Twilight fell lazily in shades of blue over the field that stretched in front of the Maple Valley Scenic Railway.

"I'm a police officer, Mara. I should be the last person committing a crime."

Mara reached for the picnic basket sitting between her and Marshall on the blanket they'd spread over the train car's floor. Her laughter bounced off the steel walls. "This isn't a crime."

Marshall propped his elbows on his crossed legs. "The depot's closed. Technically, we're trespassing."

"Technically, we're not doing anything that hundreds of Maple Valley teens don't do every year." According to Jenessa, anyway. She'd said it was practically a rite of passage for local kids to come out to the heritage railroad stationed at the edge of town at night, hang out in this empty boxcar.

"Look for the black freight car with the orange stripe down the middle. The door's heavy but it'll slide open."

"We won't get in trouble for it?"

"Nah, but if it makes you feel better, I can give Case Walker a call. He runs the depot. He has a soft spot like you wouldn't believe, and frankly, it'd probably relieve him to know it's adults sneaking into the boxcar this time instead of hormonal teenagers."

Mara wouldn't have thought of a boxcar as romantic, but the low glow of the lantern was enough to make out the hundreds of scraped markings all around its interior walls. Initials, names, hearts and plus signs.

That, along with the view, along with the handsome man sitting across from her—and now, along with the rain —made this night perfect.

Or at least as close to perfect as it could be before she knew how Marshall would react to what she was about to say. To ask him. Ever since talking to Lenora yesterday, since concocting this plan, she'd been rehearsing her words. Summoning the bravery to . . .

Well, to push open another door. Take a step through it.

Mara was grateful Lenora had understood. In fact, she'd been the one to urge Mara not to wait. To take her car that had been parked at Davis Saddler's house for weeks and hit the road at the crack of dawn this morning.

But Lenora wasn't here to prod Mara on now. Maybe it'd be better to wait until tomorrow to present her plan. Maybe they should just enjoy this date. Talk like normal people getting to know one another. She could ask him about his job—what had made him want to be a detective? What was his most interesting case? Maybe he'd even open up about Laney and—

"Mara? You going to open that picnic basket?"

She blinked. Laughed again. "That depends. Are you going to keep grumbling about how we're committing a crime?"

Why did his smile seem so strained at the edges? "You call it grumbling. I call it responsible thinking."

"I can't believe the same man who didn't give a single care as to whose property we went sledding on a few weeks ago is suddenly worried about trespassing." On her knees, she started pulling items from the picnic basket. Chicken caesar wraps. Pasta salad. Fruit.

"No cereal?"

She met his eyes. Even in the faint light, she could see the tension hovering in his gaze despite his teasing. *He's just tired. He's been working so hard.*

Or perhaps his captain showing up earlier today had taken some kind of stressful toll on him. She'd gotten the feeling after the fact that they'd been in the middle of an intense conversation when she'd arrived.

Or maybe there was something else going on. She

closed the picnic basket. "Marshall, can we talk for a sec before we eat?"

He let out a long, slow breath. "Actually, yeah. That'd be good."

She lowered to the blanket, folding her legs like Marshall, her knees nearly brushing his. *Just say what you came to say.* "Lenora wants to sell the Everwood," she blurted.

Marshall peered at her. "That's . . . unexpected."

"You're telling me." She smoothed out the blanket, moved her fingers through its tassels. "The thing is, I understand her reasons. I can't blame her. Even if it does break my heart a little."

To anyone else, her words might sound dramatic. But Marshall would understand. He'd witnessed firsthand her love not only for the house, but her place in it. He'd watched her pour her heart into reviving it. He knew her hopes for the future.

Some of them, anyway. He knew she'd hoped to stay and run the place longterm.

But did he know her hope had expanded to include him? If he didn't, he was about to.

Because that was the other thing she'd come here tonight to tell him. Another door she wanted to walk through. No, run through. Take a giant, romantic leap and let him know how she felt.

Oh, how she prayed he felt the same. If Lenora was right, if God didn't just see her but cared—deeply, intimately—about all the details of her life then surely He heard her heart's hopeful desire. And He'd point Marshall's heart in the same direction. Wouldn't he?

"If Lenora sells, what are you going to do?"

"Lenora said I could stay with her. She'll need some in-home assistance for a while." *No more stalling.* "But what I really want to do is stay here. I want to buy the Everwood. I know it's a little crazy since I don't exactly have a pile of cash handy, but we figured out how to save the Everwood once. If we put our heads together—"

"We?" He wasn't looking at her. He was looking at his lap, at his tightly folded hands.

She closed her eyes just long enough to catch her breath and beckon whatever bravery she had left. "I was, um . . . I was hoping you'd stick around. We've made a really good team so far, haven't we? We'd be perfect business partners. More than that, we'd be perfect—" She made the mistake of looking up.

And what she saw snatched the rest of her rehearsed words.

Marshall still wasn't looking at her, but his palms had moved to his knees, knuckles as tight as the rest of him. Instead of leaning toward her as he had earlier, his spine was straight, his shoulders stiff.

Oh. *Oh.*

This wasn't the look of a man who was ready to be on the receiving end of any kind of bold declaration of love or even just affection.

The same sickening feeling she'd had as a twelve-year-old, wearing that silly dress, sitting at the silly overly ornamented table, waiting for Dad to say he'd stay, finally realizing he never would—it staggered through her all over again, finding all her tender places.

She scrambled backward, slid the picnic basket back into place between them, mindlessly reached inside. "Sorry. It was nervy of me to think . . . to assume . . ."

"It wasn't—"

"You have a whole life in Wisconsin and great career. Of course you don't want to give that up to help run an old B&B."

"Please don't put words in my mouth, Mara."

"But you're leaving, aren't you? It's written all over you. I can see it now." *Please argue.*

He didn't argue.

She closed the basket. Stood.

"Mara—"

"It's okay. I get it. But now it feels kind of weird to have this date. Let's just go back and—"

"Believe me, I've thought about staying. For days, weeks now, I've been thinking about it." His tone was agonizingly apologetic. The freight car rattled as he rose. "But I'm not the kind of person you need. As a business partner or as . . . anything else."

"Why do you get to decide what I need?" She pulled on her spring jacket and tipped its hood over her head. "And who said anything about need anyway? I *want* you to stay. Because I care about you." *Maybe even love you.*

And she'd thought he felt the same. She tried to zip her coat, but it snagged halfway up. With a huff, she snatched the picnic basket and hopped from the freight car. Marshall could grab the blanket.

"Mara, wait," he called after her. "Please don't be mad."

"I'm not mad." She was embarrassed. Hurt. And, well, fine. She *was* mad. But not at him.

She was mad at herself. For letting her heart run away with her. For letting herself need something he apparently couldn't give. Like she'd needed Dad. And Mom. Even Lenora, in a way.

Marshall caught up to her, his long strides slowing to match hers, the blanket draped over his arm. "I have some money." He took the picnic basket from her hands. "Life insurance. I've never been able to bring myself to spend it. I can give it to you. You can use it for a down payment and—"

She halted, rain slicking over her hood and down her jacket, seeping through her canvas shoes. Gone was the last light of dusk. "I can't accept your money." Not if he didn't come with it.

As if he'd heard that last part, he winced. "You have to know I care about you too. More than care. I . . . " His Adam's apple bobbed. "But that's why I have to go. You deserve someone who isn't broken on the inside."

"We're all a little broken on the inside, Marshall. But Lenora would say that God—"

"You don't get it. I haven't even told you . . . Look, remember the night I had that really bad migraine and fever and I snapped at you about not wanting any meds? It's because for two years I survived on sleeping pills and painkillers. The reason I was on the road when I came here in the first place? Captain Wagner forced me into administrative leave because of how often I messed up on the job."

She stared at him through the rain, her heart aching for him. For herself.

"I've been living in a bubble here, Mara."

"Knowing those things doesn't make me think less of you. It makes me want to help. Maybe if you open up more, if you talk about Laney—"

"I don't want to talk about Laney." He swiped moisture from his face.

She was out of arguments. Out of her last reserves of emotional strength. "Then let's just get out of the rain and go back." She strode toward Lenora's car without looking to see if he followed. She dropped behind the steering wheel, closed the door harder than she meant to.

Stared ahead at Marshall's still form. Standing in the same spot she'd left him. Getting soaked. And hurting. Oh, he was hurting. Never mind the rain and the dark. She could see his pain so clearly.

But she was hurting too. And there was nothing she could say to comfort him. Nothing she could do to help him see himself the way she did. Maybe that wasn't her job anyway. Perhaps the best thing she could do was let him say the goodbye he meant to.

And later, when he was gone, when the FOR SALE sign went up in the Everwood's yard, when she was alone, she could let her sorrow free.

The vibration of her phone cut into her anguished silence. She yanked it from her pocket, answered without even looking at the screen. And froze at the voice on the other end.

"Hi, Mara. It's Dad."

22

*M*arshall hadn't been to church since the day of Laney's funeral. But it was Easter Sunday and his sister was persuasive.

Or, rather, the cute voices of his niece and nephew on the phone last night were impossible to resist. They'd begged him to come to the morning service and lunch afterward, both talking at once. Beth had set him up good.

He slid his finger under his collar. Either he'd wound his tie too tightly or he'd grown way too used to not wearing the thing during his weeks in Iowa.

Beth elbowed him in the side. "The service hasn't even started and you're already fidgeting?"

"I'm here, aren't I? Isn't that enough?" His nephew climbed onto his lap, holding a hymnal, looking like a little man in his gray vest and clip-on bowtie.

"You may be here, but you're not *here*."

Up on the stage, choir members were filing onto a set of risers.

I thought it might feel weird—going back to church after so long. But I felt strangely at home. Back in Wisconsin for nine days and he still couldn't get Mara's voice out of his head. He'd mostly stopped trying.

If only he could stop reliving those final moments over and over.

They'd stood on the porch, his bag at his feet, Captain Wagner waiting in the car. Mara had hovered in the doorway, hugging her arms to herself, resignation written all over her.

"Mara, are you sure I can't convince you to take the money? If it'd make you feel better, it could be a loan instead of a gift. Complete with interest. We could get one of those generic legal contracts and make it all formal and official and everything."

She'd shaken her head through all of it. Just like she had the night before when he'd asked if she wanted to talk about the phone call from her father. Nothing stubborn or angry in her refusal. Probably just self-preservation.

Because if she felt for him even half of what he felt for her then she most likely needed the emotional distance.

He should've followed her lead, heeded his own caution, instead of reaching for her then. Pulling her into a goodbye embrace despite her closed-off stance. But she'd eventually given in, dropped her arms from around her torso to encircle his.

Finally, he'd dropped a kiss on her cheek. *"Bye, Mara. Thank you for everything."*

She'd nodded against his chest and stepped back.

And that had been that. He'd walked away without a backward glance, heart numb as he dropped into Captain Wagner's car.

His nephew dropped the hymnal to the floor now, its thump enough to jerk Marshall to attention. His sister was staring at him. Drove him crazy how perceptive she could be. It's the reason he'd avoided her so much since returning to Milwaukee. He'd had supper with her family his second night home, but other than that, he'd stuck around the townhouse.

Brooding, she'd say.

But that's not all he'd done. He'd cleaned out a couple of closets. Found some of Penny's belongings—items she must've forgotten about. He'd boxed them up and written her name in marker. Impressed himself by not feeling the mix of anger and rejection he usually did at the mere mention of her name.

"You know, I'm actually a pretty good listener, Marsh." Beth scooted Makena off her lap and onto Alex's on her other side.

"The service is going to start in a few minutes."

"Not now, obviously. After dinner? You've hardly said a word about Iowa. I'd love to hear about—"

She broke off. Probably because she'd just seen what he had.

Penny walking down the church aisle with a man who must be her fiancé—or maybe even husband by now. Not as tall as Marshall, but older, more distinguished. He held a baby carrier.

"Marsh—"

"I'm fine, Beth."

"I didn't realize she'd be here. I thought she usually came to the late service."

He glanced at his watch. Still another couple minutes before the opening song. "I'm going to get a drink." He shifted Ethan off his lap and onto the pew. He gave Beth a strict look. "I'm *fine.*" He just needed a second.

Yet as soon as he crossed into the church foyer, the temptation to keep walking right on past the drinking fountain was simply too much. He already had his tie loosened when he spotted the exit, all the way off by the time he pushed through the glass doors.

"Marshall!"

He halted, eyes closing, fingers tightening around his tie. He made himself turn. "Hey."

Penny hurried up to him, her heels clicking on the cement sidewalk. She wore a light green sweater over a simple sundress with a flowery pattern. Not one he recognized. "I just wanted to make sure you weren't leaving because . . ." She pushed a wayward curl behind her headband. "I didn't realize you'd be here."

"You didn't chase me away, Penn. I just needed some air." The faint strains of music drifted from inside the church.

"You're sure?" She tugged her sweater closed despite the warmth of the April breeze. The gold band around her ring finger glimmered in the sun.

Well, that answered that question.

She caught his stare. "Um, we had the ceremony a week ago. Not even a ceremony, really. Just a quick thing at the courthouse."

"But . . . you're happy?"

"You care?"

"What? Penny, of course, I—" He pressed his lips together, bunched his tie in his hand. There'd be no salvaging it at this point.

Once he would've been able to read the collection of emotions that trailed through Penny's eyes as she watched him. He could've sorted through them to find the one she felt the deepest and truest. And he would've known how to respond.

But he wasn't her husband anymore. And for once, the thought didn't feel so fraught with jagged edges. When had that changed? He'd certainly still felt enough anger toward her when she'd come to the Everwood weeks ago.

But now? He couldn't read his own thoughts any more

than he could hers. "The service is about to start. You should get back inside."

"What about you?"

"I'll be in in a sec."

She turned to walk away.

He felt the breeze lift his hair and billow his shirt. The smell of lilacs drifted from a nearby bush.

"Penn?" He didn't mean to say her name or drop his tie while rooted to the sidewalk. He should let her go, follow her back into church. Slide into the pew before Beth came looking. But unbidden need pushed out his next question before he could stop it. "How'd you do it?"

She turned back to him, a clump of clipped grass tumbled over the sidewalk in between them. "Do what?"

"How'd you move on?" He rubbed his hand over his mouth and his clean-shaven jaw. "I can't figure out how to do it. I thought maybe I was getting closer when I was in Iowa, but then . . . the hospital . . . it made it all come back. I can't even talk about her. Mara asked questions sometimes and I couldn't even . . ." Was he making any sense at all? "What do I need to do? Go to counseling or something? Take more time off work? I don't know what to do."

She neared him once more. "I don't know, Marsh. I—"

"Think, please." Voices were singing inside the church now, a drumbeat nearly matching the rhythm of Marshall's racing heart. He thrust one hand in the direction of the building. "Was it this? Church? God? If so, I need you to tell me how in the world you can keep trusting God after everything that happened."

She watched him for a long, quiet moment. Finally, she took a breath. "I did see a couple of counselors, Marsh. The first one—he wasn't so great. At our first session, after I told him all about losing Laney, I asked a similar sort of question—how could a good God take away my child? The counselor launched into this theological analogy about God being like a father who helps a child learn to ride a bike." She rolled her eyes. "He asked if it's the father's fault when the child tips off the bike or if it's just gravity, and he said living in the world we do is like living with the reality of gravity and yada-yada, and I'm telling you, I left that appointment even angrier than when I'd walked in."

Marshall crossed his arms. "Because how's a lame analogy supposed to help?"

"Right. But later, I couldn't stop thinking about it. Not the analogy, but the memory it brought to mind. Of Laney learning to ride her bike."

Oh, Laney had loved riding her yellow bike almost as much as she'd liked running. He still had that bike in the garage, hanging from a hook in the ceiling. Like the sled he'd rescued from his totaled truck.

Penny pushed her blowing hair out of her face. "I remembered this one time when Laney was out riding on the driveway and I was raking leaves and you were inside. She fell off, started wailing. And you came sprinting from the house."

"I remember that." Laney had cried more from the shock of it than actual pain, though she'd scraped both knees and one elbow plenty good. He remembered his relief as he'd checked her over—no broken bones. And like the brave little thing she was, she'd been back up on the bike twenty minutes later.

"That's what I couldn't stop thinking about, Marsh. The way you ran toward her. It was this vivid, alive image in my head. And I started thinking, what if that's like God? What if when we've fallen, when we're hurt, when we're in our greatest pain, He runs toward us?" Penny's soft tone reached toward him. "What if it's not about me pulling myself together and getting up, but just . . . looking up? To see Him. Running to me."

Her voice caught. She swallowed. "I think maybe that's how I kept going. By clinging to that picture in my mind until I believed it. And felt it. And experienced it." She touched his arm, just barely. "It's not that I'm over losing Laney, Marsh. It's not that I've moved on. Laney will always be a part of me. But when I was in my deepest pain, God came for me. He didn't leave me in an injured pile on the sidewalk nor did he stand around waiting for me to get up and move. *He* came running for *me.*"

A hot tear trekked down his cheek. Another. And another. And he saw himself just like Penny said—a broken heap on hard, cold cement. *Just look up. See Him. Running.*

Could he believe that? Could he look past all the hurt in his heart, the stubbornness in his head, and let himself see a God who still cared? Cared enough to come for Marshall, kneel beside him, touch him with His kindness and presence.

He wanted to try. *Oh God, I want to try. Help me see you. Somehow . . . help me see.*

He swiped the back of his hands over his eyes. "I have so much I need to apologize to you for, Penn." He choked out the words.

"We both hurt each other. But it's Easter today. A day for grace and forgiveness and new life."

"Penny?" The voice came from the church entrance. Penny's new husband stood in the doorway, one arm holding the door open, their baby propped in the other.

Marshall's breathing hitched once more. But he made himself exhale. "You should go in."

"You coming?"

"In a minute." He looked from Penny to her new family and back again. "Maybe after church I could, um, meet

Jason and . . . the baby. You said his name is Noah?" It would be awkward and uncomfortable for all of them.

But like she'd said, it was Easter. A day for forgiving and being forgiven.

There was something healing in Penny's smile. "After church then."

"Are you sure you don't want me to stay with you?" Jen dumped one sugar packet after another into her Americano. "I don't mind sticking around. Really. Otherwise, all I'm going to do is shop and spend way too much money on a pair of leather cowboy boots. Preferably red ones."

Mara laughed despite the nerves that'd kept her from ordering a drink of her own at the small Nashville coffee shop. The last thing she needed right now were extra jitters.

"You don't have to stay, Jen. Shop to your heart's content. Dad'll be here soon."

He'd texted a few minutes ago that he was running late. But he'd be here. He wouldn't have bought her the plane ticket if he planned to back out on her.

She still couldn't believe this was really happening. His phone call had been stunning enough.

"Hi, Mara. It's Dad."

She'd been waiting years—decades—to hear those words.

"I'm sorry to call out of the blue. I just got your email. I wish I would've seen it earlier. I'm horrible about reading my messages. But I'm so glad to hear from you."

She hadn't known what to say. It'd been a brief, awkward call. Crammed with uncertainty on both ends of the line.

The next one two days later had been just as stilted. But the third one, just a few days ago, had been a little better. That's when he'd asked if he could see her. He'd offered to fly to wherever she wanted or pay for a ticket for her to come to him.

Considering how lonely the Everwood had become, she'd chosen the latter.

And of course, as soon as Jen had gotten wind of it, she'd asked to come along. A perfect chance to visit Nashville for the first time, she'd said. But really, it was a show of friendship for which Mara had been grateful every minute of the three-hour plane ride.

"I don't know how I got so lucky to end up with a friend like you," she said, giving Jen a quick side hug as they moved away from the coffee shop counter.

"I'm the lucky one. Do you know how long I've had to put up with two males for best friends? It's just not the same as having a female kindred spirit." Jen took a sip of her drink and winced. "And this coffee is not the same as Coffee Coffee's." She gave Mara a measured look. "Nor is our little friend group the same without Marshall. I still say he deserves a kick in the pants for leaving."

"No, he really doesn't." Surprisingly, she meant it.

In the little over a week since he'd been gone, she might've finally begun to understand why he'd left. He'd said he'd been living in a bubble. The more she thought on it, the more she could almost see the truth of it. She'd done the same thing for months after first arriving in Iowa.

The Everwood had been a haven but it'd also been a hideout. Maybe that's why Lenora had asked her now and then about her hopes, her dreams, where she'd be if not there. She'd been trying to pop the bubble.

Maybe that's what Marshall was doing in leaving. And though Mara's fragile heart yearned for a love that might've been, she kept thinking about what Lenora always said—that God was with her.

"He's been with you all along . . . even in the hallway. His love is an always and everywhere kind of love."

If that was true, then Mara had never been fully alone or fully abandoned. When Dad had left and Mom stopped seeing her and Lenora disappeared and Marshall went home . . . she'd still had *Him*. Even if she hadn't seen him.

Could she find comfort in that now? *I'm trying.* She was trying and waiting and listening for His voice, His assurance despite such a painful closed door.

Jen's purse swung from her elbow. "You have to defend Marshall because you're in love with him, but—"

"Am not." At least, she was trying not to be.

"Kindred spirits don't lie to each other. And when kindred spirits pry, it's only because they care."

"Well, then from one kindred spirit to another, how about we talk about Lucas for a minute?" The moment the teasing words left her lips, her attention hooked on the figure walking through the coffee shop's door. *Dad.*

Eighteen years had marked their presence upon him—in lines on his face, in the gray he hadn't bothered to hide in his hair. He didn't seem as tall as she recalled.

But then, she'd been twelve when he'd walked away the second time.

"Why would we talk about Lucas?" Jen asked, oblivious.

"Uh, Jen, that's my dad."

"Ah, okay. Right. Do I meet him before scramming or just disappear now?"

It was too late for the latter. Dad had spotted her straightaway, and he made his way to her now. His grin was almost too wide. As if he was trying to rally a confidence he didn't feel.

They met near a waist-high table. Empty. Two chairs. "Hi, Dad."

His smile faltered. "I didn't know if you'd—"

"Show up?"

"Call me Dad."

Was he actually blinking away tears? Mara shot a *help me* look at Jen. She didn't know what to say or do. Shake his hand? No, that seemed too formal. But she wasn't ready for a hug either.

Jen plunked her coffee cup on the table. "Hi. I'm Jenessa. Mara's friend."

Whoa, that warning tone. Jen had gone on the offensive and defensive at the same time.

Dad blinked again and gave her a simple nod. "Nice to meet you. I'm glad Mara didn't have to make the plane trip alone."

"Well, she would've been perfectly fine on her own. She's used to it."

Oh dear. "Uh, Jen, weren't you going to do some shopping? Remember? Red leather boots?"

Jen lifted her cup once more. "Yes. But if you need me—"

"I'll text you."

Jen squeezed her arm before moving away. Finally, they were alone. Well, alone in a crowded coffee shop. But surely this was better than someplace private. If it got too weird or something—

"Mara?"

It was somehow comforting to see her own hesitation mirrored in her father's expression.

"Should we sit?"

She nodded and towed herself into the high chair. She should've ordered a drink. It would've given her something to fidget with. The strums of a country song hummed along behind the chatter of the shop and the groan of coffee machines. Sunlight streamed in the long windows, interrupted by people walking past on the busy sidewalk.

"I'm so happy you were willing to come all this way," Dad finally said, breaking their strained silence. "Your email alone was more than I've hoped for in years now. So to actually be sitting here across from you—"

"What do you mean you hoped for an email?" The purse on her knees slid forward. She barely grasped it before it dropped to the floor. "You were waiting for me to reach out? You could've emailed. You could've called."

"Mara—"

"I deserve an explanation, Dad. I deserve to know why I wasn't worth sticking around for. Birthdays, holidays, graduation—you missed all of it. You didn't even come to Mom's funeral."

"I tried to."

Her knuckles were white around the strap of her purse. "What?"

"I thought I could do it. I wanted to be there, I did. I started the drive, but . . ." He pushed up the sleeves of his sweater. "I relapsed on the way. Didn't even make it as far as Kentucky. Ended up in a hospital. I was so bad off that time they put me in the psych ward."

Were Mara's lungs still working? "What do you mean you relapsed?"

Dad's pale eyes met hers. "She really never told you?"

Did he mean Mom?

"Mara, I was in treatment. On and off for years. I'm an alcoholic. Seven years sober now, but—"

"What? No . . . that can't . . . You're a country music singer. You're a Grammy-winning songwriter. You went to Nashville to chase your career."

"I went to Nashville to enter a rehab center to get help for my addiction."

Too many questions clogged in her throat. Words that didn't seem to compute knocked into each other. *Alcoholic. Addiction. Treatment.* None of it matched up to the image of her father in her head.

"It was a year-long program. I stuck with it all the way through the first time. Then I came home, remember?"

"Remember? I've relived that night a thousand times, Dad. We dressed up. We made pot roast. It was all a plan. To try to get you to stay."

He scooted his chair closer to her. "I wanted to stay. But your mom. She could tell I'd already been drinking before I showed up at the house. One week out of rehab and I was already at it again. She told me to leave and I don't blame her."

"But why didn't she tell me? Why didn't you tell me?"

The tears were back in his eyes. "I wish we would've. I was so ashamed at the time. I have to believe your mother thought she was doing what was best for you."

"She let me believe you didn't care. That you'd walked away."

"She was hurting too. Hurting people do inconsiderate things sometimes."

Inconsiderate? "But your career . . ."

"There was a volunteer at the center who had connections at The Bluebird. He heard me playing guitar at chapel one night. The rest is history." He placed one palm on the table, close to where her hand now gripped the table's edge. "I lost my family because of my addiction and my shame. The career happened somewhere along the way, but it's nothing to me compared to what I lost."

Too many emotions pressed in. Hurt so long buried. Confusion. Disbelief and realization knotting together. How could Mom have let her think . . .

She shook her head. Mom wasn't here. Dad was. "I still

don't understand why you haven't tried to contact me. You said you've been sober for seven years."

He cleared his throat. "I told myself I didn't want to intrude on your life. That it wouldn't be kind to you. That you were better off. But I think the deeper truth is that I was just a coward. And a fool. I may be sober but . . ." He lifted his gaze. "There's no excuse. Not for any of it. If I could change the past decades, I would, but all I can do is sit here now and try to tell you how immensely sorry I am. How much I've missed being your father. How many times I hoped that you'd hear one of my songs and know . . ."

His voice cracked and he looked away as he pulled a tissue from his pocket.

"I hoped you'd hear one of my songs and know that your dad loved you. Even if he was too much of a mess to ever show it."

"Dad." She didn't know what else to say. Or even what to feel. It was going to take a while to tunnel through all the new details of the past, find her way to new footing in the present.

But for now, maybe it was okay just to *be*. To be here. With her dad.

"Could I get you a coffee, Dad?"

"So what are you going to do?"

The question burst from Jen before Mara had even closed the hotel room door or the sound of Dad's retreating steps faded. She slid the chain lock into place and turned to see Jen sitting cross-legged on the queen bed closest to the window, shopping bags spread around her.

"Did you find those boots?"

"We'll talk about my boots—all three pairs—later. You can't just text a friend that your dad, whom you haven't talked to in almost two decades, asked you to move to Nashville and then not elaborate."

Mara plopped on her bed, muscles still sore from the cramped plane trip earlier this morning, but heart over-flowing. She'd talked with Dad in that little coffee shop for more than three hours. In fits and spurts, snippets of their lives shared through the awkwardness of not really knowing one another anymore.

But he loved her. He'd always loved her.

No, knowing so didn't erase eighteen years of pain just like that. But maybe pain wasn't a thing to be erased anyway. Maybe in facing it and understanding it and walking through it instead of around it, a person could find new purpose.

He'd be back in another couple of hours to take her and Jen to dinner.

She laid on her back, gaze on the popcorn ceiling. "Apparently he has a really nice guestroom. He offered it when I told him about Lenora selling the Everwood." She bent her knees, her toes tangling in the bed sheets and her arms crossed over her head. "Honestly, it was pretty weird. He kept looking at me like he couldn't quite believe I was real. We sort of tiptoed around each other."

"Now I feel bad for being rude to him." Jen moved to the edge of her bed, feet touching the floor. "Him looking at you like he couldn't believe you were real, though? It makes sense. You're probably a miracle to him. He thought he'd lost you for good."

And Mara had thought she'd lost him. All this time, if she'd only reached out . . . if he'd reached out . . .

No, she'd already decided not to go there. At least not

now. Today was a reunion, a celebration she'd never seen coming. She wasn't going to get caught up in *if onlys.*

"So, you could move to Nashville. You could move to Illinois with Lenora. You could stay in Maple Valley." Jen held up a finger for each option. "You could chase Marshall to Milwaukee."

"Uh, no."

"Well, obviously, happy as I am for you and your dad, I have to cast my vote for Maple Valley. What are you thinking?"

Mara sat up. "I have no idea what I'm thinking."

"Don't you have some little inkling, though? A gut instinct?"

"I love Maple Valley. It's the first place that's felt like home in . . . forever, it seems. But without the Everwood, what would I do there?"

"Move in with me? Help me clean out my parents' house?"

Mara laughed.

"You think I'm kidding, but I'm totally serious."

Moving to Illinois would be the safe choice. She'd have a new place to belong. Lenora would dote on her and Mara would be the daughter she'd never had. It was the very thing she'd longed for at this time a year ago.

But for some reason, "safe" didn't hold the same allure now.

"I want to get to know my dad. I really do."

"You'd move to Nashville? Just like that?"

"I've moved plenty of times before." She turned to the window, the lights of Nashville and the sprawling airport nearby glittering against a sunset abounding in every shade of pink. What did she want?

Marshall's face filled her mind in an instant. Just like it had so many times in the days since he'd left. Those gray eyes of his —stormy at times and at others as soothing and mellow as one of Dad's songs. His smiles, so rare when she'd first met him and ever-varied—crooked and teasing, dimpled and sincere.

Marshall Hawkins. Thirty-five. Milwaukee.

But Marshall was a *who*, not a *what*. And he had his own road to walk right now. Besides, while it might sound romantic to go chasing after him, there was something else tugging on her soul now. Something urgent and beckoning. Voices, memories rising up.

Jen as she helped paint. *"I think there must be something magical about this house. Even Lucas seems happier since he's come here."*

Lenora as she pointed Mara toward faith. *"I think God led you here, Mara."*

And Marshall. *"You're not just saving the Everwood, Mara. Every day that I've spent here—with you—I've felt a little more whole."*

And one more voice. A whisper. The one she'd been waiting for. *I carved out a place for you. Because I love you.*

She watched through the window as a plane lifted into the pastel sky. God, who'd loved her with an *always and everywhere* kind of love, even when she hadn't seen it, was summoning her from the hallway once more, wasn't He? It was time to stand up and walk through another door. She didn't have to know how it'd all work. She just had to take the next step.

Mara reached for her braid, pulled its tie loose and helped it unravel. She brushed her fingers through unruly waves as she turned to Jen. "Come on, friend. Let's get ready for dinner with my dad."

23

LENORA

*D*avis's great-grandchildren—four girls and a boy who is awfully good-natured for being so outnumbered—are racing around my chair as I guard my teacup. Their parents are out on the lawn playing a game of bocce ball while Davis's adult daughters—my cousins!— keep me company in the living room.

I can't get over how closely they resemble me.

I can't get over how Davis's wife has taken to mothering me just as much as she mothers them, never mind that we're all so close to our seventh decade.

I can't get over this family. *My* family.

After George died, I asked God to send me a person. Just one person to care for. He sent me Mara. And he sent me this.

"Kids," Davis says as he and his cane thumpety-thump into the room. "Time to stop making Eleanor dizzy. Great-Grandma has snacks for you in the kitchen."

Eleanor. The poor man has tried so hard to call me Lenora. But sixty-odd years of thinking of me as Eleanor are hard to undo. Over and over I tell him I don't mind.

He settles into the recliner next to me, his daughters caught up in their own conversation over on the sofa. "You miss her," he says simply.

And that's another thing I can't get over. How an uncle I didn't even know months ago can now hear my unspoken thoughts. But he spent all those weeks praying at my hospital bedside. Maybe, even when I was unconscious, God was knitting us together. Grafting me into this family.

But not so long ago, He grafted Mara into my life too. And Davis is right. I miss her.

Yet I'm happy for the decision she's made. It'll be official soon. All the paperwork completed and signed. She's found her open door. She's taking her next step.

Most of all, she's discovered the One who's present in the hallway every bit as much as the other side of all of life's doorways. I hear it in her voice when she calls. In her newfound confidence and her gentle strength.

"I miss her," I confirm to Davis now, setting down my teacup. "But she's right where she's supposed to be. And I'm right where I belong. And—"

A high-pitched tone blasts from the pocket of my cardigan. Of course, that phone Mara insisted I buy and Davis keeps trying to teach me to use. Never mind that I had the annoying thing figured out the day it came in the mail. Just because I don't like technology doesn't mean I don't know how to use it.

But it makes him happy to teach me and so I let him.

"The green button, Eleanor," he says. "The one with the little image of a phone."

It's not ladylike to roll my eyes, so I don't. I lift the phone. "Hello?"

It's not the voice I expected. It is, however, another answered prayer. I hang up a few minutes later and turn to Davis. "I hope you don't mind company."

24

These long road trips were getting old.

Marshall jumped down from the driver's seat of his new truck. He'd test driven three different vehicles a few days ago just to make the salesman at the used car lot happy, but all along he'd had his eye on the ten-year-old hunter green Ford. The thing had plenty of miles on it and a few scratches on the dash, but it suited him.

A gentle rain pattered on its top, and he pulled up the hood of his jacket. Despite the rain, stubborn sunbeams pushed through the clouds, and he moved without hurry to the little yellow house.

All it had taken was some Googling and a couple of phone calls to find this address and confirm that the woman he needed to speak to was, in fact, in residence. He'd thought about having this conversation over the phone but it didn't feel right. Instead, he'd asked to visit.

So here he was, once again road-weary and approaching an unknown house in the rain.

But oh, how different this was than the night he'd stumbled upon the Everwood. This time, his head was clear and his steps sure. This time, he wasn't running away from a life he could barely bring himself to care about anymore. He was walking toward a life he couldn't wait to begin living.

Or had already begun living, really. Easter Sunday with Beth and Alex and the kids had been the first holiday in years he'd actually enjoyed. And that night when Alex had dropped him off at his townhouse, it wasn't loneliness that awaited him, but instead, action. He'd started packing boxes and hadn't quit until sunrise.

He'd spent the following days making calls, meeting with a realtor, breaking the news to his sister and Captain Wagner. He'd even called Penny.

And of everyone he'd talked to, of all the encouragement he'd received, hers were the words he'd replayed over and over in the days leading up to today.

"She'd be so excited for you, Marshall. She'd start jumping up and down and running from one end of the townhouse to the other."

"And the neighbors would bang on the adjoining wall."

"And she'd only run faster."

He hadn't been able to see Penny's face, but surely there'd been tears in her eyes too. Just like in his. Tears a little more sweet than bitter, although there'd always be some of both.

But he could finally truthfully say it was better this way. Better to feel—to feel all of it—than nothing at all.

"You should go see her before you go, Marshall. Tell her yourself."

He almost hadn't been able to do it—stop at the cemetery to see Laney before hitting the road this morning. Any other time he'd tried in the past two years, he'd never made it farther than the iron fence encircling the graveyard.

But this time, he'd gone through with it.

And now, hours later, despite limbs stiff from too many

hours in the truck and a growling stomach, he was still wrapped in the tranquility of that place, the impact of those moments.

Knees in dew-tipped grass. A hushed breeze in the trees. It was strangely solacing, the way grief and love had entwined around and inside him as he stared at his daughter's tombstone.

"I will love you and miss you always, Laney Grace Hawkins. Always. But for you, I'm going to choose hope today. I'm going to choose to believe that there's still something good for me here."

Rolling clouds had drawn his gaze to the azure sky. And for a wonderful, spellbinding moment, he'd been able to picture it so clearly. Laney pumping her little legs and running through the heavens, moving clouds and lighting the sky with her laughter.

Goose bumps had covered every inch of his flesh and those words he'd hurled at God in the hospital chapel came flooding back. *"If you want me to believe . . . you're going to have to give me something. Anything."*

The wind had picked up and the grass and trees around him bowed. And he could still see her running even as a sob, somehow grateful, stole the breath from his lungs.

This was the gift. The something, anything, he'd begged God for. He'd see Laney run again someday. He knew he would.

He'd wept until he was spent, and when he'd finally stood, he was a man ready to keep living in the *now*—in all its abundance and possibilities and longings too—even as he held on to the hope of *then*.

He shook the hood from his head now, amazed at his lack of a headache. The drive should've done it, if not the tears.

Marshall paused on the front steps of the yellow house. A wreath of sprigs and little white flowers decorated the front door and a silver mailbox to the side was half-open, catalogues and envelopes sticking out. He cleared his throat and lifted his hand to knock.

But the door swung open before he could. "Marshall Hawkins. It's about time you got here." Lenora Worthington clucked her tongue. "And look at you, you're all wet."

"Even if I didn't already have the best reason ever to be here in Iowa, this coffee alone would make the whole thing worth it."

Mara laughed at the pure appreciation on her father's face as he popped off the lid of his paper cup and made a show of smelling Coffee Coffee's house blend. She tucked her mocha into the cupholder between her seat behind the wheel and Dad's.

Dad. Here. In Iowa.

He'd flown in this morning and they'd gone straight to the bank. He hadn't even seen the Everwood yet, though he'd have plenty of time to explore the house in coming days. He planned to stay for the whole week.

She planned to stay . . . for a whole life. The papers she'd just signed at the bank—her signature next to Dad's—gave her roots here. Gave her purpose and direction and so much excitement.

She owned the Everwood. She *owned* the Everwood. She shifted in her seat to face her father. "Dad—"

"Please don't thank me again. All I did was cosign."

"That's hardly *all* you did. There's that little matter of the down payment." A breeze brushed in through her open window, carrying the scent of freshly mowed grass from the sloping knoll across the road.

The riverfront bustled with activity today—someone walked a dog along the path that traced the river, shop doors opened and closed as townspeople took advantage of the sunlit morning. City employees were at work, filling the flower baskets hanging from lampposts and tending to the riverbank.

Mara drove her father through the downtown— showing off the town square where she'd been in that hilarious pet fashion show. They passed the bakery where she'd first met Jen and Sam, Jen's newspaper office, The Red Door where Mara had made her speech. When they reached the edge of town, she pointed out the sign for the Valley Orchard, where Lucas worked with his sister.

She skipped taking him past the depot, though. Memories of that particular Maple Valley landmark were still a little too fresh.

She'd almost texted Marshall so many times in the past week. She'd considered calling. Emailing. *Just to tell him the good news. To tell him about Dad and the Everwood and . . .*

But every time, she'd stopped herself. He'd made a decision, and she needed to respect it.

Finally, she pointed her car toward the lane that led home. "That's the Everwood Bed & Breakfast up ahead."

Fresh white paint gleamed against the backdrop of the grove. Purplish-blue shutters bordered all four windows at the front of the house on the second floor and sunlight glinted from the attic's circle window. Clusters of hedges and flowers surrounded the house, and new pavers led the way from the parking lot to the porch. All Marshall's doing while she'd been at the hospital in Illinois.

"It's beautiful, isn't it?" And it was *hers*.

Of course, there was still so much more work to be done on the inside, and taking care of the grounds alone might end up being more challenging than she realized. She might need to hire someone, take on an employee or two. She'd have to figure out how to pay for the extra help. Maybe in the off-season she could find a part-time job.

"Lost in thought?" Dad asked.

She rolled up her window as she neared the parking lot. "Oh, just a little reality setting in. That's all." But this was a good reality. A really, really good reality. Only one thing— one person—could make it any better.

Or maybe two. It'd be lovely to have Lenora here, as well.

But Lenora had her own new beginning to enjoy. They'd stay close, visit each other. Mara had convinced Lenora to buy a cell phone. Davis had promised to teach her to use it.

A promise he'd clearly followed through on considering the number of texts and calls Mara had received.

Dad leaned forward, his crinkly-eyed gaze peering through the windshield. "Say, I thought you said you only had one guest at the moment."

"Yeah, though we've got a couple more coming in. But not until the end of the week."

"Then why are there two trucks in the parking lot now?"

Huh. She recognized Lucas's truck, but the other . . .? "Maybe we have an unexpected guest. Yikes, at some point I'm going to need to figure out what to do when I'm not here. Just lock the doors and put up a Closed sign? I should ask Lenora what she did back before I arrived. She manned the place on her own for a few months before—"

Surprise stole the rest of her words as the porch came into better view. Since when was there a swing on the porch?

"Mara?"

"Uh, sorry, I'm just confused all of a sudden." She pulled

into the lot and shifted into park. "There wasn't a porch swing when I left the house this morning."

It swayed just slightly in the breeze. Had Lucas hung it? Sam? But what would've made them think to do it? She'd had the thought a couple times that the far end of the porch would be the perfect spot for a swing, but she didn't remember mentioning it to anyone. It reminded her of that magazine ad she'd seen on Marshall's nightstand.

She slipped from the car and started toward the house, the sound of her dad's closing door clanging behind her.

At the bottom porch step, she stilled. Two porcelain dolls, situated in the center of the swing, green and yellow pillows on either side.

"Marshall Hawkins." She breathed his name in a whisper, her heart beginning to thud.

She raced up the rest of the steps. "Sorry, Dad," she called over her shoulder. "I have to check on something. I have to find . . ." She barreled into the house, toed off her shoes. "Marshall?"

She veered from the lobby toward the open staircase, started up and immediately tripped over something. *Lenny!* She caught herself on the banister, stepped over the cat, and ran back down. No point in looking upstairs first. Marshall was probably in the den or the kitchen or maybe out back. "Hey, Lenny," she called over her shoulder. "Sorry to run you over."

Dad stood in the open doorway, and she barely caught the look of amusement plastered on his face before swerving into the sitting room. Empty.

Dining room. Empty.

She burst into the kitchen.

And smacked into a wall of plaid. *Marshall.*

Did she say his name or only think it as she toppled backward amidst a shower of . . . cereal?

His low rumble of laughter was pure music as he grasped her hand just before she hit the floor in the most un-graceful move of her life. He hoisted her upright, but one foot landed on the cereal box he must've dropped, which nearly sent her sliding again.

And maybe that wasn't a bad thing. Because Marshall tightened his grip and pulled her to him. And what had only been a blurred view at first came into focus. His bristled cheeks spread into a grin, complete with those grooves that were most definitely dimples. Gray eyes etched with flecks of gold she hadn't noticed before—like a sunlit calm after a summer rainstorm. Plaid shirt rolled to his elbows, unbuttoned and loose over a dark tee. A piece of cereal caught in the cuff of his jeans.

Her gaze traveled back up. "You . . . you're . . . you're eating my cereal."

"Well, I was until you spilled it."

"Good thing I always keep a backup box in the pantry." He still held her hand and she stood so close to him she could swear she heard his heartbeat, pulsing nearly as loudly as her own. "There's a porch swing."

"So there is."

"And . . . and dolls."

"So there are." He tugged her free from the mess of cereal around their feet until she stood with her back against the kitchen wall.

"Are you going to explain?"

"Shouldn't I get a 'Hi, Marshall' first? An 'I'm glad you're back' or an 'I'm happy to see you?'" His free hand came up to the wall beside her. "I mean, that is, assuming you are happy to see me. If you aren't—"

"Of course I'm happy to see you, you exasperating man."

He released her hand and brought his to his chest only long enough to say, "Me? Exasperating?" And then that hand was on the wall too—on her other side, hemming her in.

She couldn't breathe and she didn't really want to. Because if this wasn't real . . .

He inched closer, the oh-so-faint tangy scent of his cologne enveloping her. Oh yeah, it was real.

"You are exasperating. The dolls. My cereal." She tipped her head to meet his gaze. "I didn't think you were coming back. You've been gone three weeks."

His lips were a breath away from hers when he spoke. "Well, I'm here now."

And then he kissed her. Softly, at first. Sweetly. But when her hands slipped under his top shirt and her fingers grasped the back of his tee, when she whispered his name on his lips, his kiss became something else entirely. Deeper, hungrier. He wrapped her in his arms, and she returned his kisses with everything in her.

Until a throat clearing in the kitchen doorway yanked her from her bliss.

And Marshall swung his gaze over his shoulder.

And Dad crossed his arms. "You must be Marshall. You've got some explaining to do."

He'd seen Mara blush before. But this was her most adorable look yet—cheeks so rosy her cute freckles almost disappeared. Her aqua gaze shot from Marshall to the man in the doorway and back to Marshall once more.

"That's my dad," she whispered, her arms still twined around him.

And it was all he could do not to completely ignore the man and kiss her all over again. But wait, her dad?

He couldn't decide whether to be overjoyed for her or annoyed on his own behalf. Sure, it'd be good to meet the guy, but they'd kind of been in the middle of a little something here.

Or a lot something.

Something that had been even better than he hoped for. He'd hoped she would be happy to see him. He'd hoped she'd welcome him back and hear him out and not hold what he'd said at the depot or the way he'd left against him.

But this . . . her . . . just now . . .

Great, was he flushing too?

He turned, reluctant to face Mara's father. "Uh, hi."

"That's all you've got to say for yourself?"

What was he supposed to say? That he was a little flustered at the moment because of what a good kisser the man's daughter happened to be?

Mara's laughter saved the moment. "Dad, this is Marshall. Marsh, this is my dad, Stephen Bristol. Shake hands or something, will you?"

Cereal crunched underfoot as Marshall stepped forward to obey Mara. They shook and by the time they parted, the older man had given up biting back his grin. "I really wanted to play the stern father role solely because I missed out on doing that when Mara was a teen. But clearly the time for that has passed."

"Um, Dad, could you give us a couple of minutes? Marsh and I need to talk for a sec."

He harrumphed. "Talk. Right."

"Dad."

He smirked before retreating.

Marshall turned to Mara, taking in everything he'd missed earlier. Her hair reached past her shoulders in loose waves. Black and white shirt, yellow sweater, black leggings.

Bare feet. His smile widened as his gaze swept upward. "Your dad is right. I do have some explaining to do. But I'm not the only one. Your *dad* is here."

"I know."

"He's back in your life."

"He is. It's still a little awkward but it's good."

"Mara—"

"What are you doing here, Marshall? You have to explain."

He took a step toward her.

She stepped back. "No. If you get too close, I'll kiss you, or you'll kiss me, or we'll both—" She shook her head. "Explain."

He pulled out a chair at the kitchen table and motioned for her to sit. "I went to see Lenora."

She sat. "You did?"

"Just yesterday." He dropped into the chair next to her, scooting it over the floor until he faced her. "I had this great plan. I was going to stop her from selling the Everwood. But she told me I was too late." He reached for Mara's hand. "Someone else was already in the process of buying it. And there was no chance in the world she'd be talked out of it."

"She told you who the someone was?"

"Yep."

"And now you're here because . . ."

He could live on the captivating mix of hope and desire in Mara's eyes. If he could just find the right words . . .

He brushed his thumb over the back of her hand and the words found him. "She would've liked you." He heard the rasp in his voice, the uncertainty. But he kissed her hand and willed himself on. "She was always saying she wished she had red hair. Like Anne of Green Gables."

He looked up to see tears in Mara's eyes. And it was all he needed to keep going.

"Laney would've loved you. She'd have loved your taste in food—sugary cereal, especially."

Mara gave a small laugh as a tear slipped down her cheek.

"She loved running. I always figured she'd end up as a track and field girl or maybe a cross country runner. I'd have to be that parent going to meets and sprinting to get pictures of her." He reached for Mara's other hand. "Speaking of which, I brought some pictures of her if you'd like to see them."

"Of course I would."

"And you're okay with me staying?"

"For how long?"

"As long as you'll have me." One of her tears landed on his knuckle. "I think . . . I think I'm still grieving, Mara, and maybe there's a piece of me that always will be. But I've spent enough time being broken. I'm ready to let God put me back together. I know now that there's life beyond the brokenness. But I can't imagine that life without you."

She was crying now, her shoulders shaking, and she pulled one hand away to swipe her eyes. He gently towed her from her chair and onto his lap and as she cried into his shirt, arms around his neck, a joy he'd thought once lost forever settled into his core.

And it reached deeper still when her fingers brushed from around his neck to his face. With both hands on his cheeks, she looked into his eyes. "Marshall Hawkins. Thirty-five. Milwaukee. I love you like you wouldn't believe."

"I love you too, Mara Bristol." He kissed a stray tear on her cheek then pulled her close. "But there's one thing I should tell you."

"What?"

"It was my birthday a few days after I returned to

Milwaukee. I'm thirty-six now. And you should probably amend the Milwaukee part too. I'm selling my townhouse. I'm hoping to talk Sam into giving me a job. Maybe just part-time at first so I can still help around here."

She laughed against his neck as his arms tightened around her. "Marshall Hawkins. Thirty-six. Maple Valley. I like the sound of that."

EPILOGUE

FOUR MONTHS LATER

*M*ara tucked her feet underneath her, the first breaths of autumn prodding the porch swing into a lulling sway. Lenny curled on her lap, purring and content. Really, Mara should be inside putting the finishing touches on the bedrooms Lenora and Davis would occupy when they arrived in a few hours.

Or helping Jenessa with the breakfast dishes.

After staying at the Everwood off and on all summer, Jen had officially moved in a couple of weeks ago, seeking solace from the disarray of her parents' house as she finally began readying it for sale. The process seemed to be dredging up painful memories, though she hadn't entirely opened up to Mara about it.

There was more to Jenessa's story than she'd ever shared. Mara was sure of it.

Same with Lucas. Though he, too, appeared to have found peace at the Everwood. He'd extended his stay through the summer while continuing to help his sister at the orchard. So far, he hadn't mentioned returning to Mexico. Did that mean he was sticking around indefinitely?

If so, maybe he'd finally tell Jenessa how he felt. What a picture they'd make. Stylish, chatty Jen. Casual, quiet Luke.

"I knew you'd love the swing."

Marshall appeared from around the porch corner. For all the guests who'd filled rooms over the summer, this was the man she kept wishing lived here up in his old room. Instead, he'd insisted on bunking in Sam's spare bedroom ever since moving to Maple Valley.

But he spent plenty of time here, helping around the place whenever he wasn't working at the police station.

He took the porch steps two at a time and crossed to the swing in long, easy strides. The knees of his jeans were grass-stained and the T-shirt underneath his open hoodie bore the evidence of how many times he'd wiped dirt-covered hands over his chest.

Over his forehead too. She licked her finger as he sat beside her and rubbed at the smudge just above his brow.

And when he smiled, she kept her palm against the warm, scratchy skin of his cheek. She traced his long dimple with the pad of her thumb. "Laney would've loved the swing too."

"She would've."

"And the purple door."

"Mara, you can call that door purple as many times as you want, and I'll still say it's blue."

She laughed and dropped her hand, settling against him as his arm went around her shoulder. "I've been terribly lazy this morning," she said. "Here you're getting all dirty planting trees and bushes and I don't even know what all, and I'm just sitting here."

"You've been working your tail off for months. I thought you were joking last spring when you said cleaning is your hobby. Now that I've seen it firsthand, all I can say is you deserve to be a little lazy now and then."

"I wonder what Lenora's going to think when she sees everything."

"She's going to think she left the Everwood in capable hands."

Mara's gaze drifted from the porch to the lawn, now dotted by scrawny trees that would one day produce bright blossoms in flamboyant shades of pink and violet. Oh, she couldn't wait for spring.

Except that she could. Because autumn promised its own gorgeous show of color, and then would come winter —sparkling snow, Christmas—and through all of it, she had this beautiful house, friends who had become like family, a newfound faith, and a growing relationship with her father.

And she had Marshall. A man she knew and loved more with every day that passed.

"I had no idea you had such a green thumb, Marsh."

"Don't ever say that in front of Beth. She's horribly jealous of it. Can't keep a house plant alive to save her life." He moved the swing with his feet. "Want to know something funny? I was working in the back yard just now and I kept looking at that wall where the hidden room juts out from the fireplace. I can't get over how obvious it is. Anybody who really pays attention to the layout of the interior and compares it to the exterior could tell there's more space there than you realize when you're in the den. It looks even bigger from the outside."

"I still wish we knew more about that room and why—"

She cut off at the sound of a car rumbling down the lane. It was too early for it to be Lenora and Davis. And they didn't have any guests scheduled to show up today.

"Hey, that's Sam." Marshall stood and tugged Mara to her feet as Sam parked his car and bolted from the driver's side. "Wonder why he's got a duffel—"

"Hope you've got open rooms, Mara," Sam half-growled

as he marched to the porch and climbed the steps. "You're gonna want to pack a bag too, Hawkins. I think I just gave away my house."

"What?" Mara and Marshall said it simultaneously.

"Harper got evicted. She was going to take Mackenzie and move in with her parents. In Nebraska. Couldn't let that happen."

Marshall's eyebrows lifted. "Uh, so they're moving into your house?"

"And we're moving out." Sam yanked open the front door and stomped inside.

Mara turned to Marshall with a grin she couldn't hide. "I have so many questions. You should go pry some answers from him, Detective Hawkins."

"I don't think he's in the mood. And why are you smiling so big?"

"Because now our whole little friend-family is under one roof. This is what I've wanted all summer. We can have meals together and watch movies and make brunch on Saturdays."

"Don't we already do all that?"

"But it'll be even better now. I've been saying all along you should stay here."

Marshall's answering smile held a playful reprimand. "And I told you, it wouldn't be smart to stay under the same roof at night. Not when I find it hard enough to keep my hands off you during the day."

"Well, who ever said I wanted you to keep your hands—"

"Mara!"

He was adorable when he was exasperated.

"Come on. Let's get gruff old Sam a room and you too. Don't worry, between him and Jen and Luke and two other guests, not to mention Lenora and Davis, I think we're set as far as chaperones go."

She started to turn away but he grasped her hand. "Or there's another option."

"You're not sleeping in the garden shed, Marsh."

He pulled her close. "The thing is, there's something I've been meaning to ask you."

The sudden husky edge to his voice added to the swirl of intent in his gray eyes. A gasp stuck in her throat and even the breeze stilled.

"I've been trying to figure out when and how and even just now when I was working out back, I was thinking about it . . . and now with Sam showing up, maybe it's a sign and—"

"Wait a second." Oh, she couldn't believe she was doing this. Interrupting him. But the lightning strike of realization was too much to ignore. "You said when you were out back, the room jutting out behind the fireplace seemed even bigger than from the inside."

"Um. Yes. But—"

She turned and towed him by hand into the house. Voices floated from overhead, and the floorboards creaked in all the familiar places.

"Mara, seriously, I was just about to—"

"I'm sorry, but I have to know if I'm right."

"Right about what?"

They reached the den, and she let go of Marshall's hand, hurrying to the fireplace. She caught a glimpse of the mantel and her favorite framed photo in the whole house. Not a photo at all, really. But that wrinkled magazine ad—the one Marshall used to carry with him. His daughter's dream house and a reminder of all the love this wonderful man had to offer.

But first, she just had to know.

She ducked under the fireplace and found the handle to the hatch. In seconds, both she and Marshall were straightening in the dark room. Without wasting a moment, she knocked on one wall. It sounded solid.

"What are we doing, Mara?"

Another knock on another wall. Not the sound she'd hoped for.

One more possibility. One more knock.

She squealed. "Did you hear that?"

"Yeah." He stepped up beside her, a hint of wonder in his voice. "It sounded hollow."

"Do you think…"

"Only one way to find out." He pulled a pocketknife from his jeans and opened the blade. He jabbed it into the wall then grinned down at Mara. "Just flimsy drywall."

He cut a hole, then stuck his hand in and with a grunt, tore away a jagged chunk of the wall.

"That just reminded me of when you pulled the cellar door off its hinges your first night here."

"Impressed you with my strength, did I?"

Her laughter filled the air around them as she helped him pull away more of the drywall. She lifted her cell phone to shine light into the hidden room's even more hidden space.

The painting.

She shrieked again, throwing her arms around Marshall's waist from the side and dropping her phone in the process. "Oh my goodness. We found it. We found the painting. We—"

He cut her off with a celebratory kiss. "*You* found it, you little genius. All I did was cut a hole in the wall."

"With your impressive strength."

"I think it's safe to say you'll never have to worry about money again, Mara." He pulled her closer. "That is, unless you don't technically own it. Does it belong to Lenora? Or does it come with the house? If it's yours, think of what you could do with the money if you sell it. You could replace the furnace. You could get that crack in the foundation fixed. You could—"

Now she was the one to interrupt him with a kiss. One filled with so much joy there could never be a house big enough to hold it, no matter how many rooms, hidden or otherwise. "You were going to ask me something."

"That I was, Mara Bristol." He touched his forehead to hers and though she couldn't see his dimples in the dark, she knew they were there. "And I don't think I can wait any longer."

"Good." Because she couldn't wait to give her answer.

THE END

ACKNOWLEDGMENTS

This is always my favorite page to write! I am sooooo grateful to the following people who provided endless encouragement and support as Marshall and Mara's story took shape ...

Mom and Dad, you are *always* listed first because you *always* inspire and uplift me probably more than you even know. And to my siblings, grandparents, and the rest of my family, as well—I love you all like crazy and I feel your support in so many ways.

Courtney Walsh, thank you for all those voxes. Thank you for brainstorming and encouraging and empathizing with the whole juggling-two-careers thing. And thank you even for convincing me to commit to a crazy hard workout program. Haha!

Rachel Hauck, Lisa Jordan, Alena Tauriainen, Beth Vogt, Susan May Warren—I love all your morning (and afternoon and evening) texts and I love each of you. Lindsay Harrel,

Gabrielle Meyer, and so many other writer friends—you make this journey richer than I could've imagined.

Charlene Patterson, you're the best editor a writer could ask for. Thank you for seeing both the gems and the, um, not-so-sparkly things in the early version of this story. And Marisa Deshaies, thank you bunches for your keen proof-reading eye.

Thank you, Jenny Zemanek, from Seedlings Design Studio for the prettiest cover ever! Truly, this is the kind of cover I pictured when I was a kid dreaming about writing books.

Readers, reviewers, and influencers—I really think writing these stories is the most vulnerable thing I do. With every purchase, review, note, and kind word, you help me shore up enough bravery for the next one. *Thank you.*

Finally, thank you to the One who keeps giving me stories to unwrap. This one feels like the best gift yet. Thank you for surprising me. And changing me. And loving me. *Always.*

ABOUT THE AUTHOR

MELISSA TAGG is the award-winning author of the popular Walker Family series, the Where Love Begins series, and the Enchanted Christmas Collection. She's a former reporter, current nonprofit grant writer and total Iowa girl. Melissa's recent releases include a 2018 ACFW Carol Award Winner (*One Enchanted Noël*), an RT Book Reviews TOP PICK (*All This Time*) and a Publishers Weekly Spring Top Ten Pick (*Like Never Before*). Melissa has taught at multiple national writing conferences, as well as workshops and women's retreats. When she's not writing, she can be found spoiling her nieces and nephews, watching old movies, and daydreaming about her next book.

facebook.com/authormelissatagg

twitter.com/Melissa_Tagg

instagram.com/melissatagg

goodreads.com/melissatagg

amazon.com/author/melissatagg

bookbub.com/authors/melissa-tagg

Sign Up for Melissa's Newsletter

Stay in the know about Melissa's book news and more by signing up for her email list at melissatagg.com.

You May Also Like . . . .

Meet the Walker Family in Melissa Tagg's
critically-acclaimed series! Set in Maple Valley,
the close-knit Walker siblings grapple with their careers,
relationships, and faith as they learn what it means to
take risks, chase dreams, and fight for their futures.

CPSIA information can be obtained
at www.ICGtesting.com
Printed in the USA
LVHW090102201120
672187LV00003B/127